= The Songline Series =

Book One: The Fall

Book Two: The Flight

Book Three: The River

=Southwestern Songline=

= The River of time =

Book Two: The Flight

A Novel :

Written by:

Denver C. Davis

This is a work of fiction. Names, characters, places and incidents are either the products of the Authors imagination or are used fictitiously.

The Authors use of names of actual persons, places, and/ or characters are incidental to the plot, and are not intended to change the entirely fictional character of the work.

Published by Denver C. Davis
Copyright ©2015 by Denver C. Davis

www. DenverCDavis.com

ISBN: 9780996198417

* This book is dedicated to a life of adventure *

*

To all of you who have been involved in the trip and are around to laugh about it still.

You know who you are.

Thanks.

To those I've lost along the way,

I miss you.

But most importantly this book is dedicated to my friend, confidante, and partner in crime for lo these many years. She has remained by my side through sickness and in health, for richer and for poorer, and through a multitude of events that would have crushed a lesser woman.

Thanks J.J. My love is great, my sympathies legion.

*

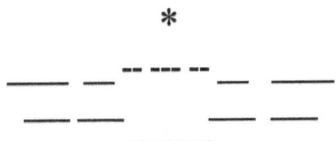

I also wish to thank Eric Adams, whose friendship and sage advice helped throw light into the dark corners of the writer's craft.

And, to the rest of you, and there are many, while there is not sufficient room here to mention you all, I trust you know who you are, and will accept my heartfelt thanks for your help and support throughout this endeavor.

Stories Happen to those who tell them.

Thucydides

When we last left Teller, he and his traveling companion Abbott had been led on a merry chase through the water-carved canyons of southern Utah by the ancient Navajo god of mischief: Coyote.

Steered by this demi-god to the hidden treasure of the escaped slave Estebanico, our friends find their future now deeply entwined with the past and their concepts of time profoundly tested. But when Abbott hurts his leg, Teller is forced to leave him in a small cave on the slopes of the Abajo Mountains to find help for Abbott's rescue, and for the retrieval of the treasure.

We now join our friends as the story continues.

= Chapter 1 =

Blaaaaat!! Blaaat! Blaaaaat!!

The air-horn of the Semi truck outside his window nearly blew James out of bed, his fists squeezing the sheets as he bolted upright in panic. His eyes scanned the room and as his heart rate began to slow the reproduction prints on the walls came into focus.

He was in a cheap motel room.

He remembered now.

That fucking pilot had humiliated him with his aerial acrobatics; and then, after introducing him to that rude woman in the diner, brought him to *this* dump.

His hand fumbled across the nightstand, bumping into the lamp as he searched for his watch. Picking it up he squinted at the Rolex's illuminated dial.

"Five a.m.?" he growled. *Goddamnit!*

Flinging the expensive timepiece across the room, he rolled out of bed, stumbling across the worn carpet to yank the curtain aside. All he could see was huge 'Safeway' logo lumbering

1

slowly across his plane of vision one giant letter at a time; and as the wall of steel passed the driver swung the wheel hard, turning onto the highway causing the dual rear wheels to drop from the curb. The trailer bounced and tipped; crumpling the corner of the motel sign and briefly mollifying James' anger. The driver continued west: shattered neon tubes and sparking wires in his rearview mirrors while chromed twin stacks left dirty exclamation marks in the cloudless morning sky.

But when James turned back to the parking lot, the smile of his momentary distraction dissolved.

The old Chevy truck was gone.

"Son-of-a-*bitch!!!*" he cried out.

Jerking the curtains closed with both hands, he snatched up his cell phone and began punching out Jack's phone number, composing a brutal verbal evisceration for desertion. But as his quivering finger hovered over the send button he was suddenly back in the helicopter flailing helplessly against the curved window a thousand feet above the trees.

With the image of Jack's calm, chillingly satisfied smile mocking him, he lowered the phone and sat back down on the bed, his balloon of righteous anger deflating as he gazed forlornly at his watch lying on the floor. Picking up the remote he flicked on the television and with the local news as background weighed his options.

He decided to shower. That might help his attitude; and while he would still be angry he would be fresh.

Pushing himself off of the bed, he picked up his watch and checked the time. If he showered and then went to the office for a cup of coffee it should be close enough to seven to call Casey to see how she and Ben were doing.

Then he would call Jack.

— — -- --- -- — —
— — — — —
-- ---- --

= Chapter 2 =

From his stool at the diner, Jack stared past the row of bottles that lined the shelf, his coffee gone cold.

First and foremost, his thoughts were on Teller, but this woman Kelly was running a close second. He wasn't quite sure just *how* she fit in, but she was knee-deep in this mess whether she liked it or not. He shook his head and smiled. *'That's what happens when you get near Teller. You get sucked into his orbit.'* Of course, James was also included in his deliberations, but he hovered peripherally; no more than aggravation with a paycheck… but as he sat attempting to match the various players in this crazy story with the events that compromised the whole thing, he became aware of a quiet, but steadily intrusive: tap-tap-tap in the background.

He looked up.

Jane was resting on one elbow over her folded newspaper, drumming absently on her front tooth with her pencils eraser as she mulled over todays crossword puzzle. The tapping stopped as she called out, "Hey Jack, what's a five-letter word for a native of Odessa or Paris?"

Jack lifted his nose to sniff the air. The aroma of Jane's freshly brewed: "Fancy' coffee" mixed with the smell of cigarette smoke that surrounded her head like a wreath always made him feel at home.

"Texan," he smiled.

Janey penciled in the squares. "Thanks, Hon."

"Sure Janey."

Getting up to refill his cup, he happened to glance out of the window to see the FedEx truck racing towards the maintenance hangar.

"Gotta run Janey, you got any go cups?"

Jane looked up from her puzzle and blew a thin stream of smoke at the ceiling. "I got Styrofoam Jack, same as always." Grinding her cigarette into the ever-present ashtray she folded the paper and tucked the pencil behind her ear. "Hang on a sec."

Moments later she was snapping a lid on the steaming cup in front of him. "There you go . . ."

"Thanks, Jane," he smiled. "What do I owe you?"

"Oh, don't be silly, Jack. By the time you get back I'll be ready to serve breakfast. I got fresh eggs, and Leroy slaughtered a pig last week. You want some ham and eggs?"

"With a side of hash browns?"

"You gonna bring Leroy's truck back fulla gas?"

"Of course."

"You gonna have your friend?"

Popping the lid off of the cup, Jack stirred a tablespoon of sugar into the black liquid. "He's not my friend."

Jane smiled around her cigarette. "Well, your client then?"

"Yeah." Jack nodded.

"Then get your butt in gear boy, I got taters to peel."

Laughing, Jack shoved his arm through the sleeve of his worn flight jacket and leaned over the counter to give her a peck on the forehead. "Just give me an hour or so Janey. It'll take me that long just to get the new part installed and get back to town to retrieve asshole. I mean, Jim." Sticking his arm through the other sleeve, he looked back up but all that was left of Jane was a cloud of smoke that trailed into the kitchen, followed immediately by the clanking of cookware. He grinned as he picked up his cup and headed out to the truck.

Driving across the tarmac, he found himself feeling pretty good about life. It was nice to be back in the company of old friends; and although this job with James was a pain in the ass, it *had* proven interesting. *And* there was a fat payday on the horizon. Of course, it was also an opportunity to see Teller again, and that was *always* an entertaining proposition.

Nosing the truck towards a group of smaller hangars clustered at the west end of the airfield, he aimed for the one with open doors.

Passing between the steel frame work that held the big bay doors he entered a massive room. Banks of florescent tubes hung high on the concave roof illuminating its interior with bright light and stark shadows. Allowing his eyes to adjust to the unpleasant light he shifted the truck into low and drove slowly, searching the emptiness for Leroy. Then at the far end of the hanger he saw two men. As the larger of the two took a package he slapped the FedEx driver on the shoulder and Jack heard a deep voice boom, "I'll see ya later, Ed!

Grinning, Jack gripped the wheel with both hands, pointed the hood ornament at Leroy, and stomped on the gas. The tires squealed on the concrete, and at the sound the big man whipped around and Jack smiled in respect.

At seventy-two years of age, Leroy was still an imposing figure. None of the muscle had gone to fat, and Jack guessed that he still stood six-six.

Finishing his turn, Leroy stood, feet spread as his prized truck came barreling towards him and did not budge an inch as the bumper came to a screeching halt just inches from the toes of his size thirteen boots. He simply leaned forward, resting his huge hands on the hot metal of the hood to stare at the windshield, squinting to see who was behind the wheel.

Unable to see through the glass he looked down at the bumper that touched his knees and frowned at his reflection in its perfectly polished surface.

Jack leaned out of the window.

"Hey, Sarge…"

Leroy looked up from the gleaming bumper; and seeing Jack's smiling face, his scowl vanished.

"Jaaack . . ."

The pleasure in Leroy's voice was music to Jack's ears, and at its tone, all of the anger James had instilled in his morning drained away. Grinning, he pointed at the box in Leroy's hand.

"Looks like my package arrived early."

Leroy bounced the cube in his bear-sized paw.

"So, this is yours?"

Swinging the truck door open, Jack jumped down onto the immaculate floor and closed the trucks door.

"Yeah, and go easy, it's fragile . . . so how you been?"

Leroy forwarded the box like a basketball and it hit Jack solidly in the chest. He gave a surprised grunt but recovered quickly, twirling it on his fingertips with a smile.

Leroy clapped his hands together. "I'm pretty damn good Jack," he laughed. "and you still got good hands . . . So Janey let you borrow my truck again huh?"

"Yeah, you don't mind do you?"

"Ahhh hell no, Jack. Just fill it with gas. Wait, you don't have that crazy friend of yours with ya do you?"

A momentary flash of puzzlement passed over Jack's face; but then he grinned, "You mean Teller? No... Why?"

"No reason." Leroy shrugged, "I just got a kick outta the guy. Janey liked him too."

Jack laughed as he opened the box. "Yeah, she said as much over coffee. Nope, he's not with me this time but believe it or not, he's a big part of why I'm here. Give me a hand with this fuel regulator and I'll fill you in."

~

Forty minutes later Leroy pulled the rag hanging from his back pocket and wiped his hands.

"There you go Jack, that should take care of it. You're lucky you caught it when you did. That kind of thing can get a fella killed."

Jack nodded and closed the cowling. "Yeah," he smiled, "I know. Unfortunately, there are some folks who just don't seem to appreciate preventative maintenance."

Leroy scowled as he stuffed the rag back into his pocket.

"Now just what kind of fool would think like that?"

Jack jumped into the truck, grinning as he leaned out of the window.

"I will personally introduce you to just such a fool over breakfast. Oh, and speaking of, Jane says it'll be ready in about an hour." Throwing a sloppy salute, he drove away.

~

The phone started ringing just as Jack pulled into the motel parking lot. Shoving the column-mounted shifter into neutral, he shut off the ignition and checked the incoming number.

No surprise. It was James.

Smiling, he gave a cheery, "Hello!"

The response, however, was not nearly as chipper.

"Jack. Where are you?"

"Oh, Hi James. Just taking care of business. Got the chopper all fixed up and ready to fly. I just figured I'd let you get some sleep in while I worked. No point in you gettin dirty. Thinking as he spoke, *fat chance of that.*

"Anyway," he continued, "Janey's got breakfast over at the terminal. How about we grab some good home cookin' before we take off?"

James' response was immediately dismissive. "Look Jack, I don't eat at diners."

Jack frowned. Then, holding the phone at arm's length, gave the voice at the other end the finger and brought the phone back to his ear. "Look, James," he sighed, "we're not talking any old diner here, we're talking home cooking. Besides, I've got someone I want you to meet."

James' voice came across both angry and resigned.

"Do I have a choice?"

"No, you do not. I'll pick you up in twenty minutes."

"Why twenty minutes?"

"What difference does it make? Just be ready."

He shook his head as he tossed the phone on the front seat; both impressed and amused at the amount of energy it must take to maintain the attitude of perpetual asshole. *'It must take a lot of work to be a full-time dick.'* He chuckled. *'Maybe that's his problem... he's exhausted.'*

7

Swinging the door open, he stepped out, but as he crossed the parking lot he saw that the curtains to James' room were still drawn tight.

'Good' he thought, 'now I don't have to talk to him.'

Flinging his room door open he peeled off his jacket, fell back onto the hard mattress, and putting the toe of one boot to the heel of the other, pushed while at the same time grabbing the TV remote.

The old tube TV hummed, and soon a perfectly coiffed news anchorman was delivering a current list of global miseries while his female co-anchor nodded with appropriate gravity: and as the clip featured a mid-eastern city being systematically destroyed; his boots popped off in sequence with the "booms" of American bombs. Jack sat up, and shook his head sadly, contemplating the mess a bunch of monkeys with opposable thumbs had made of an otherwise perfectly lovely planet.

"And now to sports," The news anchor announced.

"And now to sports . . ." Jack repeated with a sigh.

Gathering his razor and toothbrush, he turned the hot water in the shower on and began humming one of Teller's tunes.

It was a song he had been reminded of during this brief conversation with James: A little ditty titled: 'Fat Chance.'

— — -- --- -- — —
— — — -- — —
-- --- --

= Chapter 3 =

Tellers fingers released the small carving, pulling his hand from his pocket... for as pleased as he was at the sight of the Scout's headlights emerging from the oncoming dust cloud, he was considerably less enthused with the Ravens appearance. Regardless of circumstance, black birds had proven nearly as troublesome as Coyotes as of late.

Slipping into the shade of a gnarled piñon tree and out of the sight of the bird still circling above, Teller returned his attention to the dust cloud rolling his way.

'Well, well, well, he thought, *'what have we here?'*

But then, above the rattling and rumblings of the oncoming vehicle, Teller heard a loud, squawking caw: one that sounded suspiciously like laughter. Peeking up through the branches, he saw the bird was gone.

'Hmmm... now what?'

His rhetorical question was answered immediately.

The vehicle materialized, and all thoughts regarding the raven were rendered meaningless. Kelly sat in the passenger's seat; her elbow hanging out the window with the fingers of her right hand wrapped around the wing vents strut: while her other hand was pressed the das; anchoring her in the futile hope of being tossed around like a rag doll.

Thrusting his hand to his vest pocket a second time, he gave the little carving a hard squeeze.

'First the river, and now here . . .? stop it already!'

From his place of camouflage, Teller could see that her lips were moving but the rattling of the Scout made it impossible to hear her voice: so, stepping from the shade, he whistled; the piercing sound cutting through all other noise.

9

Kelly's eyes went wide as her head whipped around and she saw him standing in the road behind them.

Shouting, "TELLER!" she anxiously slapped at the door handle but couldn't get it to work. Finally it swung open and by the time Billy slowed Lulubelle down she had exited and was racing across the sandstone leaving the door swinging on its hinges.

Billy brought the Scout to a stop and stepped out, laying his elbows on Lulubelle's faded roof and laughing quietly as Kelly hit Teller at a dead run. The momentum of the impact spun them around several times; Kelly kissing him the entire time. Teller's laughter rang out, and as he brought them to a stop she pulled back, looking at him in disbelief.

"Tell! What are you doing *here?!!?*" and as she held him, she looked over his shoulder. "*This* is what the coyote told you about?" she asked Billy.

Already beyond surprise by Kelly's arrival, Teller's laughter stopped and he unwrapped her from his neck.

"Wait a fucking minute…!" he growled. Then, stepping back and holding her at arm's length he squeezed her shoulders to verify she was real. Satisfied, turned to the dark man.

"Just *what* is she talking about?"

Stepping away from the Scout. Billy held out his hand: his smile dazzling white beneath the shade of his battered Cowboy hat. "Hello Teller, you are *very* much as Coyote said you would be."

Teller said nothing. He simply stood, taking slow measure of the man in front of him. Then, gently pushing Kelly away; he took the smiling strangers hand.

"And you are…?" But before Billy could answer, Kelly jumped between them.

"God, Teller, it's good to see you!"

Teller released Billy's warm hand, wariness diminishing his joy. "You too Kell." he nodded. "But if I may be so bold, what are *you* doing *here,* and just *who* is this gentleman?"

10

Kelly's eyes sparkled with delight and relief. "Oh Tell, it's a long, long story."

Teller suspicions faded, but only slightly.

"Oh, I have no doubts about *that*," he smiled. "But you haven't answered my question."

While Billy had remained silent during Teller and Kelly's exchange, his smile never faltered.

"Miss Kelly is correct, Teller. It *is* a long story, and a very large puzzle. And it is *you* who hold many of the missing pieces. But I think it would be best if we went back to my home to discuss these things."

Teller looked at Kelly, then to Billy, his curiosity displacing doubt. "What *things?*"

Billy's eyes twinkled as he laughed and there was something so pure in his laughter that Teller's misgivings dissolved. Turning, he looked at Kelly; and her joy, combined with this old Indians smile, quelled his apprehensions.

"Coyote has told me much," Billy said, "But I need *you* to fill in the rest. Please, get in and I will drive us home. I'm quite sure you are tired of walking."

That much was true. He was tired of walking; but the past ten days had left him a bit skeptical when it came to Demigods.

"Coyote huh?" he frowned, casting another glance Kelly's way. But she simply smiled and gave him a sweet, reassuring kiss. "Get in Tell, there's beer back at the store."

With that, the last of his objections vanished. Opening the Scouts passenger door, he helped her slide in; but as she scooted across the bench seat she brought her hand to her mouth.

"Beer! Oh God! Teller, where is *Abbott!?*"

Teller smiled, pulled the door shut, and looked calmly over at Billy. "The coyote didn't mention Abbott, huh?"

Billy simply chuckled and started the Scout.

Executing a perfect three-point turn he pointed them back downhill. "Oh yes," he nodded. "Your friend was included. But *you* are Coyote's main concern."

11

They bounced across the mesa; Kelly stroking Teller's arm while pressing him further about Abbott whereabouts, but Teller remained elusive.

"Abbott's okay, Kelly. He hurt his ankle, but I left him reasonably well provisioned. He'll be fine for now, but I *do* need to get back asap."

At her puzzled expression Teller gave her cheek a light kiss and leaned forward to see the old fellows profile.

"So," he said, speaking loudly enough to be heard over the squeaking and rattling of the Scout. "A coyote told you I was up here?"

Billy's black eyes glittered beneath the shade of his hat. But offering nothing more than an enigmatic smile, turned his attention back to the rough road before them.

— — -- --- -- — —
— — — —
-- --- --

= Chapter 4 =

James sat on the hard bed, tired of his conversation with Casey long before the knock came on the door.

"Alright, sure, I'll call when we get there. No. I will . . . Bye." He hung up just as a second knock hammered the door.

"Relax, goddammit!" he shouted, throwing the phone onto the bed. "I'm coming!" He stood and marched across the worn carpet: cursing the existence of all the little people that were making his life miserable.

What he found on the other side of the door did nothing to improve his attitude. There, rocking on his heels while whistling a merry tune, was Jack.

Curling his lip as if he had just found a dog turd on the step James glared. Then, without a word turned, and went back into the room.

Jack stopped his whistling and stepped into the room.

"I'm *very* unhappy Jack." James growled over his shoulder; stuffing his shaving kit into his bag and zipping it closed with a hard pull.

Jack's good mood was evaporating fast.

"And why is *that*?"

"I don't like the fact that you're treating me like a fool." James continued. "You seem to forget that *I* am the man financing this trip." Glancing around the room he sneered, "Including *this* shithole."

Slinging his bag over his shoulder, he pushed past Jack, pushing him into the doorjamb as he passed.

Jack's temper flared at James blatant rudeness: but when he dragged his suitcase across the fender of the truck as he threw it into the bed, his patience vaporized along with what little good humor he still held.

James however, didn't even notice the small scuff he had put in the paint: he just turned to Jack with a smug look, wrapped his fingers around the chrome door handle and jerked.

Swinging open on well-oiled hinges the door quickly reaching its full extension and sprung back, clipping James' elbow and knocking his briefcase from his hand.

At first, James just stared at the door in shocked disbelief. Then, kicking the tire in frustrated resentment, he picked up the briefcase, tossed it onto the seat, and slid in, slamming the door hard behind him.

That did it.

The disrespectful shove in the doorway had both surprised and shocked Jack; the scuff on the fender angering him further. But with the slam of the truck's door his initial shock became full-blown fury.

Stepping from the doorway, he started across the parking lot; fully intent on dragging James out of the truck, cold-cocking his arrogant ass and terminating this disagreeable business arrangement altogether. But the sight of the truck door slapping the briefcase out of James' hand nearly brought a smile: and James' childish reaction deflated his anger further still… by the time he reached the truck he was still pissed but he was no longer homicidal. Instead, he slid in, gritted his teeth, gave a quick ten count, and gently closed the door. This was a replay of the flight over the La Plata's Mountains; except *this* time the ground was only a few feet down; and regretting the current lack of elevation, wondered now if he might have made a mistake in not opening that helicopter door when he had the chance.

Tucking away his disappointment over lost opportunity, he turned to James, his eyes cold and his jaw set.

"I thought we settled this back in Durango, Jim."

James' reply was quick, his was steady.

14

"We did. What I'm talking about here, Jack, is respect. I want to be kept informed of any and all changes involving this charter; because that's all this is, Jack. A charter. I expect to be treated professionally, and that includes *not* being referred to as 'Jim.' My name is *James*." Snapping his wrist, he checked his watch, and returned his attention to Jack.

"Now, you said the helicopter is ready to continue the trip. Is that correct?"

Jack's lips tightened. Less than an hour ago, in the light of this fresh new morning, his good mood had brought with it the thought that perhaps he had been too critical, that he had somehow misjudged his client. But evidently his first impression was an accurate one. The guy was a world-class prick.

Pushing his aviator shades firmly in place he eased the old truck into gear.

"Yes *James,* your airship awaits. But before we fly I believe that I mentioned Janey is cooking breakfast," Turning, he gave a cold smile. "And don't worry*, James,* it's on me."

He didn't bother to wait for a response.

"Also, I want you to meet Leroy. He's not only the head honcho here, he's also the chief mechanic, the husband of the woman who's cooking, the owner of this here truck, and a *very* good friend of mine."

His voice grew suddenly frosty. "It would be incredibly bad form for you not to meet the man and thank him for his assistance. And, manners aside, I would take it as a *personal* insult." As he turned onto Main Street, Jack could feel James's eyes drilling into the side of his head: but he kept his gaze on the road.

Finally, James spoke. "Are you fucking with me, Jack?"

His eyes straight ahead, Jack answered, his voice ice cold.

~

Jack's mood improved between the hotel and the airport. It was *still* a beautiful morning and he was *not* going to let *this* asshole ruin it. As they pulled up to the terminal, he glanced

15

over his shades at James and smiled, but the expression held no warmth. "I'm going to let Leroy know we're here. You go on into the bar and tell Janey that we're leaving at ten hundred hours."

While reluctance was plain on James' face, Jack's tone was firm. "Go on, that's where we're eating. You can leave the briefcase, I'll be back in a few minutes." James glared, and stepped out; holding the briefcase to his chest.

"No thanks, I'll keep it if you don't mind."

Jack just shook his head and stomped on the gas.

James' foot was still on the running board as the truck jumped forward, throwing him backwards; but somehow managing to keep his balance he stood, watching the truck roar away, the door still swinging until Jack punched it. The old truck leapt forward, slamming the door closed.

Left standing in the exhaust, James bit his lip, cursing under his breath as he turned and walked up the steps through the glass doors. The place was as empty as it had been yesterday; but the quiet ambiance *was* a pleasant change from the hectic madness of the Denver airport.

Shouldering his bag, he stood in front of the flickering Coors sign and wondered if this was all a big mistake. He sighed. It didn't matter now. It was done. But as he pushed the door open he was pleasantly surprised to find the smell of fried ham now overrode the odor of cigarettes; the counter and stools had been wiped down; and he could hear the rattle of pans in what he supposed must be the kitchen.

Suddenly, with a cough and a clatter, the batwing doors flew open and the same skinny woman from yesterday came bustling through, carrying a handful of silverware and trailing a plume of smoke. The doors came to a creaking stop and she looked up. Giving a nod of recognition she laid out four place settings, the cigarette between her lips bobbing as she smiled.

"Morning slick. Want some coffee? It's the fancy kind."

James was still annoyed from the morning's events and the 'slick' crack irritated him all the more. But her smile was genuine so he held his tongue.

"Sure, I'll have a cup. Thanks."

Reaching under the counter Jane pulled out four cups along with a big glass sugar dispenser, and setting them next to the silverware, smiled sweetly, "Sorry slick, no honey. Be right back." Fixing the cigarette between her lips, she turned and went back through the swinging doors. Following a few minutes of banging around, she came hustling back to the counter with the coffee pot, set her cigarette in the ashtray in front of him, and filled his cup.

"So, where's Jack?"

The smoke from her cigarette curled up into James' face and giving a small cough, he looked at the ashtray with the disdain one might give a dead rat.

"Aren't all public areas no smoking these days?"

Jane's attitude was one of absolute nonchalance.

"Don't know, slick," she said, picking up the cigarette and taking a long drag. "I don't get out much. So, where's Jack?"

James frowned and pushed the ashtray across the counter.

"I'm not sure, he said he was going to go see somebody named Leroy. Oh, and he said to tell you we're leaving at ten hundred hours."

Jane raised her eyebrows and looked up at the bar clock.

"That old thing runs ten minutes fast so you got about an hour. How do you like your eggs?"

James did *not* care for this woman's attitude. She was just like Jack, no respect; but on taking a sip of coffee he smiled for the first time this morning.

'*Hmmm not bad! Maybe things are looking up.*'

Lowering his cup, he smiled. "Poached."

Turning towards the kitchen, Janey laughed as she disappeared behind the swinging doors. "Good, over easy, just like everybody else."

James gripped his cup so tightly it nearly shattered.

He was *not* used to being treated this way, and he did *not* like it. This was the same disrespect that Teller had always displayed. The difference, however, was that he held a certain grudging admiration for Teller. *These* people, on the other hand, he didn't know, or give a shit about; thus making their attitude *entirely* unacceptable. And, as he sat on the stool, forced to be in a place he did *not* want to be, he grew angrier and in no time he was furious. It was at that moment Janey came back through the swinging doors, her arm full of plates and trailing a cloud of smoke. Cigarette dangling from her lips, she leaned across the counter and began laying out place settings.

James' hands trembling in fury, he watched the blue smoke trail up into the yellowed acoustic tiles of the ceiling; dispersed into a low cloud by the wobbling fan.

That was it... Enough!

He lifted himself from the stool and was just about to reach across the counter to pluck the cigarette out of this old crone's mouth and grind it into the counter top when the door of the bar swung open and laughing voices spilled into the room. Recognizing one of the voices as Jack's, he dropped back onto the stool. *'Good!* he growled, baring his teeth in a semblance of a smile. *'Now maybe I can set these people straight.'*

Spinning around, he jumped up and stormed towards the voices outside the diner's door; his jaw and fully prepared to inform Jack in no uncertain terms that he was *done* putting up with this *bullshit* from both he, *and* his hick fucking friends. But before the first word left his mouth one of the biggest men he had ever seen squeezed through the door, eclipsing all light within the doorframe. His jaw snapped shut and through confused shock he heard a voice call out.

"James! *there* you are! good, we were looking for you."

Emerging from the shadow the giant cast; Jack threw a friendly arm over James' shoulder and turned him to face the man in the doorway.

"James, I want you to meet my dear friend, and brother in arms, Mr. Leroy Smith." Then, turning to Leroy, his smile increased, savoring this introduction.

"Leroy, I want you to my client, and the man who embodies all the qualities of judgment you questioned earlier regarding the oil sensor, Mr. James Carson. But all his friends call him Jim." James was so utterly overwhelmed by the mans size, that Jack's comment didn't register. He simply stood, gaping at the enormous hand that engulfed his. Gulping as his hand went numb, James eyes went first to the man's thick wrist, then, moving up a muscled arm, traveled across a massive chest to rest for a moment on the mother-of-pearl snaps that gleamed from the pockets of Leroy's cowboy shirt. Then, moving up a bull-like neck, they settled on a surprisingly pleasant face.

Forcing a smile, he stammered out a weak, "Pleased to meet you," while at the same time thinking, *'God, I'm glad I didn't say anything to this guy's wife.'*

Leroy nodded; holding James' hand in a grip that felt like a calloused vise.

"So this is the guy?" he said, glancing over to Jack

Jack simply gave a nod.

With Leroy's steel-gray eyes boring into his, James struggled to quell his quaking heart. But then, with a nearly imperceptible smile, Leroy gave James' sweaty hand a final squeeze.

"Well, some folks just don't know much 'bout motors, but it's nice ta meet ya Jim." Turning away, he laid a meaty paw on Jack's shoulder. "I know you two gents are in a bit of a hurry. I'll go see what's keepin' Janey."

With grace honed by years of practice, Leroy stepped behind the counter; maneuvering between the bat-wing doors and into the kitchen. The doors were still swinging when his voice boomed, "Hey honey, these boys need to git. Where the hell's breakfast?"

Melting back onto his stool, James gently probed his hand for anything broken; his previous resentment replaced by shock and pain. Then, adding at his misery, Jack's cheerful voice piped up.

James shrugged, "I don't . . ."

Jack didn't bother to let him finish. "Never mind, I'll check."

Glowing with unapologetic delight, he motioned at James hand. "But he's in a good mood this morning Jim, and I think he likes you. Otherwise he probably *would* have broken it."

Reaching under the counter he brought up an empty cup, and laughing, disappeared into the kitchen.

James glared in the direction Jack had gone; intimidated, furious, and unable to see the smile of immense satisfaction on Jack's face.

= Chapter 5 =

Breakfast had been somewhat of a homecoming for Jack; with the three of them laughing as they reminisced over shared experiences but becoming somewhat subdued when talking about personal events: particularly the reason that Jack was in Cortez in the first place. And while the conversation was both lively and solemn in turns, James sat silently. The food was good, but there was no denying that he was the outsider.

Jack noticed this as well, and while he wasn't in any way fond of the man, he still couldn't justify prolonging his misery. Taking a last, reluctant last sip of his coffee, he glanced at his wristwatch and pushed his plate away.

"Well guys, it's time to hit the sky."

Leroy nodded, spinning off of his stool as he threw his napkin on his empty plate. "Yeah," he grumbled, but Jack saw a hint of moisture in his eyes. "I need to get back to work. Those engines ain't gonna fix themselves." Laying a gentle hand on the back of Jack's neck he gave a fatherly squeeze; then turned to James, his eyes a cold mix of humor and menace.

"Jim, you seem like a nice enough kid, but don't you be gettin this here boy into any trouble. Understand?"

James nodded. He may not *like* the implied threat; but he understood.

Janey slapped Leroy's arm. "Shoot Leroy. What kind of trouble could Slick here get Jack into that he couldn't get into on his own?" Picking up the dirty plates she turned to James and gave a dismissive wave of her free hand. "Don't pay him no never mind Jim, he's just a little over protective."

Bumping the saloon doors with her hip, she disappeared into the kitchen.

~

Twenty minutes later Jane stood on the tarmac. Leroy had important business elsewhere, she said, handing Jack a little travel cooler with a thermos and giving him a kiss on the cheek.

Jack returned the kiss. "Now Janey," he smiled with an expression of reprimand. "Let's not forget that the road goes both ways."

A whisper of melancholy crossed her face as she placed an unlit cigarette between her lips. "Oh hell, son. Me and Leroy, we can't never leave. He's always up to his elbows in some engine and I got the place to run." Sighing, she waved her arm to encompass the airfield. "Nope, this here's my little slice of paradise." Reaching into her bag, she dug for a lighter; but Jack quickly pulled a pack of matches from his pocket and with a strike, held the wavering flame under her cigarette.

"Aw, this place isn't so bad."

Jane inhaled, coughing as she laughed. "I ain't complaining Jack. I watch the news, *and* I got a daughter who lives in New York. Believe me, the stories she tells! I know what goes on in the rest of the world, and if you recall we lived in California back in the sixties... I know *exactly* what I'm missin,' and I don't miss it at all. No Jack," she said, turning her head to blow a plume of smoke over her shoulder, "I like it just fine right here. But I'll tell you what, I *will* try to talk Leroy into pulling that old Caddy out of the garage and taking me up to Flag for a visit."

Jack couldn't help but smile. "He still has that beautiful hunk of Detroit iron?"

"Yep." Janey's eyes lit up in fondness. "And he loves that old thing 'bout as much as he loves me, and almost as much as that damn truck."

"Well Jane," Jack laughed as he reached down to pick up the little cooler. "If that's the case, then you're in good hands.

Tell Leroy adios, and thank him again for his help. *And* the use of his truck." He kissed her again on the forehead.

"And thanks for the sandwiches."

Nudging James with his elbow, he walked away.

James had stood silently in the sage-scented wind, massaging his hand. And as he listened to the two old friends banter he realized how completely he had alienated every friend he may have had. *'Hell, maybe Teller was right about what he had said back at the bar that night.'*

Jack stopped and looked over his shoulder. "Come on James, let's go."

James blinked, and silently obeyed. But as he turned to get in the chopper, Jane stepped up onto the landing rail; surprising him from his self-pity as she put out her hand.

"Nice to meet you slick."

James hesitated at first, but taking her small hand in his, held it limply. Feeling uncomfortable he tried to pull away, but Janey held tight; looking deeply into his eyes as if she were searching for something. With a sigh, she released his hand and turned to Jack. "Well Jack, we'll see you in Flag. You take care now."

Jack grinned, gave a thumb's up, and hit the ignition.

The blades began their 'swoop,' slowly gaining momentum, picking dust up off the tarmac: and as the rotation increased, the hem of Janey's dress began to lift.

Putting a hand to her knees like a modest schoolgirl, she backed away, waving goodbye as her hair broke loose from its ties, the stray locks whipping in the wind.

The helicopter rose and banked towards Lake Powell.

Jane couldn't see through the hair in her eyes, but as the helicopter lifted James pressed his forehead against the window and waved back.

= Chapter 6 =

Billy negotiated the Scout around rocks and scrub oak; bouncing across the sandstone as Teller gripped the dash with both hands, staring intently through the windshield trying to see a road Billy seemed to follow instinctively: a road that was no more than vague tire tracks that appeared randomly in the sand-filled gullies. Turning his gaze to Billy's profile he grinned.

Both of Billy's palms hovered lightly above the steering wheel, allowing it to spin as the Scout bounced crazily, knowing that it would straighten itself out without the risk of a broken finger or unnecessary wrist fatigue.

'Smart man,' Teller thought. 'He knows what he's doing.'

His eyes flicked over to Kelly. Tucked between them she had her right hand tucked between his legs in order to keep from being tossed back and forth too violently, but the smile on her face showed she was enjoying the ride: and seeing that pleased him greatly.

Unable to help himself, he leaned forward.

"So, Billy." He shouted over the creaking and rumbling of the vehicle. "You from around here?"

Billy, catching on to Teller's game, grinned.

"No Sir, not from these parts." But before Teller could respond he shouted, "Hold on!" and spun the steering wheel. Everyone in the cab was thrown roughly against one another; rebounding against doors and shoulders until the Scout bounced back to a relatively straight course.

Straightening his hat, Teller leaned forward and smiled, "Yeah, I thought as much."

Suddenly, the nose of the Scout dropped over a ravine.

24

Kelly screamed, grabbing Teller's arm as they bounced down the slope, while he laughed and whooped like a kid on a roller coaster.

Billy, Zen-calm, downshifted. "Why do you ask?"

Not missing a beat, Teller leaned forward. "Cause you drive like a lost tourist."

The image was so wonderfully absurd that, combined with Teller's delivery, the old Navajo's smile increased by a thousand watts and he began laughing so hard tears welled in his eyes until he was unable to see. Forced to pull over, Kelly, elbowed Teller in the ribs squealing, "Let me out!" through her laughter.

Taking the sharp jab, he shouted, "Hey! What was that for?"

But Kelly, one hand clutched between her legs and still giggling, slammed her elbow into his ribs a second time.

"Now!!"

Fumbling with the door handle, he finally swung it open; and as his boots hit the dusty ground he laughed, "Jeeze woman! What's the rush?"

She slid out, still laughing as she raced around the vehicle, unbuttoning her pants as she ran. "I gotta pee!" she shouted and ducked behind the rear of the Scout.

Teller, hanging on the open door, rubbed his ribs as he looked at Billy and shrugged. "Weak bladder."

Billy nodded. "But strong heart."

Teller smiled. With that, he agreed.

Walking around to the front of the Scout he leaned back on the hood and looked up at the clouds, rolling his head to loosen his neck muscles.

"So, you said something about a coyote?"

Billy still smiled, but much of the humor that lit his eyes faded. "Yes, I did. For reasons I cannot understand, Coyote has taken a great interest in you."

Teller's eyebrows rose, and he gave a half-smile. "So I've noticed. Well then, with that in mind I'd like to show you something."

Reaching into his vest pocket, he removed a small blue sculpture. Lifting it between two fingers, he smiled.

"What do you think of this?"

= Chapter 7 =

Staring at the last of the smoking coals, Abbott realized he had no choice. He needed more wood. Steeling his nerve, he hobbled to the caves entrance: where, upon peeking cautiously out, saw a scattering of dead branches beneath a stand of Pine trees. Keeping an eye peeled for large, feline carnivores, he shuffled out, quickly loading his arms and limping back to safety.

Once inside, he revived the flames and was soon sitting in front of a crackling fire carving meat from the carcass of the wild pig Teller had provided. And as he laid thick slices into the pan considered his position.

Counting this dawn, Teller had been gone now for three days: and, with this morning's gathering he had collected the last of the easily accessible firewood.

With a sigh, he rotated his foot.

'I'm not going to be able to walk out of here on my own.'

Cursing the thought, he looked down at the pig that popped and sizzled it the pan. *'Thank God Teller managed to get this meat.'* he mumbled. Then, glancing over his shoulder he looked at the little pool of drinking water. Clear and fresh, it flowed slowly from a crack in the sandstone wall... a steady drip that echoed throughout the cave.

With each reassuring 'plink' he thanked Teller again.

'I suppose I shouldn't complain. He chuckled *This would be penthouse living for ancient man.'* He looked first at the sink-sized depression full of water, then turned to gaze out across the rugged expanse of rock and the snow on the mountains shining in the distance. *Yep, pretty good living really. Running water with a view. This is some high priced real estate.'*

Suddenly, the scream of the Mountain Cat echoed through the canyon, shaking Abbott from his musings.

Looking down at his only weapon; the spear that now served as a rotisserie, he frowned. *'Yet I'm quite sure I'm not as adept at this as my ancestors were.'*

Scuttling around the fire, he put his back to the wall. And while he wasn't really frightened, he still eyed the entrance warily. "Teller . . . where are you?" he murmured.

— — ·· --- ·· — —
—— —— —— ——
·· --- ··

= Chapter 8 =

Teller pressed the turquoise coyote into Billy's outstretched palm. "Okay, Chief, what do you think of that?"

Billy's dark eyes narrowed, moving up from the coyote to come to rest on Teller's face.

Teller waited, perplexed by Billy's expression. But then he broke into a huge grin. "What? Oh, come on! Don't tell me I've offended you?"

Billy laughed, closing his hand around the carving. "No, no, Not at all! I am glad to see you are not hampered by this foolish age of political correctness. Leader, Captain, Boss, Chief, they are all terms of respect, although your *use* of the word is somewhat cavalier. But I suppose that is to be expected from a man that Coyote has taken such an interest in." He paused to look down at the small sculpture in his palm.

"Coyote's sense of humor is also curious."

Teller's smile faded away. "So I've discovered."

Sensing the change of mood, Billy examined it more closely.

Teller was unsure just how much to reveal. After all, he had just met the man. But before he could say anything, Kelly popped up from the back of the Scout. Catching a glimpse of the carving, she hastily buttoned her pants and hurried over.

"Wow! That's beautiful! Where did you get it?"

Teller smiled. "It's good to see you again, Kell." Giving her a light kiss, he turned back to Billy and plucked the carving from his hand with two fingers. "But that, my friends, is a *very* long story, and I would much prefer to tell it once we're back to wherever it is we're going." He opened the Scout's door and gave a grandiose sweep of his arm. "Hop in girlie, let's go!"

The first few miles of the ride consisted of Kelly grilling Teller on what had happened, while he deftly avoided giving answers and growing tired of her questions long before she tired of asking them. Finally, he pressed his finger on her lips and smiled. "Give it up Sweetheart. I'll tell you all about it once we're there and I have a cold one in my hand. As I said, it's a long story, and I doubt you'll believe half of it anyway." He rubbed his forehead. "Hell, I don't know if I believe some of it myself."

Conversation ceased as the Scout's nose took another dive, and they began their final descent down the long, tilted slope of red sandstone that ran to Billy's store and the lake beyond. Kelly pressed her palms against the dash for support as Billy shifted into low gear.

Giving Teller a look of forbearance she said, "Alright Teller, I guess I can wait." But turning to Billy, smiled. "What do *you* think, Billy? think we can believe him?"

Billy unleashed a magnificent grin, but kept his eyes on the gritty expanse of rock. "Oh, I doubt it will be believable, but I'm quite sure it will all be true."

Breaking into a grin, Teller slapped the dash. "Amen to that, Billy boy! Amen to that."

Laughter filled the Scout as they pulled into the shed that served as its garage; but Teller leapt out before Billy could put it in park; bolting through the big doors towards the lake and pulling off his shirt as he ran. "I'm going to hit the water kids!" he hollered over his shoulder, "it's hot and I stink!"

With that, he was gone.

Kelly stared in the direction Teller had gone, then turned to Billy. "Well he *does* stink." she shrugged. But her expression quickly turned pensive. "What do *you* think of that carving?"

While some of Billy's humor lingered, his tone was thoughtful. "What I *think* hardly matters Miss. It is what your friend will tell us that will provide answers." Turning away, he pushed the door of the Scout shut and gave its faded yellow roof a pat. "Good girl, Lulubelle."

Kelly cocked her head. "You need to thank her?"

"Couldn't hurt." Billy smiled, and ushered her out into the bright Sun.

As they walked, Kelly quizzed Billy regarding the odd circumstances of finding Teller on the Mesa, but he remained evasive as always. She was about to try a new line of questioning, but as they came around the front of the store she saw Teller and lost her train of thought. He was standing in the shade of the wooden porch, dripping onto the deck and holding the remains of a six-pack by the plastic rings.

He held out the remaining four as an offering.

"Sorry, I couldn't wait. Want one?"

Billy declined, but Kelly accepted with a smile. "Thanks, Tell."

He nodded, took a seat on the bench, and patted the area next to him. "Take a load off, Toot's"

Kelly sat and Teller motioned for Billy to take a seat in the chair across from him. Once Billy was settled, Teller put his elbows on his knees and leaned forward.

"If you don't mind," he smiled, "I have a few simple questions of my own... Once *those* have been answered, I will regale you with my tales from the twilight zone. Agreed?"

There were nods of assent from his two listeners.

Satisfied, he turned to Kelly. "Okay, first, who all is here?"

"Well, right now everybody's here but Benny. Why?"

Teller took a drink. "Because most of this is for your ears only."

Billy's expression didn't change but Kelly protested,

"Teller, *everyone's* going to want to know what happened! You've been gone nearly a week, and now with Abbott missing you can't just act like nothing's going on!"

Teller gave her knee a firm squeeze.

"I understand, Kell, but I'm serious. We can share the general story but let *me* tell it. No one but the two of you need to know about some of this. Are we agreed?"

She nodded her head hesitantly

31

Billy, however, nodded with no hesitation at all.

Teller put a great deal of trust in his intuition; and his faith in such a nebulous concept had saved him on more than one occasion. Having decided that Billy was a man he could trust despite their having just met, he continued,

"All right then Kell, what happened to you guys after Abbott and I left? And how does Ben fit in?"

Kelly proceeded to give him the full story. The trouble in the rapids, the loss of gear, and the damage to the boat. She praised the crew's ability to keep it together, told him of some of her concerns, and finished with their final arrival at the marina.

Billy sat in silence as Kelly shared the story of their meeting. She left out the awkward moment at the counter, moving on to tell what little she knew of Ben's rescue and with a sigh, finished. "That's it for me, Tell. Billy took care of Ben and got a helicopter to fly him to Denver for help."

At the word 'helicopter' Teller leaned forward excitedly.

"A helicopter! Where the hell did you find a helicopter? That is *exactly* what we need to go get Abbott!"

Kelly glanced over to Billy. "Out of Flagstaff, wasn't it?"

Billy nodded.

Teller's eyes went to the rafters of the porch and he muttered,

Billy and Kelly looked at one another, puzzlement plain on their faces. Kelly turned to him but he just shook his head and the question died on her lips as Teller's eyes drilled into Billys.

Billy had questions for Teller as well, but now the direction of the conversation had shifted.

"A fella by the name of Jack" he smiled. He lives up in Flag. I've known him for some time, and he helps me out now and again."

There was a moment of pure silence. But then Teller's smile grew into a laugh of unadulterated joy.

Leaping to his feet, he shook his hair like a dog, splattering Billy and Kelly with the drippings of lake water while preceding to do a comical rendition of the dance the old prospector did in 'The Treasure of the Sierra Madre.

"Hee heee! I can't believe it!!" He guffawed. "You called Jack Hawkins! Hee *heeee!*"

He began dancing around the porch, the beer in his fist held high, foam spilling up and out of the can as he hopped about the wooden floor, his boots thumping on the deck as he pumped both fists in the air. Hee heee!! he hooted.

Kelly looked over at Billy, who, between the sight of Teller's dance and the expression on Kelly's face, had broken into joyous laughter

"TELLER!" she shouted in frustrated amusement, "What are you *doing?*"

"Ahhh, Kelly!" Teller laughed, "The gods are truly crazy!"

Throwing his now empty can on the floor, he danced over to her and taking her by both hands drew her up and off of the bench. Billy watched for a moment, then stood. For a moment Teller thought he might join them. But he simply flashed his radiant smile.

"Yes, Teller... but which ones?"

Finishing his impromptu jig with a little heel to toe, Teller released Kelly and came to a stop in front of the weathered old Indian. Cocking his head, the twinkle in his green eyes reflected in the black depths of Billy's and with a grand smile he winked,

"All of them Billy, *all* of them . . ."

= Chapter 9 =

Jack reached behind his seat, grabbed the thermos Janey had provided and poured a cup of coffee, sneaking a glance in James' direction.

He looked terrible.

Slumped in his seat, his head was pressed against the convex glass, staring at the tree-covered slopes of the Abajo Mountains; disheveled and lonely. A far cry from the take-charge asshole he had been in Durango.

Almost feeling guilty for finding satisfaction in James's misery he pulled off his headset.

"You're kinda quiet James, you okay?"

James lifted his head from the glass but continued to stare out the window. "Just thinking."

"Nothing wrong with a little introspection." Jack nodded, checking his watch. Refitting the headset, he reached for the volume knob on the cassette deck. "We'll be at the marina in about three hours." But as he turned the knob, he heard James' muffled voice. "You got a girlfriend?"

The question caught him off guard; and coming from James, made him more than just a little uncomfortable.

He slid the cup from his ear again. "I don't know Jim . . . excuse me, James."

James waved it off. "Forget it Jack, just forget it. Call me Jim. It doesn't really matter. Just answer the question."

This shift in attitude immediately raised Jack's suspicions but his curiosity overrode his paranoia.

"Well, there *is* this woman up in Flagstaff . . . she and I have had this little game going for a while. But no, not really, why?"

"Ever been married?" James asked, his voice flat.

Jack now regretted that he had bothered to break the previous silence. Through gritted teeth he answered, "Yeah James, I have. But that is something I do *not* wish to discuss, and definitely not with you."

James' interest spiked at the tone of Jack's voice. He straightened and turned. "Didn't end well huh?

Jack sighed, "Let's just say she's in Las Vegas starring in the Cirque' du' soulless." Snapping the headphone cup back over his ear, he flipped the intercom off. As far as he was concerned this conversation was over. Incredibly, it took less than a second for James's arrogance to return full bloom. He reached over and punched the eject button on the tape deck.

The cab went silent.

Stunned, Jack yanked off the headphones; but the second they came off, James held up his hand, and with every ounce of his previous smugness, spoke. "No, no, no, Jack, it's not that easy. You have been riding my ass since I first called you, and from that point on you have provided me with *no* respect. So, I would appreciate it if you would at least talk to me, man to man. Hell, we've all had woman troubles."

Jacks anger subsided slightly. And while his skepticism remained, he relaxed enough to give an honest answer.

"Yeah, you're right James, I have been a bit tough on you. But, in my defense, you have been a right prick since the moment we met."

James' eyes went cold and he gave Jack a hard look. "I don't allow many men to talk to me like that Jack."

But his expression suddenly lightened, and he chuckled softly. "By the way, what happened to 'Jim'?"

Jack smiled. "No fun if it doesn't piss you off."

James' eyes narrowed.

"You remind me of someone I used to know . . ."

Not liking the direction the conversation was headed, Jack made a show of checking the instrument panel, tapping on the glass of the newly installed gauge and changing the subject.

"Fair enough. So, James, just what makes you ask about my love life?"

James stared at Jack for a moment more, then turned back to the window; taking a few minutes to organize his thoughts.

He cleared his throat and spoke softly.

"Because, Jack, I no longer have any friends to talk to about these kinds of things."

Jacks eyes rolled behind his shades, thinking, *'Jeeze, there's a surprise.'* Keeping his opinion to himself and hoping that James had not decided to include him as a new confidante, he attempted a quick exit. "I don't think I can be of any help James, I'm not exactly a relationship expert."

James either didn't hear or didn't care. He continued talking to his reflection in the glass. "My problem is a complicated one Jack. I'm in love with one woman, and I live with another."

Now Jack was thinking, *'oh shit . . . '*

"Uhh, James," he sputtered, "I *really* don't think I can help you with this," he wiggled his headset back over his ears but James' muffled voice still came through.

"Don't get me wrong," James continued, ignoring Jack completely. "Casey is beautiful, *and* rich, but there is just *something* about Teller's girl that-"

The music was off, but the song 'Layla' played in his head. Jack tried to drown out James' voice. But when James said, "Teller's girl." He lost it. Shouting, *"Teller's girl!?"* Jack yanked off his headphones and slammed them against the console, staring at James in disbelief.

"Mo-ther-*fucker,* did you say *Teller's* girl ?!?"

The intensity of Jack's reaction rocked James back and with backpedaling caution, stammered, "Yes . . . why?"

Jack looked to the heavens and slammed his fist into the roof of the cabin. "Oh, for Christ's sake James! You're in love with *Teller's* girl!?"

Now James was not only confused, he felt suddenly exposed.

"Wait, wait, wait! You *know* Teller?"

36

Jack saw the immediate need to diffuse the situation.

"Yeah, Jim. I know Teller. He's an old friend of mine . . . I do not, however, know his girlfriend. Although I *have* heard that he is quite fond of her."

James' face went red. "And you knew of this when we started this trip?"

Jack held up his hands in a gesture of peace. "Relax James. Yes, I heard that you were Teller's old partner. I also heard that Kelly was on the raft trip with your nephew. And I *do* believe that I mentioned that when we first spoke on the phone. I *also* said that the river rats were a small group, and that news traveled fast." The color in James' face began to fade as he remembered the conversation.

Seeing this, Jack continued.

"All I *knew,* James, was that you, Teller, and Kelly were involved somehow. And keep in mind that *you* called *me* for a ride. I did not seek you out. But what I did *not* know was that there was some sort of romantic triangle going on."

In a furious flush the color in James' face returned. "We are *not* talking triangles, Jack!" he shouted, slamming his fist on the console.

Jack's hand shot out, grabbed James' wrist, and squeezed.

"Take it easy, *Jim.*"

James yanked his hand away, struggling to process this new information while attempting to cover his shock; and endeavoring to regain control of the conversation he changed subjects. "So, do you think Teller's at the marina?"

Jack's breathing calmed as well.

"I have no idea." he shrugged, "the only people who were there when I picked up your nephew were the guys that found him and an old Navajo friend of mine. Matter of fact he's the guy who called me in the first place." Pausing, he raised his eyebrows. "But if *Ben* was on a raft trip with *Kelly,* it only stands to reason that she's probably still down there."

A smile crept across Jack's face.

"Ahhh, *that*'s why we're going down there now isn't it? This isn't about finding those fishermen at all."

At James' silence, Jack leaned back into the pilot's seat.

"Yeah, that's it . . ." He shook his head. "Listen James, it's really none of my business. But you're the one who started this conversation regarding women in the first place. So my advice is this. You stick with this Casey girl that you're living with. You said she's good-looking *and* rich. That's an enviable combo, and I shouldn't need to mention the obvious bonus of not needing to go through Teller to get to *her*."

James' eyes went cold.

"And I've *got* to ask." Jack continued, "what kind of asshole leaves his hospitalized nephew and girlfriend behind while he chases his ex-partners girl around anyway?"

James jaw clenched. "Drop it, Jack."

Jack thought briefly about taking James' advice because honestly, he didn't really give a shit. But because this involved Teller, and because this guy had just proven himself to be *exactly* the kind of prick Jack had suspected he was from the beginning, he decided not to let it go quite yet.

His voice rose above the noise of the rotors.

"No *Jim,* I don't think I will. I tried to stay out of this little drama. I *wanted* to stay out of it. But you insisted on dragging me into the mix. So here's my opinion. *You* are a complete fucking idiot."

James' eyes bulged in fury, but Jack pressed on.

"First of all, *my* marriage fell apart because my wife and I wanted different lives. *You,* on the other hand, are just another pathetic, self-centered jerkoff with an overblown sense of entitlement. Secondly, I don't know *where* Teller is, but the smart money is on his being somewhere near this Kelly girl. And, as his ex-partner, you should know better than to mess with him or something he loves. And last, but most *certainly* not least, how the *hell* do Kelly and this girl Casey feel about this?"

James' hostility dwindled to a deflated frustration. "She ignores it." He mumbled, "dancing around the subject and always bringing Teller into the conversation. And, like you, she thinks I'm a fool. But as the saying goes, "The heart wants what the heart wants."

Jack gave a bitter laugh. "Bullshit Jim, you just want what you can't have. Grow a pair and get over it." Dismissing James with a shake of his head he checked the compass and reset his course six degrees north.

James looked at the side of Jack's head for a moment, then turned away: away from Jack, and the conversation. But on seeing his reflection in the glass, thought, *'that's what Casey said...'* With the memory of the scorn Casey's voice held resonating in his mind, James spoke.

"Forget this conversation ever happened Jack. Just get us to the marina. And do me a favor, don't mention any of this to Teller."

Jack looked at James, his disgust turning to amusement.

"And just *why* would I do *you* any favors Jim?"

James attempted to appear intimidating, but the fear in his eyes betrayed him and his voice reflected that desperation.

"Because there's an extra five hundred in it for you."

Jack gave a sharp laugh. "Keep it. Our original deal still stands." He reached up and put his finger on the headphones toggle switch. "The reason I won't mention it to Teller is because he's a friend and there is absolutely *nothing* to gain by my doing so. But you know what? I'll bet you *that* five hundred, and five more that he already knows." He made a slight adjustment to their heading, then turned and looked at his client as if he were covered in excrement.

"Seriously Jim, have you ever asked yourself *why* you don't have any friends?" He let the question hang and flipped the communication switch to off.

— — ‐‐ ‐‐‐ ‐‐ — —
— — — — — —
‐‐ ‐‐‐ ‐‐

39

= Chapter 10 =

Finishing the last of his crazy prospector heel-to-toe, Teller wiped away the sweat that his dancing around the deck had produced, pulled the last beer from the plastic retainer, and flopped onto the bench next to Kelly. She looked at him as if he had lost his mind while Billy just sat with his million-dollar smile radiating from under the shade of his hat.

Teller stood and took a bow. His smile remained, but his demeanor grew slightly more serious.

"Okay, Chief, as much as I would love to discuss the various gods and their manipulative habits, I need to call Jack post-haste. Where's a phone? Oh, and I'll need the number too."

Billy lifted himself from the chair; amusement plain on his face. "Come back to my office, Teller. I've got the number written down, and you can use the phone at the desk."

Teller turned to Kelly and grinned. "See? Things always work out."

"Yeah," she nodded. "But for who?"

They trailed Billy as he went through the screen door, following him past the aisles of snacks and through the swinging doors at the rear of the store where he opened the office door and motioned toward the desk.

"The number is in the book next to the phone. Make your calls and come back down to the trailer when you're done. I've got to make a trip to the garden." With a smile, he turned and walked away. The sound of his boot heels on the wooden floor grew faint, and on hearing the tinkle of the bell above the screen door, Teller turned and kissed Kelly on the forehead.

"Interesting guy." he grinned as he went around the desk and pulled out the high-backed chair. "You sure know how to pick em' kid."

Savoring the feel of his lips on her skin, Kelly leaned against the doorjamb and sighed. *'Yeah, I sure do . . . .'*

Fanning through Billy's book, Teller eventually located Jack's number. Kicking his boots up on the desk, he set the old rotary phone in his lap and with a grin looked up at Kelly, winked, and dialed. But after five long rings his grin faded: on the eighth ring he was in the process of hanging up; but an answering machine picked up.

"Hi, this is Jack's Tour and Rescue Service. I'm either out having fun or saving someone's butt. If this is a dire emergency you'd better call 911. If you would like to talk to me, call me on my cell. The number is 928 B-I-R-D- that's 928-2473. Or, just leave a message with your name and number. I'll get back to you."

Teller stared at the ceiling as he sat through the recording, and the moment it ended he blurted, "Hey Jack, this is your old partner in crime and this *is* an emergency. I'll try your cell, but if I don't get you call me back at" He looked up at Kelly. "Shit! Kell, what's the number here?"

"How would I know?" She shrugged.

Teller growled into the receiver, "Damn! Sorry Jack, I'll try the cell. If I don't get you I'll call ba-" the 'beep' of the answering machine cut him off. He glared at the receiver for a second and dropped it back in its cradle.

"Hey Kell, do me a favor. Go find Billy and get this number. I'll give Jack's cell a try." He picked up the receiver for the second time, stuck his finger in the ninth hole on the plastic dial and looked up at her. "Well, what are you lookin' at? Get goin' sweetheart."

Kelly gave an exasperated sigh.

"It's good to see you again Tell." Turning, she walked away, and watching her go a lusty grin spread across Teller's face.

'And it's mighty good to see you again too . . . yes indeed!

"Come on Jack, pick up . . . Pick up . . ."

"Hello, this is Jack."

Teller waited a moment, fully expecting to go to voice mail.

"Hello? Jack here…"

"Jack! Goddammit lad, it is you! Long time no talk to. Listen, I've got a problem and I need your help."

It was suddenly quiet, but he could still hear the rotors whipping in the background. "Hey Jack? Can you hear me? It's Teller and I need your help."

Jack came back, abruptly cutting him off. "Yeah Billy, I got the kid, and I'm on my way back."

Teller shouted into the receiver, "This is Teller, Jack! *Not* Billy. Listen man, I really −" Jack cut him off again, "I know who this is, *Billy* . . . like I said, I'm on my way back to the marina. Yeah, I've got a client . . . yeah, he's the boy's Uncle. Name's Carson, *James Carson."*

Teller's mouth dropped open and he muttered, "No shit."

Jack continued, "Yeah, *Mr. Carson* wants to come down and talk to the fishermen that found the boy. Are they still around? You don't know huh . . .? Where are you?"

Teller's smile widened, and he leaned back in the chair.

"Believe it or not buddy, I'm sitting in Billy's office as we speak."

This time Jack's jaw dropped. "No *shit!"*

Teller gave a short laugh. "Yeah, no shit."

Glancing over to James' puzzled and mistrustful expression, Jack put the phone against his chest and smiled. "Nothing to worry about James, Just Billy. Called to see if I got your nephew to Durango alive."

James gave Jack a skeptical once-over. He was suspicious, but he had bigger problems. He returned to the paperwork on his lap and Jack turned his attentions back to the phone.

"So, anyone else down there?"

Now Teller was curious. "Who and why Jack?"

"The uncle wanted to know. Apparently, the boy was with a group of rafters led by a woman by the name of Kelly something-or-other. You seen anyone like that?"

Teller sighed and leaned forward in his chair. "James is looking for Kelly huh?"

"It appears that way."

He pinched the bridge of his nose. "What a prick."

Jack's snort came over the line, "You know, it's funny, I said the *exact* same thing when I heard."

A warm grin crossed Teller's face as he reclined back in the chair. "I almost forgot why I love ya Jack."

His eyes drifted to the ceiling as a rough plan began to formulate.

"Alright Jack, both Kelly and I are here, and I guess the rest of the crew are somewhere around here as well. By the way, I just met Billy. What's your honest opinion of the man?"

Jack's voice came back with no hesitation whatsoever.

"I'd trust him with my life."

Hearing that, Teller relaxed for the first time in days and a smile of true pleasure crossed his face. "High praise indeed Jack, and that's great news because I really need someone I can trust right now. How soon will you be here?"

Jack flipped his wrist and checked the time.

"Hour, hour and a half, depending on the wind."

"Good. And don't say a thing to James. *I'll* take care of him. Oh, and once you drop off your present cargo, get the chopper ready to fly out as soon as possible. We need to rescue a wounded bear."

Jack did a mental double take. "A what?"

"Don't worry, Jack," Teller laughed. "He's tame. See you soon."

The line went dead.

Intertwining his fingers behind his head, Teller leaned back in the chair. *'I'll be damned. That son of a bitch is coming down here for Kelly. And with Jack no less!'*

Taking the little coyote out of his pocket, Teller held it up and put a finger on its nose. "I'll say one thing my little stone friend, you sure know how to make us dance. But it's a dance I know the steps to, and I do truly appreciate your sense of humor."

He laughed quietly, his boots coming off the desk just as Kelly walked through the door.

"You talking to yourself again Tell?"

He quickly closed his fist around the carving. "No Kell, just talkin' to God, or something like him."

But the flash of blue had caught her attention, and before he could slip the carving back into his pocket she reached out.

"Let me see the little dog."

Teller's hand clamped over her wrist in mid-reach. "Not dog, my dyslexic wench. God. But to be more specific, *this* is a coyote."

She gave a wicked glance at the hand holding her wrist.

"Well then. Let me see the little coyote."

He nodded and placed the small sculpture in her hand.

Kelly expected the stone piece to feel cool but it held the warmth from Teller's body; and as she noted the unexpected weight, she also noticed that not only did it feel warm, the damn thing felt nearly alive. Surprised, and just a little nervous, she examined the incredible detail of the piece, turning it over in her hand. "This is amazing!"

Teller nodded, "Yeah, it really is . . .."

Holding the coyote in her palm, Kelly spoke quietly, her voice tinged with awe. "I mean, look at the detail Tell. His little gold eyes seem to be looking right at you."

Teller nodded distractedly, for with Jack's impending arrival, and all its implications, he wasn't really paying attention. But when the words: "little gold eyes looking," sunk in, he snatched the carving out of her hand.

"Wait a minute. What gold eyes? He's sleeping."

Kelly immediately grabbed it back. "No, he's not! He was looking straight at me!" But as she re-examined the coyote it

44

was just as Teller had said. The eyes were closed as if in sleep. Her forehead furrowed, "something's very strange here Teller. I *swear* to you that his eyes were open and he was looking at me. And not only that, I got the feeling it was slightly amused."

His expression doubtful, Teller held out his hand and wiggled his fingers, "Give it back Kell." She dropped the figurine into his palm but did not let go of her belief.

"I'm not crazy Teller, that things eyes were open!"

Teller smiled and pulled her close, kissing her on the nose.

"After what I've been through Kelly, I don't think you're crazy. But the story you and Billy are about to hear, is."

Slipping the coyote back into his pocket, he put his arm over her shoulder. "Come on, let's go find him. As I said earlier, I need to tell both of *you* the story first. The rest of the crew does *not* need to know all of the details." Teller talked as they walked, but she only heard half of what he said. The coyote's eyes still bothered her. *'Had they been open?'* she asked herself; but the tone of Teller's voice changed and her attention returned, more sharply in focus.

"By the way," Teller continued. "I've got some great news. I got hold of Jack and he's headed this way. That means I can go get Abbott. But you won't *believe* who he has with him."

Kelly sighed, "James."

Her calm utterance stopped him dead in his tracks; his immediate reaction surprise, followed instantly by anger.

"How did *you* know that?"

She placed a hand on either side of his face; holding his cheeks firmly while looking deeply into his eyes.

"Think, Teller! Ben *is* James' nephew."

Teller's anger grew. "Exactly! So what that backstabbing prick *should* be doing is taking care of his family! *Not* coming down here looking for *you!*" Kelly found the fire in his eyes unsettling.

"James and I had this conversation the night I split," he continued, "and I assure you, Kelly, I left no room for *any*

45

misunderstanding." He tilted his head, his lips tight, suspicion evident in his eyes.

"What's going on Kell?"

Taking his hand, she pulled him towards the door, smiling reassuringly. "Let's go outside, Tell, it's *not* that big of a deal!"

"Come on!"

Leading him to the porch, she asked him to sit. He did, but when she started to explain he interrupted. "Kelly, sweetheart, I just can't believe that arrogant bastard has the balls to hire a helicopter to fly down here just to look for *you!*"

Her eyes flared.

"Wait, wait, wait." he backpedaled, "I didn't mean it that way! It's not that you're not *worth* it..." As always, his humor began to return. "I would scour the deepest reaches of hell for you if the situation required, and I suppose in a different universe James may have only magnanimous reasons regarding his concerns for your safety. But really, Kelly, you and I both know that James' actions are always in *his* best interests. And surely you are aware of his feelings towards you, regardless of the apparently insignificant detail of his already having a lovely lady." There was a very short pause. "*Whom* he lives with."

He crossed his arms and waited.

Humor lit Kelly's eyes and a feminine smile crossed her lips.

At the flash in his eyes, she rested a hand lightly on his thigh.

Teller threw his head back and laughed. "That's why I love you girl. You're not swayed by the rich pretty-boy type."

"Lucky for you." She smiled.

Teller's gave a teasing grin, grabbing her hips to pull her across the bench and slide his hand beneath the hair at the base of her neck. "Lucky for me is right."

He gave her a long kiss that was sweetly reciprocated: but their passion was doused as a faded red F-150 towing an empty boat trailer banged into the parking lot, raising a billowing cloud of dust that floated in obscuring everything within a thirty-foot radius. As the dust slowly settled, a curly head of blond hair leaned out the window.

"Hey you two! Get a room!"

"We were doing fine until you got here!" Teller shot back. "Go away!"

"Hi Dave!" Kelly laughed, and pushing Teller away with both hands jumped up to greet the new arrival.

The trucks door swung open and a lanky frame unfolded onto the parking lot, standing to stretch as Kelly rushed in to smother him with a big hug. Dave laughed and hugged her back, looking over her head to see Teller coming down the stairs.

"Hey Teller!" he grinned. "long time no see!"

Teller smiled, holding out his hand. "Well Dave, I've been busy, and the world's an easy place to get lost in."

"Yeah," Dave nodded, "But I'm glad to see Kelly found you, so welcome back." Gripping Tellers hand solidly with one hand he slapped the hood of the truck with the other. "Come on and give me a hand."

Teller followed to the rear of the truck where Dave dropped the tailgate, smiled at Kelly, and gave a sweep with his arm.

"Here's the stuff you asked for."

Teller grabbed one handles of the large cooler and pulled, expecting to lift it, but only got it an inch or so off the bed.

Dave hopped up into the bed for better leverage.

"Oh, not much. Let's see. We got eight bottles of red wine, some steaks, two cases of beer, and twenty pounds of ice."

Teller laid his arms on the side of the truck bed and looked at Kelly questioningly, but she just raised her arms and shrugged.

They both looked at Dave, but he just slid the cooler onto the lip of the tailgate and held out his arms to expose his sweat soaked shirt.

"Yeah, I know, but I like beer, the steaks go with the wine, and the ice is self-explanatory."

47

"Can't argue with his logic." Teller shrugged, grabbing one end of the cooler. "Well then, come on Dave, let's get this into the shade."

Soon they were sitting in the relative cool of the porch. Dave pulled three beers out of the cooler, passed them around and set the wooden rocking chair in motion.

"So guy's. What's the story?"

Teller looked at Kelly and raised his eyebrows. "You called him, Kell. I just got here, remember?" He waited, but Kelly's expression pleaded with him to take the lead. Taking pity, he nodded, "Okay, but you owe me big time, sweetheart."

Giving a quick synopsis of the journey to date, Teller glossed over the core of the trip; leaving gaping holes in parts of the story and no explanation at all of other events: so, ultimately, Dave received nothing more than a watered-down version of a boat ride. He sat quietly throughout the telling while sipping his beer and grunting at the appropriate moments. But once Teller finished, Dave leaned forward and put his elbows on his knees.

Teller stammered out an indignant, "What?" to which Dave cackled, "I said your fulla shit, Teller. First of all, Kelly didn't leave with you. Matter of fact, as far as I know, when she left she didn't even know where the hell you *were*. Second, James was completely bent out of shape when he found out that his nephew Ben had ended up in the hospital and Kelly had disappeared." He paused, reached in the cooler, took out another beer and pointed the can at Teller.

"You know, it was kind of weird. James seemed a lot more worried about Kelly here than his nephew."

Teller's eyebrows lifted and he gave Kelly a: "I told you," look. Dave looked at one, then then other, and pressed on.

"So, what's the *real* story guys? After all, I *did* drive all the way down here to get the boat." He glanced around. "*And* a crew. Neither of which I see anywhere. So... what's up?"

Kelly started to speak but Teller cut in. "Look, Dave, you've known me for a long time, and you also know James and I have had our little differences, right?"

"Oh yeah" Dave laughed. "On both accounts."

Teller nodded. "Alright then. As a personal favor I'm going to ask you to let the details rest for a while. James is on his way here as we speak."

Dave leaned in. "Really? I thought he was in Denver with Casey and Ben."

"He was." Teller said, tilting his head in Kelly's direction.

Dave gave Kelly a concerned look, but Teller continued.

"Anyway, the upshot is that he doesn't know *I'm* here. And that's an advantage for our side. And, better still, he's flying down here with an old friend of *mine*." his grin grew larger.

"Of which, he is *quite* unaware."

They both turned curious eyes his way, but it was Kelly who spoke. "What are you thinking about doing, Teller?"

He stood and kissed her on the forehead. "Fret not my dear, for soon all will be revealed." Then, with a smile, he turned to David. "So, Dave, do you think you can just do what Kelly asked you to do for now? I can't promise you the full story yet, but you'll get what information you need as I can give it, and I *personally* assure you that you will be well rewarded for both your patience and your loyalty." Reaching into his pocket, he felt the weight of the gold coin.

"Right Kell?"

She looked bewildered but nodded in agreement.

"Good!" he laughed. "Where *is* the boat anyway?"

She pointed across the parking area towards the river. "It's on the bank tied to a log next to our tents."

Teller gave his most charming grin. "In that case, babe, why don't you take Dave, locate the rest of the crew, load up, and get ready to get out of here. *I'm* going to go find Billy. As soon as you have everything ready you come find us." He turned back to Dave, who gave a casual shrug.

"Sure Teller, whatever you say. You've never lied to me, but eventually I'll want the whole story."

"You got it Pard." Teller laughed. "Okay then, off with the both of you!" The two of them stood and started to leave, but Teller grabbed Kelly by the arm and pulled her in for a quick kiss. "Hurry back." but then, as an afterthought asked, "Where do you suppose I could find Billy?"

She pulled away. "Down in the garden." Her arm slid through his grip, but he caught her wrist and drew her back.

"Not much help sweetheart. Where is the garden?"

Giving a coy smile, she brought her warm lips to his ear and whispered, "Behind the store, past the trailer and down in the Arroyo." Then, with no warning, a wet tongue snaked into his ear, wiggled about, and popped out. In his surprise, she broke free of his grip and bounced down the stairs, seizing Dave's arm and laughing as she went. "Come on Dave, let's go!"

Teller watched as she led Dave away; him twisting around to give a helpless shrug as she pulled.

Looking to the heavens, Teller lifted his arms in dramatic supplication. "Why me Lord?" he moaned. Then he chuckled.

A few minutes later he was standing behind the store, looking down the slope at the old Airstream trailer that shone silver in the sunlight. Seeing the 50's trailer sitting next to the six-sided Hogan, Teller made the same observation Jack had made a few days back.

'Life on the reservation. Always an interesting blend.

Scanning the convoluted landscape, he saw the arroyo that Kelly had mentioned, and following what looked to be a trail soon found himself standing at the head of worn steps that were carved into the soft sandstone. He paused and gazed over the edge.

Hidden in the small canyon was a glass and timber building surrounded by a white painted fence. The building itself was interesting enough; but it was the small stream that coursed down the stained red rock to disappear beneath the structure that captured his attention. Teller smiled, sat down, and let his legs hang over the edge.

He could not help but admire the beauty of the concept and was particularly impressed with the clever use of materials that had obviously been salvaged. Again, his eyes followed the placement over the water source. *'Brilliant design . . . this guy is no dummy.'* With a sigh, he squeezed the coyote in his pocket. *'I just hope he is as clever when it comes to explaining you.'*

Finally he stood and started down the stairs into the canyon below. But as he did, he caught a glimpse of movement higher up on the cliff face. Watching, he saw a lone figure in a battered cowboy hat emerge from the shadows of a hidden cave.

Teller was sitting in the shade, his back against the wall of the building when Billy walked through the garden gate.

"Hello William…"

Billy seemed not at all surprised. He gave a casual smile and nod. "Hello, Teller. Have you come to help me harvest a few vegetables?"

Teller was equally nonchalant, smiling as he gave a glance up to the deep shadow on the massive wall from where Billy had emerged. "Sure, glad to help. So, what's in the cave?"

Billy followed Teller's eyes up the sandstone wall as he held open the door to the greenhouse. "That is a sanctuary of sorts. It also provides a lovely view. Perhaps later we can go up for a sunset."

Teller nodded and stepped into the building. "Yes, I would like that. Thank you." but as he crossed the threshold he came to a complete halt; gazing around in both surprise and amazement. This was *much* more than he had expected.

Beneath clear corrugated roofing lie a veritable cornucopia of goodies. Green beans and sweet peas hung from trellises, raised beds held carrots while multiple strains of lettuces grew in rows next to miscellaneous veggies that were ripening on long hydroponic tables.

He remained just inside the doorway, his smile growing.

"Quite the little enterprise you've got going here."

Billy's eyes warmed. His smile was humble, but the humor in his voice was evident. "Thank you, Teller. It *does* help alleviate the humdrum of mutton every day."

"Uh-huh…" Teller said, giving a measured smile as he stepped past Billy and made his way to a pair of water-filled bathtubs plumbed with copper tubing. He followed the shut-off valves; tracing the pipes as they ran through stud walls to an array of solar panels mounted on a large, south-facing slab of stone. From the panels, the pipe returned: water passing through a control unit to flow back to the bathtubs.

Teller's eyes went from the tubs to Billy, who stood with a Cheshire cat's smile; brilliant white against his dark weathered face. And, while this gardens simple existence provided questions enough, the smile on Billy's face intrigued him further.

Returning his attention to the tubs, he noticed a line holding a submerged thermometer. He glanced over at Billy, who simply stood, his smile in place. Teller grinned back and pulled the line out of the water, holding the dripping glass tube to his eye.

72 degrees.

Pushing aside a blanket of floating algae, Teller was greeted by the sight of at least a dozen lobsters crawling over one-another along the bottom of the tank.

He looked up at Billy.

"Nice sheep."

"Well, they *do* supplement the mutton," Billy smiled.

"I'm quite sure they do." Teller nodded, sticking his finger in the water and bringing it to his lips.

"I thought lobsters were salt water specific."

Billy rolled up his sleeves and stuck his arm elbow deep into the tank. The water roiled and he pulled out a lobster that easily weighed well over a pound. Twisting and squirming, the muscular crustacean flipped its tail, sending water in all directions. Teller tried to dodge the splattering but his efforts proved futile while Billy, holding the creature with both hands laughed joyfully as it struggled to break free.

"These are known as 'Short Lobster. They are really just freshwater crayfish . . . I've done some selective breeding to get them to this size. But they are easy to raise, and they taste very much like the ocean lobster."

Teller reached out, humor and heartfelt admiration shining in his eyes as he removed the bug from Billy's grasp.

"Amazing, but let's put dinner back in the tank for now, shall we?" The bug twisted as it exchanged hands and Teller dropped the squirming creature back into the water.

With a splash, it made good its escape.

Teller's expression turned serious. "But let's switch species for a moment. I would *really* like to talk to you about a certain mammal that seems to be plaguing my life as of late."

Billy walked away, wiping his hands on his shirt as he went went to one of the tables. "Of course we can talk, Teller. You refer to Coyote..." He smiled, picking up a woven basket, letting it swing freely between his thumb and forefinger.

"But are you sure that Coyote is 'plaguing' you? it seems to me that he has added a great deal to your life."

Teller nodded. "Well, I suppose that would be *one* way of looking at it. Like everything, it's all in your perspective."

Billy's smile gained wattage. "I assumed you already understood that."

Picking up two plump tomato's, Teller laughed. "Oh, I do, Billy, trust me, I do."

Throwing them it into the air, he began juggling the two in a high arcing oval. Once he had established a rhythm he picked a third and added it to the loop.

"Depending on your perspective, my entire life fluctuates between insane and sublime," He laughed. His smiling eyes following the red fruits as they continued their elliptical orbit. On the fourth loop, he caught the tomatoes one by one and dropped them into a basket. Then he turned to the old Indian.

Billy's dark eyes grew playful. "No Teller, you are in the same league…" He paused, searching for a fitting metaphor and after only a moment's silence flashed a triumphant smile.

"Coyote is just your new coach!"

Billy's smile was infectious; and with the absurd perfection of the concept, Teller's apprehension vanished and heartfelt laughter accompanied a fresh appreciation for the man standing in front of him. But the laughter gave way to unease.

"With that imagery in mind," Teller said, raising his brows, "it seems my new coach is playing a *very* different game."

Billy's joyful expression gave way to earnestness.

"No Teller. It is the same game, it is simply that Coyote doesn't care who wins or loses. He simply likes to play."

His humor returning, Teller nodded; but an edge crept into his voice. "And *I* have no choice in the matter?"

For the first time since their meeting, Billy saw a different facet of the man in front of him. A deep seriousness that lay beneath the caviler façade. This subtle revelation brought a smile; for it helped to clarify something that had bothered him from the beginning of this event. Coyote was fond of chaos, but not of shallow men. With this new insight Billy nodded. Perhaps Coyotes choice was not as random as he had first thought.

"Please, Teller. Do not misinterpret what I am saying. Coyotes intentions are far from malevolent, he plays simply for the game. Coyote is mischievous; not cruel, and his motives are rarely anything more than his own amusement. But for some reason he has chosen *you* as the focus of his attention." Cocking his head, he pinned Teller with a questioning gaze.

"Do *you* have any idea why this might be?"

"No," Teller smiled, "but I'm getting the impression that *you* might be inclined to hazard a guess." Setting down his basket, he leaned against the table and crossed his arms.

A full minute ticked by: each man searching the thoughts of the other; with Teller raising his eyebrows, prompting Billy to proceed while Billy waited with frustrating calm for Teller to voice a guess.

Finally, it was Billy who broke the stalemate with his trademark smile. "Coyote chose well!" he laughed. "Let's go up and continue this conversation from above. There we can rest comfortably. And, as I said before, I believe you will appreciate the view."

Uncrossing his arms, Teller pushed himself from the table.

"Whatever you say Chief, but Kelly will be looking for us soon." Billy simply smiled and opened the door, motioning him to step out.

"Do not worry, Teller, leave your basket on the table for now. We will be able to see her when she arrives.

— — ▬▬ ▬▬▬ ▬▬ __ —
___ __ __ ___ —
▬▬ ▬▬▬ ▬▬

= Chapter 11 =

Abbott cringed at the call of the mountain cat. It came screaming through the weak light of morning; a crazy cross between a growl, a howl, and a purr, and sounding as if it originated from the shelf above his refuge.

It had now been four days since Teller walked south; and Abbott's most sincere desire was that he would have returned by now. But he also realized that it was, at best, wishful thinking. After all, not only did he need to traverse miles of rough canyons to reach the marina, he also needed to find some sort of transportation suitable for a return rescue.

Abbott shook his head.

'Not a simple task; even for a man such as he.'

With a groan, he leveraged himself up, putting his weight on the cane Teller had given him and limping to the cave's entrance to cautiously poke his head out. Glancing both ways, he looked for any indication that the Cougar was lying in wait with Abbott tartar' on the menu. But by all appearances he was safe for now.

Cautiously making his way to a nearby Juniper he leaned against the tree to relieve himself. As the sound of his water splashed against the tree, he couldn't help but be impressed by Teller's resourcefulness. The makeshift cast was solid, allowing almost no movement of his ankle as well as helping to distribute his weight properly.

'I knew when I met him that he was a remarkable man, and he has since proved it many times over' Zipping up, he hobbled back to the smokey fire. *'Let's hope his skill and luck hold.'*

Throwing a few fresh sticks onto the flames, Abbott laid back and put his hands behind his head; staring up at the stone ceiling to let his mind drift to the puzzle of Estebanico and his odd grave.

= Chapter 12 =

It had been well over thirty minutes since they had passed over White Mesa and James had not said a word, sullenly gazing out the window since they had left Cortez.

To his right the rock outcroppings that lent Bears' Ears its name protruded, while west of the Abajo's a massive bank of threatening clouds towered into the stratosphere.

Banking the little bird a few degrees south, Jack's eyes skimmed over the altimeter to his client.

He decided to risk it.

"So, James, what if Kelly's not there?"

James answered without turning, his voice bouncing off of the convex glass. "She'll be there, just fly this thing."

Against his own better judgment Jack found himself feeling sorry for James. Sure, the guy was a jerk, and had shown extremely poor taste in his actions. But being a man himself he didn't have to search very far back to find one or two situations where he had either been the sucker in some woman's game or had treated one badly. Nothing on the scale of *this* guy's stupidity of course, but if he were being honest he *may* have been an ass on one or more occasions.

He tried again.

"Listen, Jim, like I said earlier, this whole thing is really none of my business. But I've got to ask you, what are you going to do if Kelly *is* there, and more importantly, what are you going do if *Teller* is there?"

James said nothing, but his body shifted slightly as he stared silently at the passing landscape. Jack noted the movement, and as he reached down to change the tape in the cassette deck he also noticed James's hands were clenched so tightly that the knuckles were turning white.

He shifted his weight into a defensive position as the music began, and James turned to look at him, his sad and somewhat desperate expression replaced by a cold, hard stare.

"You are absolutely right Jack. My affairs are *none* of your business. I'm sorry I asked your opinion earlier, so consider my personal history no longer any of your concern. Kelly *will* be there, and I'll be taking her back to Telluride with me. You may also consider this your notice that I'm booking your services in advance for the return flight. Not that I care for your attitude, but you're convenient."

Jack's eyes narrowed as James continued.

"As for Teller, with any luck at all that son of a bitch will still be in Texas or wherever the hell he was when he sent her that last post card. Your job is nothing more than pilot from this moment on. Not a comrade, not a counselor, not a consultant, not even a fucking sounding board. Just get us there as quickly as possible and let *me* take care of things after that." With cold dismissal, he returned to staring out of the window at the mounting cloudbanks to their right.

Jack absorbed the outburst, suppressing his own anger as he pushed the throttle forward for added prop speed. Clenching his teeth, he turned a fierce smile to James.

"You got it."

Cranking up some old Creedence he silently nodded. *'Okay asshole, so much for compassion. Teller, I certainly hope you have a very special greeting planned for this prick.'*

— — ▬▬ ▬▬▬ ▬▬ __ __
▬▬▬ ▬▬ ▬▬ ▬▬ ▬▬▬
▬▬ ▬▬▬ ▬▬

= Chapter 13 =

Teller walked to the lip of Billy's cave and looked over. The cliff wall dropped several hundred feet with the land spreading out for miles.

"Wow!" he grinned, "You weren't kidding when you said nice view." But as he took in the immense vista something tickled the back of his memory; vaguely familiar: creating a sense of belonging that circled around at the edges of his subconscious; bumping like a moth against a screen. He gazed across the beauty a moment longer, but the feeling neither gelled nor went away.

With a shrug, he turned to join Billy.

Like most Anasazi dwellings this one had the traditional Kiva dominating the center. But Billy, in a bizarre piece of craftsmanship, had constructed a complex latticework of willow branches, laying it over the Kivas opening like a large, convex spider web.

Teller stepped up, peeking between the wooden webbing at what seemed a bottomless pit, and now closer, he saw that to add to the mystic ambiance Billy had placed a series of symbolic carvings and fetishes in seemingly random positions across its surface; each piece representing some facet of the spiritual world and each eye-catching in its own right. But most conspicuous was a twelve-inch-tall, dancing figure. Dressed in full costume, it possessed a coyote head replete with feathers, fur and beads, and was placed in the exact center of the wooden web.

Teller had seen many different versions of Katchinas over the years... at many festivals, on different tribal reservations, not to mention more than one cheap replica for sale in souvenir stores. But *this* one seemed different. More 'alive' somehow.

Circling the kiva for closer inspection, he tilted his head in the direction of the figure. "Zuni?"

Billy sat cross-legged, concentrating on tamping some type of leaf into an intricately carved pipe.

"My Grandmothers." he smiled.

Teller nodded as his eyes went back to the figure centered in the web above the dark hole.

"Why the coyote?

"Because the Coyote is my family's totem." Billy answered.

"As a child I was called, 'Tso seh Ma'i. In English it roughly translates to, 'Small Coyote.' but 'Ma'i' can also mean mischief."

"Hence your ability to talk to Coyote?" Teller grinned.

Billy's return smile illuminated the shadows. "Have I ever told you I could talk to Coyote?"

"Well, not in so many words," Teller shrugged, but when Billy placed the stem of the pipe between his lips, Teller raised his eyebrows. "That's not...?"

A slow smile parted Billy's lips as he scratched the large Blue Diamond stick match with his thumbnail. It popped, sparking and flaring before settling into a steady flame.

Teller smiled, and lifting his nose, quoted a comment made by Mark Twain on his 1860 trip to the Kilauea volcano on the Big Island of Hawaii.

"The smell of sulfur is strong, but not unpleasant to a sinner."

Billy laughed as the demon odor dissipated in the breeze

"It does not surprise me that you are a reader of Mr. Twain, Teller. I too, find his writings thought provoking." Waving the match above the bowl, he lit the pipe. "However, no... it is only some white Sage and a few herbs I have dried and mixed together. It will help with what we are going to talk about." He inhaled, then presented the pipe to Teller with a light cough.

Teller nodded. "Not to worry Bill, just had to ask. I like to know what I'm getting into."

The statement, coming from the man who sat across from him, caused Billy to laugh again

"And this concern began when?"

Teller grinned as he took the pipe. "Just now."

Smoke curled lazily in the air, enveloping them in the sweet smell of sage, then wafting through the arched opening to cloud the mountains in the distance. Tellers gaze followed the smoke as it ghosted into the sky. But just as he began to pass the pipe back to Billy a large raven swooped through the haze; landing with a loud caw and tipping a shining black eye to Teller.

A moment passed and Teller turned to Billy.

"You *sure* all that's in here is sage?

The raven cawed again, bouncing up onto a flat stone that had tumbled from the Kivas stacked wall, fixing Teller with its glittering black eyes; tilting its head left to right as if making a decision.

Silence hung thicker than the smoke.

The bird inclined its head once more, blinked, then cackling happily, hopped back to the cave's ledge. Looking back at Teller one last time the bird spread its wings and leapt from the edge of the stone lip. A few moments later it rose back into view, flapping westward towards the San Francisco Peaks.

Teller sat, staring at where the bird had been, then turned and looked at his companion. But Billy's gaze followed the raven, watching as it grew smaller against the backdrop of the sky and stone.

Finally, it was gone.

A smile touched Billy's lips and picking up his pipe he tamped it, struck another match, and re-lit.

Teller continued to gaze in the direction the bird had flown. Then, with a nod, snatched the pipe from Billy's hand, inhaled, and blowing a long stream of smoke at the ceiling, pointed the pipe stem to the spot where the bird had been.

"*That* is *exactly* what I'm talking about!"

Pushing himself up, he went to the cave opening and stood; silently gazing in the direction the raven had flown. Staring at the white-capped peaks in the distance, his anger clashed with his curiosity. Then, suddenly, it all came back to him. Those mountains were the very same spot the raven of his vision had dropped him after he went over the waterfall.

'On those very peaks, right above the town of Flagstaff . . . this cannot be coincidence.'

Shaking his head, he brushed his palms together and as if he were flinging away the past he opened his hands into the empty space. As he did so he saw movement down near the greenhouse. It was Kelly opening the fence gate.

He turned. "There's Kelly. Mind if I invite her up?"

Billy took a puff on his pipe and gave a nod.

"Good." Teller said gruffly. "She may as well hear this at the same time. It's far too long a story to tell twice."

He gave a loud whistle; and when she looked up, he motioned her to join them.

~

Time passed quickly as Teller spoke, the air cooling as shadows poured into the canyons below them, filling the empty space like ink. And with Billy and Kelly sitting silently, Teller paced back and forth in front of the cliff dwelling's entrance, recounting his experience in true storyteller fashion, with broad strokes and expansive gestures, but also with attention to the smallest of details. It was long in the re-telling, and with so many odd events being part of the past two weeks, even *he* had trouble believing some of it. And, to make things more difficult still, by trying to include Abbott's dreams it seemed he was telling two similar, but separate stories. But by weaving the two together he eventually reached the point where the Scout had come bouncing across the mesa: the very spot the fates had placed him.

Kelly was most intrigued by the discovery of the cave and its contents; and while Billy's primarily interest was Coyote, he was intensely fascinated with the dream sequence and pressed Teller for more detail. Unfortunately, Teller had not dreamed Abbott's dreams, so his description held far less visual clarity; thus, making the telling considerably less dramatic. But eventually the tale was told; his two listeners either satisfied or confused into silence. And Teller, unsure as to which it was, looked from one to the other, waiting for comment.

Billy sat silently while Kelly turned one of the gold coins over and over in her fingers. Finally, she looked up.

"Wow." she whispered. "How many of these did you find?"

Teller squatted at her side. "Not really the point now Kell. Let's just say that restocking Billy's store cooler won't be a financial burden." She grinned, and when he turned back to Billy his questions died on his tongue.

The old Indian sat perfectly still, eyes closed, lips moving slightly. Teller whispered, "Billy . . .?" but received no response. Turning back to Kelly he quietly mouthed, "what the…?"

She shrugged.

Suddenly Billy's black eyes snapped open and he spoke, his voice commanding.

"Teller, please, give me the Ma'i."

Teller hesitated for a heartbeat; a dark, subliminal feeling of proprietorship clenching his heart. But then, seemingly out of nowhere, the 'thwop' of helicopter blades could be heard in the distance.

Billy's expression grew stern. "Jack is returning but he brings with him a man who deserves no trust. Please, Teller, the Coyote."

Teller was torn, but Jack's words came back.

"I'd trust him with my life."

Teller nodded. But as he placed the little coyote onto Billy's outstretched hand an inexplicable pang of loss enveloped him and he pulled back.

63

Billy's black eyes glittered, but held no demands, only understanding.

Calling on his inner strength, Teller dropped the Coyote into Billy's palm. Folding calloused fingers over the small object he gave Billy's hand a firm, final squeeze. Then, with a nod, turned to Kelly.

"Jack has brought James with him." he said, reaching down and pulling her to her feet. "If we hustle we can meet them in front of the store. I don't want James to see this place. We need to go, now!"

"You are right, Teller," Billy agreed. "We must leave."

They followed Billy as he maneuvered down the steep hand-carved steps, Teller gripping Kelly's hand tightly as they passed the greenhouse to race away. They rounded the massive boulder that shaded the trailer at a lope, only to find Fred sitting quietly at the beat-up table playing solitaire with a ragged deck of cards, while country music jangled from a cheap transistor radio that sat next to his drink.

"Time to go Fred!" Teller shouted as he passed.

Fred looked up, and seeing Teller surprise lit his face.

"Teller! What are you doing? I mean, when did *you* get here?"

Teller returned and squeezed Fred's shoulder. "Long story Freddy, and I'm not going to tell it again. Put the cards down, we've got company."

Startled by Teller's sudden appearance and disturbed by the urgency in his voice, Fred hesitated; but when the muted sound of the chopper's blades echoed across the mesa he threw the cards onto the table and swung a leg over the bench.

The other three were already halfway to the store by the time he caught up, Teller hitting the steps of the store at a trot. He entered the shade of the porch, and came to a quick stop.

Skip and Lori were stretched out on the floor while Dave, sprawled out on the bench with his shirt rolled up behind his head and a beer resting on his stomach, lifted his head and gave a puzzled look. "Whoa guys, what's the hurry?"

Teller clapped his hands twice. "Sorry to disturb your rest kids, but you all need to get up and get into the store."

Lori gave an annoyed sigh, followed with a tired, *"Why?"* just as the whip of the chopper's blades came over the building.

Teller took one step forward. "I don't have the time to explain Lori!" he snarled. "Just get in the goddamned store!"

Between the tone in his voice and the cold flash in his eyes Lori shut her mouth and scrambled through the door.

Turning to the rest of his troupe, Teller barked, "Fred, you join them in the store. Take everyone to the office and tell them to stay put! Billy, you go greet our guests. Jack's expecting you, so do what you can to stall them for a few minutes."

Putting on a luminous smile Billy walked down the steps and into the parking lot, pressing his hat to his head to keep the prop wash from blowing it into the river beyond.

Kelly looked expectantly to Teller. "What about me?"

He smiled a wicked smile. "You, beautiful, are the bait for the rat."

Her jaw tightened. "Gee, thanks."

The helicopter was now hovering above the hard-packed dirt.

Teller looked into her eyes. "Kell, we both know why James is here. Just act happy to see him and get him to go down to the trailer to wait for you." She poked him in the gut with a sharp fingernail. "And just *what* makes you think he'll do as I say?"

Resting a hand on either shoulder, Teller kissed her on the forehead. "Sweetheart, the man flew all the way down here for you... he'll do whatever you ask. Just tell him you and Billy have something you need Jack to look at, and then suggest he go down to the trailer for a drink and to clean up. I assure you, he'll do it."

She gave a halfhearted smile. "I *really* don't want to talk to that man, Teller."

"Just think of it as setting a trap, Kell."

"And I'm the bait."

Teller gave her a wink. "Just say cheese."

With a flash of charismatic grin, he blew her a kiss and trotted into the store.

Once inside he went to the office and told the crew to stay put for another thirty minutes. Unhappy as they were with his demand no one argued and he didn't stay long enough to answer any questions.

His first stop was the cooler.

Yanking the door open he saw there were only four six-packs left. Grabbing two, he went to the counter, picked up a bag, and went down an aisle, scooping medical supplies into the crook of his arm. Considering the mood of he and James' parting, and now with his arrival here at the lake, Teller was honestly not sure how this might turn out. He was furious with the man, and more so at the extremely poor judgment he had shown in coming here for Kelly.

Loaded with Band-Aids, peroxide and iodine, he dropped them all into the paper bag that held the beer. Reasonably satisfied, he jogged through the back door and down the stairs, racing down the path to the trailer and the picnic table beyond.

Kelly might be the most attractive bait: but she wasn't the only trap being set.

— — ▬▬ ▬▬▬ ▬▬ — —
—— —— — —— ——
▬▬ ▬▬▬ ▬▬

= Chapter 14 =

The moment the skids touched the ground, Jack unclipped his harness and dropped a heavy hand on James' shoulder. "Stay seated!" he shouted above the chop of the blades.

Flinging his door open, he jumped onto the landing rail to grip Billy's arm and pull him close.

"Where's Teller?"

"He is here." Billy said, motioning with his eyes in the direction of the store.

"What about this girl Kelly?

Billy smiled. "She is here as well."

"Good." Jack grinned then looked at James, the blades reflected in his sunglasses making one final rotation.

Turning back to Billy, Jack smiled and patted him on the shoulder. "Well. It looks like it's time to let His Majesty from his coach." Tugging on the bill of his cap, Jack swung the passenger door open, instinctively holding out his hand to help James down. But having already unclipped himself from his harness, the instant the door opened James pitched his satchel solidly into Jack's chest. The impact sent Jack stumbling from the landing rail: and before he had a chance to react, James jumped to the ground and marched straight up to Billy.

With no preamble he shoved his face so close it was shaded by Billy's hat.

"Where *is* she?" he demanded.

Expressing surprise but not insult, Billy took a step back, pushed his hat up with his thumb, and turned to Jack; disregarding James completely.

"Excuse me Jack, but who is this *rude* Billagaana?"

Struggling to suppress a smile, Jack stepped between them.

"I am *very* sorry to have to do this to you, Billy. This is James Carson, the uncle of the boy whose life you *saved*..."

Then turning to James, he spoke evenly. "James, this is Billy Knowles. He's the man who kept your nephew *alive*," putting heavy emphasis on the word, 'alive.' But James, perceiving only insult ignored the pointed comment entirely.

Turning his angry red face to Jack he barked, "*What* did he call me?"

It took a moment for Jack to realize that he was referring to having been called 'Billagaana.' and as it dawned he grinned,

James nearly hyperventilated.

'Were all of this pilot's friends this disrespectful? First those hicks back in Cortez, and now this old Indian!?'

Looking first at Jack and then at Billy's smiling face, James' fists clenched as he sputtered in fury, "He called me *what!?!?*

Billy stood, his eyes wide with shocked embarrassment.

"No Jack! That is not at all what it means..."

Now James just stood helplessly; confused, off balance, and completely out of his element.

Jack couldn't maintain a straight face any longer. He burst into laughter. And Billy, while unhappy that his comment had been wrongly translated, saw the look of bewilderment on James' face began to chuckle. And James, his anger and frustration mounting looked as if he would burst.

Finally, Billy spoke through his brilliant smile.

"No, Mr. Carson, it is simply Navajo for white man."

Sucking in a deep breath, James snarled, "Good!" then, struggling to regain some sense of control, reined in a small portion of his resentment and pinned Jack with a withering look of disdain. But instead of the cowering he hoped for, Jack simply smiled; infuriating James all the more. Glaring at the pilot he turned back to Billy, repeating his question.

"Where *is* she?"

Billy however, was the picture of innocence.

"Are you speaking of Miss Kelly?"

James was on the verge of tearing out his hair.

"Yes goddammit! Is-she-*here!?* "

Billy smiled and tipped his head in the general direction of the store. "Yes, I believe the young miss is here. Last I saw her she was in the shade of the porch."

Loosing an angry exhale, James gave the two of them a dismissive look of hatred, picked up his bag, and he turned to march away. He was still within hearing distance when Billy called out, "although, Mr. Carson, as with many languages, words like Billagaana can have *many* meanings."

The expression that clouded James' face caused Jack to burst into laughter all over again.

Kelly, who had been watching the exchange from the shadows of the porch heard the tall, lanky pilot laugh and by the expression on James' face, he did *not* appreciate the joke.

She hesitated, unsure just how to proceed. But then, in a sudden flash of inspiration, she pulled her hair back, snapped it in place with an elastic band from her back pocket, and hurried towards them feigning distress.

"Oh good, *there* you are!"

Both Billy and Jack turned, while James dropped his bag and took a few quick steps towards her, holding out his arms.

"Kelly! Thank God you're alright!"

The level of her disinterest could have blistered him; but unable to avoid his touch, she reluctantly allowed him to give her a hug, immediately pulling away to restore the distance between them.

"James!" she said, her revulsion palatable. "What are *you* doing *here*?"

His spirits sagged. This was not the reunion he had fantasized. But sadly, it was the one he had expected. Burying his disappointment, his eyes traveled reflexively over her body, his hunger plain beneath his concern.

"How are you?" he asked, reaching out a second time.

Unable to escape his visual scrutiny, she took a quick step back. She could avoid his touch at least.

Hurt by her evasion, anger colored his face. "And what in the *hell* happened!!?" he snapped.

She took another step back, looking at his drawn, but still handsome face. *'It really is too bad you are such an asshole.'*

"*I'm* fine, but the raft was badly damaged. As a matter of fact, I need these two guys to come down to the river and help me with a problem." She turned to Jack, hoping her eyes would convey her meaning.

He nodded. "I'm sure we can help."

The lustful scrutiny James had displayed for Kelly shifted to clear distaste as it swept over the two men, and it was with barely contained jealousy he turned back to her.

"Can *I* help?"

"No, James," she said, forcing a smile. "But thanks. I think the three of us can handle it. Tell you what tho,' there's a cooler on the porch with some wine. Why don't you take it down to the Airstream trailer behind the store and clean up? I'm sure you could use a shower after your trip. Go on down, clean up, and relax. We'll take care of this and join you shortly." She looked over to Billy. "That's okay with you isn't it?"

Billy smiled at her, winked, and turned to James, assuming the role of genial host. "Of course. Mister Carson, please, be my guest. The clean towels are in the small cabinet in the bathroom and the clean glasses are in the kitchen to the right above the sink."

James knew he was beaten. He cast a suspicious look at the three of them, then looked to Kelly with a petulant frown.

"I hope you have a good red in that cooler." He snarled, his tone that of a dissatisfied customer speaking to an incompetent waiter. Kelly closed her eyes, touching her forehead as if she felt a headache coming on, and struggling to maintain her smile, she nodded. "I'm sure you'll find something *acceptable,* James."

Turning as if it might make him disappear, she looked at Jack, smiled, and held out her hand.

"Hi, I'm Kelly, nice helicopter!"

The warmth evident as the three introduced themselves left James feeling displaced yet again. He turned, and as he walked towards the store his misery increased with every step.

'I should have known better.'

Kelly watched him go. Then taking Jack by the arm, hustled both he and Billy towards the river. As she did, she looked over her shoulder to see James trudge up the stairs; the slump of his shoulders indicating the level of his misery: the intensity making her feel that much better. Smiling, she turned to Jack.

"Teller has talked about you."

"And I've heard about you as well,' Jack replied. "Although you *are* as beautiful as described."

Kelly turned a puzzled, yet defiant expression on him.

"And just what is *that* supposed to mean?"

Jack laughed, stepping beside her to lay his arm lightly around her shoulder as they walked. "Well, Willie told me about you, and you know how musicians exaggerate."

Her smile returned, instantly put at ease with his company and just a quickly understanding why this man and Teller were friends. "Well," she said, looking him directly in the eyes. "There are some things even Willie can't lie about."

Jack chuckled. This woman was Teller's match. With complete sincerity he responded. "No, but in this case he didn't even try."

Billy was following a few steps behind; thoroughly enjoying this exchange and thinking that the more he discovered about Teller and the people he surrounded himself with, the more he understood what had attracted Coyote's attention. But on thinking of Coyote he quickened his pace, stepping in beside them and directing his attention to Kelly.

"So then Miss Kelly, what do *you* think of Teller's story? is it a lie?"

There was no hesitation whatsoever in her answer.

"No Billy," she smiled. "Teller only stretches the facts if he thinks it makes a *better* story. This one needs no exaggeration.

71

Besides, with the coyote carving and the gold to back it up, I think it's the truth."

Billy nodded. He also felt what Jack had felt: that this woman was different; and the fact that Kelly believed what Teller had told them without question or doubt proved that she too, was worthy of Coyote and that Teller was a very lucky man indeed.

But Jack, having no idea what they were talking about, stopped in mid-step.

"What the *hell* are you two talking about?"

Billy stopped beside him, smiling as he turned his attention back to Kelly. "Just what was it that you needed *our* help with?"

Kelly slowed to look back over her shoulder; but seeing no sign of James, she stopped and placed a hand on both Billy's and Jack's chest. "I don't. Teller just wanted me to get James to go down to the trailer alone."

Jack's first expression was that of curious suspicion. But then a smile took its place. "Any Idea what he's got in mind?"

Kelly's eyes reflected a momentary concern. She was well aware of the animosity between the two men. But thinking of Benny, alone in a hospital in Denver, they hardened.

"No, I don't. But whatever it is he deserves it."

Dropping her hands, she turned and began walking towards the river. "Come on guys, we've got some beer in my tent."

Jack looked at Billy, then took a couple of quick steps to catch up. "Great," he breathed. "I could use one. And I don't know what that guy did to piss you and Teller off, but I can understand. I sure wanted to slap him more than once."

Kelly raised an eyebrow. "And why didn't you?"

Jack smiled, but it was devoid of humor.

"Cause the bastard hasn't paid me yet."

"That's reasonable," Kelly nodded. "How about after he's paid you?"

The three of them stepped into the welcome shade of a large Cottonwood tree and the temperature dropped by several degrees. Jack smiled, leaned against the trees rough bark, and took off his cap.

"Well," he said, running his hand through his hair. "I guess that'll all depend on if Teller leaves anything to slap."

Kelly liked this man more already.

= Chapter 15 =

James watched Kelly walk towards the lake with the two men. His annoyance with Jack had returned. And now this old goddamned Indian seemed to be mocking him as well.

He plopped angrily onto the bench next to the cooler.

Did everyone Teller associate with lack respect?

The thought that perhaps *he* might be the problem flitted on the edges of his subconscious for the briefest of moments but was just as quickly shoved back into his ego's sack of self-denial. He buried his face in his hands. It seemed that his entire life was coming unwound.

'This isn't working out as planned. I had hoped she'd at least be glad to see me. The only thing in my favor now is that Teller's not around.' With that realization his thoughts went to Jack. *'Ha!'* he smiled bitterly. *'Guess I won't have to pay that jerk-off pilot the extra five bills.'* It was small consolation; but with everything else going wrong, screwing him out of the bet provided a small degree of satisfaction. Buoyed nominally by the thought, he decided that he would not fall victim to weakness. Taking a deep breath, he opened the cooler.

His newfound gratification was immediately extinguished.

"Christ," he grumbled. "Who drinks this crap?"

Cursing his luck, he dug through the ice, despising all the peons that drank mediocre wine. But as he dug deeper his efforts were rewarded. Pulling up a bottle of Fetzer Cabernet, he checked the vintage and smiled for the first time since their arrival. *'Hmmm, an '87', maybe things are looking up.'*

Lighter of step he bounced down the stairs towards the trailer, his sense of optimism renewed.

'Yes Sir, a long hot shower and a glass of decent wine. That'll help wash the taste of Jack, and all of his disrespectful friends shit out of my mouth.'

As James made his way down the path, his devious mind worked every angle that might turn Kelly to his side. But as he rounded the corner his happy schemes were torpedoed.

It was worse than he had expected.

There was nothing but an old trailer next to a giant boulder with a beat-up table at the foot of its stairs. But his initial disappointment was over-shadowed by a sense of danger.

His pace slowed… something was wrong.

On the table were four empty wine glasses next to a plastic five-gallon bucket: bottles of Coors poking out of the ice.

James came to a full stop and looked to his left.

Any simple curiosity he may have had regarding this unexpected table setting was jettisoned. There, a man crouched on one knee at the fire pit; his back to James.

The man lit a match and held it to the kindling.

The small flame flared and the man lowered his face to blow on the diminutive flame until the kindling caught. The fire grew quickly, crackling throughout the carefully arranged wood and sending tendrils of smoke curling into the dusk… and from behind that smoke came a voice.

"There." It said, its tone so cold it seemed to suck the heat from the air. "Now the mood is set."

The flames lighting his face, Teller turned, his smile so predatory James heart nearly stopped

"*Hel-lo* James." he said, slowly rising. "Fancy running into *you* here. My, my, my, it seems a smaller world everyday does it not? Don't bother answering that Jim. That you're here is proof enough. But, disturbingly, your being here also raises a much larger question… one that forces me to ask this. Have you *already* forgotten our last conversation?"

James' grip on the wine bottle increased, turning his knuckles white as fear rose in his throat. Struck speechless, he took a step back; fighting the instinct to bolt. But there was no place to run.

Teller moved in James' direction, speaking softly, but every word radiating danger.

"So then James, what happened? I thought that I made myself *quite* clear of the outcome, should our paths cross again."

James finally found his tongue.

"Hey Teller. I'm not looking for trouble."

"Trouble?" Teller said, shaking his head as the slightest of smiles touched his lips. "Trouble...? You know, James, it's a funny thing. I've recently found that what a man is looking for, and what he finds, are often two *completely* different animals."

"Have a seat, Jim." he smiled. "We need to talk."

Teller released his grip and James collapsed onto the bench, shoving his hands under the table to hide their shaking: for while he considered himself no coward this was simply too much. He had most certainly *not* forgotten Teller's threat back at the bar in Telluride. Yet here he was. Sitting across a table from the same man once again: and, if possible, under even *less* friendly circumstances.

The air seemed to mute every sound but the pounding of his own heart; and trying to calm it he looked across the table to where Teller sat, his face unreadable.

James flinched as Teller suddenly reached across the table, but it was only to pull a beer from the sweat-covered bucket. Then, in a gesture that comforted James to a small degree, Teller tilted his head, silently indicating that James was welcome to help himself.

James gave a meek shake of his head.

"Suit yourself." Teller shrugged.

Nothing more was said as dusk settled across the land, shadows masking Tellers features as he studied James in the same way a leopard studies a cornered gazelle. And as the seconds ticked by, James felt his web of lies growing tighter, constricting his throat as Teller leaned forward, closing the gap between them, his cold eyes chilling James to the marrow.

"So tell me James," Teller said, breaking the silence. "What *exactly* is it that tempts you from your Kingdom up in the cool green of our beloved Rockies to *this* over-irrigated hellhole?"

Shifting uncomfortably, James mumbled, "I wanted to come down to talk to the guys that rescued my nephew."

Teller leaned back, scratching his whiskered chin: an air of supreme amusement lighting his face. "Really!? that's mighty considerate of you James. Surprising however... As a matter of fact, it's completely out of character. Hmmm. Thinking of a reward perhaps?"

"N-n-no." James stammered. "I hadn't thought about that."

Teller's smile dropped. "No, I don't suppose you would have. Not your style. Nope, not your style at all. And speaking of a pathetic lack of style, how *is* little Benny anyway?"

Having decided that Teller was not going to kill him, James' anger was slowly displacing his fear. But wariness held his temper, and his tongue, in check.

"He's alive. He's being cared for in Denver General."

"Really?" Teller's eyebrows rose. "Did Jack fly him up there?"

Now James was losing his cool.

"Yeah, Teller, he did, and if I had known you and that asshole pilot were buddies I would never have hired him"

Teller's eyes sparked.

He was out of his seat so fast that James didn't have time to register the move. One moment he was facing Teller and the next he was leaning backwards, nearly off the bench with Teller's hands planted firmly on the table, smiling menacingly and wilting what little was left of James's attitude.

"Yes, James," he said, slowly lowering himself back into his seat. "That *asshole* is a *very* good friend of mine. And I'm quite sure that if he had known what a backstabbing cocksucker *you* are, he would have tossed your sorry ass out of the helicopter on the way here."

James flashed back to that horrific moment hanging over the La Plata Mountains, and the ice in Jack's eyes.

Had he really come that close? He wondered, momentarily humbled. But quickly succumbing to ego, his fear turned anger to arrogance.

"What the hell do you want, Teller? and what are you doing *here?* You're supposed to be in Texas!"

James's predictable reaction diffused Tellers fury; turning his rage into amused annoyance. Settling onto the bench, he gave a cold smile. "An enigma wrapped in a mystery, remember? Besides, you know how I feel about Texas." Seeing the throbbing pulse in James' throat slow, Teller slid the corkscrew across the table.

"Open your wine, James."

Snatching up the corkscrew James pulled the cork; but when he tipped the bottle his shaking hand spilled as much as got poured in and Teller's mocking smile didn't help.

Gathering every molecule of self-control, James set the bottle down. Griping his glass tightly, he lifted it to his lips and drained it. His hands were still shaking as he refilled the glass, but he spilled less on the table.

Teller waited until James finished his third glass of wine then leaned back, casually checking the fingernails on his left hand.

James grip nearly shattered his glass as he leaned forward.

In a playback from the bar in Telluride, Teller's fists shot out, taking James by the collar and yanking him halfway across the table to bring his shocked face within inches of his own.

"Because he was an arrogant, two-faced little prick, just like his uncle. The only difference between the two of you, is that *he* was too stupid to steal without getting caught."

Throwing James roughly back, Teller placed both palms on the table. "*You* only took my idea, James." he said with deadly calm. "But you took it with my help, and eventually, my approval. Ben, on the other hand, tried to steal from me like a coward. A literal thief in the night. So yeah, I cracked his jaw. But I did *not* try to drown his worthless little ass."

Teller picked up his beer, his eyes never leaving James' stunned expression.

"No, he disappeared one night with a knife, and *I* am the one who went looking for him. I have no idea how he got to wherever those guys found him, but I assure you I did *not* try to kill him." He paused giving with a cold smile while his eyes bored into James' heart. "Although the thought *did* cross my mind."

James stared at Teller; guilt and suspicion weighing equal in his devious mind. But it was fear was that kept him silent.

Teller held James' eyes for a moment more, then continued,

At this, James jumped up.

"Now wait a goddamned minute!" he shouted, lifting his fist to slam the table. But as it touched the woods rough grain, Teller's hand shot out, snatching James's fist so quickly James had no time to react. Squeezing like a vise, Teller smiled as he pinned it against the tabletop. "As I was saying; you can either catch a ride with them, *James*, or you can join your worthless fucking nephew in the hospital."

"Fuck you Teller!" James squealed as he attempted to jerk away. "You can't do-" but his objection quickly became a whimpering mewl of pain as bones began to crack.

Cold satisfaction in his smile, Teller slowly squeezed harder, the pain of every incremental micro-ounce of compression reflecting in James' eyes

"And one other thing." Teller growled, pulling James closed and forcing him to look into eyes that were colder than his smile.

"I told you once to quit doggin' Kelly, James, and I meant it. I know *why* you came down here, so you can save your breath trying to tell me it was out of concern for that dipshit nephew of yours."

Teller's eyes turned to glittering ice.

"I *gave* you the keys to Telluride, James, and that should have been enough; even for *you*. Try and show some dignity for Christ sake. This is the *last* time we are going to have this conversation James. Next time you'll go home neutered."

He released James' fist.

"Do we have an understanding, 'Partner'?"

James stuck his hand into the ice bucket and glared, "I am *not* riding back with *those* people." He growled through clenched teeth. Then, pulling his dripping hand from the bucket, he smiled smugly. "I've hired the helicopter to take me back."

Teller looked at James in disbelief, then broke into extravagant laughter while James' arrogant grin faltered.

It took a moment for Teller to catch his breath.

"Your flight's been canceled." He smiled. "That bird's been requisitioned for other purposes."

James sat in shocked silence as all of his anger, fear, and frustration coalesced. Finally, he screamed, "You son of a bitch! You can't do that!"

"But I can." Teller grinned. "It's a simple matter of priorities. You see, I need to help a friend who is in distress."

James jumped up, banging his fist on the table and hurting again as he did. "But I need to get back to Telluride!"

Teller's smile vanished and all of the menace that had left his eyes resurfaced. "I said I need it to help a *friend,* James. You removed yourself from that group some time ago. What*ever* your needs, they mean less than *nothing* to me. So, *your* best choice is option number one."

Swinging a leg over the bench, he took a few steps, then he stopped and turned. "Of course, if you *insist* on pushing me, we still have option number two."

James began to argue. but the throbbing in his hand made him think better of it. "*Fine.*" he hissed. "I'll ride back in the truck."

Teller was no more than a shadow in the night by the time he answered, but his voice was bright. "Wise choice, Jim."

Chapter 16

Jack flipped his wrist, checking his watch for the third time. "Think we should start diggin' a hole?"

"Nah," Kelly laughed. You know Teller, his bark's worse than his bite."

"You're wrong there, Kelly." he said, raising one eyebrow. "I've *seen* that dogs bite. The bites survival all depends on how far he gets pushed.

"Really?" Kelly frowned, nibbling the end of a frayed nail.

"No," Jack said, shaking his head. "It's not like that. Teller doesn't go crazy. *That's* what makes him so dangerous. He stays calm, but if the person doing the pushing isn't wise enough to stop, Teller'll take the time to explain to 'em. Then, if they're foolish enough to continue, well, let's just say it's not long before they wish they'd paid a little more attention." He paused and took a drink. "Think James will push too far?"

Kelly hesitated. "Well, they've known each other a long time and it hasn't happened yet."

Jack nodded, admiring Kelly's profile. Her beauty made it easy to understand how a problem could develop between two men.

He finished his drink. "Yes dear," he smiled. "But there's a first time for everything. I think we should go on down and see." He bowed and swept his hand toward the trailer. "Shall we?"

A whisper of a smile crossed her lips and she walked over to where Billy rocked back and forth.

"You coming?"

Billy rocked to a stop, then taking the carving from his pocket, held it to his eye.

"No, you two go on, perhaps I will join you later."

He turned the coyote slightly and Kelly could have sworn she saw the little statue shimmer... Billy looked up, winked, closed his fist around the little statue and turned his attention to Jack.

Kelly's face went white. "Oh shit!!" she cried. "I forgot about Abbott!"

Jack, on the other hand, looked baffled.

"Who's Abbott?"

Both guilt and anxiety colored Kelly's face. "Abbott went with Teller to look for Benny."

To Jack, this meant absolutely nothing. He turned to Billy for clarification but Kelly grabbed him by the sleeve. "Teller can explain. Let's go!"

Jack was no closer to an answer, but giving a shrug, he poked the cooler at this feet with the toe of his boot.

"Shall I bring this?"

"Does it have beer?"

Jack lifted the lid. "A little."

"Then it's enough for now." She nodded, then turned. "Hey Billy, did you say you had more beer somewhere?"

Billy was elsewhere; lost in the Coyote.

"Billy . . ." She said, kneeling in front of him. "Beer?"

His eyes came back into focus, and he looked up.

"Oh, yes, down in the Hogan... besides the walk-in it is the coolest place here. You will find more beer there." He wrapped his fingers around the sculpture and closed his eyes.

Kelly stood. "You'll need to take beer for Abbott."

The comment jogged his memory. Teller had said something on the phone regarding the rescue of a bear. Cocking his head, he looked at Kelly. "Abbott's a beer drinking bear?"

A bewildered look crossed her face, but then her eyes lit up.

"Yeah," she laughed, "I guess he is!"

Then taking him by the elbow she tugged. "Let's go!"

Jack lifted the cooler onto his shoulder as Kelly asked, "How in the world did you come up with that?"

Jack's expression was one of puzzled humor.

"When Teller first called me, he said something about our needing to fly out and pick up a bear. Then when you said we needed beer, well…"

Kelly giggled, her smile one of warmth and love. The guy never ceased to amuse.

"Well, I'll let *him* explain about Abbott." She said, hurrying her pace. "Provided he hasn't killed James yet."

Jack set the cooler down and took three quick strides, stepping in front of Kelly to take her by the shoulders.

"Do you have any feelings for him, Kelly?" He probed her heart with his gaze and was pleased to see the bewilderment in her eyes was sincere. "Who? James?"

He nodded.

Kelly reacted as if she had been slapped.

"Of course not!!" she cried, pulling away. "He's my boss and I tolerate him; even though he's a pig. But no! Not if you mean it like it sounds."

Jack's smile returned. "Well then," he said, picking up the cooler. "If that's the case then James is likely to survive."

= Chapter 17 =

Jack, hard on Kelly's heels rounded the massive stone that sheltered the trailer, walking into the low-lying smoke that hung heavy in the air. Air redolent of cooking meat.

Teller glanced up. "*There* you are! he grinned, shoving a fat stick into the flames while glancing to the trail behind Jack.

"So, where's Billy?"

Kelly's head swiveled, looking for James. Not seeing him, she experienced the instant, while unlikely, thought that it was he that was cooking on the grill. But on seeing only steaks sizzling over the coals she exhaled a sigh of relief, chuckling at her paranoia.

"He's up at the store communing with your Coyote." she said, her eyes darting about. "But where's James...? is he alright?"

Teller held up his spatula, the picture of innocence. "He's in the shower cleaning up. And why wouldn't he be?"

"You know damned well why, Tell." she laughed, throwing her arms around his neck. He returned the hug but on looking over her head at Jack, his grin increased a thousand-fold.

"Jack! Good to see you again old chum! Hang on just a sec."

Beaming with happiness, he gently unwrapped himself from Kelly's arms and kissing her solidly on the lips strode towards Jack, wiping his hands on his pants as he walked.

Jack stood where he was; his eyes unreadable behind the sunglasses. But his smile grew larger by the second.

Tellers pace never changed. He simply stepped up, wrapping muscular arms around Jack's waist and lifting him off the ground with a bone-crushing hug that made Jack wheeze like a punctured Accordion.

"How the *hell* have you been Jacko?" Teller laughed as he put him down.

Jesus, Teller" Jack coughed, struggling to regain his breath. "Take it easy! Kelly tells me we need to fly outta here tomorrow... James busted my balls all the way here, I don't need you bustin' my back!"

Teller reached into the beer bucket, pulled out two bottles and handed one to Jack "Glad you still *got* balls Jack. And speaking of, how's the wife?"

Massaging his side, Jack winced as he took the proffered beer. "She's gone off to Las Vegas Teller, and it's a story I'm sure you would appreciate. But now is not the time. And speaking of time, it seems we are pressed for it." He threw a thumb in Kelly's direction. "Kelly here says you have a beer drinking bear in need of rescue."

Teller followed Jack's thumb to Kelly. "What's he talking about?"

"Abbott," she grinned.

"Oh!" Teller laughed, of course! *that* bear!"

Twisting the cap from his bottle, he took a seat on the bench.

Jack gave a nod. "No problem Tell. We have the chopper, so all we need to do is fuel up and do a flight check. What kind of medical you think he'll need?"

Kelly smiled, slid over, and snuggled under Teller's arm.

"I don't know for sure, Jack. Teller said, kissing the top of Kelly's head. "I left him with water and food and put a cast on the ankle, but still . . ."

"You put a cast on him?" Jack asked, cocking his head.

Teller's smile was both proud and humble, but mostly amused. "Come on, Jack, you know me. The child of the mother of invention. That, and I now possess a custom-made short sleeved Pendleton."

With a shrug that spoke of his many years of experience with Teller, Jack didn't try to understand. He simply smiled.

"You've always been a snappy dresser Tell, *and* a survivor." He paused and looked around. "And speaking of surviving, where's your buddy James?"

Fury flashed in Tellers eyes only to be quickly replaced by a chilly smile. "James? Oh, he has, through deep reflection, seen the error of his ways and so, will be joining the rest of the crew for the ride back. Although quite reluctantly I might add. It seems he finds travel with the lower classes somewhat distasteful. Oh, and by the way. I suppose I don't need to say it, but he no longer requires your services."

Jack tipped his beer in Teller's direction, then turned to Kelly.

"See what I mean about barks and bites?"

She just smiled and shook her head.

Jack turned back to Teller. "Understood, and I thank you. He might not have survived the return trip. So, you said he was in the trailer?"

Teller nodded. "Last I saw."

Jack tipped his bottle up, swallowed and stood. Then, with a cold smile, cracked his knuckles. "Well then if you two will excuse me, I believe I'll go collect for services rendered."

Teller's grin radiated amusement, but on glancing at the grill, smiled, "A capital idea my friend, but make it quick. Those steaks'll be ready in about ten minutes." He kissed Kelly on the forehead and stood. "Hey babe, there's a basket of veggies on the table there. Would you mind finding some bowls to whip up a salad? And you got a knife by chance?"

She gave a shrug and a smile. "Sorry Tell. Everything's in the trailer."

He picked up the wine bottle. "Well go get it then. I'll pour some wine and check the meat. And see if Billy has any steak sauce in there. Oh, and salad dressing too."

Kelly snatched the wine from him and pulled it to her chest.

"If you don't mind, Tell, I think I'll just wait out here."

"Why would you…" he stopped mid-sentence, then smiled as his eyes went to the closed door of the Airstream. He was not the only one with a formidable bite.

"Good Idea." he nodded and giving Kelly a quick kiss, moved the steaks to the outside edges of the grill.

A moment later the crew's laughter echoed through the dusk and within minutes Fred, Skip and Lori came around the corner. As usual, Fred was the first to speak up.

"Mmmm. Smells good. When do we eat?"

"Soon, Fred," Teller smiled, "Soon."

Everyone but Lori stopped at the table: instead, she stepped around, picked up two glasses, grabbed the bottle of red and poured, keeping one and handing the other to Skip, who accepted with a grunt; his smile barely visible through an unruly tangle of newly grown beard.

Teller frowned as he watched. But Fred just took the bottle from Lori and poured himself a glass.

"So," he said, turning to Teller. "What happened?"

"About what?"

"About why we had to wait in the back room of the store. That's *what.*"

Teller shrugged. "I just needed a little privacy to explain something to my ex-partner."

Kelly grinned into her empty glass. But when she saw that Fred was about to ask for more details she gave a delicate cough; catching his eye and giving slight shake of her head while mouthing the word, "Don't."

Fred wisely acknowledged and changed the subject.

"So, when do we eat?"

A burst of light suddenly swept across the table as the trailers door swung open. Jack stepped out, then pushed the door closed, extinguishing the light.

Teller watched, then laying his palms on the table, pushed himself up. "Fred, why don't you go check the steaks? Leave mine off if you would, I'd rather have it cold than overcooked." He looked down at Kelly and smiled. "I'll be back with the salad bowls."

Kelly watched him go then picked up the now half-empty bottle. "Hang on Fred, I'll help."

Teller met Jack halfway between the trailer and the fire.

Jack gave a snort. "Which news are you talking about? The grim fact that you're here, or the unpleasant reality that he no longer has a flight back to Telluride?"

Teller's smile shone in the half-light of evening. "Fuck *those* details! I'm talking about the fact that the tight sonofabitch had to pay you!"

Everyone at the table glanced their way as Jack erupted with laughter. "Oh, that..." lowering his voice he chuckled, "He asked me if I would take a check."

Tellers incredulity inspired a few more moments of uncontrolled snickering, then Jack smiled. "I told him I'd need to ask *you* if I could trust him."

At that, they both broke into sidesplitting laughter that left them both speechless for the next few minutes. Finally, the hilarity subsided and Teller managed to ask; "So how much does he owe you?"

Jack brushed a tear from his cheek and gave what he considered a fair figure. Teller nodded, reached into his pocket, took out one of the coins he had taken from the chest in the cave, and flipped it in Jacks direction.

"This should cover it."

The toss was a little high, but snatching it as it sailed by, Jack gave Teller a dubious glance as he rubbed away some tarnish with his thumb. "Where did you get *this?*"

Teller's face clouded with weariness. "That, my friend, is a long . . ." he halted in mid-sentence. "I am *really* getting tired of saying that." But his angst vanished, and he burst into an enormous smile. "But now that I think about it, that just might be the perfect epitaph for my headstone:

"Here lies Franklin James Teller. It was a *looong* story."

Laughing, Jack turned the coin over. "This is cool, Tell, and you say it'll cover my expenses with asshole?"

"Yeah Jack, it is and it will, and there's more where that came from. But I'd rather show you than tell it all again. So for tonight, just let it rest. I'll give you the gist of it all tomorrow when we're in the air. But for now, I'm going to go in and get a personal check from James. In the meantime, if you know anyone who will fly down here and take that miserable prick back to Telluride, call 'em up. I'm sure James would be more than happy to have an alternative to the truck ride with the crew, and not having *him* along would no doubt make the trip home considerably more pleasant for them as well."

James nodded. "Yeah, I sure as hell wouldn't want to be stuck in a truck with him for eight hours. I'll call an old friend up in Junction, He's a little expensive but he's got a nice chopper and he'd probably do it for the right price."

Teller shrugged. "That's his problem. He pays or he stays." Setting foot on the first stair to the trailer, he turned. "I've got to collect a check and some dinnerware. Go see if Kelly needs a hand, wouldja?

Jack nodded. "Sure, Tell."

On his way back to the table Jack made the phone call to arrange for James' return flight. He laughed, hung up, and walked over to where Kelly stood at the grill. Picking up the empty bottle he dangled it between the two fingers of his left hand. "Teller asked me to come help you out. How may I be of service?"

Kelly tipped her head at the empty bottle. "You can open a fresh one of those for starters. Where is Tell anyway?"

"He's in the trailer." Jack smiled, pulling a bottle out of the cooler and checking the label.

"Any preference on vintners?"

"Na, long as it's red and chilled."

Smiling, he handed her the magnum. "This one's both."

"Then it's perfect." but glancing around for a corkscrew frowned. "Damn! Must be in the trailer. Think it's safe to go in yet?"

Jack just shrugged.

Kelly waited a minute, then looked at him with semi-serious concern. "Well, we haven't heard any bloody screams yet."

This time Jack added a depraved smile.

"Teller would never allow his victim to scream."

Kelly made a face. "That's awful, Jack."

Jack thought for a moment, then, with a conciliatory nod, grinned, "Cry like a little girl maybe, but never scream."

She shook her head. "That's no better."

"Sure it is." he laughed,

At that moment the trailer door flew open and James stepped out, his arms loaded with plates and bowls; unharmed but clearly chastised. Seeing the expression on his face, Jack leaned into Kelly's ear. "But not far from the truth."

Kelly politely covered her mouth, stifling her laughter to avoid embarrassing James any further.

Jack's grin grew as he set the bottle on the table and stood.

Halfway between the fire and the trailer, Jack confronted James; James tried to sidestep, but Jack stepped in the same direction, clamping a hand on James' bicep bringing him to a reluctant halt where he somehow managed to cringe and appear arrogant at the same time.

"So, Jim," Jack smiled pleasantly. "Since this emergency of Teller's came up, I took the liberty of contacting another pilot up in Grand Junction and made arrangements for him to fly down and pick you up. Hope that's okay."

James' eyes went from Jack's face to the load of dishes in his arms. "Do I have a goddamn choice?" he growled, shoving the plates at Jack.

Jack stepped back, holding his hands up as if he were being robbed at gunpoint. "'Course you do, Jim. You can ride back in the truck or you can fly back with my friend. It's your call. Personally, I don't give a shit."

90

James juggled to keep the stack balanced as the plates shifted, a bowl dropping into the grass at his feet. Glowering, he gave it a kick. "What's it going to cost me?"

Jack picked up the bowl and placed it on the top of the wobbly pile, reaching around the stack to tuck one of his business cards into James' shirt pocket.

"I wrote his number on the back of that." He grinned. "You can call him yourself and negotiate the price." Stepping back, he touched the bill of his cap. "Good luck Jim."

Turning towards the trailer, he took a few steps but then stopped and turned, his smile radiating generosity.

"By the way. Remember that extra five hundred you owe me from the bet? Keep it. You can apply it to whatever he charges you. Merry Christmas, James." Touching his cap again, he whistled up the three steps and disappeared into the trailer.

James, fuming at his state of total helplessness, stood there, his arms full of plates, watching Jack duck through the small arched trailer door; and as it closed, shutting off all light, he wondered where it all went wrong.

~

Teller lay on the small bunk staring at the rounded ceiling. His head was crowded with questions; but on hearing the sound of feet coming up the stairs he tucked them away and sat up, folding James' check and tucking it into his shirt pocket.

The door opened and closed, and Jack went to the tiny kitchen without a word. Teller sat for a moment, then rolled off the bed to take the few steps it required to cross the trailer.

Five drawers had been pulled out and Jack was rummaging through the sixth.

"So amigo, what do you think?"

At first, Jack said nothing. But when he turned around, he held up a folding corkscrew and pushed the drawer closed with his hip. "I think I've found what I was looking for."

Teller gave a tired smile. "That's it? Your quest is now complete? Fuck Jack, I had somehow hoped the meaning of life involved more than a corkscrew."

Jack shrugged, slipped the device into his pocket, and opened the trailer door. But as he stepped out he turned and gave Teller a world-weary smile. "I'm quite sure it does, Tell, but I wasn't looking for the meaning of life, I was looking for a corkscrew. Which, by the way, is *much* easier to find. So, I am *now* going to continue my endless search for earthly pleasures in the depths of the fermented grape. Come on out and join me. We can always search for the meaning of life tomorrow."

Jack's smile struck a note of kinship; and having his trusted friend back at his side helped shake Teller out of his malaise.

"Sure." Teller grinned. "But tomorrow we search for Abbott. The meaning of life will have to wait for another day."

_ __ \-\- \-\-\- \-\-__ __
___ __ \-\- \-\-\- \-\-

= Chapter 18 =

Abbott was bored.

Having completed his daily shuffling loop around the cave he now sat on a flat stone; examining the ugly mix of black, yellow and purples that colored his ankle. Clenching his teeth, he rotated the foot. It was painful, but manageable. That was good news; but the damn thing still hurt and he was far too weak to walk out of here on his own. Stabbing the last of the rabbit carcass with the charred stick that served as his rotisserie, he slowly turned it over the flames, unconsciously lifting his nose to the aroma of the meat as it warmed.

Watching the smoke rise as he waited, he thought again of Estebanico and the bizarre circumstances under which they had found his remains. He let his mind wander, his thoughts gathering with the smoke that pooled in the pockets of the rock ceiling, following the contours of the weathered stone and out into the air; where his musings had more room for analysis.

Looking back, nothing seemed out of the ordinary.

The entire thing had started as a simple rafting trip. At least until Teller had appeared... it was at that moment *everything* had changed. But now, with time to consider things fully and after the fact, he could see that his life, and his decisions, followed a definite pattern. One that had culminated in his final decision of joining this particular crew.

~

As a ranking member of the Denver Museum of Natural History's Archeology Department, Abbott was well liked and well respected. But his position within the faculty held minimal prestige and sadly, his pay was reflected in that minimalism. Fortunately, however, he felt that while the pay was inadequate, that in, and of itself, was a minor issue: no more than a small brushstroke in a much larger picture. For with low profile came anonymity; and it was that anonymity which provided him with what he liked to refer to as his: "Cloak of invisibility." For the fact that he did *not* draw high payroll was *precisely* the same reason he was left alone. And being left alone allowed him the freedom to pursue his own projects while still fulfilling his museum duties. This combination resulted in his superiors rarely pressing him for details of his work, nor asking where he was working. And that resulted in Abbott's being able to claim the entire southwest as his office; with his answering machine being his endlessly indulgent secretary.

It was the perfect example of intellectual bureaucracy.

And, best of all, it provided him with the time to pursue his current fascination: a series of petroglyphs that not only depicted the creation of the Hopi and the history of their people; it told of the white mans arrival and the unfolding events that will lead to the end of the world... all on a simple slab of ancient sandstone known as 'Prophecy Rock.' So, after months of administrative paperwork and the endless cajoling of his superiors, Abbott had finally wrangled a pittance of additional funding for a loosely related dig that just happened to be in the area of his pet project.

Once packed, he had disappeared.

~

Despite the fact that Abbott had been less than one hundred percent clear on the nature of his: "official" museum sanctioned project, he was an honest man. And thus, at the close of the third week on his authorized assignment, he had decided to take a side trip to the Hopi Reservation where years earlier he had met one of the village elders. The men had taken an immediate liking to one another. They were kindred souls, and before long were as close as brothers. And, to add to Abbotts pleasure, the old fellow was not only talkative, he always seemed delighted to converse on the subject of Abbotts current obsession: Prophecy Rock.

Having spent three glorious days listening to the elder tell of the creation of the Hopi, with countless hours of interpretation by the old fellow's grandson, he had left the old man's Hogan with a notebook filled with condensed scribbling and the promise to return just as soon as he could manage: and included in that promise was the delivery of the old man's double vices: Licorice and tobacco.

It was a promise he had intended to keep.

And so, after leaving the Res, he had found himself driving Highway 550. Lost in the scenic splendor of the high country and more reluctant than usual to return to the Museum. He hadn't realized it at the time, but now, sitting in this cave alone with nothing but time to contemplate his existence, he recalled a subliminal nudging; a suggestion that there were greater things than hurrying back to work. As a matter of fact, in retrospect, he recalled that the desire to return to the canyons was practically irresistible.

And now, staring up at the gathering smoke, he realized that there had been something else. It had been more instinct than conscious decision that had prompted him to take the turn-off outside of Ouray, and following *that* reflex, to make the detour to Telluride: led by impulse over Dallas Pass and into the crushing beauty of that dead-end valley.

Once arrived he had given himself to the fates; parking his truck and making his way to his favorite bar where, once settled onto a stool prepared to enjoy the first of what would be many cold brews. And he intended on doing it while watching the new, and lovely, bartender.

She was truly beautiful as well as funny, and like every other man in the room he nursed a slight crush as he watched her work. The difference between he and the other barstool occupants however, was that he could see that she clearly had no interest whatsoever in any of the men vying for her attentions. She simply went about her job, delivering clever banter, serving drinks, and turning down even the rudest advances with poised panache.

He chuckled as he remembered that on his first visit he had covertly checked her left hand for a ring; and seeing none his hopes had soared. But, being a realist had quickly calculated his odds of success... and as he accepted those odds to be somewhere below zero, he let those hopes crash; and joining the rest of the men in a pleasant but fleeting fantasy went back to simply enjoying the view: content in the hum of bar noise and watching her work her magic.

Then things changed.

Picking up his third empty she wiped a rag across the bar, pointing to his dusty hat and asking him where he had been. Surprised, and practically glowing at the attention, he told her his story, quickly becoming the envy of every male patron in the place; and when the exchange went beyond his drink order and to the details of his adventures, he could almost hear their jealous grumbling.

The time passed quickly for them both. He appreciating her wry sense of humor, and she fascinated with his knowledge of the area and its history. The exchange deepened as they found shared common interests, and upon discovering that he was a white-water enthusiast she became more animated still.

He remembered that moment with absolute clarity.

She had been refilling his mug while he told the story of one of his more spectacular trips down the Yellowstone River: and as he reached the harrowing climax, her emerald eyes had opened wide. And now, as he lay on his back staring up into the smoke, recognition dawned: *'The very same color as the stones Teller found.'* The thought was accompanied by the absolute certainty that it was no coincidence.

With that, his memories returned.

He had no more than finished his story when she smiled, "Some friends and I are going to take a trip down the Green River day after tomorrow. Would you like to join us?"

His mind was made before she had finished the sentence.

"I would enjoy that *very* much," he had answered with eager anticipation.

~

Abbott's thoughts returned to the present. *'Fate intervened at that moment. And now here I am, awaiting the yang to her yin for my rescue, and both now the subject of mythical intervention.* Abbott's eyes followed the wisps and curls of the smoke as they blended together, only to separate again... much like his life.

He thought further.

'All led to an amazing discovery that will certainly shake up the historical community; and as resulting consequence, that cache of stones and chest of gold will change our financial futures irrevocably.'

He thought again about the stones tumbling across the floor when Teller had unrolled that hide; as well as his comments concerning the skeleton.

"You're going to be in National Geographic, Grizzly," he had laughed. "But leave me out of it!"

A smile parted Abbott's beard and he sighed.

I am afraid there is no way you will be able to avoid the spotlight, my reluctant friend.'

Shaking himself back to the present he looked up.

"Damn it Teller! Where are you?"

The mountain cat that had seemingly taken up permanent residence on the rock overhang howled in emphasis, and Abbott shivered as he watched the smoke continue to roll across the cave's ceiling, and out into the darkening sky.

— — -- --- -- — —
—— —— ——— —— ——
-- --- --

= Chapter 19 =

An uneasy truce had been established between the two men.

Teller smiled. It was typical James bullshit and he knew she saw it as such. He also knew that James' display of ego and self-promotion was unlikely to win her over.

"Hey...earth to Tell." Jack smiled, nudging Teller's shoulder.

"Look, Kelly, we really need you up there." James pleaded. "I've hired a helicopter to come down tomorrow. Fly back and help me finish this season. Then if you want to quit I understand; but nobody knows the sponsors better than you. They all like you, and they all like working *with* you. Please, think about it."

Kelly laid her arms on the table and leaned forward.

"That's it? She asked.

James was caught off-guard, but he quickly regained his self-assurance. Leaning back, he smiled, "That's it."

Kelly stared at him for a moment, then dismissed him with a shake of her head. "Sorry James. Not enough."

Teller stifled his laughter as James blinked, stammering out,

Draining the wine in her glass, Kelly popped her lips, stood and stepped away, looking down at him, dripping disdain.

"Not enough, James. That's all, just not *enough.* You are un-fucking-believable. Everything, and I mean absolutely *everything* is about *you!*"

He started to argue, but she overrode all denial.

"You and Teller have a disagreement and he walks away. Wrong, and very stupid in my opinion, but not my decision. And the result is what? You don't give a shit that you lost a friend and partner. You're just happy because it leaves more for you! And *then* you have the balls to try to take his place with *me*?" She looked at him as if he were roadkill.

"And *then* what happens? I take a rafting trip, so *you* send your nephew along as some sort of spy. And when he gets hurt you leave him in Denver with your fiancé and chase *me* down *here*! And now, with Teller sitting at the same table, you try and talk me into flying back to Telluride with you!" She turned furiously in Teller's direction, but he just continued to smile. Livid, she focused her anger back on James, who sat speechless.

"And you know what *really* pisses me off?"

James shook his head.

"The fact that you didn't even *try* to offer me more money! You cheap *son- of- a- bitch!*"

At that, both Teller and Jack broke into the laughter they had been struggling to suppress. Teller, throwing his head back in howling amusement tumbled backwards from the bench into a wheezing heap, while Jack fell forward, pounding the table with his fists. Choking back tears of hilarity, Jack regained his breath and through short gasps, wiped his eyes and asked, "You okay Tell?"

Teller, still chuckling, lifted his head.

"Yeah, I'm fine, but do me a favor."

Jack offered a hand up, but Teller waved it away. "No, not that. I'm gonna stay down here where it's safe. Just hand me a beer." Jack glanced over at Kelly, who looked ready to kill, and then to James, who looked as if he expected it.

Grabbing the six-pack from the table, Jack handed Teller a can.

"Good idea Tell. I think I'll join you."

He had just started to slide under the table when Kelly walked over and put a heel on Teller's chest.

"Get up!" She growled.

Pinned beneath her shoe, Teller attempted a smile of contrition. "Why, I would be more than happy to do that sweetheart, but I seem to have this tremendous weight on my chest. It must be the great love I feel for you overburdening my poor heart."

Grinding her heel into his chest, she gave a final twist and stepped back. "Dammit Tell" she snarled, "you're impossible!"

She hesitated a moment, growled, "impossible" under her breath, and grabbing his wrist, jerked him into a sitting position.

Rising reluctantly, he kissed her on the nose.

"No Kell. James and I have already come to our parting of the ways, this is completely you. I don't think I've left any doubt where I stand on this matter. If you feel obligated in any way to finish the season then do so. I guarantee James will be the perfect gentleman in your presence." He turned to James, who sat looking pale and confused. But under Teller's gaze he wilted and nodded his head.

At that, Teller smiled graciously. "As for more money, I think I can convince him to give you my percentage of this last show. After all, I still hold fifty percent of the company."

James sputtered, "What!? but was looking more deflated by the moment.

Teller walked over and took a seat across from him.

"Whataya say James? Fair deal? You give Kelly here my piece of the pie for this year's show. You do that, *and* quit bothering her, and I'll sell you my shares of the company for fifty cents on the dollar this Christmas."

All conversation ceased. Everybody stopped what they were doing to gape at him while James' narrowed his eyes.

"What are you trying to pull Teller?"

Reaching into the bucket, Teller fished out a beer as he shook his head woefully. "You know James, I pity you, I really do. You seem to think that everyone is driven by the same greedy motives as you are . . . fortunately, that's simply not true."

He twisted the cap and held it, his eyes never leaving James' face. "No, the truth is not everyone is an egotistical, controlling, money hungry bastard. I do *not* have a secret agenda, nor do I harbor any nefarious schemes to screw you out of *anything*. We were friends once, and right or wrong that still counts for something to me. So, it really is as simple as I've said. You give Kelly my share of this year's profit, as well as her salary, *and* return your attentions to Casey. You do that, and at the end of the year I'll let you buy me out. I'll sign off on everything and just walk away." He paused and took a long drink. But as he brought it down to the table he looked straight into James' eyes.

"It's either that, or I will come up to Telluride, castrate you, and take away everything you *think* you own."

A flash of angry caution crossed James' face; but was quickly replaced with a smug smile. "What are you talking about Teller? *I* own that company! My lawyers would eat you alive."

Laughing, Teller leaned forward with a ruthless grin.

"You know what the problem with a shark is, James? The problem with sharks is that they'll turn on whoever is bleeding the most. And brother, I've now got the means to cut you to ribbons."

James's jaw tightened. He wasn't sure just what Teller meant, but he knew him well enough to know he was dead serious. He knew, but his ego wouldn't let him stop.

"Is that a threat?"

"I'm only speaking metaphorically."

James relaxed slightly, glanced at Kelly, and decided to push it. "You wouldn't stand a chance in court, Teller."

"And why is that James?" Teller raised his eyebrows. "On paper we're equal owners, remember?"

"Doesn't matter," James said, a sneer of self-satisfaction spreading across his face. "Money talks. Bullshit walks."

James' arrogance only made Teller's smile grow.

Reaching into his pocket, he slowly removed his fist and placed it on the table between them. "You're a gambling man James, how'd you like to place a little bet?"

James' eyes went to Teller's fist and he scooted back on the bench.

Teller chuckled. "Oh, don't be such a fucking coward James. If I were going to hurt you this conversation would have been over long ago." Unfolding his fist, he revealed one of the rough-edged coins; tipping it up between two fingers.

It glittered in the firelight, the King of Spain's Royal Coat of Arms stamped on one side, and the Crusaders Cross on the other, shinning as bright as it must have done five centuries earlier, when it had first been hammered out.

The coin glittered in James' eyes; reflecting his money lust. He leaned forward. "Where did you get that?"

Teller shrugged. "*That* is none of your concern, James. But I do have a *lot* of them. So, you may now consider the economic playing field leveled."

He cocked his head with a reckless smile.

"Hell James, I'll even sweeten the deal. How's this sound? We flip this coin. Heads, you simply do as I requested and the deal I offered stands. Tails, you fly out of here sole owner of the company and you don't even have to buy me out. Deal?"

The silence around the table was deafening.

But James, being both suspicious and greedy, couldn't help himself. True to form, he had to add a caveat.

"Only if I get to call it."

A coyote's laughing howl pierced the darkness at the same moment the demand left his lips.

Looking over his shoulder, Teller smiled as the strange laughter died. When he turned back, his eyes shone.

"Whatever you say…"

"Wait! Wait!" James shouted, grabbing at Teller's arm.

Teller didn't bother to answer. With a flick, the coin spun into the air, glittering as it made its arc, and as it fell Teller caught it in one hand and slapped it onto the table.

Everyone stared at the hand covering the coin.

"The cross is heads," Teller smiled. "Your call."

There was no sound but for the crackling of the fire as the seconds ticked by, James staring at the hidden coin, agonizing over the choice.

Finally, Teller broke the silence. "Come on Jimmy, choose!"

Being called 'Jimmy' snapped his concentration. He had hated that nickname since childhood. He glared at Teller's confident smile. "Alright. But just so we're agreed. I win and you sign everything over to me. No strings attached. Is that correct?"

Teller tilted his head. "That's right. But, if you lose, you do *exactly* as I said or I promise one morning I will be on your doorstep. And you know me, James, I don't make promises I don't keep."

"I believe you Teller. I believe you."

Hesitating for a fraction of a second more, he pointed at Teller's hand.

"Heads."

Teller slowly pulled his hand off the coin.

In the flickering firelight gleamed the coat of arms.

For a moment, complete and utter silence hung in the air; but then another howl split the night and as it echoed across the mesa James seemed to collapse into his Patagonia windbreaker.

Then leaning down, he gave Kelly a kiss.

"Well there you are my dear. I think we've reached an understanding."

Turning back to James, Teller pressed both palms flat on the table and leaned in close, his eyes ice cold.

"Isn't that right?"

James nodded. "Right."

With that, Teller smiled brightly and clapped his hands.

"Good, then it's all settled."

He gave Kelly another kiss; this one on the top of her head.

"It's your choice now babe, I'm going to go find Billy. He's got something of mine and I want it back."

Jack stood to follow. But on seeing Teller's eye shift towards James, he nodded and stepped up to the table and coughed, breaking the hush that had settled on the rest of the crew.

"So, Fred, how're those steaks coming along?"

= Chapter 20 =

Kelly caught up with Teller halfway between the trailer and the store, grabbing him by the arm and yanking him around to face her. She was furious.

"Just *what* in the hell was that about?"

Teller, as usual, was oblivious to any problem.

"What do you mean?"

"Goddammit Tell! I mean that whole thing! Almost giving away your half of the company? Are you crazy?!"

Grinning, he slipped his hands around and under her butt, lifting her and pushing his face between her breasts, savoring the warmth beneath her shirt.

Pulling his head back, he looked into her eyes.

"But I didn't give it away kiddo, I negotiated a pay bump for you, *and* provided an acceptable exit for myself."

He tried to set her back on the ground. But she locked her legs tightly around his hips, putting a hand on each cheek to look deeply into his eyes.

"But you could have lost it all! what if he had won the toss?"

Teller shook his head. "Honey, for me it was a no-lose situation. Either way I'd be shed of that miserable prick. I don't know what happened to the guy, Kelly. When we first started he was a different man. Or at least that's what I thought." With a shrug he added, "I guess that's what success does to some people. Anyway, *you* now have the option of going back and making some decent money while Jack and I go get Abbott."

Kelly slid down his legs to the ground.

"What makes you think I want to go back?

Teller exhaled slowly. "Cause that's what I want you to do."

She relaxed slightly and allowed him a smile.

Finding that smile encouraging, he elaborated.

"May I point out that it *would* be beneficial to our cause if you would go back for just a little while longer and work this last show. Because I can absolutely *guarantee* you he's going to try and pull some sort of legal bullshit in my absence." He ran his hands up her arms until they rested on her shoulders. "But with *you* there to keep an eye on him he'll be a lot less likely to jump right on it."

She nodded in silent agreement.

"And besides, I'm only pretend rich right now. The coins are very real, but at the moment they're a not a bird in the hand." He reached down and slid his hand between her legs.

"They're a bird in the bush."

She squeezed her legs together. "Mmmm, So?"

"So," he lifted her chin with the finger of his free hand. "I can't whisk you off to a life of luxury quite yet. *You*, my dear, need to go back and protect your interests."

She tilted her head. "What do you mean *my* interests?"

Teller returned her question with a sigh and a smile.

"I'm giving *you* my fifty percent dear heart. *That* gives you a vested interest in the company, and therefore a damn good reason to keep an eye on our buddy James. You know as well as I do that he's bound to try something snakey."

Kelly's mouth dropped open and she stuttered, "Y-y-you're giving me what?"

Teller put his finger on her chin and lifted, bringing her lips back together. "I am giving you my half of the company. I'm done babe. I'm done. I want you to have it."

Kelly was stunned at the generosity. But then her eyes narrowed. "So I will keep an eye on James..."

"Well, yes and no. I want *you* to have it because, one, I am tired of the whole thing, and two, I've grown rather fond of you. Besides, someone *does* need to keep an eye on that bastard because he *will* try to steal that fifty percent. It's a given Kell, and we both know it."

She nodded in agreement. "But what am *I* supposed to do to prevent it?"

Teller took her by the hand and started up the hill.

"Nothing. Just having you there will keep him pretty much in line. He'll be spooked for a week or so, and by the time he feels comfortable enough to start something I should be back."

Kelly dug in her heels, bringing him to a halt. "Back from where?"

"Well, first from rescuing a beer drinking bear."

That got a smile.

"Then, from trying to find someone who will buy an impressive pile of gold coins and gemstones."

He took her hand and started back towards the store, but she dug her heels into the dirt again. "So the story about the cave and the treasure is true?"

At first, Teller stood there looking hurt, as if he couldn't believe she would doubt him. But his smile returned and gathered her into his arms. "Of course it's true. I may be a world-class dreamer and a reasonably competent bullshitter, but this has been something even *I* couldn't make up. Come on, let's go find Billy.

~

Billy was not on the porch where they had left him, nor was he in the store office and after splitting up for a quick search around the building, they met back on the porch.

"No sign of him, huh?"

She shook her head.

Teller rubbed his stubbled chin. "Hmm. Well, he can't be too far. Let's go back to the trailer and grab a bite. Tomorrow's a busy day." He started back down the trail.

Kelly took a fast step to follow, talking as she walked.

"But what if I don't want to go?"

"Go where?"

"Back to Telluride with James!"

Teller kept walking. His mind was on things other than this conversation. "That's your call, kid. If you don't go with James, then you can stay here with Billy until we find Abbott and bring him back. Eitherway's fine by me."

Kelly came to an abrupt halt, the hurt obvious.

"You don't care!?"

Teller whipped around, weary anger in his eyes.

"Goddammit Kelly!" He snarled. "Stop it!"

He was tired; and getting more so every day. It was becoming impossible to deal with so many people on so many levels.

"Of course I care! I just don't give a shit whether you go or stay."

Her eyes widened as her lips formed a small 'o'.

Teller found this gesture many times more disturbing than anything she might have said. Closing his eyes, he sighed and began massaging his forehead with his fingertips.

"That is *not* what I meant!"

Kelly knew him well, and it gave her a perverse satisfaction to see him this frustrated. With a tilt of her head and her tone honey sweet, she asked, "Then what *did* you mean?"

Her smile relaxing him marginally, he growled, "You know *exactly* what I meant you little bitch."

Stepping forward, she stood on her toes to give him a kiss.

Teller gave a smile of surrender. She was a woman after all, and there was simply no way to win. Laying his arm over her shoulder he pulled her close, and they walked back towards the trailer. "First light. Abbott's been out there four days now."

Kelly took his fingers and crossed his hand over her chest.

"He'll be alright Tell."

A coyote yipped across the distant mesa, and Teller allowed himself to smile. "Yeah, you're probably right."

As they walked he found himself more at ease than he had been in days. At least now he had a plan of sorts. The severing of any last ties with James had begun, his old partner Jack had flown back into his life, and Kelly was here beside him again.

Laying his arm across her shoulders, he clutched her hand; and feeling the warmth he allowed himself to relax. It might be the last time he would get the opportunity.

His fleeting sense of peace was cut short as they entered the halo of firelight. "Hey Teller!" Fred hollered. "Your steak's cold!"

Freeing his hand from Kelly's, he went over to the grill.

Picking the meat up with his fingers he put it back on the grill. "But fortunately, it's also adjustable."

As the meat warmed, Teller, Jack and Kelly moved three lawn chairs away from the table, setting them up to discuss the best approach to Abbotts rescue while the others sat laughing at another one of Fred's stories.

Everyone except James.

He sat alone in a chair outside the light of the fire, hidden in the flickering shadows: nursing the expensive bottle of wine he had taken from Billy's trailer earlier that evening.

Isolated by more than just the distance between he and the rest, he plotted his revenge.

— — ‑‑ ‑‑‑ ‑‑ — —

— —   — —

‑‑ ‑‑‑ ‑‑

= Chapter 21 =

Ben's eyes snapped open.

Bringing his arms up to cover his face he cried, "No!" and lunged from the bed. His momentum carried him forward until a web of tubes, monitor wires, and a catheter brought him to an abrupt halt. But not before the bed crashed against the wheeled stand that supported the I.V. bags; tipping it over and nearly striking Casey who dozed in the empty bed next to his. She was up and at his side within moments, pinning his arms as he flailed at his imaginary attackers.

"Benny! Benny stop, its alright! I'm here, it's okay! I'm here…" Ben's eyes came into focus and a flash of recognition crossed his face.

Cashey?" he mumbled through his wired jaw.

Relief sweeping through her heart, she scooped him into her arms, "Yes Ben, it's me, you're alright. You're safe …"

Ben's grip of panic was slowly replaced by confusion, and he seemed a lost child. "Where am I?" he whimpered.

Stroking his hair, she reached up to give the nurse's call button a push. "You're in the hospital Benny, but everything's going to be fine. Just rest and hold still."

~

The portly nurse's pager went off. Recognizing the room number, she stubbed out her cigarette as a look of supreme annoyance crossed her face.

"Looks like an emergency up in the luxury suite," She sneered, "Must be time to empty the kid's piss bag.*"*

Tossing her pizza crust onto the table, she wiped tomato sauce from her chin as she struggled to extricate herself from the plastic chair she had stuffed herself into.

With a monumental grunt of effort, she popped free.

The woman she was with took a drag of *her* cigarette, exhaled, and waved her off.

"See you at lunch."

~

Casey was perched on the edge of the bed, her phone to her ear when the door swung open and the nurse waddled into the room, making no secret of the fact she was clearly upset at being disturbed. Glancing up, Casey nodded acknowledgment, and turned away as the sixth ring jangled on James' cell phone.

"Damn it James, pick up." she whispered angrily.

The nurse wrinkled her nose in Casey's direction; but on seeing Ben lying in a heap of tangled tubing and monitoring equipment, her irritation dissolved.

Showing surprising agility, she rushed to his crumpled form and gathered him up, tucking him into bed and checking all vital signs while reattaching essential connections in a fluid motion.

Throughout this flurry of action, Casey still held the phone to her ear.

James picked up on the seventeenth ring.

"Hello?"

Covering the phone with her hand, Casey hissed, "Where *are* you?"

James pushed himself out of his chair and walked away from the minimal warmth of the fire. "I'm stuck down here at the lake." He growled. "Why?"

"Because Benny just woke up and you need to get back here."

James stopped, turned, and walked back to his chair, snatching the wine bottle from beneath it.

"Why?"

Casey was seething. "Because *James*, he's *your* nephew and he wouldn't be here at all if it wasn't for *you.*"

Upon hearing those words, all of James' anger, frustration, and indignation merged with the feeling of helplessness that being here with Teller had instilled.

"*I* did *not* put him in that goddamned *hospital!*" James shouted into the phone, "*I* am down here right now trying to find out just how he ended up there! So don't give me this shit that this is *all my fucking fault!*" Holding the phone at arm's length, he squeezed as if he could crush not only the problem from existence but her whining voice with it.

Failing, he cursed under his breath; and tipped the bottle up, pouring half of its contents down his throat. His adams apple bobbed maniacally. Gasping, he swung the bottle down to his side; exhaling heavily as he stared out into the night, listening to the crickets' chirp.

It was then that he noticed that they were the only sounds.

Turning back to the fire, he saw that the conversation at the table had ceased and all eyes were on him. Glaring back, he slowly brought the phone back to his ear and struggled to speak more calmly.

"So, how is he?"

Casey's voice was razor sharp. "He's in with the doctor now. I really don't know *how* he is."

"Well then. There really isn't much *I* can do *is* there?"

"No," she hissed. "I guess *not.*" Her voice transitioned from cold to ice as she asked, "Did you find Kelly?"

Upending the bottle, he drained it. "Yeah," he coughed, "I found her. And I found Teller as well."

Casey couldn't resist a smile.

"Well, *that's* interesting… What now?" The satisfaction in her voice only fueled his resentment.

"Don't gloat quite yet Casey," he growled, "She still may come back to Telluride for the season."

There was a moment of silence, and a bitter laugh came over the phone. "*That's* not what I found interesting, *James*. So tell me, how *was* your reunion with Teller?"

James gritted his teeth and decided to keep the coin toss to himself. "It went more or less as expected, but it looks as if he's willing to dissolve the partnership."

There was another laugh, but this one held genuine amusement. "Oh, I'm sure he is sweetheart, but on whose terms?"

James' anger returned full force.

"Mutual agreement, Casey. I'll tell you all about it when I get back. Plans have changed and I'll be there as soon as I can. Just call me when you know more about Ben, okay?"

He stabbed the 'off' button.

Aggravated and angry, he tipped his bottle up, holding it over his mouth, shaking it fiercely.

Nothing.

Glaring at the cork hole in the empty bottle above his head, James stared at the shimmering red drop hanging on the lip that was so inconsequential even gravity ignored it.

Slowly lowering his arm, he stared at the glass container.

Its emptiness seemed to represent his life at the moment. And as every insult of the past two weeks, real or imagined, paraded past his resentment and bitterness mounted. It was with the power of their combined force that he threw the bottle into the desert. It whistled in the wind as it spun, only to land in the soft sand with a thud, denying James even the minuscule pleasure of breaking glass.

'*Goddamn Teller!*' he screamed.

— — -- ---- -- — —

— — — —

-- ---- --

= Chapter 22 =

'Asshole!' Casey whispered angrily, shoving her phone into her purse and snapping it shut.

The nurse, who had quietly waited for the call to end, saw Casey lower the phone and stepped from the door, fussing with her necklace as they walked down the hall.

"The doctor has examined him thoroughly Miss Carson. Everything seems to be fine."

"I am *not* Mrs. Carson." Casey snapped. "James and I are *not* married."

The pudgy nurse frowned. "Oh, I see. Well. Regardless, young Mr. Carson seems to have stabilized. If you don't mind my asking, what happened to upset him so?"

"I've no idea." Casey answered. "I was napping on the other bed when I heard a crash and woke to find him lying on the floor."

The nurse nodded. "I see. Well, the doctor has given him something to calm him so he should be fine for the next few hours. I'm sure he will sleep so if you need to leave for any reason, now would be a good time to do so."

Casey yawned, shaking her head as she returned to the room.

"Thank you. But I think I'll stay. I want to be here when he wakes up."

"I understand." The nurse nodded. Then, clutching the small silver cross that hung from her neck, gave a tilt of her head.

"Thank you, but that won't be necessary." Casey smiled, pausing at the threshold to lay her hand on the door knob.

"I'll ring if I need you."

She closed the door gently, took a seat on the freshly made bed, and studied Ben's face. His color had returned to a small degree; and while he *was* breathing, it seemed dangerously slow and shallow.

'*Oh, Benny, what happened?'*

Anxiety threatened to consume her. But conceding there was nothing to be gained by worrying, she let her mind wander; picturing the meeting between James and Teller.

'I would have loved to have been a fly on the wall for that.' She smiled wickedly. But as her amusement grew, a wave of exhaustion washed over her and her eyes fluttered closed.

~

Ben's eyes snapped open… engulfed by panic, he held his body absolutely still as the room came slowly into focus.

No canyon. No river. No Coyote… but where am I?

What . . .?

As his fingers traced the cold steel halo that circled his skull his panic returned. He jerked; attempting to sit up but found he was strapped to the bed by restraints that resembled seatbelts. Unable to move, Ben let his mind shuffle back through the few foggy memories he was able to gather.

He relaxed as he remembered he and Kelly alone on the river… the memory made him happy. He had finally gotten her to open up and she was even flirting with him just a little.

But then her old boyfriend showed up out of nowhere and ruined everything!

As Ben lay there, jealous anger jogged his memory.

When his uncle had first asked him to tag along on the trip he was thrilled. After all, Kelly was the most beautiful girl he had ever seen. He had been in love with her from the moment he had first laid eyes on her and for him, the thought of being on a raft with her would be almost heaven. Of course, he knew that his uncle also had the hots for her, but *that* old horn dog chased anything with tits. And the *only* thing that had kept his uncle in line was Teller. And even though they were partners, the tension between them was thick when it came to Kelly. But then Teller disappeared and Ben thought that he might have a

115

chance. But instead, his Uncle James' pursuit became nearly obscene.

Ben glanced over at Casey, asleep on the bed.

And he was so stupid that he didn't think she even noticed.

The only thing that had made it bearable was the fact that Kelly wanted nothing to do with him, and she had made that *very* clear on more than one occasion, and in no uncertain terms.

But Uncle James had continued his ridiculous chase, all the while telling *him* that it was the oldest game in the world for women to play. But *he* didn't see it that way, and by her actions, neither did she. And then his relentless badgering had finally driven her away.

That's when his opportunity had arisen.

Uncle James' suggested that he accompany her on the rafting trip. He had jumped at the chance and was doubly thrilled when she mentioned she would like to have him come along.

But then Teller had shown up.

Canyon King! Jeez, what a crock! But there was no mistaking the look on her face when he had walked out of the darkness and she realized who it was. Too bad she hadn't shot him before she recognized him. Then she *really* would have needed some comforting. A cruel smile played across Ben's face as he fantasized holding a distraught Kelly in his arms while standing over Teller, lying in a pool of his own blood.

~

He was shaken from his daydream when the door to the room squeaked open and a fat-faced nurse peeked in. Her beady eyes darted about and as the door was pulled closed he quickly tried to re-visualize the imaginary scene.

Teller lay dead, while Kelly cried, wrapped in his arms, gratefully accepting his comfort while showering him with kisses of appreciation . . .

Squeezing his eyes shut, he strained to re-immerse himself in the fantasy, but found it impossible now that he had been brought back to the reality of being strapped to a hospital bed.

He heaved at the restraints. *'How did I get here!?'*

Finally, a lone image came clearly through the haze . . . it was the image of the coyote from his dream.

Now he remembered! The magnificent animal had appeared out of nowhere, trotting up and sitting like a well-trained dog waiting for a treat. The Coyote's strange yellow eyes had pierced his soul, sifting through the accumulated waste of repressed desires until it settled on one powerful image.

Kelly.

Giving an ambiguous canine smile, the Coyote had cocked its head and suddenly the idea of stealing the boat floated through Ben's mind.

Yes! That was the answer! Simply take the boat; and Teller, being the hero that he was, would go looking for it. A man like Teller would do nothing less.

All Ben would need to do is to make sure the raft was stuck between some big rocks somewhere downriver then hide above the boat and wait.

The plan formulated subconsciously.

As Teller rounded the rocks to retrieve the boat, Ben would simply bash his head with a large stone and push him into the current. His body would wash downstream never to be found. And even if it were, it would be chalked off to another accidental fall and unfortunate drowning. Then he could have Kelly for his own.

Ben blinked. After that, everything seemed fuzzy. He remembered being wet, cold, and unable to breathe. Then, somewhere in the haze, he recalled being fed some soup followed with bitter crunched-up pills. Then nothing. Nothing but swirling colors, followed by the frightening sensation of being lost... but then, out of the fog of this fitful dream, the Coyote had come once more. But *this* time the coyote told him he must run, take the knife, steal the boat and go! And he had

117

tried. But the boat was full of rocks and he was too weak to empty it. Then, in the darkness of his pain Teller had appeared in the night, hunting him.

He had to run! Teller was going to kill him! He must swim!

Ben closed his eyes.

Nothing . . .

Nothing at all.

Until now . . . *Now* he was in a hospital. That much he now knew. But how he had gotten here, and what had transpired was a mystery.

He looked over to the figure in the bed.

Maybe Casey could answer his questions. Ignoring the pain, he turned his head and faintly called her name.

— — ‒‒ ‒‒‒ ‒‒ — —
— — ‒‒ — —
‒‒ ‒‒‒ ‒‒

= Chapter 23 =

Billy Knowles shook his head in amazement.

Sitting on the meditation rug that lay on the stone floor of the ancient Anasazi dwelling, he pondered the events of a half millennium. Things that had been set in motion so long ago were now coming to a head.

Coyote's patience was endless, as was his penchant for chaos. But all of time is a circle, and now here he was; somewhere on that endless loop.

He smiled. At his feet lay a pile of wood shavings. Curled pieces of mesquite that had fallen away as he had carved a small figurine: a sculpture that now rested in the peripheral orbit of the Coyote fetish that was balanced at the very center of the willow branch web covering the kiva. The carving represented Teller of course; and his placement on the web was no accident... surprising perhaps, but not completely unforeseen. And as Billy studied the webs intricate pattern, the smoke from his pipe drifted up, gathering under his hat to funnel out through a small tear in the brim; creating a halo that floated above his head.

The puzzle that had been introduced on the day two panicked fishermen delivered a nearly drowned boy was now coming together. Billy had known that Coyote was involved the moment he had sensed the sickness in the child, but at the time he had no way of telling just how deeply, or how completely, Coyote may have dedicated himself to this group.

But it was now clear.

As he puffed his pipe, he gazed across the land of his ancestors. His people had been here since time began: or at least since the first medicine bundle, when the mud people had crawled from the earth to create the world.

Coyote began the game, Billy thought, drawing on the pipe stem and releasing a thin plume of smoke towards the sky beyond the entrance. *And has been poking his nose into the affairs of man ever since.*

His heart warmed as he remembered lessons taught by his grandfather. A quiet man of easy laughter. He was a man whom Billy had deeply loved, and deeply respected. It was he who had first told him of Coyote's ways, and of man's place in the universe.

And, as usual, Billy thought, *Coyote has brought great change into the people whose lives he has intruded upon.*

Lifting his eyes to see the constellation Orion low in the sky, he considered the bow of stars cocked towards the heavens, ready to let fly his arrow. The Hunter had always been Billy's favorite heavenly body for no other reason than its relationship to man and as a child he had often wondered if Orion let loose his bow, if the arrow would strike the sun and kill it.

Perhaps, he now thought, that is how the world will end. In darkness due to a god's errant missile.

He shook himself back to the problems of the present.

Never in his many years had he seen Coyote become this involved in one man's life, or bring so many others into his circle.

'Teller must be a unique individual for Coyote to take such an active role in his future. Why, the simple act of leading him to the black man's cave, and the chest of gold was a thing unheard of.'

The creases in Billy's weathered face grew deeper as he smiled and blew another stream of smoke towards the stars. For while the gold was immaterial to Coyote, it was not to man.

'This will change Teller... whether for good or for evil I cannot see. But I believe him to be a truly honest man, and do not feel his soul will be crushed by this fortune.'

Billy still possessed the Coyote carving he had taken from Teller upon James's arrival.

'But this small carving is the true prize.'

Centering the turquoise statuette in his palm he reached out and held it in the beam of moonlight that shone through the caves entrance, and as the light struck the carving, the stone seemed to absorb the pale light and he could have sworn, just for a moment, that the curled, sleeping sculpture opened one glittering yellow eye and gave him a wink.

Lifting his eyebrows, Billy's lips pulled back to reveal his brilliant smile and he spoke to the little god.

"I do not pretend to know what you are up to, my playful friend, but I thank you for bringing me into your game."

Closing his fist around the small statue, he rose from his rug, bowed his head, and spoke a short prayer of his clan; and as the last melodic phrase left his lips a coyote howled in the distance.

Cocking his ear, Billy put his nose to the light breeze and inhaled. The smell was one he recognized.

Change . . ..

Tapping the ashes of his pipe into a stone bowl, he tucked the pipe into his shirt pocket and opened his hand one last time to gaze at the small figure.

The small coyote now lay peacefully asleep.

His black eyes twinkling, Billy headed back to his guests.

— — -- --- -- — —

—— —— —— ——

-- --- --

= Chapter 24 =

Teller and Jack leaned close at the table, deep in conversation, Kelly's head resting on Teller's left shoulder. Lori and Skip had left earlier, leaving only Fred who now sat cross-legged before the fire feeding small sticks into the flames.

James was nowhere to be found.

Suddenly Billy materialized out of the shadows of the bluff to sit silently across from Kelly. She turned tired eyes to him and he coaxed a weary smile from her.

"Alright then, it's settled." Teller said, slapping the table and turning to Billy as if he had been there all along. The sudden movement disturbed Kelly's comfort, eliciting a groan of displeasure.

"Sorry sweetheart." He smiled, kissing her on the top of the head. "We'll go to bed soon." She stretched her arms over her head. "Good…" she mumbled through a yawn.

Teller directed his attention back to the old Navajo.

"Billy, Jack and I are leaving first light. I would consider it a great favor if you would watch over sleepy beauty here in my absence."

Billy nodded, and reached across the table, taking Teller's hand and placing the carving onto his palm.

"Thank you for letting me commune with your coyote, Teller." he said, a grand smile lighting his face as he gently closed Teller's fist over the carving. "And as for keeping Kelly company, I would consider it a great pleasure. This young woman," he gave a slight nod in her direction, "and you, have brought a great deal of entertainment into an old Indian's lonely existence." Suppressing a smile, Teller said, "Lonely old Indian my ass…" but holding Billy's hand, he could feel the warmth of the figurine radiate through their entwined fingers. The sensation was so pleasant he held a moment longer.

"You may be alone Chief, but you're not lonely. Trust me, I know the difference."

Billy simply smiled as their grip released.

Teller tucked the carving into his pocket, swung a leg over the bench, stood, and took Kelly by the hand, pulling her up.

"Come on sugar."

She allowed herself to be hauled from the bench and leaned into him and slid her arm around his waist. "'Bout time . . .."

Teller put a hand on Jack's shoulder and gave a heartfelt squeeze. "It's great to see you again Jack."

Jack nodded and put his hand on the top of Tellers.

"It's good to see you too, Tell."

Billy could almost feel the warmth of Teller's smile as he turned and asked, "You got somewhere for this man to get some rest?"

Billy tipped his head towards the Airstream.

"He can sleep in the trailer."

Jack looked over at Billy, his eyes showing exhaustion as well as gratitude. But he shook his head. "Thanks Bill, but where are you gonna sleep?"

"I have somewhere I need to go." Billy said, an enigmatic grin creeping across his face. "Please, take the trailer."

Jack didn't need to be asked twice. He nodded and smiled, "Thanks."

Billy turned. "Missy here knows where the coffee is. Kelly, if you stay, please watch the store, if not, please lock up and leave the keys in Lulubelle."

Kelly gave a sleepy nod, and Billy looked at Teller, his black eyes shining in the night. "I will see *you* when you return." He took a few steps into the darkness; but before vanishing, he paused and turned, the light of the fire illuminating his smile.

"I am very much looking forward to meeting your Bear."

His smile flashed once more in the firelight and was gone.

Turning from the darkness Billy had melted into, Teller took Kelly's arm. "Well then, I guess it's settled. Jack, I'll see you in a few hours. Kell, let's go find a bed."

Kelly slid under Teller's arm as he called back over his shoulder, "G'nite Fred." but Fred just stared into the fire, seemingly mesmerized. He responded only with a quiet, "G'nite guys."

Kelly suddenly stopped. "Where's James?"

Teller nudged her forward with a shrug of indifference.

"He slinked away awhile back. Don't worry, Jack's got an eye on him."

"Good..." She let him pull her along for a few steps, but then shrugged away and turned to face him.

"Tell, do you think I should stay or go back?"

"Like I said Babe, that's your call, not mine."

"Damn it," she hissed, "that's not what I asked!"

Pulling her roughly to his chest, he turned her face to his, placed a hand on either cheek, and gave her a kiss that left her breathless. Then, smiling, he slowly drew back and laid his forehead to hers. "Tell you what, let's sleep on it and we'll decide in the morning. The blood seems to be rushing from my head and I'm suddenly not thinking too clearly."

Kelly's hand slid down below his belt. "Hmmm. I'm surprised you can think at all." A sly grin crept across her lips as she reached up and tapped his skull with the finger of her other hand. "There must be very little blood left up here."

Teller waggled his brows. "You're right, I do feel a bit lightheaded. Any idea where we might be able to lay down and take care of this? To our mutual satisfaction of course."

She gave him a tug. "Glad to hear you've got *both* of our interests at heart, cowboy. You know, I think I remember a cot in Billy's office. How's that sound?"

"Like heaven sweetie, you lead."

With her hand on his belt buckle, she led him up the hill like a lamb to slaughter.

The cot proved more than adequate.

~

Looking up from the crook of his arm, Kelly traced a finger up Teller's chest, her warm, contented eyes examining his.

"So, what's next?"

Teller released a massive yawn.

"I already told you kid, I've got to go get Abbott."

"I know *that* Tell." She smiled, touching his lips with her finger. What I mean is what *happens* next?"

He frowned, exasperation in his eyes.

"I don't need riddles in the sand, Kelly. Speak up! get it out. I would really like to get a couple hours shuteye."

Kelly's expression grew uncompromising. "You know damn well what I mean Teller. Of *course* you need to find Abbott! But *then* what?"

He yawned again. "Then what, what?"

She pounded his chest in mock frustration. "I'll tell you what!" Sliding her hand beneath the damp sheet, she grabbed his balls. "Straight answer Teller. What then?"

Teller's exasperation turning to painful surprise he reached down to gingerly take hold of her wrist.

"Careful, careful, gently now... easy girl. You need to be more specific, that's all."

She relaxed her grip, but only marginally, and Teller breathed easier. "There, that's *much* better. Now, what was the question?'

Her fingers ratcheted up a notch.

"Okay, okay, okay! Seriously though, what do you mean? There are a lot of variables here Kelly. It depends on Abbott's condition. It depends on if I can find the cave again. Hell, it depends on whether you go back to Telluride or not."

At that, her fingers loosened. "Do you think I should?"

He said nothing at first, then gave a slow nod.

"Yes. I think you should. I would feel much better knowing there was someone I could trust watching James."

He looked down to gauge her reaction. And although the situation was less than romantic, he smiled at her loveliness. He kissed her again and she slid her hand from beneath the sheet to touch his chin with her finger. And Teller, more comfortable with both hands where he could see them, smiled.

"Fifty percent of that business is a healthy chunk of change sweetheart. And If I can't find that cave again we're going to need every dime."

Her eyes brightened. "Did you say, 'we'?"

He nodded. "Unless you want to stay in a snowbank. Me? I'm going to be the King of somewhere hot."

Kelly rose up on one elbow, her eyes serious.

"And where does that leave me?"

Teller laced his hands behind his head, his eyes focusing somewhere beyond the ceiling. "Let me put it this way. Since I've no doubt James will try to screw me out of everything, I am going to do everything *I* can do to prevent that screwing. And I *will* prevent it, Kell. James might be smart but he's greedy, and *that* is his Achilles heel. I'll outfox him babe, of that you may be sure. And if all goes well, once I relocate that cave, I will be very, *very* rich. And what is a King without a Queen?"

He grinned. "What say you to that?"

Kelly gave a wicked smile, laid her head under his chin, slipping her hand beneath the sheet to run a fingernail up his thigh. "I say that I believe as future Queen I should verify that this King is fit to rule." Her head slid down his chest and under the sheet.

Teller smiled and closed his eyes. "Now I'm *never* going to get any sleep."

From beneath the sheets he heard Kelly's muffled voice.

"Bitch, bitch, bitch."

= Chapter 25 =

Teller was pulled from his light slumber by a bird trilling outside of the little window above his head; and creaking open one eye, he saw the faint light of dawn lighting its glass. With a grunt, he rolled over, snuggled into the warmth of Kelly's back and reached over to cup a breast.

She purred and wiggled against him.

Teller lay very still, feeling the beat of her heart while trying to clear his mind. But the inner emptiness he sought was impossible to maintain... every space he succeeded in voiding was instantly filled with random, unfiltered thoughts.

"Nature abhors a vacuum," he grumbled.

Moving his hand to her bare shoulder he gently rolled her over, wrapped his lips around a strawberry nipple, sucked it in, and released it with a wet 'pop.'

"Get up girlie, I gotta move."

"No." she mumbled through a smile, pulling the sheet back over her head.

"Yes!" he laughed, yanking the sheet away and slapping her lightly on the rump. Then, swinging his legs off the bed, he leaned back onto her, squashing her into the mattress as he lifted his legs to slide on his jeans.

Kelly pounded on his back; laughing as she grabbed at the sheet while pushing him away with her feet.

"Get offa me you big oaf!" she shouted. But Teller snatched the sheet from her hands, wadded it up, and threw it onto the floor.

"From King to oaf overnight huh?" He slapped her on the butt again, but this time with a little more force.

"Arise wench! You're not Queen yet!"

Her eyes sprung open. "Oowwww!" she squealed, taking a half-hearted swing at him.

Still laughing, Teller pulled back; grabbing her fist as it sailed by and pinning her to the bed while holding her down and kissing her neck. "Oh don't be so melodramatic," he whispered in her ear. "Where's the coffee?"

Glaring, she picked the wadded sheet from the floor and wrapped it around herself. "*You* are an evil tyrant." she grumbled, rubbing her eyes as she went to the sink to put the coffee pot under the faucet.

"How long will you be gone?"

Teller looked up from lacing his boots. "Don't know."

Kelly frowned, turned on the water and dumped the beans into the grinder. She hit the button and the machine began to whir. "Give it a few minutes." She said through the noise.

Teller looked up from his shoelaces thinking again how great she looked just out of bed; all rumpled and sexy. But as he studied her, she happed to look over, and seeing his expression, tilted her head. "What?"

He grinned and pulled on his t-shirt.

"Nothin' sweetheart, just you . . ." his tousled head popped through the neck and the smile grew serious. "But I imagine once we get Abbott, depending on his condition, we'll fly back here to refuel. Then we'll decide *where* we need to go."

Kelly leaned against the counter; one hand gripping the knot in the sheet. She stared at him for a moment: then, with a tiny sigh, she tucked the sheet under her butt and flopped onto the cot.

Tellers brows furrowed. "What's the matter?"

Kelly met his gaze, her eyes warm but tinged with anxiety.

"Damn it, Kell," he growled, his temper starting to rise. But the coffee maker beeped, and he cooled.

"Good. Coffee's ready . . ."

He poured two cups, mixed milk and sugar into both and handed her one with a kiss. "You really do need to go back, and you know why. But you don't have to fly with James. Just ride back with Dave and the rest of the crew in the truck. I'll be up to get you as soon as I can." As he waited for a response he took a drink and broke into a delighted smile.

"Wow, this is *really* good."

Taking a sip, she nodded, forcing a smile. "Yeah, Billy has great taste in coffee *and* wine." but unable to keep up any semblance of a happy facade her smile vanished. Turning her blue eyes to his, she asked, "So really Tell, about how long do you think?"

Teller's forehead creased. "Again, I really don't know. We *should* locate him by tomorrow afternoon, so with any luck the three of us will be back here the following day."

Her eyes brightened and he smiled, "Does that make you feel any better?"

Kelly nodded, "Yes, Teller, it does."

"Good. But after that I don't know. Abbott made it clear that this *is* an archeological find. So if word gets out who knows *how* many bureaucracies we'll have to deal with."

Taking another sip, he set his cup down and walked over to the chair where his deerskin pack lay. "But *that* is Abbott's problem... whereas *these,*" He reached into the pack, shuffled through it for a moment, and pulled out a rough green stone the approximate size of a quail egg. Tossing it to her, a sly grin crossed his lips. "Are *my* problem."

Catching the stone, she bounced it in her hand and held it to the light of the window. "Impressive." She nodded. "But just *where* are you going to go with these?"

Teller's grin increased. "Come on Kell, I know people I haven't even used yet. I'll find someone."

She giggled, but then they heard a voice on the porch.

Palming the stone, she looked at Teller as the voice came again, calling in a loud whisper, "Teller . . . hey, Tell, you in there . . .?

Teller leaned towards the small window, cupping his hand to his ear like Errol Flynn's Robin Hood. "Ahhh mi lady, I fear I must take your leave. My coach awaits!"

Tipping his cup back, he swallowed the last of his coffee and went to the pot. Lifting it to gauge its weight he filled his cup and grinned, "Hey, this thing is stainless and the lid cranks down, think Billy'd mind if I took it for a spin?' But before she could respond he shoved it into her hands.

"Never mind. Better to beg forgiveness than to ask permission. Make a fresh pot and bring it to the helicopter."

Kelly shook her head as he ran out, calling over his shoulder,

Jack was already walking back down the stairs when Teller came through the screen door. But the spring hinge snapped the door back; clipping his arm and splashing coffee out of the cup, onto his shirt, and across the wooden planks of the floor.

Hearing Teller's curse, Jack turned on his heel to see Teller wiping at his shirt with his hand.

"There you are! I was just headin' down to the river to look for you."

"No need to seek further amigo," Teller said, looking up from the stain. "you've found me." He patted at the shirt a few more times, but seeing that his cleaning efforts were in vain he gave Jack a dismayed smile and shrugged, "So, how do you want to do this?"

Jack motioned towards the now empty cup.

"First things first pal. Got any more of that java?"

"No," he frowned. "Well, yeah, we will. Kelly's making a fresh pot and we'll be taking it with us. Are we fueled and ready to fly?"

Jack laid a hand on his old friend's shoulder.

"*You* just make sure we have the coffee, Tell, *I'll* take care of the gear. So, why don't you go grab whatever you need and meet me at the chopper in fifteen minutes."

Slapping Teller on the back, he walked down the steps. But halfway he turned to shout over his shoulder; "And Teller, *don't* forget the coffee!"

Teller grinned. He was glad Jack was here, for without him Abbott's rescue would be considerably more difficult. And with that thought his mind reeled with the bizarre sequence of events that had brought them all together… He could not have seen this coming in his wildest dreams.

'There are no numbers to equal the odds that Jack would be the guy that Billy would call to pick up the kid who tried to steal the boat that Kelly was piloting down the one river that I happened to choose to get away from it all . . .then, compound those odds by ten million and you still wouldn't get close to the second set of odds that Abbott would be on that same boat.' He thought of the coyote in his pocket. *'And then to have James call Jack to fly him down here! Why, the mind boggles at such cosmic accord.'*

Suddenly the memory of shooting out into space over the waterfall, and of the coyote's golden eye winking as he fell flashed through his mind and he could not help but shake his head at the crazy spin the course of his life had taken. *'Makes one wonder about the entire concept of coincidence.'* His grin was one of wondrous joy as he re-entered the store and headed towards the cooler; for Fate, coincidence, or spiritual manifest notwithstanding, one thing was certain. Abbott would want beer.

— — -- --- -- — —
— — — — —
-- --- --

= Chapter 26 =

The sun was rising, and it was a glorious sight.

From the entrance of his shelter, Abbott watched the sky grow lighter; splashing the horizon with colors. But sadly he was in no mood to enjoy it. He was hungry, thirsty and worse still, lonely.

He looked over his shoulder into the shadows of the cave.

The last of the javalina sizzled in the pan, while cool water plinked steadily from the crack in the wall and into the hole Teller had dug, forming a clear little pool.

He was grateful of course, but he was sick and tired of pig dammit! And *now* the dripping water reminded him of the waterfall logo on a can of Coors.

'I want a beer!'

His thirst aside, he was also becoming concerned. His confidence in Teller was being replaced by paranoia. *'How long can it take to get to the marina? He's been gone now for four days! Hope he's all right. One more day, that's it! If he's not back by tonight I'm leaving!'*

These brave thoughts were much easier to contemplate now that the mountain cat had departed. At least it seemed as if she had gone... he hadn't heard any of the animal's low, throaty growling since yesterday, nor had he hadn't seen any fresh prints in the damp dirt.

He shivered.

For three long nights he had listened to the strange guttural sounds of the beast, imagining its intentions. But now that he was alone he found that he practically missed its fearsome company. He almost laughed, and limping further out, peeked up to scan the ridge above.

No sign of the cat.

'She probably got tired of waiting for me to come out and decided to go find something smaller and easier to kill.'

But looking down at his dirty and disheveled self, he scowled with no small measure of disgust.

'And no doubt less pungent!'

Cautiously crossing the open space between the entrance and the trees, he selected suitable vegetation for his morning constitution and crept off into the brush.

— — ⸺ ⸻ ⸺ — —
—— —— —— —
⸺ ⸻ ⸺

= Chapter 27 =

Jack tapped the glass on the oil pressure gage with his knuckle. The needle bounced a few times then settled in where it belonged. He smiled and recanted the curse that sat on his tongue. That problem solved, he turned to see Teller coming in his direction: a cooler balanced on one shoulder and a small pack slung over the other. Reaching over, he threw open the cockpit door, shouting over the chop of the rotors. "Where's the coffee?"

Teller grinned and dropped the small cooler into Jack's hands. "Relax Jack, Kelly's got it."

"Good." Jack gave a nod as he put the cooler in the back, but when he reached out to take the pack that was slung over Teller's shoulder, Teller slapped his wrist. "*I'll* hang onto this Jack."

Surprise colored Jack's face. "Whatever you want, Tell."

Teller smiled, threw the pack onto his seat and as it landed Jack touched its soft, supple hide.

"Wow, what is that? calfskin?"

Teller smiled. "Nope, deerskin. Long ago I showed a kindness to a fellow traveler in need, and during the two weeks he stayed at my house he made me this. Beautiful isn't it?"

Jack rolled the butter-soft hide between his thumb and forefinger. "Yeah Tell, it *really* is. Got a nice look and the stitching is top notch. The guy was good."

Teller nodded in agreement. "Yep, a talented fellow who really knew how to show his appreciation." He turned his eyes to the sky. "I wonder what ever happened to that guy?" The thought was fleeting, followed by a shrug.

"Oh well," he smiled, another lost boy."

But as he crawled in, he reached into the pack and extracted a worn velvet Crown Royal bag. "Hold out your hand."

Jack was wary but did as requested.

Teller pulled the drawstring open and few loose stones dropped into Jack's palm.

Jack looked to Teller, and then at the stones.

"What are these, and what are they for?"

"Down payment, Jacko. There's a bit more to this trip than a simple rescue. Quite a bit more really, but I'll explain that along the way. Kelly will be here shortly with the coffee so you can say your temporary goodbyes. I'm sending her back to Telluride to keep an eye on things."

"What about James?" Jack said, rattling the stones in his hand like dice.

Teller gave his lopsided grin. "*That's* who she's keeping an eye on. Anyway, once we find Abbott we're going to need to find someone who is willing to take these rough stones off our hands. Do you remember that guy we used to deal with down in Tucson?"

Jack nodded. "Jimmy?"

"Is he still around?"

Jack put two fingers to his chin, tapping slowly. "I don't know Tell. I heard he went semi-legit and moved to Vegas."

Teller pulled the drawstring tight, returned the bag to the pack, and presented Jack with a grand smile. "Then we'll just have to go and find him then, won't we?"

A look of dismay darkened Jack's face. "Aww Tell, I *really* don't want to go to Vegas."

Teller was about to ask why, but before he could press for an answer Kelly came running up with Billy's coffee pot in one hand, and two large Styrofoam cups in the other.

"Hope you don't mind the mix, Jack." She smiled, "I made it the way Teller likes it."

"He'll like it or he won't drink it." Teller laughed as he took the pot and gave her a kiss. "Thanks, babe."

135

Jack nodded. "I'm sure it's fine Kelly." Giving her a smile, he took the two of them in, noting the fresh glow of her skin, and her obvious affection for Teller. Then looking at his rough friend, he grumbled, "Just *how* did an old dog like *you* find a beauty like *this?*" adding with a grin, "And does she have a sister?"

"Jack," Teller laughed, "*Some* of us old dogs still have a modicum of charm and luck." He winked at Kelly. "But it's mostly luck. And sorry chum, but this woman is one of a kind."

Kelly shrugged and gave a smile that nearly broke his heart.

"Sorry Jack, no sisters."

Jack nodded. "Some guys have all the luck." but then looking at Teller with just the slightest hint of envy, smiled, "But why do *you* get so *much* of it?" Jack expected some smart-assed response, but an expression of sincere bewilderment crossed Teller's face.

"I often wonder that myself."

Jack lifted his cup and touched it to Teller's. "Well, maybe some of it will rub off on me. You ready to fly?"

"Ready as I'll ever be." Teller grinned. "Just give me a minute, will you?" He jumped out and headed back to the store.

Jack watched Teller go and as soon as he was out of sight, he took Kelly's hands into his. "Just my opinion," he smiled, "but he's not the only lucky one." He gave a nod in the direction Teller had gone. "That one is a rare find as well."

"Yeah," Kelly nodded. "he's one of a kind all right..."

Jack gave her a light kiss on the cheek.

"Yes, he is, and you have my deepest sympathies."

Just then Teller ran up. "Ready when you are Jackie boy," he grinned, adjusting his pack. Then turning to Kelly, his cavalier grin grew slightly more serious. "I gotta go babe, but I'll be back just as quick as I can." She nodded, then tipped her head in Jack's direction.

"I'll miss you Teller, but you're in good company."

Teller cupped her ears and pulled her lips to his. "The best," he laughed. Then giving her a kiss that warmed her soul, he ran towards the chopper. "See you in Durango!" He shouted as he jumped in, and they were gone.

Minutes later they were racing up the canyon, nose tipped forward, moving along at fifty feet above the waters slow current; sheer walls on either side. Jack looked over at Teller's expression. It was that of a dog on his way to the park.

Turning his attention back to the controls, he tipped the bird radically from port to starboard, partially to accommodate the geography but more for the sheer joy of it. And joy was unquestionably part of the picture.

~

Jack was in his element when he sat at the controls of a helicopter; a natural with unerring instincts. This was a talent Master Sargent Leroy Smith had recognized in Jacks first week of training. Taking a personal interest, he saw a little bit of himself in the boy; a talented kid who was a little arrogant, but fearless. Tame the arrogance, Sargent Leroy had thought, and that fearless streak could be put to use. And so, Leroy had Jack transferred to his unit.

Jack bucked the authority at first, but before long learned to respect Leroy. A tough man and an uncompromising leader. But he held a soft side as well, and the life-long friendship that followed was simply a bonus for them both

~

Glancing over again at Teller, Jack smiled. It was good to have him near again, and not only was the expression on his face priceless, the enthusiasm he exuded proved contagious. Thrilled as always to be in the air, Jack's face split into a huge grin as he saw an opportunity to pull the kind of prank that used to terrify the green recruits back in Hanoi.

Seeing that Teller's concentration was on the river below, Jack kicked up the rotor speed and aimed directly towards the massive wall that loomed a few hundred yards ahead of them;

137

and watching through the corner of his eye, he counted slowly backwards from ten.

Teller glanced up at the fast approaching wall and calmly reached between his feet and picked up the coffee pot.

Pouring himself a cup, he turned to Jack and held out the pot.

"Want some?"

Jack held his smile; but it tightened as the sandstone wall grew larger through the windscreen.

'eight . . . seven . . .

"No, not yet," he said, counting as he waited for Teller to react. Teller glanced at the wall again, but his expression didn't change in the slightest.

The wall was now less than thirty feet ahead.

Five . . . four.

Teller still didn't flinch.

It was now or never. Jack yanked back on the control stick, hauling the nose up, jerking the copter violently while clearing the wall by mere inches. However, the shift in angle and gravity caused Teller's coffee to lift up and out of his cup, hanging suspended for a fraction of a second before the contents splashed down his chest and lap.

Looking down at the wet stain that was spreading rapidly through the weave of his Pendleton, Teller's bottom lip protruded slightly, but other than that his expression remained one of calm detachment.

"Damn it Jack, I really liked this shirt."

Jack's apology was delivered through a suppressed grin.

"Sorry Tell, but that rock just jumped out in front of me."

Teller gave a composed nod and handed Jack his now empty cup. Jack took it, and Teller reached behind the pilot's seat, pulled Jack's duffle bag onto his lap, and carefully removing one of the neatly folded t-shirts began to dab at the spill on the tight plaid wool.

"I understand completely, Jack." Teller smiled. "The rocks in this part of the country are quite unpredictable, always leaping to and fro . . . why, there are times when it's difficult to even walk. Thank God you're a trained pilot."

With Jacks t-shirt having soaked up the greater percentage of the spill, Teller refolded the soggy, and now stained item and stuffed it back into Jack's bag.

Jack was annoyed but at the same time supremely amused.

He couldn't help but smile. Some things never changed, and it pleased Jack to no end that Teller was one of them.

"I missed you Buddy." He laughed.

Teller zipped the duffel bag closed and gave Jack a genuine grin of his own. "I missed you too Jack. Want some coffee?"

"Love some." Jack grinned. "Thanks. Now put on your headset and let me know when to leave the river."

Teller poured, snapped a clear plastic lid onto the cup, and handed it across the cockpit.

"Will do."

— — -- --- -- — —
—— —— —— ——
-- --- --

= Chapter 28 =

For most, the high country of the Umcompangre Plateau was an impassable maze of dry watercourses and twisting dead-end canyons with no discernible landmarks other than the high peaks that lay at the four compass points of the horizon. But for Teller, with his unerring internal compass and remarkable memory for nearly indistinguishable landmarks, the view from the air was akin to following a road map. As they flew, his eyes scanned the landscape, retracing his path back to the place he had left Abbott.

"There!" he called out, pointing to a rock outcropping.

Jack tipped the bird starboard. "Where?"

"There! see that rock that looks like a camel?"

Jack pushed his sunglasses up and squinted; "What camel?"

Teller barked. "Right there!"

"Don't see a camel, Tell."

Teller shrugged, "Eh, doesn't matter, camel or not, head about five degrees port."

"Aye, Captain." Jack chuckled.

Teller gave Jack a sideways glance.

"That's funny. That's what Abbott calls me too."

Jack just grinned. "That's 'cause you're a natural leader of men."

"Fuck you, Jack."

Jack gave a short laugh. "I'm serious Tell. You don't understand because you don't follow *anybody*. Christ, the beat of your drum drowns out the rest of the band altogether. But that sure doesn't mean that *other* people don't hear it, and some of us find it interesting enough to march along."

Teller gave a half smile but said nothing.

Adjusting course the requested five degrees, Jack squeezed the joystick between his knees and poured himself another cup of coffee.

"It wasn't meant as an insult partner. Like it or not, you *are* a leader."

Teller continued to scan the terrain. "Yeah, Kelly said the same thing."

"I'd pay attention to that girl, Tell. She probably knows you better than you do."

Teller finally smiled and laughed, "Yeah, she thinks *that* as well. But I'll tell *you* the same thing I told *her*."

Reaching behind Jack's seat, he pulled the binoculars from the deerskin pack; and as he panned the rough country below, he said, "I don't need, nor want followers… but if you choose to follow, I take no responsibility, liability, or blame for broken hopes, crushed dreams, or missed connections."

Jack gave the side of Teller's head a quizzical look. And Teller, feeling Jack's stare, lowered his field glasses and turned to Jack, his green eyes twinkling.

"I'm serious. But I will also take no credit if you end up deliriously happy." Pulling out one of the gold coins from his pocket, he flipped it in Jack's direction.

Jack snatched it out of the air and Teller grinned, Happy?"

Jack tucked the coin into his shirt pocket.

"Ecstatic."

Teller winked and lifted the binoculars to his eyes.

Staring at Teller's profile for a moment more, Jack turned his attention to the landscape below; while considering what Teller had said.

'Well, at least you know where you stand with this guy, and that's a rarity in this world.

Teller's voice intruded on his thoughts.

"Slow it down a little and follow that ravine."

Jack brought the air speed down slightly and banked in the direction indicated. "We close?"

Teller said nothing but held the field glasses to his eyes. Then, suddenly, he gave a backhanded slap to Jacks upper arm, gave a hoot of joy, and held the binoculars to Jack's face.

"See that large, hairy, naked creature sunning himself on that rock shelf over there?"

Taking the glasses, Jack held them to his eyes one handed while trying to keep the chopper stabilized. "Where?"

Crawling back over the seat, Teller opened the cooler while laughing wildly, "Right there! You blind? The fuckin' guy stands out like a clown at a funeral! *Look!*"

Another pass with the field glasses brought Abbott's prone, naked figure into Jack's view.

"So *that's* our bear huh?" he said with a bemused smile

Sliding back into his seat with a beer can in his hand and a broad smile on his face, he laughed, "That's him! Albeit a bit pinker than most bears, and furrier than most men... but that's our guy!"

Jack handed the glasses back. "Well, he looks healthy enough."

Teller shoved the beer between his legs and looked through the binoculars one last time.

"Yep, and he's still got the cast."

Hanging the binoculars around his neck, Teller slid the door back. "Hover over him, Jack. We're going to provide an emergency air drop."

Jack laughed, gave thumbs up, and dipped towards the ground.

— — -- --- -- — —
— — — —
-- --- --

= Chapter 29 =

Abbott had finally had enough of the cave.

The past twenty-four hours had been quiet... so quiet in fact, that he had started wondering if the cougar might have gone in search of less timid prey. But even if that *wasn't* the case, even *if* the damn cat was waiting silently above to pounce upon and swallow his stinky carcass whole, he was tired of sitting and waiting. Defiant, he pushed himself up with his cane and limped to the shelters entrance. Gazing out at the flowers that dotted the meadow beyond, he recalled the Chief in the movie 'Little Big Man.' Stepping from the cool shade into the morning sun, he stood with eyes closed and arms akimbo,

"It is a good day to die." He spoke bravely.

Nothing happened.

Waiting for a few more seconds, he squeaked open one eye.

A snarling death ball of claws and teeth failed to appear; and in its absence his grisly demise was circumvented.

Opening his other eye, he lowered his arms and took a tentative step forward.

Still nothing...

Apparently, the feline had skipped town. And whether she had done so due to boredom or repelled by his aroma was immaterial. He was alive; and turning his face to the sky, smiled. It was a beautiful day, and, by all appearances, he was going to live to enjoy it.

Well, Abbott sniffed, *my bravery paid off!*

Taking a deep breath, he took a step forward: this time with conviction. And, as his foot touched earth, the pain he expected failed to drop him to his knees in agony, and with that, his smile grew bold. his spirits soaring, he decided to attempt the climb to the top of the ledge before him: the very ledge the Mountain Cat had occupied.

~

Twenty minutes later, wheezing and covered in sweat, Abbott stood atop the cliff, his hand resting on his brow to shade his eyes. Teller had gone down the drainage that snaked through the landscape below; of that he was sure. But it then branched off in multiple directions not a half mile further on... so, to the direction he may have taken at that point there was no way of knowing. Perhaps, he thought, he might be able to track Teller: but even though his ankle felt much better *now*, he doubted the wisdom of attempting a trek cross-country in his condition, and with very few supplies. His earlier conquering hero attitude withered as he considered his scope of options.

'*Which lie somewhere between zero, and none.* he reluctantly admitted. But lifting his face to a sun that hung in the clear, cobalt sky, he allowed his looming depression to be burned away by its warm rays; replaced with thoughts of Teller and beer.

Closing his eyes to enjoy more fully these more pleasant contemplations, he could almost hear Tellers voice:

"*Have a little faith, Grizzly!*"

Swelling with newfound confidence, he began removing his clothing. '*Well, it is a lovely day after all . . ..*'

Moments later, Abbott lay naked, stretched out on the rough stone as warmth soaked into his body: and taking his imaginary Teller's advice, let his eyes flutter closed as he placed his trust in fate.

~

A soft, steady whisper tickled the edges of Abbott's subconscious... slowly opening one eye, he rolled his head to the right and froze.

There, only a few feet away, sat a large coyote; its thick, plush tail slowly swinging back and forth. Swish, swish . . . its long fur sweeping across the sandstone with every pass.

Swish, swish . . .

Mesmerized by the steady metronome sweep of the animal's tail, Abbott nearly missed the toothy grin and wink of a golden eye as the Coyote leapt up and dashed into a copse of Juniper trees.

Yet the brush-like whispering continued:

Swish, swish, swish, swish . . .

Abbott squinted at the wall of shade into which the Coyote had vanished.

"That's odd," he thought, the sound growing louder still.

Swish, swish, shish SWISH!

Realizing that the sound he was hearing was real, he shook himself from his strange dream and opened his eyes wide.

To the south he saw the glint of sun on glass.

Abbott shook his head... it looked like a helicopter... a helicopter? What would a *helicopter* be doing out here?

Then, in a rush of realization, he smiled.

Teller!

His first reaction was to leap up. But thinking of his ankle, and then his image, he decided to play it cool. Lying back, he closed his eyes and put his hands behind his head, waiting for it to come closer; and as it passed directly over him, he opened his eyes, gave a casual wave, and closed them again: the epitome of cool... a relaxed, naked man in a makeshift cast, casually sunning himself on a rock in the middle of nowhere. Not a care in the world.

Teller pointed and laughed. "Now *there's* a class act, Jacko!" With a grin of unfettered joy, he gestured towards Abbott; shouting above the rotors noise as he stepped through the open door and out onto the landing rail.

"Get close enough to ruffle his fur Jacko, then hover."

Giving a nod, Jack put the bird directly over Abbott's recumbent form.

Abbott's cool was shattered. He began scrambling to get out of the prop's wash as it began picking up debris in a swirling tornado of dust .

Teller, balanced on the skid above, hung precariously from the door, a cold can of beer pinched between his thumb and forefinger. Moving it below his eye like a bombardier, he shouted, "Hey Grizzly! Incoming!!" and released.

Abbott, now standing had one hand raised in an attempt to shield his eyes from debris; and in doing so had caught sight of Tellers release of some object: and while his ankle may have been damaged his reflexes were still surprisingly quick. His hand whipped out, fingers managing to grip the slippery, fast-moving cylinder as it passed. Bringing it to eye level, he cautiously unclenched his fist. An enormous grin split his dirty beard upon recognizing the logo, and he swallowed it in two gulps. It was wet, cold, and tasted of a thirsty man's fantasy.

Crushing the empty can, he held it up while shouting, "God bless you, sir! God *bless* you!!"

Laughing so hard tears filled his eyes, Teller stuck his head back into the cabin. "Find a place to set this bird down brother, we got us a bear to feed!"

Jack couldn't help himself. Joining in Tellers laughter he shaking his head in amused admiration. *'With no other man on earth but Teller could it possibly come to this.'*

Following a quick look around he saw a suitable landing spot.

"Hang on, Tell," he shouted "we'll be earthbound in a few."

But Teller was already standing on the landing rails; one hand holding his hat, and a six-pack in the other.

-- -- -- --- -- -- --

—— —— —— ——

-- --- --

= Chapter 30 =

Kelly sat in the wooden rocker, coffee cup between both hands, her gaze on the spot where the helicopter had been. The dust from the chopper had barely settled and she already missed him. Damn! The man was impossible!

She kicked the rocker into motion.

The past few months had been a whirlwind of conflicting emotions. She had no doubts that Teller loved her; but following his disappearance in Telluride she had been forced to take stock of her life. And that involved not only some honest soul-searching, it also required a serious revaluation of their relationship.

She did a mental count.

One: The man was not dependable, at least not in any conventional sense. Yet he had never let her down. When she had needed him most he had always been there.

Two: He was most definitely not predictable. Solid as a rock, but as unmanageable as the wind.

Kelly brought the dark liquid to her lips and smiled as her heart opened to the truth of the matter.

Number three, and possibly the most endearing:

He was not boring.

Yes, she thought, it was that very trait that ultimately overshadowed all of his other failings. And as aggravating as it might be at times, it was *that* small, but fundamental quality that kept her from becoming complacent; resulting in a far more interesting life. Sliding to and fro in the rocker, her finishing thought came with a degree of comfort. *And I've always known where he stands on things. He's steadfast in his beliefs. And from that perspective alone he's a better man than most.*

Thinking of the kiss he had given her just before he jumped into the chopper she closed her eyes and his playful smile appeared. With that image warming her heart, she tipped her cup back, let the last of the liquid dribble onto her tongue, and rocked forward. The momentum carrying her up, and out of the chair, she went into the store for a refill.

~

James trudged uphill towards the store, plotting his next move while hoping to find some coffee. He was beyond being mad, he was furious, and on the verge of desperation.

Following hours in the shadows outside of the firelight, he had waited until Kelly, Teller, Jack, and that rude Indian had all walked away; leaving him alone and forgotten.

He sniffed it self-pity. That was *exactly* what he was; alone and forgotten. And, to make matters worse, the duffle bag with all of his new outdoor gear was still in the trunk of the rental car with Casey. And so, embarrassed and angry, he had waited, and once alone he had sat near the small fire, huddled deep in the coat he was fortunate enough to have shoved into his carry-on; and with only his anger and self-incriminations it had been a desolate night indeed.

But now, with the Sun cresting the line of buttes to the east, he huffed up the hill, his phone pressed tightly to his ear, waiting through a seemingly endless series of rings until finally stabbing the 'off' button.

Before he was simply furious. Now he was homicidal.

He had left a long string of messages on Casey's cell: each more aggravated than the last, and *still* he hadn't heard back! The *only* communication he had received in the past few hours was from the owner of the helicopter he had been forced to charter. The pilot told him he would be there within the hour, and *that* was yet another source of his mounting rage. It had cost him a bundle to charter the damn thing, and he felt the fee was bordering on usury. According to the pilot, the charge was

148

due to short notice and rising fuel costs. But James wasn't fooled. *He* knew it was because the pilot was a friend of Jack's, and those motherfuckers were *all* in a conspiracy with Teller to make his life miserable. *And Goddamnit, they were succeeding!*

He hurried his pace. He needed to get back to Telluride quickly. He and his high-dollar attorneys needed figure out what legal options were available to prevent Teller from taking his percentage of the company and giving it away. *Giving it away!!* The man was crazy!

But as he puffed up the hill his train of thought turned from persecution to calculation... perhaps having Kelly as a partner might *not* be so bad. She would be easier to control than Teller ever was. And working closely may give him another shot at winning her affections.

At that, he smiled and slipped into a fantasy he had secretly harbored for the past two years but was now slightly modified.

He and Casey shared the beautiful house her parents had built in Telluride; and she, with the business skills learned from her father, hired the help necessary to keep the books for the concert revenue as well as manage the mansion and it's grounds. And, being an appreciative open-minded woman, grateful for the life he had provided, would discreetly overlook his taking a mistress.

James smiled as the fantasy coalesced.

And, to make things perfect, with the bizarre bet he had made with Teller, Kelly would see just what an irresponsible vagrant he really was, and would be more than happy to remain in Telluride as his partner (in name only, of course,) and lover . . .

A smile blissful smile crossed his face.

Then his phone rang.

~

Billy had walked through the night, crossing the moonscape of the mesa until he found the arroyo he was looking for. Bending to one knee, he examined the soft sand for prints.

149

Hmmm, Fresh tracks. *Interesting . . ..*

Standing, he adjusted his beat-up old hat and looked into the shadows of the narrow slot canyon. His smile flashed beneath its brim as the old Navaho sprinted into the gap.

~

Ben's croaking call shook Casey from her exhausted sleep. Pulling herself from a fog of fatigue and worry, she rolled off of the tightly made bed; padding across the floor in stocking feet to lay her hand on his forehead.

"I'm here Benny."

Attempting a weak smile Ben mumbled through his shattered mouth, "Wha happem?"

Sighing in relief, Casey stroked his hair.

"We were hoping you might be able to give *us* the answer to that, Ben."

He made the attempt to shake his head in the negative, but it only brought a grimace of pain.

Casey's eyes reflected his misery. "Shall I call the nurse?"

He squeezed her hand, "No, pease do'n."

It wounded her to watch his eyes struggle to focus.

"Wherehs Unca bames?"

"He's not here, Ben" she smiled, "I've been waiting for his call," Patting his hand she picked up her purse. "Let me check." Opening the phone and seeing the number of missed calls she whispered, "Oh no . . ." She must have hit the mute button when she had lain down.

'Damn!

As she listened to her voicemails the anger she had felt just moments ago evaporated. James's messages were many, each sounding more harassed and angry than the last.

Guiltily, she dialed his number.

= Chapter 31 =

Trudging up the trail, James paused and bent over, panting as he placed his hands on his knees, sweat dripping from his forehead to make little wet craters in the dust at his feet. Suddenly the phone in his pocket rang. Glaring at his watch as he fumbled it free he punched the on button.

"Where the *hell* have you been?" he barked.

At the antagonism in his voice, Casey's anger flared. But noting anxiety in his tone as well she remained civil.

"I'm at the hospital, James. Benny woke up again and wants to see you." She paused, concern overriding her anger.

"Why are you breathing so hard?"

"Because I'm walking in the goddamn desert Casey! How is he?" Ignoring his attitude, she answered.

"He's in pain, James. He's confused and he's scared."

James slowly pushed off his knees and stood straight, modulating his voice while taking a deep breath.

"Look, Casey, there have been some developments that require my immediate attention. I need to fly back to Telluride and I need to do it today. As a matter of fact, I've chartered a helicopter out of Grand Junction and I'm expecting it any minute now."

Frowning, Casey put her phone between her ear and shoulder and held a cup of water to Ben's cracked lips. He took a small sip, smiling a weak 'thank you' and closed his eyes

Cassy laid a finger to his cheek returned her attention to the phone. "What happened to the helicopter that took you down there?"

James' anger flared and he ground his teeth so hard he nearly cracked a molar. "Goddamned Teller happened to it!"

He nearly screamed, running his tongue along the tooth to check for damage as he struggled to regain his composure.

"Look Casey, it's a long story and I have neither the time, nor the desire to go into it right now. Can Ben travel?"

Casey's brow furrowed and she set the cup on the side table. "I don't think so."

Following a long pause on James' end, he came back sounding exasperated. "Well then Casey. What would *you* like to do? do you want to stay with him, or come back to Telluride?"

"You are *such* an *asshole*."

Surprisingly, James' self-control held. He had always prided himself in his ability to work under pressure and right now the petty problems of an unhappy woman and an injured boy were nothing. His empire was threatened, but his priorities were in place. The boy was in good hands with the hospital staff and Casey could either stay or go. It was up to her.

"I may be an asshole, Casey, but I'm a *rich* asshole and I intend on remaining that way. Teller is trying to destroy *my* company, and I will *not* allow that to happen. You have enough credit cards to last the millennium, and Ben needs to remain under medical care anyway. So you do whatever you feel is necessary. The decision is *yours*; not mine."

The "thump" of an approaching helicopter suddenly filled the background: growing louder by the second and threatening to drown James out altogether. He shouted into the phone, "I've gotta go."

Suddenly there was complete and utter silence.

Flipping her phone closed, Casey shoved it into her purse. As much as she hated to admit it, he was right.

Looking down, she saw that Benny had drifted off into a morphine sleep; and seeing him lying there, multiple tubes running from the assorted bags that hung from the steel rack next to the bed, she knew what to do. Her decision made, she leaned over gave him a light kiss, and walked out to the nurses' station

~

"Yes Mrs. Carson, we'll take good care of your son."

"Pierpont."

"Pardon me, Ma'am?'

"Pierpont... My name is Pierpont. Not Carson."

"Oh, yes. Mrs. Pierpont then. Your son is in good hands here, don't you worry."

Casey didn't bother to correct the chubby nurse. Let them think she was his mother. Maybe they would care for him differently. Tearing a piece of paper from the notepad on the counter, she scribbled down three sets of digits.

"Here are the numbers where you may contact me. Please call if there are any changes. I can be here in a matter of hours."

The nurse took the note, adding it to the file tucked beneath her arm. "I'm on my way to check on him now Ma'am,"

She took a few steps towards the room, stopped and turned.

"Someone will call if you're needed."

"Thank you." Casey called to the woman's retreating back; and as the door swung shut, relief washed over her; her part was done. Stepping into the waiting area, Casey took the phone from her purse and dialed.

"Hello, Daddy? Would you send the jet? I want to come home for a few days."

— — -- --- -- — —

— — -- --- --

= Chapter 32 =

Hovering above the spot they had last seen Abbott, Jack held the chopper in place; rocking over a thick cloud of dust and debris that the spinning rotors created, unable to see anything below the landing skids. Turning, he was about to shout at Teller to close the door when he saw him leap into the churning sea of dust.

Teller dropped blindly, keeping his knees loose and trusting he had gauged both the distance and the landing area favorably. There was a split second of doubt during his free-fall; then he hit ground. Smiling, he crushed his hat to his head, tightened his grip on the six-pack beneath his arm, and set off in a crouching run in the direction he remembered Abbott being.

Unfortunately, with the taste of long-awaited beer, Abbott's taste buds had gone into hyper-drive; and that enthusiasm sent him hobbling towards the noise of the helicopter with surprising speed.

Blinded by dust, both charged towards their goals; Teller moving low and fast while Abbott, leaning forward for maximum momentum, stabbed the ground with the cane: and unable to see through the dust, they slammed into one-another full force.

The solid impact knocked Abbott onto his back with a grunt while Teller ricocheted sideways, bouncing onto the hard surface and landing solidly on the bruise the tree root had inflicted only a few days before.

Howling, he rolled onto his side, clutching his shoulder awhile a punctured beer can spun in tight circles, spraying beer foam in a six-foot radius: turning the dust that settled on him into mud.

He lay there for a moment, watching the can come to a slow, fizzling stop. With a groan he sat up, licking the dirty foam from his mustache as a sudden breeze began to clear the dust.

Picking up his hat, he chuckled at seeing Abbott laying on his back, Stunned, but otherwise unharmed.

Slowly pushing himself up onto one knee, he saw Jack emerging from the dust cloud that still floated behind Abbott's prostrate form; a wraith-like figure slowly gaining solidity until coming to a halt to gaze coolly down at the two of them.

Looking first at Teller, and then at Abbott, he shook his head.

"My, my, my. Just when I thought it couldn't get any weirder. Teller, you've outdone yourself."

Teller grinned through the dirt and pain. "Of course I have Jack, that's what I do . . ." Pinching the brim of his hat, he yanked it down, picked up the three surviving beers by the plastic ring. "Christ!" he moaned, massaging his ribs. "That was like running into a furry brick wall." Jack chuckled and they both looked down at Abbott, who lay on his back in the beer-splattered dust, moaning softly.

Teller stood, pulled a can from its plastic ring, and snapping the tab, took a long swig. "So, how're *you* feelin' Griz?" he asked, wiping the muddy foam from his mustache with the back of his hand.

Abbott still appeared dazed, gazing blankly at the scattered mess of woolen sleeves and fragmented mud that had once constituted his cast. Then, with a shake of his head, he propped himself up on his elbows and wiggled his toes. "Like I just got hit by a freight train," he groaned. But then, smiling through his mud smattered beard, chuckled, "Not exactly the most subtle form of cast removal doc, but certainly effective." Gesturing to the remaining beers hanging from Teller's hand, he sighed, "Would you be so kind as to pass me one of those?"

Jack reached over, took the beer ring from Teller's filthy hands, opened a can and handed it to Abbott, who smiled gratefully, closed his eyes, and drank.

Tilting his head in Abbott's direction, Jack grinned, "So, this big naked fellow is the one we're here to rescue?"

Teller's eyes went wide, then he began looking nervously about; feigning anxious worry. "Egad's Jack, I certainly hope so! You don't suppose there are more of them, do you?"

Jack laughed and looked down at the man before them.

Abbott sat naked in the mix of mud and dirt; his pale skin barely visible beneath a thick coat of curly body hair; happily guzzling the cans contents.

Teller's semi-serious expression became an enormous smile as he laid a hand on Abbott's furry shoulder and gave it a hearty squeeze. "Yep... This is the man we came to find. 'Course I never expected to find him like *this*."

Jack's expression turned quizzical. "What, naked?"

Teller laughed. "No! walking. I really didn't think he'd be on his feet yet."

Jack's mouth opened as if he was going to say something but he just stuttered and blinked, triggering yet more amusement on Teller's part. "What?" Teller grinned, "The naked part? Hell, Jack, He's a beer-drinking bear! You can't expect him to be civilized!"

Reaching down, Teller splayed his fingers over the top of Abbott's head, gripping it firmly to rotate it towards Jack.

"Grizzly old pal, I'd like you to meet a true friend, an ace pilot, and my partner in crime, Mr. Jack Hawkins."

Lifting his other hand, he motioned to Abbott.

"Jack, I'm pleased to introduce Sir Abbott."

He stopped in mid-sentence, looking somewhat at a loss.

"Hell, Grizzly, I don't even know your last name."

Shaking free of Tellers grip, Abbott stood and held out a large hand. "Pleased to meet you Sir. The name is Livingstone, Abbott Livingstone."

Seeing Teller's brows lift, Abbott turned to him and waggled a finger. "Please, Captain. No lame jokes."

Teller's face lit with humor. "Why Mr. Livingstone, I would *never* be so presumptuous."

Abbott groaned and turned to Jack, who simply shrugged as Teller gestured again in Abbott's direction.

"Well there you go Jack! Meet Professor Abbott Livingstone. My newest friend, fellow time traveler, and present cohort in the discovery of previously lost riches . . . not to mention his status as Royal muse *and* Court Magician: personally appointed to such lofty position by the Canyon King."

Taking the proffered hand with a smile, Jack shook his head. "That is one hell of a title."

Opening three beers, Teller looked at Abbott and grinned. *"That,* my friend, is one hell of a man."

Raising his can he proclaimed, "To the future!"

The other two men joined the toast.

His eyes still twinkling with amusement, Teller gave Abbott a slow once over. "Now then, with all introductions now complete, how's about putting on some clothes, Sir Knight? Your nakedness is not nearly as pleasing for us as it may be for you."

Abbott, overjoyed as he was with the rescue and still muddled from the collision with Teller, had completely forgotten that he was without clothing. He gave an embarrassed smile. "Sorry."

Teller just set his empty can on the ground and crushed it with his foot. "No need to be sorry Griz," he smiled. "Just get dressed while 1 go get the first aid kit from the chopper. Then we can take a look at that ankle." he paused. "But not until you've got some pants on." He turned and walked towards the helicopter. Both men watched for a moment, then Jack turned back.

"Well, Sir Abbott," he laughed. "where *are* your pants?"

But Abbott was already limping in a circle, searching for his cane, not his trousers. Hearing Jack, Abbott turned and muttered, "Pardon?" Jack averted his eyes from Abbott's hobbling nakedness; and in doing so spied a small pile of clothing neatly folded in the shade of a Piñon tree.

Gathering them up, he brought them to Abbott.

"Here you go."

"Thank you, Jack."

Jack shrugged, "No big deal." and twisted the last beer from the plastic ring. "I imagine you would like this."

Abbott, who was now sitting on a rock, pulling his pants gently over the tender foot, looked up, gratitude plain in his eyes. "Only if you don't."

"It's yours Abbott. I'm not really a beer guy, and Teller made sure we brought plenty. Not much else, but plenty of beer."

A radiant smile burst through Abbotts tangled beard. "Ahhhhh, that's my King," he laughed. So," he smiled, pulling is pants up. "you've known Teller a long while?"

"Yeah Abbott," Jack nodded. "Quite a while."

"And he's told you nothing of our adventure?"

Jack reached into his pocket, and removing the gold coin Teller had given him, held it up. "All he has shown me is this."

Buttoning his pants, Abbott limped over and took the beer; his smile growing ever wider as he gently removed the coin from Jack's fingers, palmed it, and made a fist. Then, with a flourish, rolled his fingers open, revealing an empty hand... he then opened the beer and drained it with one long swallow.

Holding out one bare hand while balancing the now empty beer can in the other, he presented them as if on a scale.

"Then you know *nothing!*"

Jack nodded, "On this subject, Master Court Magician, you may be right. But before we head back to the chopper I have two things to say." Abbott dropped the empty can onto the ground and put on his shirt. "And those would be?"

158

"Give me back my coin, and who the hell is the Canyon King?"

Abbott laughed aloud and reached over, putting his fist next to Jack's head and performing the old magicians trick of plucking a coin from the subject's ear. It flashed brilliantly in the sun; and with a grin Abbott slipped it into Jacks shirt pocket. "There is your coin, good sir," he laughed. "But the story of the Canyon King is a tale in, and of itself." Lifting a filthy arm, Abbott bowed his head.

"Some help, please?"

Jack nodded and slid smoothly under Abbott's arm.

Following an awkward first few steps, they quickly found a rhythm: and as they shuffled towards the helicopter, Abbott began his elucidation.

"Teller is the Canyon King, and Kelly is, of course, his Queen." Cocking his head to look into Jacks face, he smiled.

"Have you met her yet?"

"Oh yes," Jack nodded.

At Jack's expression, Abbott chuckled. "Yes, lovely woman. Anyway, it's a long story Jack. Our meeting, the gold, oh, and are you aware of the Coyote?"

"The little statue?"

"Yes and no Jack. Yes and no . . ." Abbott shook his wooly head. "I believe we will need all of the beer you may have brought, and Teller as well, to relate the tale in its full scope. But in the meantime, I'm ravenous! Did you bring any food?"

Lowering Abbott into the shade of the helicopter, Jack stood and stretched his back. "I'm not sure. Teller packed... speaking of, where *is* he?"

Both men looked around and Jack frowned as he scanned the area. "Wonder where he got off to?"

He circumnavigated the helicopter and by the time he completed the circle, Abbott was pulling out his second six-pack, along with a big bag of peanuts from the cooler.

Ripping the bag open, he poured out a handful and popped them into his mouth. Grinning, he held out the bag in Jack's direction. "Want some?" he mumbled as he chewed.

= Chapter 33 =

Teller having vanished, they had little to do but wait.

Palming some of the cold water from the cooler he splashed his face and sat next to Abbott, giving silent thanks that he was now fully clothed. "So… a beer drinking bear, huh?"

Cracking another peanut, Abbott added it to the handful he held and tossed them into his mouth. The papery skins floated onto his beard, settling like downy feathers in a bird's nest. A rapacious crunching followed, then looking at Jack, the skin at the corners of his brown eyes crinkled.

"Yes sir." He chuckled, his smile shining through his whiskers. "Our friend Teller has an interesting sense of humor."

Jack, taking in Abbott's considerable mass, along with his tanned face framed by a head of unruly curls and beard sprinkled with peanut skins, as well as the littering of shells and empty beer cans that now littered the area, smiled.

"And a keen sense of observation as well."

Abbotts chewing ceased: then realizing the inference, chortled, "Ha! Yes. I suppose the Captain's comments are not *all* based on prejudice and bad taste." Brushing the peanut remnants from his beard, his eyes went to the cooler. "You *did* say he brought an ample quantity of beer, did you not?"

"Yes, Sir Abbott, I did. Help yourself."

Abbott happily complied, opening another can and offering one to Jack who waved it off.

"No thanks. I've got to fly us out of here."

"Oh yes, of course." Abbott smiled, tipping his can.

Sliding sideways to remain the shade of the chopper., he asked. "So, Abbott, why Captain?"

161

"Why what?"

"Why do you call Teller, 'Captain'?"

"Ahhh" Abbott smiled, rubbing his beard. "Well, shortly after I first met him he managed to steer our craft through some extraordinary rapids with Miss Kelly."

Jack nodded, waiting, but Abbott said nothing more.

"I see. So, it's a long story?'

Abbott grinned. "A *very* long story Jack." The pause was perfectly timed. The two men, bonded now by mutual association, looked up just as the man in question's head popped up over the edge of the cliff not twenty feet away. Pulling himself up over the ledge, he walked towards them; two beautiful rabbit pelts tucked in his belt and a satisfied smile on his face. "Hi ho gents!"

"What you got there, Tell?" Jack said, pointing to the pelts.

Teller didn't answer. Instead, he looked down at the mess that was Abbott.

"Thirsty? "he said, his lip curling in distaste.

Abbott burped. "Enormously."

"Well, go easy big fella, we still got a long way to go."

Abbott responded with another burp.

"You're disgusting." Teller sighed.

During the exchange, Jack had reached up, plucked one of the silver-white pelts that hung from Teller's belt and was stroking the extraordinarily soft fur.

"Where the hell did you get *this?*"

Having turned away, Teller was gazing west. Mentally orientating a tall, red-rock spire that was silhouetted against the sky in geographical relation to his topographical memory map. Satisfied with the match in location, he turned back to Jack.

"I killed a couple of 'em before I left so Abbott wouldn't starve." "And it did *not* go unappreciated Captain." Abbott interjected, shaking the last of the peanuts into his maw.

"Good" Teller grinned, looking down at Abbott's dirty, shell-littered face. "I would hate to think my considerable efforts were for naught."

162

Looking back and forth between the two of them, Jack found it impossible not to smile; but he also felt the need to get moving.

"Gentlemen," he smiled, "as entertaining as this reunion is, it's time to go." He handed the pelt back to Teller. "Tell, I don't know if you had thought any further than the rescue of your friend here, but we really do need to get on with whatever it is we're doing."

Teller nodded. "Yes, Jack, I have, in fact, thought beyond the location and possible evacuation of this here beer swilling bear." He smiled down at Abbott. "And, as it seems the nearest medical facility is not an immediate necessity, I believe our next step is to relocate the final resting place of a certain rogue slave." His eyes left Jack and focused on Abbott. "You up for such activity Abbott? After all, you *are* the archeologist."

Crumpling the empty peanut bag, Abbott tossed it onto the ground and reached out his hand for some help up.

"Yes, Captain, I think my foot has healed sufficiently to travel, as long as I am not required to walk any great distance."

Pulling Abbott smoothly to his feet, Teller patted the side of the helicopter. "Walking is no longer necessary my scruffy friend. *That* is the whole point of the expensive piece of machinery; machinery the two of you are using for shade." But as he was about to hand Abbott his cane he looked down at the mess that surrounded the big man. Poking the empty peanut bag on the ground, Teller rotated the cane and jabbed Abbott solidly in his furry belly.

"Damn it, son! I should beat you with this stick for that!"

Chastised, Abbott picked up the crumpled bag.

"Sorry Cap'n."

Teller poked him again, then spun the stick so the handle was within Abbott's grasp. "Just hobble over to the chopper and climb in the back. I'll get this."

Taking the cane, Abbott shuffled towards the helicopter.

Teller sighed. "Hey partner," he said to Jack. "give me a hand with this mess wouldja?" Jack picked up the crumpled bag.

"I *really* want to hear this story, Tell."

"I know you do Jack, and hear it you will. But first things first. How far can we fly on the fuel we have?"

Jack thought for a moment. "Are we searching blindly, or do we know where we're going?"

Teller smiled. "Oh, I have a pretty good idea where we're going."

"Well then," Jack nodded. "Given a relatively straight line and fair cruising speed, we ought to be good for about two hundred miles."

Teller dropped the crushed empties into the cooler.

"We don't need to go anywhere near that far."

"Well that's good news." Jack said, "but just where *are* we going?" But before Teller could answer, Abbott's voice called from the helicopter, "Don't forget my helmet!"

Teller glared, but then gave an amused shake of his head.

"Hang on Amigo." He said, then turned to Jack.

"Excuse me." Going to the cliffs edge, he hopped over.

It was a short hike, and at the caves entrance he paused. This shelter had likely saved Abbotts life. Thanking the powers that be for his luck he kicked dirt over the still smoldering coal of the fire and gathered Abbott's gear. But when he picked up the Conquistador's helmet, he saw that a mouse had tried to remake her home in its confines in the short time he was gone.

"Industrious little bastards," he muttered; shaking the dried grass and droppings onto the dirt he tucked the helmet under his arm and made his way back to the chopper; picking up rubbish and cramming it into the helmet as he went. Once there, he slid the door open and tossed the helmet onto Abbott's lap.

"There ya go…. Then, turning to Jack; smiled.

"Let's fly."

= Chapter 34 =

Standing just inside the rocks narrow passage, Billy gazed into the shadows, allowing his eyes to adjust to the darkness.

To anyone walking above, the slot canyon in which Billy now stood would appear nothing more than a slightly larger crack among the many that riddled this desolate landscape. But from Billy's perspective, the narrow gap through which the light managed to filter was thirty feet above his head: bouncing with eerie intensity from water-sculpted walls. And with the sun directly above, the beams that slipped through that narrow crack drew lit the paw prints pressed into the sand at his feet.

Smiling, he followed them in.

The distance between the walls at the slots entry left barely enough room for his shoulders: and as he went further, not only did the space get tighter, the light from above was squeezed out, growing fainter with every step until reaching a bottleneck that pinched tighter still.

Turning sideways, he exhaled, working through the narrow space until his back and belly rubbed the walls on either side. He squirmed through the narrow gap, a button scraping from his shirt to fall at his feet. Unable to retrieve it, he pushed it deep into the sand with his foot as he inched along.

'This was much easier as a younger man,' he grunted. And with a final exhalation, pushed into a large chamber.

His eyes having adjusted to the thin light that filtered through the crack behind, the room that he now found himself in seemed supernaturally bright. Dust motes sparkled as they floated through a single beam of light that passed through a hole in the ceiling to light what served as an altar. An altar of stacked stones for legs, with a slab of carved stone the size of a church pew as its cap. As always, he paused to mumble a quick prayer.

Before him, beneath a fine coat of dust and in the exact same position they had been placed over four hundred years ago, were five green glass plates. Each in line with its twin: each serving as a translucent base for an ancient pottery bowl: each bowl filled with gold coins. In the beginning, each bowl had held five hundred coins. But over the years that number had diminished.

That Billy knew of these bowls was no accident; for it was his ancestor who had placed them here so long ago.

Billy's grandfathers, grandfather's grandfather had served as not only Estebanico's trusted guide, but his counselor as he had trekked through this strange, and uncharted territory. And, having also been with him on the day Estebanico walked into the Zuni village of Hawikuh, he was one of the fortunate few to have escaped the wrath of the warriors who poured from the walls that morning, slaying all that resisted, and making slaves of those who did not.

Originally, there had been ten plates and twelve bags of coins. But before entering the walls of Hawikuh, Estebanico had taken three of the plates, leaving his guide with the others, insisting that his friend and companion hold the rest of these mysterious treasures while he went to speak with the leaders of 'Cibola.' But in the mayhem that ensued, Billy's ancestor was forced to flee, taking with him the objects with which he had been entrusted.

Initially, the coins were little more than pretty baubles. Interesting, but holding no value to the people. The glass plates, however, proved to be far more troublesome: with the smooth, translucent green objects creating envy among the women of the tribe from the very beginning.

Following an argument between several of the Chief's wives, he had taken one of the plates, and in the wisdom of Solomon, broke it into pieces, giving one piece to each of the wives. But his hope for unity or satisfaction amongst the

166

women was short-lived... each woman had greedily taken her piece of glass: but the following day each returned, complaining that the other wives was larger; and each now demanding that they deserve a whole, unbroken plate.

In answer to their squabbling, the Shaman kept one plate for ceremonies, entreating the surviving guide to hide the rest of the bothersome items where they could not be found.

And so he had done. In this place, so very long ago.

Billy's family was of the Coyote water clan. And because the spirit of Coyote had been present in the village of Hawikuh that fateful day, it was his family that was given the charge of their keeping. Thus, over the centuries, Billy's clan had remained the custodians of these odd treasures, and the narrators of the legend that was passed down by the elders. From generation to generation; to this day.

Time passed; with the People continuing to move in the prescribed circle of existence. And as it passed, the stories of the bloody events of Hawaiki faded into distant memory. But the circle had been broken as the disturbing rumors of a strange new trespasser washed over the land.

In the beginning, only a few of these odd creatures wandered into the remote home of the Diné; but as they were considered nothing more than amusing oddities, they were allowed passage; but within a few seasons these peculiar white men covered the land like ants, stealing everything they could find.

For the People, the objects these strange beings coveted were of no real use... and while their greedy obsessions were perplexing, they seemed harmless. Sadly, the error of that belief came too late; for the speed in which these creatures multiplied was astonishing; their endless numbers and senseless actions quickly overwhelming the People.

But worse, these strangers possessed no soul.

167

Seemingly intent on destroying the harmony of the Earth they forced their ways upon everyone, forever changing man's place upon it, and ending the manner in which the People had always lived.

Over the course of the past one hundred and forty years, Billy's family had used the coins to help the families of the remaining clans to survive. And while they had been required to use caution, they *had* survived. And, while greed was not unknown among the people in these new and complex times, Billy's position as guardian of this wealth had taught him the wisdom of patience.

Through trial and error, he had discovered that presenting too many coins, to any one collector, at any one time, raised unneeded suspicion that required explanations. Explanations he had no desire to provide. Consequently, over the years, and with the help of his contact in Tucson, he had covertly funneled monies into hospitals, as well as programs for the education of the children within the imaginary walls of the reservation. And at nearly two thousand dollars per coin, the occasional sale to a discrete collector also subsidized the meager profits of his snack and bait store, allowing him to keep the old Scout running and indulge himself in the quality of coffee and wine his new friends had so recently enjoyed.

Kneeling to remove four coins from each bowl, Billy's hat blocked the light that fell across the stone alter. A call to Tucson and within the day half the money would be wired to his account in Flagstaff while the other half went into a Native trust he had created long ago.

But as he rose, the shadow of his hat lifted, allowing the Sun's bright beam to light the surface of the center plate.

'What's this??. . .'

Bending, he saw an irregular shape in the dust; and upon closer inspection, he recognized it for what it was.

The nose print of a coyote...

A smile spread across his face.

You just can't keep it out of things, can you?

Pocketing the coins, he squeezed back towards the entrance.

— — ▬▬ ▬▬▬ ▬▬ — —
— — — — —
▬▬ ▬▬▬ ▬▬

= Chapter 35 =

Sitting at Billy's desk, Kelly stirred sugar into her coffee, her mind on leaving. The spoon clinked as she stirred, splashing small drops of warm liquid onto a stack of papers that were lying on the desk. Dabbing at them, she noticed Jack's phone number scribbled in Teller's quirky print. Her first instinct was to call: but tucking the number into her back pocket, decided instead to return to the porch, and the rocker. But as she pushed through the swinging doors with her hip she nearly ran into Dave. They both came to a startled stop and uttered the same phrase simultaneously: "Shit, you scared me!" Then, simultaneously shutting their mouths as well, looked at one another and laughed. David's laughter faded into a chuckle, and he pointed to the cup in her hand.

"I came in for some of that."

"Well Dave," Kelly smiled, lifting her cup. "you're in luck. I just made some." She turned around, and he trailed her back to the office where she picked up the water-spotted glass carafe that had replaced the stainless steel one Teller had absconded with., "You planning on leaving today?" She asked as she poured.

He took the cup, gave a nod of thanks, and shrugged.

"That's kind of up to you Kelly, I came down here to get the boat, remember?"

The fingers of her right hand went to her forehead as she squeezed her eyes shut.

There was just too much happening at once! Teller . . . Jack . . . James!!

"Dammit Dave. I'm sorry I guess I forgot."

"I understand." he smiled, "There's a *lot* going on down here. So, what about you? What are you gonna do?"

Kelly flopped back into the desk chair.

"I don't know... I thought about waiting here for Teller but it seems like I'm needed back in Telluride more than I'm needed here. Now I just have to decide whether I should ride back with you, or fly back with James."

Dave lowered his cup. "Wait a sec. I thought Teller took off in the whirlybird."

"He did," She nodded. "But James found another one up in 'Junction. It's coming sometime this morning."

Dave's eyebrows rose. "Really? I can't say that hurts my feelings any."

Kelly smiled. "Well, he's got the money, and it *would* be a long, crowded ride in the truck."

"True enough." Dave nodded. "And eight hours with that guy would make for a miserable ride. So then, what about you? You ridin' with us or flyin' with him?"

Kelly gave a little shrug. "I don't know yet, let's see how the morning goes." Holding up the glass coffee pot, she shook it. "Want some more?"

"No thanks, Kelly" Dave said, tapping the crystal of his watch. "I'm going to head down to the boat and see what I can do to fix it. Then I'll load up and head back to Telluride."

He smiled. "Anything else I can do for you?"

"No, Dave. that will help a lot, and if you need a hand Skip and Lori are around somewhere." She set the coffee pot down.

"Come on, I'll walk you out."

Parting on the steps of the porch, Dave headed towards the river while Kelly walked back into the store muttering under her breath. "I wonder where Teller is?"

James hadn't bothered with saying goodbye. He just jammed the phone into his pocket and cocked his ear in the direction of the distant "thwop" from the east; for while he could *hear* the chopper, the glare of the sunrise prevented his seeing anything. Assuming it would land near the store, he began trotting in that direction; and as he crested the hill the roar grew closer. His trot became a run, and as he passed between the store and the garage the sight of a new EC135 Hermes hovering above the parking area greeted his eyes. It swayed side to side as the pilot looked for someone to provide landing instructions.

James jogged into the cloud of dust, waving his arms in order to get the pilots attention while pointing to the parking lot.

Spotting him, the pilot gave a thumb's up and settled the craft to the ground, dirt and gravel spraying in a wide circle as he shut the engines down. The props slowed to a lazy swoosh, a door slid open, and a tall young man jumped out, smiling through his neatly trimmed beard to extend a gloved hand.

"James Carson?"

Waving away the dust with one hand, he shook the soft leather with the other. "Yes I am. And thanks for coming."

The pilot returned a firm grip. "Sir," he grinned, "for the money you're paying me I should be thanking *you*!"

It was exactly the wrong thing to say.

James' jaw tightened. He was in full agreement and grumbled as much through tightly clenched teeth; while the pilot, delighted with the agreed upon fee, prudently overlooked James' reaction and adopted a serious, professional manner.

"Excuse me Sir. Pleased to be at your service. Now, may I ask where we going and how many will be flying with us?"

James turned from the pilots smile and looked across the packed dirt lot.

Dave's truck was still sitting where he had parked it yesterday, and looking to the porch, saw no movement. Turning, his expression was so rancorous that the pilot's smile vanished.

"*I* am going to Telluride." he growled. "As far as any other passengers, I'm not sure. Give me a minute and I'll check."

Turning, he marched away, leaving the pilot holding his sunglasses in his hand: wondering whether to follow his new client or just wait.

He wisely decided to wait.

James stomped up the stairs, nearly colliding with Kelly as she came through the screen door at a trot. Taking a quick step back and appearing only slightly apologetic, she looked over his shoulder.

"I heard the helicopter . . ."

Against all odds she had hoped it was Teller returning for her; and although she was disappointed she was not surprised.

Biting the inside of her cheek, she looked glumly at James.

"So. You're all ready to go?"

Sensing her contempt, he nodded as he went to the bench where he had set his bag the night before.

"Yes, Kelly, I am."

He slung it over his shoulder. "Are you coming?"

She was torn between her desire to wait for Teller's return and her full understanding of his request... that she keep an eye on the man in front of her.

Kelly knew money was the very least of Teller's motivations; a fact he had proven many times over. And he was absolutely correct regarding James... money was his number one priority; a fact he had demonstrated on a daily basis. And as Teller had made quite clear after winning the wager last night; she now had a vested interest in the outcome. Therefore, his reasoning was sound. She made her decision.

She would go.

Looking hard at James, she gave a provisional smile. "I'll go with you James. Give me a few minutes to get my things together." She turned and went into the store; but as she did a tight smile crept across James' face: his manipulative mind already working.

Billy crested the rise, holding his hand up to shield his eyes against the morning's bright rays as Jack's helicopter disappeared into the Sun; taking he and Teller towards the Abajo Mountains.

Just why Coyote had taken such an interest in Teller was still a mystery: but Billy felt fortunate to have been drawn into this adventure with him.

Closing his eyes, a luminous smile spread across his face.

'Use caution Teller. Coyote may lead you on a merry chase, but as long as you pay attention you will come to no harm.'

Teller's fingers drummed on the console as he stared at the passing landscape; concentrating on remembered landmarks.

"What's the matter Tell?"

"Huh?"

"I said,"

Teller waved a hand in Jacks direction but didn't take his eyes from the windscreen. "I heard you . . ."

Jack shrugged and looked over his shoulder at Abbott, who simply smiled as he took a bite of the stale, plastic clamshell encased sandwich he had grabbed in a last-minute stop at the cooler of Billy's store.

Teller's voice rose over the chop of the blades, "Hold steady for a minute, Jack."

The craft came to a swaying stop, hovering in place as Teller put the binoculars to his eye and slid the glass slowly across the landscape.

A second later Teller's finger shot out. "There!"

In the distance a sandstone cliff rose from a meadow; its crest dotted with Piñon and Cedar. There was nothing remarkable about the site other than the fact that its face was a washed out white with yellow highlights as opposed to the more common red and pink sandstone that colored the surrounding cliffs.

Jack tipped the chopper forward in the direction of Teller's finger.

At first glance, the distant wall appeared small. But as they approached, Jack realized that it easily rose fifty feet from the tall Ponderosa pines growing along its base; stretching for nearly a quarter mile: the snow in their shadows unmelted while the meadow that spread to the south was lush with the grass and wildflowers blossoming in profusion.

"Beautiful." Teller smiled. Then pointing to an open spot below a cave opening that had been invisible until now slapped Jack on the shoulder.

"Set'er right *there*, Jack!"

The moment Teller said, "There!" Abbott crammed the last of his sandwich into his mouth, and squeezing between the seats, chewed madly, trying to swallow while gazing anxiously through the windscreen.

Shouldering Abbotts head out of the way, Jack leveled the bird, and swaying a dozen feet above the grass turned to speak; but as he did Teller unbuckled his harness, flung open the door and leapt out.

"*Dammit* Tell!" Jack hollered while turning dials and flipping switches; landing lightly onto the meadows soft grass. The 'copter rocked to a stop and Teller stuck his head back through the door. "Give me my pack, Abbott. Please."

Abbott held it out and Teller grabbed it, slung it over his shoulder and shouted Thanks! as he sprinted towards the same cave they had spent a cold and miserable night only eight days ago. Abbott chuckled as he watched Teller cut across the meadow and melt into the caves entrance.

With a sigh, he crawled out of the chopper, looked at Jack, and tipped his head towards the cliff. "See ya there." he smiled and limped away.

Jack glanced over to where Teller had gone, then watched Abbott follow, shuffling through the trail of crushed flowers Teller had left. With a shake his head he shut the machine down and with a final check of all instruments, rapped the oil sensor with his knuckle one last time. With a nod of satisfaction, he took off his headphones, wrapped them on the joystick, stepped out onto the lush grass and looked up.

The sky was the brilliant blue of the Southwest; accompanied by flat-bottomed cumulus clouds that seemed to glide over an invisible sheet of glass as they marched west, gathering against the mountains in the distance.

'Teller's right. This is beautiful' Jack smiled to himself. Then, putting on his shades, he followed the trail of crushed grass his companions had left.

At the sound of Jack's boots crunching through the dry pine needles, Teller looked up. Crouched next to Abbott just inside the entrance; half in and half out of the Sun, Jack's shadow eclipsed them as he laid a hand on Abbott's shoulder.

"That'll have to wait compadre," he chuckled, pushing himself up and looking to Jack. "Glad you could make it." Is all he said, and with that, disappeared into the darker reaches of the cavern. Jack stared into the shadows for a moment, then looked down at Abbott.

"Give him a minute." He smiled.

Jack nodded and sat, his back to the wall. "So, Abbott, how long am I going to have to wait before I hear the story?" He had no more than finished his sentence then Teller emerged from the shadows like something from a storybook.

"Not too much longer amigo . . ." He smiled.

He carried a six-foot long, polished ebony staff in his left hand, using it as a walking stick; while tucked under his right arm, the gold bands of a carved wooden chest gleamed.

He handed the staff to Abbott. "You'll be needing this, old bear." He grinned, squatting to shove the chest into his pack. From his crouched position, he looked up into Jacks eyes.

"There's something you need to see old friend." He smiled, placing his hands on his knees to push himself up, groaning as joints creaked and popped from a lifetime of mishaps.

"This gettin' old shit is highly overrated." he grumbled as he stood. Then placing a hand on Jacks shoulder, tipped his head.

"Come along, Gent's."

The two men followed as Teller led them out of the cave, weaving through the sweet-smelling Ponderosa Pines that towered along the base of the cliff wall. Abbott followed, second in line: still favoring his ankle, but with his mobility much improved by using Estebanico's spear shaft as a cane while Jack, bringing up the rear, wondered just what the hell Teller had gotten him into *this* time.

~

The original tracks Teller and Abbott had made in the mud had hardened, making them easy to follow; and while Abbott's limping gait slowed them, the three soon stood at the small entrance of Estebanico's tomb.

Teller took off his pack and pushed it through the hole.

"I'll go first and get some light set up. Abbott, you follow. That way if you get stuck again I can pull, or Jack can push. Either way we'll get you in." With that, he lowered himself onto his belly and snaked through the tight opening. The soles of Teller's boots disappeared, and Jack turned to Abbott.

"You're next Sir Abbott." He motioned gallantly. Abbott nodded, handed the staff to Jack, dropped to his knees and reluctantly stuck his head through the hole.

He had expected darkness, but to his surprise and great relief, Teller had stacked rocks around the bases of four flashlights, angling them upright. The result was that of mini spotlights fanning the stalactite-covered ceiling. Creating an odd blend of spooky comfort.

"Cool." He muttered.

Abbott's entry was made much easier due to the one positive regarding his accident. He had lost weight. Thus, eliminating the embarrassing need to be either pushed or pulled, he elbow-walked in and stood cautiously, allowing his eyes to adjust to the minimal light.

Considerably more gracefully, Jack followed, and glancing around, passed the polished spear shaft to Abbott.

"Nice job Tell." He grinned. "you always did have a thing for lighting."

"Thanks Jack." Teller smiled, reaching into his pack and pulling out an old handheld lantern he had found in Billy's garage and cranking the handle. A soft glow enveloped them.

In the warm halo of light, Teller poked Abbott in the belly. "Well Griz. seems that pig and water diet did you no harm."

Puffing out his chest in indignation, Abbott rose to his full height. "Yes," he glared, "and those are pounds that I fully intend to regain the very moment we return to civilization and I have access to something tastier than the aforementioned products."

"Abbott, my friend." Teller laughed. "Once we have found the right person to help us safely distribute our loot, you shall be at liberty to collect calories at will, in any form you prefer."

Abbott's face broke into a grin.

Turning to Jack and placing his hands his shoulders, Tellers smile of amusement and indulgence was reflected in the lanterns glow.

"Jack, throughout these many years, you are the *one* man who has never abandoned me in times of crises, nor have you ever lost faith in me, regardless of what less forgiving souls may have deemed questionable pastimes."

A warm smile spread across Jack's face. "That is because I have never doubted your intent, *or* your ethics, Tell."

Teller's expression grew uncharacteristically serious, and his hands slid down Jack's arms, putting pressure on the elbows.

"Precisely my friend! Precisely! and *that* is why I now grant you title of third Musketeer in Grizzly's and my little secret." Turning to Abbott for confirmation, Abbott gave a slight, and single, bob of his head.

Teller smiled, nodded back, and spoke, his voice firm.

"The story of *how* Abbott and I came to discover this place is a tale for later. For now, I want you to understand that what we are about to show you will change your life irrevocably; and it is of the utmost importance that you realize that it will do so." The gravity in Teller's tone made Jack uncomfortable.

"Whoa Tell," he said, holding up his hand. "I don't want to get involved in anything *too* life altering."

Teller's smile returned, and his voice softened.

"Relax Jacko, this will alter only your financial realities. What you *do* with this gift is a purely personal choice." Again, he looked at Abbott. "What do you think Griz? a third okay with you?"

Abbott had been leaning on his spear shaft, smiling beneath his beard. But as he answered, he stood straight. "That's fine by me Teller. Any friend of yours is a friend of mine."

Teller's grin radiated absolute contentment. "I thought as much. Well then, it's settled. Jack, you are now one-third partner in the treasure of Estebanico. Follow me."

Jack looked to Abbott, Abbott gave a nod, and they hustled to catch up with Teller.

A few minutes later they entered a larger cavern; where small beams of light filtered through the tumbled rocks that blocked the opening in the caves ceiling; illuminating the room in dim light. But the snow melting through those same cracks had pooled, creating a thin layer of ice that spread across the floor. Teller sidestepped the little pool as he called over his shoulder. "Watch yourself gentlemen."

The warning reached Jacks ears just in time, sparing him a fall. His eyes were turned to the ceiling where the ladder met the blocked entrance. Giving a dancing sidestep he glanced back at the reflective surface. "Thanks for the heads-up." He said. "That coulda hurt."

Teller threw his thumb in Abbott's direction without bothering to turn around. "It was a favor to us both. I've already lugged *his* big ass across the desert. I'd hate to have to leave *you* here at this late date." Jack laughed. "But I've got the helicopter, remember?"

Teller turned and shone the beam of his flashlight in Jack's face. "All the more reason for you not to break a leg."

Redirecting the flashlight, he played it's beam across a wall, lighting the cubbyholes that held the painted gourds.

"But, lookie here . . .

"Wow!" Jack whispered.

"Yeah" Teller smiled. "but that's not best part. Check *this* out."

Teller reached under the shelf and pulled out a second hide.

This was the skin that he had found while Abbott was occupied with his skeletal exam of Estebanico on their first visit; and one that Abbott had not yet seen.

Carrying it to the center of the room, Teller's eyes glittered in the beam of Jacks flashlight; and glancing up at his companions he gave a wink, unrolled the old hide, and spread it flat.

There, among the loose hair and droppings of countless generations of rodents, lay an impressive pile of rough emeralds; dull green rocks; each a different size with none smaller than his thumb. And, if that weren't enough a great number of hand-polished turquoise stones were scattered in amongst them. Picking one up, Jack rubbed his thumb across its smooth blue surface. "Wow again." he smiled.

Teller nodded. "Eloquently stated, Jack."

Abbott, however, was stunned.

"When did you find *this,* Captain?"

"While you were examining Estebanico's remains Sir Archeologist. You were so enthralled with that pile of bones that I saw no point in disturbing your joy for such a trifling."

Turning to Abbott, Jack mouthed, "Trifling?"

Abbott simply sighed, shrugged, and held out his hands, palms up; and Teller, seeing the exchange, laughed and dug into his pack, pulling out the rabbit hides from the hunt earlier and the hammered spear tip he had pocketed from their last trip here.

The silver spear tip flashed as he stuck it between his teeth and rubbed his hands together.

"Alrighty boy's, Showtime's over. Time to get to work."

Stretching one of the rabbit skins between his knees, he reached into his pocket, removed a little cloth bag he had taken from Billy's store, and pulling the drawstring, sprinkled the salt it held onto the hide.

181

Rubbing it aggressively into the silver-red membrane with the heel of his hand, he scraped the excess into the dirt. He had been unhappy from the very beginning with not being able to cure the rabbit skins to his liking. But now the salt would help keep them supple enough for his use. Wiping. his hands together he took the spear-tip from between his teeth and began pushing the sharp point through the perimeter of the hide, making a small incision every inch or so.

Both Jack and Abbott watched in silent curiosity.

Teller, intent on his job, spoke over his shoulder.

"Get me some of that lashing from the ladder…"

Without questioning why, Jack went to the rickety stick ladder, took out his pocketknife, and putting the flat of the blade between the pole and the rawhide, twisted.

The old leather snapped.

"Kinda brittle, "Jack said with a shake of his head. "This'll never work."

Teller pointed the spear tip in the direction of the melted water floating on top of the ice patch.

"See if you can moisten it with that mud."

"Okay…" Jack nodded. Kneeling, he pressed the leather thong into the icy mud; working it into the string-like thong.

The warmth from his hands thawed the mud into a slippery consistency; and as he massaged the strip it began to soften.

Surprised, he chuckled. "Hmm, this seems to be working."

Soon the thong was like a wet piece of pasta; and wiping it on his pants leg, handed it to Teller. "Well whattaya know. It worked."

Teller waggled his eyebrows. "Ya gotta learn to trust me, Jack." Then lacing the slippery strip through the holes in the hide, drew them taut.

"Excellent." He grinned.

— — -- --- -- — —

— — _ — —

-- --- --

182

= Chapter 37 =

Kelly's forehead rested against the tinted glass window of the lavishly appointed helicopter, watching as the landscape flowing by below changed. The alkaline soil of what was once an ancient seabed stretched across the valley to the ragged rise of the high country: ravaged by ten thousand cuts and gouges The language of time carved into the earth.

The rugged topography gave way to a patchwork of cultivated squares: green squares that spread out on either side of a once wild river that ran through the small town of Delta; and seeing it brought Teller back front and center in her thoughts. A smile lifted the corners of her lips as she recalled the heat of his skin the night before; and closing her eyes, she basked in the memory.

"So, now that you're fifty percent partner, just how do you think you should be involved?"

James' voice was like ice water pumping into her heart. Wrenched from her pleasant musings she turned from the window.

"Pardon?"

Taking pleasure from disturbing her, James let a smug smile cross on his face as he leaned back in his plush seat; rattling the ice of the Bloody Mary he held.

"You're a full partner now Kelly! enjoy yourself!"

He held the drink out to her, but she waved it away.

"Fine." He shrugged, motioning to the opulent surroundings.

"But don't tell me you couldn't get used to this."

Kelly sighed. "What do you want, James?"

Pleased that he had her attention, he smiled. "I want to know how you would like to handle things now that you're a partner in this Company." Raising the glass to his lips, his eyes searched hers, waiting.

Kelly stared back, her eyes betraying nothing. Hoping he might reveal some weakness: some chink in his armor that might help her to bring him down... but seeing nothing, she swiveled to face him, her eyes cold.

"I don't know, James. I haven't had the time to give it a great deal of thought. What do *you* have in mind?"

A hint of a smile twitched the corner of his lips; but he stifled it, struggling to appear nonchalant. But his manner betrayed him. Everything in his bearing showed that he had put much thought into what he was about to say.

Reclining, he tapped his heavy gold ring against the crystal glass he held, allowing the suppressed smile to surface.

"Well, you've been doing great in the public relations arena for some time now, so I see no reason for that to change."

Kelly said nothing.

Taking silence for acquiescence, and having dreamt variations of this scenario for years, he continued, quite pleased with himself. "And, as Teller was never directly involved with the financial aspects of the business, I see no reason for you to assume that burden either." He brought the edge of the glass to his lips, waiting for her reaction.

Still nothing.

"Well then..." he smiled, swirling the ice in his glass.

"All in all, I suppose nothing changes except in title. Teller's name will be erased from the books." The thought nearly made him giddy: but seeing something in Kelly's manner shift he submerged his joy and reverted to a more solemn, business-like demeanor. "And, of course *your* name will be inserted in its place."

Kelly's eyes drilled his, but she displayed no emotion.

"Whatever you say, James."

That was *exactly* what he wanted to hear, but *something* in her phrasing made him inexplicably nervous.

Suddenly, and with no preamble, Kelly reached over and took the drink from his hand; then turning back to her window, dismissed him entirely.

James sat absolutely frozen.

Offended, confused, and utterly speechless, he found himself unable to muster any reaction at all; while Kelly, seeing James 'expression reflected in the window glass could almost hear Teller laugh.

Lifting the drink to her lips, she winked at her own smiling likeness reflected in that same window, repeating quietly,

"Whatever you say…"

With that last syllable, she blew softly onto the window, smiling as her warm breath fogged over his unhappy reflection. Once gone, she leaned back into the seat and closed her eyes.

Uncomfortably confused, James studied her profile: his desire nearly overriding his suspicion.

— — -- --- -- — —

— — -- --- -- — —

= Chapter 38 =

Teller poured a handful of the stones into his newly made pouch and bounced it up and down, testing the ties.

"Looks like it'll work. Soften up some more rawhide old chum, whilst I make another bag."

Jack threw a loose salute and went back to the ladder: but as he cut away the frayed lashings he looked back at Teller, who, kneeling over a century-old hide, casually worked rabbit skins into a pouch to carry priceless stones as if it were just another day in the office. Chuckling, he sawed off another piece of leather. Working the strip into the mud, he looked around.

"Hey, what happened to Abbott?"

Lifting his eyes from his work, he glanced around. "Abbott?" he shrugged, "Hell, I don't know. He's bound to be around here somewhere..." Turning towards the shadows, he shouted, "Hey Abbott!"

"Back here!" a voice called from the darkness. "What's the problem?"

Teller smiled and returned to his rabbit skin. "Nothin.' Jack was just worried about you."

Abbott was so thoroughly engrossed in his examination of Estebanico's skeleton he didn't catch the sarcasm in Teller's voice.

"I'm fine Jack." Abbott called. "Thanks tho'."

Jack squeezed the moisture from the thin strips of rawhide and dropped them onto the pile of stones at Teller's knees.

"There you go smartass."

Teller laced the second bag. "Ahh, come on, Jacko," he grinned as he scooped up a handful of stones. "Have a little fun."

186

Then rattling the gems in his hand, he poured them in his newly made pouch.

"Just like old times huh buddy?"

Jack scanned the caverns interior.

Abbott, who barely visible in the caves shadows was hunched over an ancient, desiccated corpse; mumbling to himself while Teller squatted next to a partially frozen puddle, humming happily while sewing rabbit furs into pouches: pouches he was fashioning in order to hold the fortune in rough stones that the aforementioned dead man had hidden: a dead man that apparently was, until now, an unsolved historical riddle… a riddle that a Navajo demi-god had led them to.

Jack the top of Teller's head a solid rap with his knuckles.

"Not even close, Tell. Not even *close.*"

"Yeah," Teller laughed. "You're right. This *is* dull in comparison to our standard caliber of adventure." Pulling the drawstrings of his newly made pouch tight, he stood.

"Now, where *is* that bear?"

Abbott was in the back of the cave, hovering over Estebanico's skeleton.

"Abbott my friend," Teller said. "the man is *dead.* Let's go." Abbott nodded slowly but was clearly distracted. Turning to the other men, his brow wrinkled as he rubbed his beard in scholarly concentration.

"Yes, yes, Captain… but I simply *cannot* understand how Estebanico ended up *here.*"

Turning his lamp on the gourds lining the shelves, Teller took one from its recess. "Well, in *my* dream," he said, shaking it, "he was released from captivity and followed the raven north."

The gourd was empty; so, placing it back on the shelf, he moved down the wall, examining each container as he went.

The hairs on the back of his neck rose as he recognized that each gourds illustration was identical to the ones painted above the entrance of the cave that contained the gold and armor during his visionary trip down the river on the back of the mystical fish. His brow furrowed and he muttered quietly, *'Just how far does this rabbit hole go . . .?* Looking at the gourd in his hand, he rotated it so the image faced Abbott.

"Professor, do any of these symbols mean anything to you?"

Accepting the gourd, he rotated it.

"Well, nothing unusual," he shrugged, passing it back." If that's what you mean."

Teller gave a second frustrated sigh. "Yes, Abbott, that would be *exactly* what I mean."

Placing it gently back in its cubby he continued down the wall, playing the flashlights beam on each gourd as he moved down the row. At first glance the gourds all looked to be uniform in same size and shape. But then the beam lit a gourd that was slightly larger than the others. Reaching into the shadows he removed it. It was heavy, and giving it a shake, rattled the contents within.

"Well hellooo!" he smiled.

"Hey Professor, what do you think of this?"

Abbott shelved the gourd he was examining and took the one Teller offered. His brow wrinkled. "This is *not* a North American image," he muttered as he assessed the multicolored drawing, rolling the gourd this way and that. "I just don't recog..." Suddenly, his eyes lit up and an enormous smile split his beard. Turning the figure painted on the gourd towards Teller, he shook it. The contents within swirled against the gourds dry interior, and as the clinking quieted, Abbott spoke, his voice a mix of disbelief and humor.

"As I said Captain. *This* is not a North American image; and certainly not one common to the Southwest. However, it *is* a character that has played a significant role in our lives as of late. Well, in *your* life in particular." Suppressing a smile, he pressed the gourd to Teller in outstretched hands.

"This is the image of the Aztec god, Huehuecoyotl."

Teller's eyes darkened, then grew amused.

"Don't tell me... another version of our friend Coyote."

Abbotts grin grew larger. "Yes Teller, the shape-shifting God of Merriment and Mischief."

Taking the gourd, Teller shook some of the contents from the gourd; the stones clinked into his palm and Jack, who had been standing quietly in the shadows, gave a quiet, "Whoa!"

Teller smiled. "Hmm, more emeralds. Seems this guy was quite the collector of valuable stones."

Abbott looked at the stones. "Well. At least we now know where the emeralds came from."

Jacks expression turned quizzical, forcing Abbott to answer his unasked question.

"South America, Jack. Most emeralds are from there."

Teller shook the stones back into the gourd, and as the last stone plinked in amongst the rest he turned to Abbott.

"So... you say this guy is the god of mischief and merriment eh?"

Abbott nodded, his brown eyes gleaming with the pride of an archeologist redeemed. "Yes, Teller, I'm quite sure of it."

Nodding, Teller shook the gourd. The stones hissed as they swirled and Teller, holding the gourd above his head, shook it with force. The sound of the stones filled the silence of the cave and he laughed aloud; his joy warming the oppressive atmosphere.

"Alright then!" he grinned to his companions, "These should pay for a *considerable* amount of mischief."

"And let's not forget merriment." Jack added.

Teller's smile grew wider still.

"Yes, indeed Jacko, yes in-*deed!* merriment galore!"

His humor waning, he went back to the incredible wealth scattered across the Buffalo hide and bending to pick up a handful of stones let them fall through his fingers: but on looking into the eyes of Huehuecoyotl's image, he added a silent prayer that trouble would not outweigh the merriment.

Thankfully, the thought passed as quickly as it had come.

Kneeling onto the hide, he looked up at Abbott. "Sir Bear, would you bring me a couple of those empty gourds?"

"Of course." Abbott smiled, and was gone.

As he waited, Teller dumped the contents of the new gourd onto the hide; mixing them with the stones already there; separating the emeralds to the left and the turquoise to his right. He soon had an impressive pile of each and was doing a rough mental count when Abbott appeared, setting a pair of empty gourds in front of him.

"Here you are, Captain."

Teller looked up with a distracted smile. "Thanks, Griz, but you made me lose count. Oh well… I'll just say that there's a shitload of each."

Abbott chuckled. "Yes. I believe 'shitload' *is* the universal denominational unit for gems; given a fudge factor of 'dammed close anyway." Teller grinned. "Good enough then. We'll break out the abacus once we've returned to civilization."

Scooping up a handful of stones, Teller poured them into a gourd; smiling at the plink of stones echoing in the silence.

Hundreds of plinks later, Teller placed a now heavy gourd into Abbott's hands. "There ya go Griz. *That* is going to buy you a whole lot of fame." Abbott accepted the gourd but shook his head, pointing to the mummified remains on the dirt floor.

"No Teller. While these stones have significant value, the man who lays there is my ticket to independence from the museum."

Teller looked down at the skeletal remains. "Different strokes my friend," he shrugged, "The choice is yours. But for me," he grinned and lifted the two rabbit-skin pouches by their lashings with one hand so they hung side-by-side, heavy with the weight of the stones; then, cupping them with the other hand he snickered, "But with *these,* gentlemen, I've got the world by the balls." His raucous laughter drowning out the sound of his companion's groans, he handed Jack one of the pouches.

"*This,* Aramis, is your half of the world."

Jack accepted the bag and Teller turned to Abbott, who stood, gourd in hand; blinking like a lost Owl.

"While Porto's seems to prefer the gourd to the sack."

Swinging his bag joyfully, he turned back to Jack.

"Now old chum. If you would be so kind, take us to our Pegasus and fly us away!"

Jack hefted the pouches substantial weight with a colossal grin, and giving a low bow, stretched his arm towards the caves entrance.

"Your steed anxiously awaits, good sir."

"As it should be." Teller grinned; and with a nod led them back the way they had come.

~

As they walked, he and Jack discussed the logistics of their future, while Abbott, close on their heels, tried to get Tellers attention, complaining about his references. Teller, however, purposely ignored him, concentrating on his conversation with Jack. But by the time they had reached the caves small entrance, he had finally had enough. With a sigh, he looked over his shoulder.

"What is the *matter* with you, Abbott?"

Abbott stood: the Aztec coyote gourd tucked under his arm, pawing in the dirt with his toe, his expression pained but defiant.

"Well sir, it's about your comment a bit ago. You are mixing your images and cultures again, not to mention your centuries. You see, Pegasus was Greek, and the Musketeers were —"

Teller just kneeled to crawl out, wiggling his way into the bright daylight; and once out, his voice came through the small opening, slightly muffled, but perfectly clear.

"Details, Professor, and inconsequential details at that. So, with all due respect, go fuck yourself.

Jack, hand the goodies through."

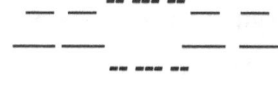

191

= Chapter 39 =

Seeing the sharp tips of the San Juan Mountains cut the sky above Dallas Pass, Kelly breathed a sigh of relief. Having suffered more than enough of James' company for a lifetime, she was almost home. But as she buckled up for the landing James turned from the window, a smile of smug self-importance on his face.

The sight of his expensive black Escalade parked in the lush grass of the open meadow vindicated him. After all he had been through it was good to be home: home; where he received the respect he deserved. Respect that Teller and his friends refused to grant. An omission he *knew* was intentional, and it was one that *each* and *every* one of them would pay for; with Teller at the very top of the list. Retribution on his mind, he gave a sideways glance at Kelly.

Her eyes were closed, but he was unsure whether she was sleeping, or deliberately ignoring him.

Allowing his ego to assure him it was sleep, he turned to the window; leaning back into his seat as the sleek craft settled into the spongy alpine peat: crushing the delicate Lupine and dandelions beneath the rails while blasting away the honeybees and butterflies that fed upon them with the rotors hurricane winds.

Unclicking his harness, James ignored the pilot's entreaties to stay seated and threw his door open, leaping from the craft and crouching low to race across the meadow; dashing to the gleaming vehicle's passenger door and yanking it open to ensure the office had included the champagne and truffles he had demanded. Everything was as he ordered, making him feel more himself.

Then the odor hit him.

Slouched behind the wheel was his brother Jonathan, a cloud of cannabis smoke surrounding a head that was bopping to the muffled music in his headphones. James slapped his shoulder, and Jon lifted his Wayfarers, exposing a pair of bloodshot eyes. "Hey Bro," he grinned.

If looks could kill, James' return glare would have gutted him on the spot; but on seeing Kelly step through the door of the helicopter he snatched the joint from Jonathan's lips, threw it into the grass and ground it under his heel.

"Goddamn it, Jon!" he hissed. "What the fuck's wrong with you!?"

Jonathan let his shades drop back on his nose.

"Whoa bro, why so tense?"

James turned the A.C. up full blast and began fanning the door, trying to remove the cloud of smoke from the vehicle while looking over his shoulder.

Kelly came down the stairs, carefully making her way through the slushy grass.

James fanned the door frantically; but realizing there was nothing more he could do, left the door hanging open and hurried across the meadow; stepping in beside her, taking her elbow and reaching for her bag. "Here, Kelly, let me help you."

"I'm fine, James." she said, pulling her bag away from his clutching hand. "Thanks anyway,"

Her attitude both hurt and angered him. Acting as if he hadn't heard, he pulled the bag from her hand and led her to the rear of the vehicle where he placed her case on the ground and helped her into the rear seat; motioning to the display of French truffles on a silver tray and a bottle of Monet nestled in a bucket of ice.

Bequeathing her his most persuasive smile, his voice was silk. "May I pour you a glass?"

Kelly simply shook her head, "No, thank you. Just take me home, please."

Burying his disappointment, he switched on the charm.

"Come on, Kelly, we're back home! Let's at least toast to your new position in the Company."

His attempt at charisma was wasted. Curling her lip in disdain she settled back into the soft seat: and as she did, she sniffed the air.

"Smells good Jon."

Jon turned to look at her over the seat. "I know," he grinned, pointing to his brother. "But try tellin' *him* that."

James gritted his teeth and tried to change the subject.

"Don't be this way Kelly... let's at least go somewhere and have a drink to celebrate your promotion."

"James, please. Just take me home."

Fighting the urge to slam her door, he gave a rictus of a smile and stepped back to put his hands on the roof and count slowly to ten. Then, putting on his best professional face, he leaned down, pushed it firmly closed, and slid into the front passenger seat. Crossing his arms tightly across his chest he growled,

"You heard the lady Jon. Take her home."

Jonathan adjusted his shades and started the car. "What about you bro, where do you want to go?"

Giving his brother a withering look, James grit his teeth. "Just drop me at the office and *take-her-home*."

～

Stepping from the Escalade, Kelly looked at the house she and Teller shared; then, with a sigh, she picked up her bag and went up the stairs to open the front door and step in.

Somehow it seemed emptier now than when she had left.

Dropping the bag, she walked into the kitchen where stood for a moment, tapping her bottom lip. Finally, she nodded and went to the pantry. *"Yes,"* she smiled. She had remembered correctly, there was a bottle of red on the bottom shelf.

Grabbing a clean tumbler from the strainer next to the sink, she poured herself a full glass, flopped onto the couch, and kicked off her boots.

'God it's good to be back.'

Tucking her legs beneath her, she raised the glass to her lips and gazed at the mountain panorama through the window.

'Teller, Teller, Teller . . . Where are you now?'

— —— ‥ ——— ‥ — —

—— —— —— ——

‥ ——— ‥

= Chapter 40 =

Teller stood with Jack, waiting while Abbott labored through the cave's small entry. He may have lost weight, but it was still tight, and the range of expletives produced as he struggled through the little hole was impressive.

"Jesus..." Teller grinned, shaking his head and stepping over to the entrance. Taking the gourd from Abbott's grasp he handed it to Jack, wrapped his hands around Abbott's wrists, and with a yank, pulled Abbott through like a cork.

"There, done . . ." he muttered.

Bushing his hands on his pants he walked away, leaving Jack standing with the gourd and Abbott stretched out in the dirt.

"Hey!" Abbott called out; but Teller kept moving up the canyon, talking to himself; oblivious to their absence.

Jack reached down and helped Abbott to his feet.

"Don't mind him, Abbott," he chuckled, handing him the spear shaft. "Once he gets something in his head he's pretty single minded."

Abbott wiped at the dirt on the front of his shirt and accepted the spear shaft cane. "Yes, Jack, I've noticed."

Hurrying to catch up with Teller, they were only a pace behind when he suddenly stopped, snapped his fingers, and turned.

"Jack, what was your argument against Las Vegas?"

The two men came to an abrupt halt, barely avoiding running into Teller; but Jack answered, "My ex-wife."

"Valid argument," Teller nodded. "Abbott, what about you?" Giving Teller a pained look Abbott wiped his forehead.

"I've nothing at all against Las Vegas, Teller, but could we slow down a little bit? My ankle is still not healed."

Teller's brow furrowed. "Ah hell, Griz, I'm sorry, I forgot about your injured paw. You want to take a break?"

"No," Abbott said, shaking his head while gripping the spear shaft. "just slow it down and I'll be fine. Now, what was the question?"

With Abbott's injury now in mind, Teller moved at an easier pace.

"The question, amigo, is what are we going to do with this booty?" He stopped again and held the pouch.

"It's not as if we can just walk into a bank and deposit raw stones and Spanish doubloons . . . we need a middleman, but we need one we can trust. Any ideas?"

Jack shook his head. "Sorry Tell, the only man I can think of that may still be in that business is our old friend Lenny, and I don't know if trust and Lenny can even be used in the same sentence."

Teller frowned and began walking again. "Yeah, I agree. I might give him a shot with a few small stones, but nothing like what we got here."

"Jesus, Teller," Jack said, "I don't know if I would trust *anyone* with what we've got here."

Teller nodded. "You have got a *very* good point there, Jack. I'm not sure of the value of what we are carrying, but I'd bet my ass that it's worth stealing."

"Or killing for." Abbott muttered quietly.

Teller frowned. "And now *you* have a very good point my friend… albeit a rather depressing one."

Walking in silence, they rounded a towering sandstone wall and came into view of the helicopter. For a fleeting moment, all of Teller's troubles vanished, and he thought again of how lovely this spring meadow looked. It was a short-lived respite however, and with a sigh he pointed in the direction of the cave that had saved he and Abbott from the snowstorm.

"Perhaps we should be none too hasty in our departure. What say we take some time to discuss the best way to deal with this dilemma?"

Abbott gave an anxious nod. "Capitol idea, Sir!"

With that he took the lead, limping hurriedly towards the cave's entrance. He was surprisingly nimble for a wounded bear.

Teller nudged Jack in the ribs, grinning at Abbott's hobbling gait. Jack nodded, and chuckling, they followed Abbott's shuffle into the cave.

Teller remained at the caves entrance in the warmth of the Sun; while Abbott, lowering himself into the shade, looked up.

"I think I may have a possible solution," he said, wiping away the sweat from his forehead with his sleeve.

Teller knelt to place the bulging rabbit pouch on the ground. "All for one and one for all Porthos. Please, share your thoughts."

A smile shone through Abbott's dirty beard as he took off his boot and began massaging his ankle. "I will be happy to do so, Teller. but would you be so kind to get me some water first?"

Teller stepped back, a look of surprise on his face.

"Water? Why Griz, are you not feeling well?"

Abbott shook his head, "It has nothing to do with how I feel Captain, it's just that I've had a sobering thought."

Tellers expression turned from humor to mock fright.

"*Now* you're scaring me..." he laughed; then patting Abbott's shoulder, smiled, "Hang on buddy, I'll be right back."

Jack watched Teller walk from the cave; then looking down at Abbott, chuckled. "And he's hard to scare."

Teller returned with a six-pack, a canteen, and a bag of chips. Handing Abbott the canteen, he tossed Jack a beer, ripped the bag open with his teeth, and sat down next to Abbott.

"Okay partner, what's your idea?"

"Just a sec." Abbott smiled, unscrewing the lid to the canteen. Raising it to his lips he drank greedily, water spilling down his chin; trickling through his beard and leaving little trails of mud.

The resulting effect reminding Teller of pictures he had seen of tribal elders in New Guinea dressed for a spirit dance. The image made him laugh.

Abbott, smacking his lips, looked up.

"Well, First you're wrong about the bank. We may not be able to deposit the stones in an *account,* but we are most certainly able to put them in a deposit *box.*"

Jack nodded. "True enough."

Cocking his head, Teller opened a beer for himself. "And?"

"And I've been thinking, Abbott continued, "not only do we have a sizeable fortune here, but,"

"Sizeable." Teller agreed, nodding his head.

Abbott fell silent. That he was thinking was obvious, but just as plain was that those thoughts were causing him anguish.

Teller let a few minutes pass. Then, nudging Abbott's foot with his toe, smiled. "Come on, Grizzly, out with it."

Abbott looked up, his deep brown eyes reflecting both sorrow and hope. "Well Captain, I've been thinking about what you said when we first stumbled across this discovery. The fame, the recognition…"

Teller's expression darkened and a look of disappointment shadowed his face. "Yeah?"

"Well, Captain. I don't think I want it!"

Teller's eyebrows shot up in pleasant surprise. *"Really?"*

Abbott pointed towards the remains of the six-pack at Teller's feet. "May I have one of those, please?"

Twisting a can loose, Teller popped the top; handing it to Abbott who took the can and nodded. "Yes, really."

Turning his eyes to the carpet of flowers in the meadow beyond the caves entrance he took a long swallow.

"If I report this find to the archeological society it may settle one question, but it will raise a hundred others."

He took another drink and sighed, "Estebanico has lain here for five centuries undisturbed until we came along."

"Until we were *led* here Abbott," Teller interjected, "Let us not forget *that* small detail."

"Yes, yes," Abbott waved his hand impatiently, "And therein lies the root of the problem. If I were to disclose the location of these remains to the archeological world, not only will I be forced to invent a far more convincing story as to my finding it, but I would also be forced to include both you, *and* the treasure."

Teller's lips tightened. "And *why* is that?"

Abbott turned his hands up in defeat. "Teller, please be realistic. Why would I be wandering out here on my own? there are no ruins anywhere near here, and *I* certainly don't have the funds to charter a private helicopter to fly me to this remote location. Besides, there are now *three* sets of footprints in that cave. Trust me, it would raise a battery of questions I could not honestly answer." He shook his head. "This would only lead to problems for both you and Jack." Pausing, he turned to Jack and raised his brows. "Unless *you* want to be famous?"

Jack lifted his hands, palms out, pushing away the idea.

"No, no, no, I'll pass, but thanks anyway."

Abbott's face reflected what he had already suspected.

"As I thought." He smiled, took another drink, and closed his eyes, leaning his head against the wall.

"Really, Teller, I think it would be in all our best interests to let sleeping dogs lie . . . so to speak."

Teller's eyes flicked back and forth between the two men, finally coming to rest on Abbott. He searched for any falsehood, but again found his new friend's face free of duplicity. Satisfied, he smiled, "So then, discretion is the better part of self-interest is it?"

Abbott looked at him quizzically; "I'm not quite sure what you mean."

"I don't *mean* anything at all," Teller smiled. "It's just that I fully agree. Neither Jack nor I have *any* interest in the fame such a discovery might bring. And speaking for myself, I would prefer to keep this loot rather than hand it over to a museum, *or* the government." His gaze went to Jack, who nodded in silent agreement. Teller nodded back and smiled. "Although I will happily donate a fat chunk of money to any program you choose. But will do it anonymously, for I wish to pursue *my* dreams on *my* terms."

Jack raised his can. "Here, here!"

Touching his can against Jacks, Teller waited for Abbott to add his to the pair. There was a brief pause, but Abbott finally raised his can, touching the other two and completing the triad.

Teller grinned. "Then it's settled. We keep our mouths shut and our pockets full."

Abbott smiled. "Aye aye, Captain. Pirates or Musketeers, it's all for one," he waited, and the other two chimed in, "And one for all!" The three cans tapped a final time, then were drained simultaneously; and as the cans were lowered Abbott released a huge burp that resonated throughout the cave.

"Well said," Teller laughed. "well said."

Undeniably pleased, Teller knelt and began drawing stick figures in the dirt as questions formed.

"What about Billy?"

Who?" Abbott asked.

Jack glanced down at Teller's sketch in the dirt.

"Friend of mine," he answered. "Why, what about him?"

Teller scratched a spiral sun into the dust above three stick figures, adding lines attaching the heads and arms of the three figures to the spiral. Finished, he looked up from the dust and raised one eyebrow. "Well. I may be stating the obvious, but there's a hell of a lot more to that man then meets the eye."

Jack gave a nod.

"Spill the beans, Jack." Teller said as he stood. "I've been around the block once or twice, and that cagey old injun is subsidizing that operation somehow. I don't know how, and I don't care. But maybe he can help us out with *our* little quandary.

"I agree, Tell," Jack nodded. "But Billy and I have never talked about one another's incomes, so I don't have a clue to what he might have going." But glancing out on the meadow, he saw that the shadows were growing long. Checking his watch, he tipped his head towards the chopper.

"It's gettin' late gents, we should get moving."

Teller nodded. "Your right Jack… it's time to fly."

Stuffing his chest into the deerskin, he stepped out into the meadow and headed towards the helicopter.

Jack followed a pace behind, and with the help of the spearshaft cane Abbott took the rear. Limping, but the smile on his face shone through the dirt.

— — ▬▬ ▬▬▬ ▬▬ — —
—— —— —— ▬▬
▬▬ ▬▬▬ ▬▬

= Chapter 41 =

The cell phone flew from James' hand, sailing across the room to bounce from a leather cushion of the couch and onto the floor. For a moment he glared at it laying there; then checking his watch, nearly howled. He had one of the most powerful law firms in the country taking care of his legal needs yet he had spent the past thirty minutes explaining his demands to that mouse of a lead accountant.

The man was useless!

All he wanted was to expunge Teller's name from any and all paperwork that had *anything* to do with *his* Corporation.

"How hard could it be?" he had asked, insisting the man need only write up a new contract; one that relinquished Teller's shares to Kelly, but under the umbrella of *his* ownership and majority control.

"But I can't do that!" the exasperated man had cried. "Mr. Teller is a fifty percent shareholder, which makes him one-half owner of the company! I'll be happy to file for an exchange of ownership, but I *cannot* give you a controlling interest without his approval."

Such insubordination was infuriating!

"Fine!" he had shouted. "Just get the paperwork together and put Teller's shares into Miss Rowan's name. I'll get back to you concerning the particulars. But I want you to draw up the papers for transfer of options *now!* One way or the other, I *will* have her sign them over to me!" Running his hand through his hair, he paced the slate floor. He considered picking up the phone and calling Kelly but thought better of it. *No. Better give it a few days, maybe Teller will get lost. Or better yet, die.*

The thought pacified him to a degree, and he smiled.

Regaining his sense of control, James walked over to the enormous picture window that constituted over half of the west wall of his living room. Savoring the view from his place on the mountain, his sense of control became a sense of power: at his feet lay the magnificent valley of Telluride: the valley he considered his kingdom.

One by one the lights below began to twinkle on.

Finding comfort in their presence, James reached down and slid open the door of the antique burled wood liquor cabinet that sat beneath that massive window. But as he did so he caught a glimpse of his reflection in the glass. Squaring his shoulders, he gave the image a nod of approval and poured a tall scotch.

Plinking two ice cubes into the cut crystal glass, he gave a final glance at his empire, kicking the discarded cell phone across a woven Navaho rug as he went to the huge leather couch and settled onto its soft cushions.

'Ahhhhh." he sighed, *"This is how I am meant to live . . .."*

A sense of self-satisfaction he had not felt in weeks washed over him as he brought the expensive amber liquid to his lips.

'Now, if I can persuade Kelly to my side and convince Casey to understand, my life will be perfect.'

— — —— —— —— — —
—— — — —— —
—— —— ——

= Chapter 42 =

"And then I told her that I'd call when I got back to town."

"Famous last words." Teller grinned.

Jack had just finished telling the short version of his meeting, the satisfying night spent in the Strater Hotel, and the inevitable goodbye with Jenny back in Durango.

"That's what she said too." Jack chuckled, "But I meant it."

Teller looked at his old friend. "Of course you did Jack. Beautiful young women are hard to find, and harder to leave."

He reached back over his seat and patted Abbott on the knee. "Am I right, Grizzly?'

Abbott opened a fresh can of his favorite beverage. "I'm quite sure I haven't had the amount of experience that you have had with *that* particular problem Teller."

A flash of melancholy crossed Teller's face. *Yes, my friend. And you are no doubt the better for it.*

He turned to Jack. "Well, lad, the pleasures of women aside, I do understand. And we will be back in Durango eventually, so you will have the opportunity to introduce us to your sweet young thing then. In the meantime, we have bigger sticks to chase. Let's get back to the lake and see if that old Shaman has any solutions to our current problems."

Jack gave a nod and turned to Abbott. "Buckle up and try not to spill that."

Abbott tipped the can to his lips. "Not a drop will be lost, Sir," he grinned, "not a drop."

Teller chuckled. "Hmmm, perhaps the bear *is* trainable."

As the engine speed increased the chopper rocked like a baby's cradle, the downdraft bending the flowers sideways against the new grass.

Without the previous problem of questionable destinations, the return flight went quickly, and Jack was soon settling the bird in front of the store; raising dust into a hot blue sky.

"Civilization at last!" Abbott cried, tapping Teller's shoulder and leaning into his ear, "Please Sire," he entreated, "would you be so kind as to let your humble but wounded magician from this craft so he may gain access onto yon porch for a comfier seat, and a perhaps a cool beverage in the shade?" Teller laughed, throwing open the door and jumping onto the rail to extend his hand. "But of course, Sir Bear, happy to oblige, but how's the foot?" Taking Teller's offered hand, Abbott pivoted on his makeshift cane. "As good as can be expected sir. And by the way, thank you."

"For what?"

"Why, for everything!"

Teller was taken again by the sincerity in Abbott's eyes.

"All for one, Porto's." he grinned, "and one for all, remember?" Abbott's smile shone through his beard, and his eyes went from sincere to merry. "Indeed, Captain... all for one." Picking up his deerskin pack, Teller pushed him gently towards the store. "Now you go relax. Jack and I have an Injun to track." Abbott hobbled away, visions of cold beer and comfortable rocking chairs on his mind.

~

Hearing the blades of the helicopter swoop over the store, Billy quickly finished the conversation with his contact in Tucson. "Yes, as always, half in the Flagstaff account, the other in the L.L.C. Thank you, William, goodbye."

Cradling the phone, Billy transcribed the figures into the old-fashioned ledger, tucked it into the desk drawer, then closing the office door behind him, pushed through the swinging doors that separated his office from the store. But as he stepped through he came to a complete halt. There to greet him was the dusty rear end of a large man, head buried deep in the wall cooler, a polished ebony stick leaning against the open glass door.

206

Billy leaned against the cool glass and crossed his arms.

"May I help you?"

the scruffy figure pulled his head from the cooler and held up two six-packs of Coors. "No sir, I have found precisely what I was looking for." But as he spoke recognition lit his face.

"Ahhh, you must be the proprietor."

Billy chuckled at the comical figure before him.

Uncombed curly hair, matted beard still littered with peanut skins, twinkling brown eyes, and the tattered remnants of a filthy Tartan wool sleeve tied around his leg.

"And *you* must be Abbott."

At first, Abbott's brows furrowed, but then his eyes caught his reflection in the convex mirror above the coolers. Spreading his arms, he gave a subdued chuckle. "Is it that obvious?"

"How could you not be?" Billy laughed. "I am glad to see our friend Teller has found you safe and relatively unharmed… and how *is* your leg?" A grin worked its way through unruly whiskers and Abbott tucked the beer under his arm, taking a limping step forward to clasping Billy's hand and shake it firmly. "Yes, I am… and you, Sir, must be Billy. Truly, the pleasure is mine. But in answer to your questions: yes, Teller did find me, thank you, and it's my ankle, not my leg. And, with all things considered, it's doing well. Oh, and by the way, Jack and Teller are looking for you."

Feeling an immediate sense of fellowship with this man, Billy gently removed one of the six-packs from Abbott's arm, then taking him by the elbow, guided him through the screen door and onto the porch.

"Please, Abbott, come with me. And they will find me when they think to look in the right place. In the meantime, let me have a look at that foot. Perhaps there is something I can do."

Once outside, Billy pointed to the wooden bench.

"Sit and take off the boot please."

Limping over to the bench, Abbott sat heavily and removed the boot. But as he unlaced, his curiosity got the better of him.

Looking up into Billy's weathered face he asked, "Pardon my ignorance Billy, but are you Navajo or Hopi?"

Squatting, Billy lifted Abbott's foot and rest it on his knee. "Why do you ask?"

"Because of Prophecy Rock."

"Ahhh…" Billy nodded, chuckling as he rolled off the sock. "Kelly mentioned your interest in that."

"Really!" Abbott exclaimed, leaning forward in his excitement; and as he did his foot fell from Billy's knee, dropping to the deck with a 'thump.' And sending a knife-like pain up his leg.

"Oowwww!" he howled in agony.

From the mesas, a coyote barked in return; and hearing it, Billy pushed his hat back on his forehead.

"Your friend feels your pain."

Lifting the foot back onto his knee with one hand while pressing Abbott back into the chair with the other, he smiled,

"Yes, really. She mentioned you were an archeologist, and that your field of expertise was Southwestern Indian culture." He cocked his head and gave Abbott an enigmatic gaze.

"Is she correct?"

Billy's hands manipulated the ankle, causing Abbott's jaw to clench; but hissing through his teeth, he answered.

"Yes, and no . . . It *is* my area of study, but while I consider myself no expert on the subject, I *am* absolutely fascinated by it."

Billy nodded, rocking back until his weight rested on his heels: and rotating Abbott's ankle slowly he pinched the Achilles tendon. "Are you alright?" Billy asked.

"Yes…" Abbott answered. "Why?"

Billy gave the back of the heel a quick, hard tug. Abbott felt something pop and the pressure vanished.

"Wow . . ." He whispered as he swiveled his ankle. The pain was gone.

"What did you do?"

"It wasn't broken."

"Yeah, that's what Teller said."

"He was right." Billy smiled, patting the bottom of Abbott's foot as he lowered it to the floor. "It will begin to feel better now."

Standing, Billy adjusted his hat, pulling an old rocker across the worn wooden floor to place it directly in front of Abbott; then, taking a seat, began rocking. The curved rails made a soft rumble on the planks of the floor as he rocked.

His black eyes shining, he smiled. "Abbott, I will answer a few questions regarding the object of your interest, but only with the understanding that we have far more pressing things to speak of: yourself, Teller, and Coyote being foremost but not necessarily in that order. But to satisfy your immediate curiosity I will tell you what little I know concerning Prophecy rock.

Abbott grinned broadly. His foot was feeling much better, and with the thought of discussing the subject so near to his heart he momentarily forgot the discomfort altogether. Reaching down to take a sweaty can from its plastic hoop, he opened one of his beers and as he did so, his eyes brightened at the sound; and as he raised the can to drink, Billy could not help but smile at his expression of sheer bliss.

'Ahhh . . .Teller's beer drinking bear.'

The image amusing him, he looked into Abbott's hopeful face and felt true joy wash through him for the first time in far too long. With a smile, he began.

"To be clear, I am of the Navajo people, and the prophecy you speak of is Hopi."

Abbott interrupted, "Yes, yes, I am aware of that."

"Yes Abbott, I'm sure you are; but please, listen for a moment."

Abbott nodded apologetically. "Sorry."

"For perspectives, as well as time's sake," Billy said, "we will consider the rock as a mixture of your Bible, and the writings of Nostradamus."

Abbott's interest spiked, and he leaned forward.

"Like the bible," Billy smiled. "The story etched onto the rock tells of Creation, the birth of man, and of man's proper place on this earth."

Abbott nodded.

"And, as in the writings of Nostradamus, the etchings go on to tell of the changes that man will bring, and the possible devastation of his actions."

Again, Abbott shook his head.

Billy smiled. "I'm glad to see you understand. So, as in your Bible,"

Here Abbott interrupted, "Not *my* Bible, Billy."

Billy paused, looking perplexed.

It was Abbott's turn to smile. "You're not Hopi, I'm not Christian."

Putting his hands together, Billy brought his fingers to his lips. "I see... Belief, but not dogma?"

Abbott raised his can. "Exactly."

"Well, then," Billy said, his smile growing larger. "This should be easy. Prophecy Rock is no more the true story of the world and its end, than either Nostradamus's predictions, or the Bible's version of hellfire and rapture. Granted, each is final, and each brutal, but each is a prediction, not a promise."

"Not to hear an evangelist tell it!" Abbott laughed.

Billy nodded, humor dancing in his dark eyes. "And therein lies the danger of dogma."

Abbott raised his can above his head. "Amen to that!"

"Yes..." Billy laughed, but his smile quickly faded.

Taking a gold coin from his pocket he held it between two fingers, and his voice grew serious.

"Now, let us discuss our more immediate concerns."

= Chapter 43 =

Teller paced the stone floor, Jacks phone pressed tightly to his ear; the time between each ring seeming longer then the last.

"Come on, Kell . . ."

Jack, sitting on a worn rug admiring the spectacular vista spreading out beyond the opening of Billy's refuge, turned. "I can't believe you can even get service out here." He chuckled.

Tellers anxiety seemed to vanish. "I know! He grinned, lowering the phone. "Amazing huh?"

Jack smiled back, never ceasing to be surprised at Teller's mercurial moods. "I'm sure she's fine, Tell. Let's go find Billy."

Teller nodded and tossed the phone to Jack. "Yeah, you're probably right. She's a smart cookie, and I'm hoping James is still a little too paranoid to attempt any clever thievery quite yet. Okay, let us continue our search. The Chief's got to be around here somewhere."

Abbott cocked his head. "Where did you get that?"

Slipping the coin back in his pocket, Billy raised his eyebrows. "*That,* Abbott, is a very interesting story, and one that ties into your recent experiences as well... you are familiar with the 'six degrees of separation' concept?"

Abbott nodded and Billy smiled. "I thought as much. Well, once you put Coyote into the mix that concept turns into a Mobius strip."

Abbott laughed aloud. "A *most* intriguing image."

"Yes," Billy said. "But more fascinating is *our* placement on the strip, and upon Teller's return is something we will all discuss at length. But until then, would you mind telling me of your meeting with Coyote?" As surprised as he was with the sudden appearance of the coin in Billy's hand, Abbott's curiosity regarding the coyote was greater.

"Well," he began, "I've not had any real meeting. Not like Teller anyway." He paused, looking at Billy suspiciously.

"How is this important?"

Billy smiled. "Relax, Sir bear."

The word "Bear" got Abbott's attention.

"How did...?"

The warmth in Billy's eyes eliminated any last misgivings that Abbott held as he pushed the remains of the six-pack towards him. "Your friend Teller has told me everything that has happened to the two of you. The discovery of the cave, the skeleton of the black guide, and the gold." He patted the coin in his pocket. "As well as the origin of your new title. But for me, the most important element is your relationship with Coyote. What can you tell me of this?"

Abbott considered the situation.

There seemed to be no reason *not* to confide in this man. He was obviously a trusted friend of Jack's, Teller had already shared a fair amount of information with him, and *he* certainly had more questions than he had answers. So, what was there to lose? Removing one of the sweating cans from its slippery ring he leaned back.

"Where would you like me to start?"

Billy's radiant smile was like a blessing.

"Why, at the beginning of course!"

After only a moment's thought, Abbott realized the only proper beginning would be the telling of his own introduction to the Canyon King.

Stepping through the door of the greenhouse, Teller went directly to the lobster tank, stuck his finger into the warm water, and brought it to his lips.

H*mmmm...*

Circling the interior of the building, he admired the ingenious water circulation system. But with no sigh of Billy, he went to one of the garden tables, popped a cherry tomato in his mouth, and went back outside to where Jack stood at the base of the sandstone wall studying the steps that had been carved in so long ago.

"Clever man," Teller murmured.

Jack turned, "What's that?"

"I said, clever man."

Jack's mind was elsewhere. "Who's clever?"

"Never mind." Teller smiled. "Let's go."

"And *that's* when Teller and I found the cave."

Abbott leaned forward; resting his elbows on his knees and placing his chin on his fingertips.

Billy's eyes locked on Abbott's for a moment more, then gave a slight nod. "And that was the whole of your experience with Coyote?"

"Yes. As I said, Teller has experienced the contact, not I... my 'involvement' shall we say, seems to be altogether secondary."

Billy tapped his fingers together. "Yes, I see... while that gives me a proper perspective it does *not* change your importance in the overall picture. You and Teller were destined to meet. Coyote simply brought you together more quickly, arranging to have you both in the same location... on the river of time, if I may use the metaphor."

Abbott considered Billy's words.

Harboring a philosophical soul, Abbott had often pondered the odd turns of fate, and the many repercussions that result from any one choice. And, due to this, had often wondered just how many of those decisions were made of truly free will. These considerations must have reflected on his face; because as they skimmed through his mind, Billy smiled.

"I understand, Abbott. I often feel the same way."

Frowning, Abbott shifted in his seat; feeling slightly exposed. "Well then. If you can read my mind, you must also know that I take minor comfort in the possibility of there being someone, or something, else to blame for my misfortunes."

Billy laid a weathered brown hand on Abbotts shoulder.

"Ahh, my friend, now you have hit upon the purpose of religion."

Abbott sat silently, looking puzzled.

Billy's warm eyes twinkled. "Comfort or blame, Abbott. Comfort or blame."

Abbott considered the statement for only a moment, then, throwing his head back, laughed joyfully. A second later Billy joined in.

~

Jack had spent the morning thinking about the days ahead. The travel logistics were one thing, but the magnitude of problems they were likely to encounter in the covert sale of precious stones and Spanish doubloons elevated the deal onto a different scale altogether; and as they walked towards the store in their continuing search for Billy, he voiced his concerns. Teller listened for the first few minutes, dismissing them all as minor problems.

"Jack..." he chided. "Quit worrying! everything's gonna work out."

"That's what you *always* say, Tell, but-" his complaint was cut short as they rounded the building, and laughter ringing in the afternoon heat.

"See," Teller grinned. "All is well."

Jack nodded; but wasn't convinced.

Teller shrugged as his boots hit the first step; and at the sound both Billy and Abbott looked up and their happy faces reassured Jack to a small degree.

Abbott's brown eyes lit up.

"Captain! Billy and I were just talking about you and religion."

"Really?" Teller sniffed. "I find that a *very* odd subject to be included in."

From his rocker, Billy smiled his million-dollar smile.

"Not so odd if you consider the context."

Teller shrugged. "I guess I'll have to take your word for it Chief."

"Yes," Billy said as he stood. "I suppose you will."

Crossing the worn floor planks, he took Jack's hand in his.

"It's *very* good to see you again, Jack."

"You too, Billy." Jack smiled back; but as Billy's palm began to slip away, Jack noticed that the warmth of his touch seemed to have absorbed the anxiety that had weighed so heavily on him earlier; and worried that it might return, he held his grip on Billy's hand a moment longer. But the comfort remained even as Billy's hand slowly slipped away and he turned to take Teller's hands in both of his, looking deeply into his eyes.

"Welcome back, Teller. I am pleased to see that your trip was successful. You have a wonderful friend here in Abbott. As a matter of fact, he was just telling me of your first meeting on the river."

Hearing this, Teller pinned Abbott with a stern look while suppressing a smile.

"Really? Well then, my first concern is what he told may have you. Grizzly here has a habit of stretching the truth."

The sound of Jack choking back a laugh rang across the porch as he looked at Teller in amused disbelief.

"Him!? *He* has a habit of stretching the truth!?"

Abbott laughed, his eyes darting between them.

"Teller, if you and Diogenes were to cross one another along the path of his search, albeit he may have finally found an honest man, I believe you would convince him that you had a better use for his lamp. But, as a cynic, I believe he would have truly appreciated your company."

"Well…" Teller smiled. "thank you, I suppose… and while I'm quite sure he and I would find much in common, *my* cynicism is thankfully offset by people such as I have here with me now."

Holding out his hands to encompass them all, he turned to Billy.

"Okay, Chief, if I may purchase the goodies I shall require from this establishment, I will endeavor to cook dinner."

He looked at the group. "How does that sound?"

Murmurs of agreement filled the air.

"You may use whatever you find." Billy smiled. "But payment is certainly not necessary. And, if you wish, I *may* have a bottle of civilized wine to have with the meal."

At that, Teller's eyes narrowed. "Funny you should mention fine wine Billy. It is details such as those that will be the focus of our conversation tonight."

Pulling a coin from his pocket, he grinned. "But I wouldn't dream of not compensating you for your hospitality." With that he flipped the coin in Billy's direction. Billy caught it, and Tellers eyebrows rose.

"I do believe that is the coin of the realm, is it not?"

Opening his fist, Billy studied the coin and sighed. "I can see that tonight's meal is going to be one of many revelations."

"One can only hope." Teller said, then, turning to Abbott, added, "Sir Magician, your job tonight is to conjure up some hops and grains for our repast. Jack, please go back to our host's modest garden and harvest a few of those succulent looking tomatoes, oh, and grab some lettuce while you're at it. Billy, you're coming with me."

Abbott stood and saluted, "Aye Captain."

Jack laughed and imitated Abbott's salute.

"Aye..."

Billy took another look at the coin. *'Exactly the same.'* he thought, then flipped the coin back to Teller, who caught it and shoved it into his pocket.

"Come on Chief."

With a nod Billy fell in step.

= Chapter 44 =

The Sun had dropped behind the towering mountains that nestled Telluride: infusing the clouds floating above those lofty peaks with pinks and golds; their reflected light coloring the surrounding landscape.

Far below, a single ray of that magical light shone through the massive glass plate window turning the ice cubes in James' cut crystal glass into large pink diamonds. It was a stunning example of fire and ice, but James was in no mood to appreciate such dichotomy.

Picking up his bottle of Glenlivet by its neck, he shook the last remains over the colored cubes while reaching into the burled cabinet in front of him and praying that he had restocked. His prayer was answered. A full bottle waited.

Scooping a handful of fresh ice into his glass, he peeled the foil from the neck, pulled the cork, and poured a healthy splash of the pungent amber liquid, rattling the ice to stir the whiskey as he went to the window to look out over his Kingdom. With a smile of self-satisfaction, he returned to the enormous leather couch that stretched across the stone-slab floor of his living room, set his drink on the low coffee table and picked up the phone.

His attorney/bookkeeper had been left on hold when he went for his drink: and now, with glass refilled and feeling superior, James returned to business, resuming the conversation.

"Alright, Carlton. You were saying?"

"What I was saying, sir, is that without Mr. Teller's signature I am unable to complete *any* transference of ownership. And furthermore, all signatories must sign any papers with a witness present, *and* have the signatures notarized."

James' fist came down the table.

"*Who* in the *hell* demanded these stipulations?" he screamed.

"*You did, asshole!*" the young man wanted to shout, but instead, he closed his eyes and held his tongue. For while he *was* thinking of leaving the company, he wished to leave under an umbrella of compensation, and that wouldn't happen if he were fired for insubordination.

~

Carlton had started this chapter of his career with the cheerful optimism of youth. And, as the 'crème de la crème' of his Ivy League University, he had been handpicked by the headhunters of this prestigious law firm and tagged as the 'up and coming' golden boy for their Western States branch.

Ecstatic was the word to best describe Carlton when he first received word of his being hired; for the opportunity to work under the senior partners of the same firm whose sires had overseen the fortunes of the JP. Morgan Empire for the past century was precisely the recognition he was seeking, fitting perfectly with his plans for the future. But secondly, and of a far more personal nature, was his attraction to the great-great granddaughter of that financial icon.

They had met at the buffet table of a catered board meeting, and from the moment of that innocuous introduction, Carlton was utterly captivated. She seemed to find his shyness charming, and he found her stunningly beautiful. And while *that* was no surprise, her receptiveness to his attentions certainly was.

At the time he had laughed, relating his life to a song that worked its way into the American vernacular; '*The future's so bright, I gotta wear shades.*' But then James had entered the picture; plucking those shades from his face and grinding them under his heel. For not only did it seem that James was earmarked as her future husband, he treated everyone like dirt. And, in a petty, dirty act, had reassigned Carl to the Telluride account as bookkeeper; demoting Carlton to nothing more than Casey's distant admirer, and James' whipping boy.

~

Carlton's thoughts were pulled back to the not-so-bright present by James' angry tone.

"Carlton! Are you there? I asked you a question. *Who* demanded these stipulations?"

"It's standard protocol on any account such as this, Sir."

James took a long drink. "Anyway around it?"

"No, not without making your intentions obvious."

Rattling the ice in his glass, James smiled. "Well, we certainly don't want that now do we?"

"No, Sir, I wouldn't think so."

"No, wouldn't be prudent." he quipped, throwing an arm up onto the soft leather cushion as he settled into the enormous L-shaped couch and brought the glass to his lips, fancying the lowly clerk on the other end of the phone to be terribly impressed with his cleverness.

"Alright then, Carlton. I want you to do me a favor."

Carlton rolled his eyes.

"What would *that* be, sir?"

"Find out, to the penny, what those shares are worth. Once you've done that, call me back with the numbers."

Dropping the phone onto its cradle, James drained his glass.

"Yes Sir." Carlton sighed, laying his finger on the plastic button of the phones cradle and setting the receiver onto the desk. He did not want to be bothered by James again today.

Leaning back, he looked to the ceiling. It was the full exhale of a man who felt he had been dealt a foul hand and was unsure whether to bet, fold, or shoot the dealer.

With a second, miserable sigh, Carl opened the large desk drawer on his right and pulled out the bottle of Pinch whiskey that was hidden beneath a stack of contracts. Gripping it tightly, he spun his chair to the long, low table behind him. On its polished surface sat an elaborately etched silver tray, a crystal water pitcher, and a pair of matching glasses.

Picking up the pair of tongs that stuck out of the sweat covered ice bucket, Carlton plunked a few cubes into a glass and poured until the Scotch reached the very rim. Corking the bottle, he placed it precisely twelve inches down, and twelve inches in from the left corner of the desktop.

His years of dealing with numbers had had left him with a subconscious obsession for precision. But now, with the subtle taste of fine liquor on his tongue, Carlton leaned back in his hand-tooled leather chair, threw his feet up onto the desktop, and let his eyes slide from the stamped tin ceiling to the opulent wood-paneled walls.

Taking another sip, he allowed himself a faint smile.

This, at least, was the luxury he had anticipated.

But as he considered James's demand, he lowered his feet back to the floor and a third sigh emerged.

'Something's got to change . . .'

Taking a deep drink, he poked at the keyboard with one finger and opened the Mac to the document file containing the requested information.

— — —— ——— —— — —
—— ——   —— ——
—— ——— ——

= Chapter 45 =

With everyone having returned from their appointed tasks, the men were now gathered outside of Billys trailer: Jack sitting backwards on the picnic table's bench, his elbows resting on the rough surface while watching Teller cooking burgers.

Standing on the upwind side of the grill, he slid the spatula under an exceptionally fat patty and tossed it into the air where it did a double flip and landed with a 'splat' on the plate he held in his other hand. Sneaking a prideful glance at the group, he frowned when he saw but no-one but Jack was paying any attention to his culinary juggling skills.

Abbott lay stretched out in a beat-up lawn chair, his eyes closed with his injured foot propped up on a worn saddle and a beer can clutched in one hand. He appeared haggard from the events of the past week but overall, he appeared healthy and content. A smile of affection touched Teller's lips as he sprinkled salt over the meat just as Billy came through the rounded door of the trailer.

A plate of sliced tomatoes in one hand and a jar of whole dill pickles in the other, he set the two down, slid out the bottle tucked under his arm and smiled, "Wine anyone?"

Teller looked across the grill. "No thanks, Chief, I'll stick with beer."

Billy nodded and looked to Jack. "You?"

"No thanks." Jack said. "If you recall, I'm more of a Scotch guy."

Billy nodded. "I *do* remember Jack, and you're in luck. I happen to have a case of unopened bottles left over from a large celebration few years back. You may remember the event."

Jack looked at Billy questioningly.

"Why would I..." then, suddenly, the pilot's unshaven face broke into a smile. "Are you talking about my wedding?"

But before he could pursue the matter any further, Teller plopped a plate of burgers triumphantly into the center of the table. "Dinner is served." he grinned, adding, "Who wants toasted buns?"

Everybody's hands went up.

"Shoulda known." he grumbled and went back to the grill.

Chuckling, Jack returned his attentions to Billy. "So, this whiskey is left over from my wedding?"

"It is," Billy nodded. "I purchased a case for the event, but then you and your bride rushed off to Mexico before I could give it to you."

Jack gave a sour snort. "Yeah, turned out she liked Mexico more than me. Boy, was *that* a poor decision."

Teller looked up from the grill. "Which was the poor decision, Jack?" he grinned, "The wedding, the woman, or Mexico?"

"Ultimately all three." Jack frowned, "but Mexico turned out to be the least expensive."

Abbott burst into laughter while Billy just grinned.

Teller just shook his head and pushed the buns outside of the flames. "Well, old sock, look at the bright side. You now have a few bottles of premium whiskey, and your Spanish is nearly flawless."

"Teller, besa mi culo." Jack smiled.

Billy joined in Abbott's laughter while Teller grinned, "See what I mean? flawless . . ."

It took a few minutes for the laughter to die down and as it did Billy wiped at his eye.

"So, Teller, what was it you wished to discuss?"

Taking a seat, Teller tipped his head towards Jack.

"Well, this thing with Jack's whiskey segues nicely into my question . . . what's with all the good wine and liquor?"

Beneath the shade of his hat, Bully's expression grew puzzled. "Pardon?"

"Why the expensive liquor, Billy? You don't drink, your visitors are few, and this," he smiled as he waved his arm to encompass the area, "Is not exactly a high-end vacation destination. No offense of course."

"None taken." Billy smiled.

Jack interrupted, "What kind of Scotch was it?"

Ignoring Jack, Billy's attention remained on Teller.

"Yes, Teller, you are correct, I don't care much for alcohol, but I *do* have friends that drop in from time to time, and a good host should have their liquor of choice on hand."

He turned his brilliant smile to Jack. "And what of you my friend? Unless I am wrong, and your tastes have changed, you lean towards the single malt."

"No, Billy," Jack grinned. "My tastes are still single malt, and, as *I* recall, you have always been an outstanding host, and most generous when it comes to your guests' preferences."

Billy's smile radiated pleasure at the compliment.

"Thank you, Jack. If you go up to the office you'll find a leftover bottle of Highland Park in the cabinet above the coffee." Arching his brows over twinkling black eyes, Billy turned to Teller. "And speaking of coffee, when may I expect the return of my coffee *pot*?"

The smile on Teller's face vanished, and his eyes narrowed.

"I *hate* it when people change the subject."

Laughing as he stood, Jack leaned in to Teller as he walked past the. "Your buns are burning . . ."

"Just go get your Scotch." Teller grumbled, gingerly transferring the buns onto a plate with his fingers while calling over his shoulder, "Hey Griz, you want mustard on yours?"

"Yes sir!" Abbott called back gratefully. "If you would be so kind."

Teller assembled Abbott's sandwich, adding the mustard and garnish; but as he delivered the plate to Abbott's lawn chair he wrinkled his nose. "It's not kindness, Abbott, I want you to stay downwind. You stink of woodsmoke and sweat. Do us all a favor and hobble into a shower after dinner."

Abbott nodded. But as he reached up Teller drew back the plate. "I'm serious, Porthos."

"Of course you are." Abbott muttered as Teller handed him the plate with a pat on the shoulder. "and I shall just as soon as I've eaten."

Teller went back to the grill, constructed three more sandwiches, and setting the platter down, joined the other two men at the table.

"Alrighty Chief, your coffee pot is still in the chopper and I'll retrieve it after dinner. And, thanks for the loan."

"You are very welcome, Teller." Billy smiled, "Now, what is it you *really* wish to talk about?"

Teller was caught off guard by this unexpected candor; and knowing how evasive Billy could be, wanted to make sure his questions were framed succinctly, allowing no room for Billy's chronic ambiguity.

Billy, taking advantage of the silence, poured a splash of wine into his glass; swirling the red liquid against the transparent walls and holding it up to the Sun on the horizon; watching the velvety liquid slide back into itself.

Teller watched for a moment, then spoke.

"Billy, what I want to ask is−" But that was as far as he got. Billy's gaze went from his wine glass, to Teller's face; the depth of those black eyes rendering Teller mute.

"I know where the gold coins came from." Billy smiled.

The neat list of questions Teller had compiled evaporated.

"Of course you do Chief. I told you all about it the other day."

Billy lifted his glass again, holding it by the stem and looking at the fire through its red depths.

225

"No, Teller, that is not what I mean. Your friend Abbott corroborated your story regarding the cave and the dead man's treasure. No, what *I* am talking about is how the dead man came into possession of the coins and stones in the *first* place."

Fully expecting a coyote to howl from somewhere out in the mesas, Teller set his sandwich down. It seemed Billy was now going to answer the questions that he was not sure how to ask. Laying both elbows on the table he leaned in and gave Billy a tight smile. "Would you mind being a *little* more specific?"

Swirling his wine again, Billy brought the glass to his eye.

"Are you sure this is the time, Teller? It is a very long tale."

Leaning closer, Teller focused on Billy's distorted eye through the wineglass. "No time like the present," He smiled, turning to his companions. "Right guys?"

Jack nodded as Abbott chimed, "Aye, Captain."

Teller held out his hands, palms up. "Well, there's your answer, Chief, please commence."

The soft breeze was the only background, with even the coyotes remaining silent as Billy told them the incredible story of his long dead ancestor having been Estebanico's guide, followed by of the sequence of events that had placed the very same gold coins that Teller now held, into *his* possession.

The telling of the tale carried well into dusk; the three men listening in amazement as Billy told of the battle outside the walls of Hawikuh and the escape that followed, leaving Billy's distant grandfather holding his dying son in his arms, with eight bags of useless baubles at his feet.

"I heard that battle," Abbott whispered. "In my dream. I was sitting on the walls of that pueblo."

Billy nodded. "Yes, Abbott… time can be nebulous."

Jack stood. While he found the tale fascinating he was not as deeply involved as the others; therefore, his level of interest was not as great.

"Excuse me, but where did you say that Scotch was?"

Billy tilted his head, "Up in the office, on the shelf above the coffee." Then, smiling at Teller, added. "and Jack, while you're there, would you please put the coffee pot back where it belongs?"

"Sure Bill." Jack chuckled and headed up the hill.

Teller watched Jack fade into the night, drumming his fingers on the tables rough surface while minutes passed in silence. Finally he stood and went to the fire pit.

Pulling the hatchet from the splitting stump he began chopping a small log into kindling. It gave him something to do while he considered Billy's story.

He swung the hatchet.

'Thump!'

"So, you have had these same coins for some time now?"

'Thump!'

"Yes," Billy said, pouring a little more wine into his glass. "For some time..."

'Thump!'

"And *that* is how you finance your life here."

'Thump'

Billy smiled, "Yes Teller." He said, taking a sip of wine. "That, and a few other things that help my people."

Nodding, Teller arranged the fresh-cut kindling, reached into his pocket and took out a box of stick matches. Shaking one free he scraped it across the striker. It ignited and he held it to the duff, watching the flame take hold; then, kneeling, he placed his cheek nearly on the ground, encouraging the fledgling flame by blowing gently on its tiny orange start. It spread quickly and soon a merry fire crackled. Giving a nod of satisfaction, Teller added a few wrist-sized sticks to the flames.

Then, lifting the hatchet above his head, he buried it deep into the stump with a powerful blow and stood, staring at the dancing flames a moment longer. Then, with a second nod, put his hands on his knees, pushed himself up, and returned to the table to take a seat across from Billy. Dispensing with any further formalities, he cut to the chase.

"Well then Billy, it seems my next question should be an obvious one. Just *how* are you cashing these coins in without raising the suspicions of any federal agencies?"

Due to years of secrecy, Billy automatically began to repeat his fabricated storyline regarding his income. But on looking into Tellers' eyes, he realized that they were far too entwined at this point to harbor any secrets. Besides, it felt good to have friends to finally share both the burden, *and* the security that the gold provided.

"I have someone in Tucson."

With a nod Teller turned to Jack who just shrugged and smiled; and in the silence that followed, Abbott picked up his staff and rose from his chair.

"Well, my friends, I believe this is an opportune time for me to take that shower." Looking at Billy, he raised his brows. "And where might one find such a luxury?"

Billy smiled warmly and pointed up the hill.

"There is an outdoor shower behind the store. As it is considerably larger than the one in the trailer, it would be a much better choice for a man of your size. You will find soap and shampoo on the cinder block to the right of the curtain."

"Thank you, good Sir." Abbott said, raising his staff. Then, turning to Teller, he gave a short bow. "And again, thank you, Captain." Pivoting on his good heel he limped away.

As he hobbled up the hill, Teller called out, "Just wash well, old Bear. Return stinkless, and I shall consider that sufficient thanks." Watching Abbott for a moment longer, he chuckled and turned back to Billy.

"A friend in Tucson, huh? Do you suppose you could convince your friend to meet with us?"

Billy poured a few more ounces of the red into his glass and nodded. "Once I have given him my assurances, and explained your involvement, I don't think there will be any problem at all Teller. Although I cannot give any guarantees he will be able to help you."

Teller laughed, the humor of experience cutting through any pretension. "I've yet to find any guarantees in *anything* Billy. And every time someone tried to sell me one, it usually turned out to have less value than what I had in the beginning, which, more often than not, was nothing at all."

Flashing his megawatt smile, Billy tipped his glass.

"You are wise beyond your years, Teller."

Teller tipped his drink in return. "Wisdom comes at a high price, Chief," he smiled, taking a deep drink and adding, "And I have paid dearly for what little I have achieved." Finishing his beer, he reached in the cooler for another. "And, if you don't mind my asking, since we are speaking of wisdom and guarantees, just why is it you are trusting us?"

Billy lowered his glass. "For several reasons, Teller. First, I've known Jack for many years, and he places a great deal of faith in you. Second, Miss Kelly also thinks highly of you, and I believe her to have a soul worth trusting." Again, the brilliant smile flashed under his hat. "And, of course, *I* happen to like you, and my intuition is seldom false."

Teller pulled a can from the ice and wiped it down. "And?"

Billy's smile vanished, the light in his eyes dimming as well. "There is one thing that outweighs all else, Teller, and voids all other concerns."

Surprised by the ominous tone in Billy's voice, Teller asked, "And that one thing is . . .?"

The slightest of smiles cracked Billy's countenance.

"That one thing, is that Coyote has led *you,* to *me.*"

Teller leaned back. "You seem to put a great deal of faith in that troublemaker."

Billy's dark eyes grew darker still. "As *you* should learn to do. I have never seen, nor heard of Coyote treating any individual as he has you." but as the words left his mouth, the twinkle returned to his eyes. "But Coyote is very old, so perhaps he is simply bored. Who am I to question?"

As he finished the sentence, his voice seemed to drift and he seemed to follow, quietly staring at his empty wineglass.

Teller sat, quietly anxious, processing the whole of the tale while waiting for Billy to continue; but just as he was about to speak a spark flashed behind Billy's eyes. Suddenly reanimated and with clear purpose, he filled his wineglass halfway and lifted, holding it at eye level between them, the ruby liquid glowing in the firelight.

Peering at Teller through the wine, Billy's eyes shone.

"*This* is how *we* see time, Teller. Murky and dimly lit, and from one side only... Coyote, on the other hand, can not only see *through* the glass, he can move around it at any time, with no constraints regarding past or present, permitting us to see him only when he pleases. But *you*, Teller, *you* he has allowed to walk around the glass with him."

Teller waited for more, but it seemed Billy was done.

Teller waited as the silence stretched.

Finally, he asked, "So what the hell does that *mean?*"

Billy's smile lit the darkness. "I have no idea!" he laughed. Then, holding up his glass in salute, pronounced, "But here's to life, and life's mysteries." He paused as a ripple of perplexity crossed his face but another smile immediately replaced it.

"And to your future!"

He drained his wine.

Teller's return laughter was uncertain, but he raised his beer in return. "Well, I guess I'll drink to that."

Suddenly a loud curse burst from the darkness, and all heads turned as one. Having stumbled coming down the path, Jack nearly dropped the bottle of Scotch cradled in his arm. It was only some quick juggling that saved it from shattering on the rocks. Entering the firelight, he looked at the smiling faces.

"What's so funny?" he growled.

"Nothin' Jack." Teller grinned, pointing at the bottle, "but go easy on that. We're flying out of here tomorrow."

Jack shrugged, plopped down on the bench and peeled the foil away from the cap. "Where are we going *this* time?"

230

Looking across the table at Billy, Teller asked, "Tucson?"

"Yes," Billy nodded. "Tucson."

Jack nodded, sat down, and pulled the cork out with his teeth. "You coming?"

Billy smiled but shook his head. "No Jack, this is not the time for my leaving." He turned to Teller. "I am going to make the call and arrange for your meeting. Have you any idea when you might be there?"

Teller shrugged and looked to Jack. "What's your best guess amigo?"

Saying nothing, Jack poured two fingers into the tumbler and raised it to his nose, taking in the hints of smokey peat and oak. Then, with a smile, he squeaked the cork back into the neck, closed his eyes, and took a sip, letting the amber liquid rest on his tongue. With an exaggerated moan of pure pleasure, he swirled the whiskey around in the glass and considered the question. Finally, he looked up. "I need some clean clothes and a few other things, so we'll need to stop at my place in Flag on the way." He paused, took another sip, and spoke through an expression of ecstasy. "Then we can grab a bite and re-fuel."

"Well, at least it's a start." Teller said, sticking his hand in the cooler and dragging it through the slush to find a beer. The noise of the water and ice cubes caught Abbott's ear as he came shuffling down the trail.

"Hey Captain!" he shouted, "pull one out for me!"

Teller grinned as he wrestled two frosty cans from the ice. "The beer bear returns."

Abbott's limp had improved considerably since Billy's manipulations, so his hobble was not as pronounced. But still favoring the ankle, he lowered himself into a chair, taking the can while shaking excess water from his hair.

"Thank you, Captain," he grinned, "I must admit I feel much better!"

"You are very welcome," Teller smiled, sniffing at the air. "And your bath has certainly made you a *much* more agreeable traveling companion."

231

He opened his beer and turned to Jack. "So, when?"

Jack did some quick calculations in his head.

"Day after tomorrow, around two o'clock."

"Well then Chief," Teller smiled, turning to Billy. "Let your friend know we'll be there for an early dinner meeting on Thursday, and tell him to pick the place."

Suddenly Teller snapped his fingers. "Wait a minute… I remember a really good Mexican restaurant down in Tucson.

As I recall it was somewhere on Speedway, although I don't remember exactly where." He turned, "You remember that place, Jack?"

Jack frowned, "Hell, Teller, that was a long time ago. The place is probably gone by now. And anyway, I don't remember the name."

Teller nodded, "Yeah, me either. Okay Billy, have your friend pick the spot."

Billy stood. "I'll see what I can do."

Teller watched as he vanished up the trail.

Teller snapped his fingers again. "Hey! While we're down there I'd like to see if there's a guy by the name of Stephen George playin' in any of the bars, he's a great steel guitar player I met once in Hawaii, and he lives in Tucson."

Jack looked up. "When were you in Hawaii?"

"I'm fulla surprises Jack." Teller grinned. "You know that."

"I also know your fulla shit."

A look of disappointment crossed Teller's face. "Ahh come on Jack. True as *that* may or may not be, I *have* been to Hawaii." A glint of pleasant reminiscence lit his eyes. "And I'll be happy to tell you all about it. Shoot, once we've cashed in some of this swag maybe I'll even take you and Griz out to the Islands for a little vacation!" He glanced over at Abbott, who was pushing ice around in the cooler in his search for another beer. He chuckled at the image of a big smiling bear slapping through in the ice with its paw, then his attention returned to Jack.

"What would you say to a little tropical adventure, buddy?"

Jack frowned, "What? This isn't exciting enough for you?

"Honolulu's full of pretty girls, Jack."

"I don't know, Tell. After all this I think I may just want to hide out for a while."

"Jaaack . . . there may be no bouncy rafts, but did I mention pretty girls in dental floss bikinis on picture post-cardy tropical beaches?"

Jack laughed and threw up his hands. "Alright Tell, you paint an irresistible picture. Sure, twist my arm, I'm in."

"Good!" Teller smiled, "But first let's see how Tucson plays out." He directed his attention back to Abbott.

"Sound fair to you, Grizzly?"

The rustle of ice stopped. "Which one?"

"Which one what?"

Abbott's voice echoed as he stuck his head in the cooler.

"Which one, Hawaii or Tucson?"

"Goddammit, Abbott, what are you talking about?"

Abbott's head popped out.

He had a beer in his hand, and a questioning smile on his face.

"You asked me if I thought something sounded fair."

Teller nodded, "Right . . ."

"So, what are you asking?"

Teller sighed, "A trip to Tucson, then Hawaii."

"Why wouldn't either one be fair?"

Taking the beer from Abbott's hand, Teller looked into his eyes, speaking slowly and enunciated every syllable.

"Do- you- want- to- go- to- Tuc-son –with- us?"

"Is Billy going?"

"I doubt it, why?"

Abbott reached out, peeling Teller's fingers from the can and pulling it to his chest. "Because if he is staying, I would very much like to continue our conversation."

He looked over to Jack. "*You* don't require my company, do you?"

Jack shook his head and poured a splash of Scotch over the ice in his glass.

Abbott looked at Teller. "Do *you?*"

Teller shrugged, "No, I guess not."

"Well then, if it's all the same to you I would rather just stay here and rest." He sighed and shook his wooly head. "I believe I've had enough of rafts, rivers, caves, coyotes, *and* helicopters for awhile." He flashed an apologetic smile towards Jack. "No offense to your helicopter, Jack."

Jack chuckled. "None taken."

Abbott turned to Teller. "Captain, if it is all the same to you, I do believe I would find the proximity of a well-stocked store, along with a wise man's company much more enjoyable than another adventure at this time. Why don't the two of you fly south without me?" but before Teller could answer, Billy stepped out of the trailer.

"Alright gentlemen, Mr. Smith is willing to meet you. I explained things briefly, telling him only that this was indeed a unique situation, that I trusted you completely, and I would be most appreciative if he would take the time to discuss an equitable resolution to your problem."

Teller's expression turned skeptical. "Mr. *Smith?*"

Billy nodded. "Mr. Smith."

"Well then. Mr. Smith it is," Teller chuckled. Then laying his hand on Abbott's shoulder, he looked to Billy.

"I've a favor to ask Chief. In our absence, would you mind housesitting a beer bear for a few days? He's reasonably well trained, and under the right circumstances he can be quite pleasant company."

"No, no, not at all!" Billy laughed, "Sir Bear and I have already begun a most interesting conversation, and I see no reason for it not to continue."

The warmth in his eyes was sincere.

"Terrific!" Teller laughed, "Well then, Griz, you stay here and recuperate, and Chief, keep a tab on our friend's beer consumption, I want to be sure you're compensated for his thirsty ways."

Billy waved the comment away. "That is really of no concern, Teller. The important thing now is for you to take care of your business with Mr. Smith, and when done, return. There are still many things you and I need to discuss." He handed Teller a folded sheet of paper.

"Why not talk before we go?" Teller asked as he unfolded the square.

"Because now is not the time," Billy said, tipping his head to the paper. "Those are the phone numbers you will need when you get to Tucson."

Teller took the note, tucked it into his shirt pocket, and looked over at Jack who sat quietly on the corner of the table, holding his glass of Scotch loosely in his right hand.

Seeing the two of them nearly side by side, Billy was not surprised in the slightest that Jack and Teller were friends. These were men cut from the same cloth, and it pleased him greatly to know that Teller would have someone of Jack's caliber to accompany him through the events to come. And of course, having a helicopter would certainly expedite matters.

Turning from Teller, Billy walked over to Jack and laid a gentle hand on his shoulder.

"Take care of yourself Jack. And watch this one."

Jack smiled, "I always have."

Teller, hearing the exchange, sidled up to Jack and gave a wink. "It's true, Billy, he's always been a bit of a mother hen." Jack threw his arm over Teller's shoulder and pulled him in.

"Just watchin' out for your huevos, pard."

"What'd I tell you?" Teller smiled. "Cluck, cluck."

Jack released Teller, picked the cork up off the table, twisted it back into the bottle's neck, and looked at his watch.

"Alright then gents, it's time to find a place to roost. Teller, have the coffee ready at sunrise and we can be at my place by noon." He looked at Billy. "Mind if I sleep in the trailer again?"

"Not at all, Jack, I'm more comfortable in the Hogan anyway. The trailer has its conveniences, but it resembles a toaster a bit too much for me to sleep in."

"Or a fifties spaceship," Teller added.

Billy considered that for a moment. "No, A spaceship I would find quite satisfactory." but when he turned to Teller, his face reflected concern. "Please, Teller, be careful."

Teller's eyes flashed.

"Why?"

Billy's smile returned the moment he realized that Teller had misunderstood his meaning.

"No, no, your meeting with Mr. Smith will be no problem. As a matter of fact, I believe that it will probably be the least complicated, and perhaps the most beneficial thing in your life right now. What I meant is to be careful in your decisions. Coyote has been quite gentle with you to this point, and that not only puzzles me, it leaves me quite curious concerning his intentions."

Teller crossed his arms. "So then Chief, what should I expect?"

A fleeting shadow crossed Billy's brow. "Ahh, my friend, therein lays the difficulty." But the shadow flew off, and his good humor instantly returned. "Expect nothing! But be cautious. Perhaps it is as I said before, Coyote may be simply bored, and has taken a liking to you."

Teller shrugged and smiled, "Well, I *have* always been a dog guy."

"At least until Kelly came along." Jack interjected.

Teller raised his eyebrows. "Screw you Jack, I'm amazed you still have both arms."

"I'm like a lizard. I chew 'em off, and they just keep growing back."

Teller loved it. For him, it felt like old times; but the jokes were between friends and meaning little to Billy, he continued.

236

"Be that as it may," he said, his eyes dancing between the two men. "Be careful. Coyote may still have a surprise in store for you."

Teller's smile faded. "I'll do what I can, Billy, but honestly, this thing has been out of my control from the moment it began." He looked momentarily forsaken, but then his smile returned. Pulling one of the gold coins from his pocket he held it up, turned it between his fingers, and placed it on his thumb.

"But, heads I win, tails I lose."

Flipping the coin, he caught it in the air and slapped it on the top of his right hand; then, looking up to his friends, slowly lifted his left hand to reveal the glittering coin.

Heads up.

A satisfied grin spread across Teller's face. "I win . . . .."

Billy looked over to Jack, who simply spread his hands. "What can you say? He's a lucky guy."

"Luck is good, Teller," Billy smiled, "but timing is everything."

Teller pocketed the coin. "Aint that the truth."

"I couldn't agree more," Jack said, checking his watch again. "And speaking of time, it's time to get some rest. We have a big couple of days ahead of us."

There was another quick discussion regarding sleeping arrangements; Teller bid two of them goodnight and was soon alone. He smiled, and again considered himself blessed. Turning from his silent thanks, he looked down at the empty cans scattered about. With a quiet curse he began picking them up and tossing them into the cooler; where they splashed in the melted ice water. the cleanup went quickly and after dropping the last can in he walked over to the lounge chair to look down at his large friend.

Abbott lay sound asleep, his head lolled slightly to the side, snoring lightly. His injured foot rested on the saddle and a half full beer was still clutched tightly in his hand.

Teller laughed quietly and went to the trailer.

Jack was already asleep, but a quick search turned up a soft wool blanket folded in the small closet. Tucking it under his arm, he walked past the bed and picked up the pillow Jack wasn't using; but deciding against it, tossed it back, and made his way back down the creaky stairs.

Standing again at the foot of the chair, Teller looked down on Abbott's peaceful face and the half smile hidden beneath the beard. "The sleep of the just." he whispered, and gently prying the can from Abbott's fingers, set the beer on the table.

Spreading the blanket across Abbott's broad chest, Teller tucked it under his beard and patted his cheek. "Your breakfast will be waiting, champ." he grinned, and began walking up the starlit trail towards the store.

Amused by life's capricious ways, Teller paused and turned, looking back towards the dwindling fire and the shadow of the large form resting peacefully under the blanket; then, lifting his eyes to the heavens, focused on the constellation of Ursa Major. The sight jogged a musical memory and he began to sing.

It was an old Randy Newman song; one he had not thought of for years but seemed to dovetail seamlessly into this moment of his life. It was a simple tune, titled: 'Simon Smith and His Amazing Dancing Bear.'

— — -- --- -- — —
— — -- — —
-- --- --

= Chapter 46 =

James was jerked awake from his booze-induced slumber by the ringing next to the couch. His hand fumbled across the side table; swiping the smooth surface while reaching blindly for the phone. On the second pass the back of his hand knocked over the glass that still held a few ice cubes floating listlessly in watered-down scotch.

"*Damn it!* Hello . . .?"

Carlton was on the line, and he smiled at James' obvious disorientation.

"Sorry about the hour Sir, but you said to call as soon as I had a dollar figure for you."

Sliding from the edge of the leather couch, James kneeled and picked up the glass that lay on its side, the expensive rug soaking up the liquid. Scooping the cubes into his palm, he dropped them back into the cut crystal.

"It's fine, Carl, it's fine . . . How much are we talking?"

"Well sir, it's substantial."

James pushed himself back onto the couch. "How *much* Carl?"

Carl gave the figure in a whisper.

There was second of silence: then it was shattered by James' scream.

"WHAT!!!"

Anticipating the reaction, Carlton had already pulled the phone away from his ear; then, counting to three, he brought the phone back and repeated the figure.

James was livid. "There has *got* to be a mistake, Carl!"

Carl's smile was one of pure satisfaction. "No sir, no mistake. After all, Mr. Teller *does* own fifty percent of the entire enterprise."

The last words Carlton heard before the phone went dead were, "Mo-ther-*fucker!*"

— — -- --- -- — —
— — -- — —
-- --- --

= Chapter 47 =

Jack looked over at Teller who held a stainless-steel carafe of hot fresh coffee between his knees. He had protested, saying that Teller should have at least *asked* to borrow it again, but Teller had just thrown his deerskin pack behind the seat of the chopper.

"Why ask?" he grinned. "He would have only said yes."

Jack just shook his head as his eyes went to the pack.

The pack held not only Teller's personal supplies, but also a single pouch containing a mix of coins and stones for this first meeting... Billy's faith in "Mister Smith" aside, experience had taught him caution when it came to matters such as these. Kelly had once accused him of paranoia: but his response was that suspicion was preferable to remorse, and that his past experiences more than justified any wariness when dealing with *other* people's trusted friends.

Jack spoke, interrupting his humming the chorus to a song he had written, titled: "Ain't my First Rodeo"

"You ready?"

"Always."

"Where are Billy and Abbott?"

"Don't know about Billy," Teller shrugged, "but Abbott's probably still dreaming the dreams of the innocent."

"Lucky man." Jack remarked, glancing at his watch.

"What, to still be sleeping?"

Jack looked up, cynicism mixed with a hint of sorrow.

"No Tell. To be innocent."

~

The two of them spent the next few hours in the air catching up. As in most true friendships, time had little meaning, and the conversation simply picked up where they left off on their last rendezvous, the events of the past few days taking a back seat to the gap between then and now…

Teller sat in the co-pilot seat, boots off, his right foot pressed against the windscreen.

"So, the wife took off to Vegas huh?"

Jack nodded and gave a 'what are you gonna do?' shrug. Any residual anger over *that* poorly thought out marriage had been exorcised and filed away into his mental box of many mistakes. He gave a resigned smile.

"Never marry a girl with fake tits and a coke habit."

"I'll keep that in mind," Teller grinned. "So, I guess she'll do well in Vegas then."

Jack looked at Teller over the top of his shades.

"Shit, Teller, that town was *built* on tits and dope. She'll do *great*."

Teller stared at Jack in total silence, then broke into a raucous laughter. "Hawkins, you crack me up . . ."

Jack couldn't help it. He joined in, the laughter and the cabin rang with merriment: but eventually the mirth subsided.

"What about you, Jack." Teller asked. "How *you* doin?"

Jack shrugged. "Me? I'm still looking for a girl like Kelly. You're a lucky man Tell."

Teller gave a short, barking laugh. "Don't let her fool you old son, she can be as evil a bitch as any other."

Jack's humor vanished.

Pushing his shades low on his nose, his blue eyes pierced Teller with dead seriousness.

"That may be true Tell. But she is a beautiful bitch, and underneath that occasional bitch is a woman who truly loves you. And for that alone you should be grateful." He stared at Teller for a second longer, then pushed his shades back up on the bridge of his nose. "And by the way, you're no picnic either."

Teller remained surprisingly quiet for a moment then smiled. "Well Jack, I will take those words of wisdom under advisement, if for no other reason than they are true. But, my many flaws aside, what in the hell *have* you been up to since our last little misadventure?"

Jack's grin dropped, and he turned back to look at Teller's smiling face. Why in the *hell* did he have to bring up *that?*

The 'misadventure' Teller was referring to was an event that *he* found terribly amusing but held no fond memories for Jack. It had all started innocently enough: and as much as he hated to admit it, it *was* fun for a while. But the fun had ended when the two of them were arrested for driving a stolen car. It was a sequence of events so outrageous that they were hard to believe, and in retrospect could have only happened with Teller.

Jack, in an act of mental self-preservation, had allowed his subconscious to bury the whole thing. And it had stayed blissfully forgotten . . . until now.

Now the whole crazy incident came rushing back.

~

Having gotten a call from Teller one afternoon, he had been persuaded to come down and "play" in a very elite, gated community that lie tucked away in the mountains near Scottsdale. Sadly, it turned out to be a textbook example of Teller's propensity for trouble.

Teller's first bit of bad luck was that the woman he had met over drinks in the exclusive golf course clubhouse turned out to be married. The second glitch followed a wicked weekend spent in her sumptuous stone and glass home overlooking the valley.

Following coffee in bed on the third morning, the woman teased that she had a surprise for him, leading him to an elevator that opened into a subterranean garage filled with expensive, and highly collectible, automobiles.

Pointing to a classic 1964 Bentley S3, she handed him a platinum AMEX card. "The keys are in it," she smiled, and with a casual wave of an elegant hand, suggested he go out and enjoy himself. And Teller, being Teller, took to her proposition with awe-inspiring commitment, pulling Jack into his wake.

Jack had to admit that he went willingly, for not only was the fun first class, it held the promise of breaking all previous records for outrageous behavior . . . until hubby returned from his Hong Kong business trip.

It seemed the husband took far more offense in the loan of his luxurious automobile than to his lovely wife's indiscretion; and this is where it had gotten sticky.

The offended businessman was a major power player in Arizona land development: and land development generated money; *big* money... and big money cultivates powerful friends. So, once home and upon learning of his wife's casual loan, he subsequently made a quiet call to an associate in the Governor's office. *That* highly placed individual then contacted the local Chief of police, who followed by having a private meeting with a small group of trusted officers. These men were then told to quietly locate and return the car and jail the bastard who was operating it.

Regrettably, that bastard was Teller.

But more unfortunate still, in Jack's opinion, was that *he* was in the inauspicious position of being in the back seat of that luxury car mixing drinks when they were pulled over by an unmarked police car as they joyfully made their way to Sedona. Incredibly, Teller's luck once again came into play.

During their booking, Teller struck up a conversation with the desk Sargent. It turned out that the man had been in the same Airborne Division as Jack. So, out of solidarity for a fellow pilot, as well as an intense personal dislike for the cuckolded husband, the Sargent made two phone calls. The first was anonymous, informing the lovely wife of Teller's incarceration. The second, and more importantly to Jack, was

244

to a number in Cortez giving both his location and the details of his dire situation.

The very next morning they were taken to the Mayor's office where greeted by an expensively tailored receptionist, they were led through a pair of paneled doors, seated in plush high-backed chairs, and served coffee. Teller accepted the steaming beverage; grinning as if he were a guest in the Kings court while Jack sat slumped in his chair. Regretting, and not for the first time, having ever met Teller in the first place.

As they waited in the opulent office, Teller attempted to engage Jack in the memory of a night a few years back when they had been jailed in New Orleans during Mardi Gras. But Jack wanted no further reminders of the many troubles Teller had inflicted upon him in the past. Sufficiently angry about their current problem, he sat, fuming in silence. But the silence had only inspired Teller to begin happily humming, 'Mr. Bojangles.'

Glowering furiously, Jack was speculating what the sentence might be for murder in a public official's office when the Mayor stepped through the double doors, eliminating any opportunity for a quick kill and stealthy escape.

Taking his seat in the throne-like chair behind his massive desk, the distinguished public official silently scrutinized Teller over steepled fingers; and when he finally spoke it was with cold contempt.

"Well, well, Mister Teller. It seems you and your *accomplice* here," the Mayor's anger was palpable as he turned his gaze to Jack, then slowly back to Teller. "have friends in high places."

"Oh," Teller smiled with innocent sincerity. "I have friends in low places as well, but in a situation such as this, they would have been of *very* little help."

Jack stifled a snicker behind his fist while Teller just grinned.

Rising to his feet, the Mayor yanked at the bottom of his vest with such force the bottom button popped loose and rolled across the expanse of desk. All eyes followed as it dropped to the carpet, and the room fell silent. The Mayor's gaze rose from the wayward button, his expression one of unmitigated fury. When he finally spoke, his voice trembled in impotent rage.

"It seems the owner of the vehicle you *misappropriated* has decided to drop all charges."

Teller stifled a laugh, his lips tight and eyes shining.

The Mayor's reaction was one of contained fury.

Quivering with indignation, he fixed his gaze on Teller's infuriating grin; and struggling to retain his dignity, reached into his vest pocket to remove an envelope.

"I have been informed that I am to have Mr. Hawkins here taken directly to the military base and put on a flight to Colorado... *You,* on the other hand, are to take *this.*"

Throwing the sealed sheath bearing distinctly feminine handwriting onto the desk, he placed a hand on either side of the envelope, leaned forward, and raised his eyebrows threateningly. The man was serious, and even Teller's smile faded as the Mayor spat out; "and leave *to-day.* As for your leaving Scottsdale, *that* is without question." He slid the letter to the edge of the desk, pressing down on the center with a heavy index finger and tapping twice. "But Mister Teller, I would strongly suggest that you *leave my state!*"

Straightening, he pulled once more on his vest and buzzed his secretary. "Miss Hanson, please see these gentlemen *out.*"

The tension in the room was thick, but the elegant secretary maintained her poise as she hustled them from the room.

For once Teller kept his mouth shut.

Deposited unceremoniously outside the building by two very large, and unfriendly, security guards, they were left standing at the top of the stairs, blinking in the bright Arizona sun while looking at the military jeep that waited at the curb.

Jack was still angry, but he was also relieved

Teller, however, had not lost his smile.

"I didn't know you were still active, Jack."

246

Jack glared at Teller, suppressing the urge to punch him. But on recalling the look of fury on the Mayor's face he smiled at their luck; marveling at the enormity of Teller's huevos.

"I'm not," he growled. "But it looks like Leroy still has some pull with the brass. But *now* I've got to go and explain what happened." He smiled with gruff affection. "And he won't be at all surprised that *you* were involved. But what the hell, it'll be good to see him again."

He looked back at the courthouse one last time, then turned.

"So, asshole. What are *you* gonna do?"

Teller tapped the envelope to his temple. "Hell, Jack, I have no idea, but give ole Leroy my best, and give Janey a big kiss from me." Jack distinctly remembered the smile on Teller's face as he ran the envelope under his nose.

"Plumeria . . . Hmmm, what have we here?'"

Tearing open the envelope, his green eyes had sparkled as he removed a stack of hundreds. Fanning them like a deck of cards he grinned. "Wow... it seems that cheap romance pays considerably more than it used to."

Peeling off ten of the bills, he had handed them to Jack.

"Here, buddy, take this. It is considerably more tangible than an apology, but I still owe you one. I'm really sorry about the night in jail."

Jack's anger dissolved. "Forget it Tell." He said as he pocketed the cash. "It's the price of having you as a friend. And, as I've said before, life around you is never boring."

He remembered the M.P. nervously checking his watch.

"I gotta go Tell. Take care of yourself and keep in touch."

The M.P. opened the door. And as he slid in, he leaned out of the window. "Stay outta trouble Teller!" he shouted.

"Can't do that, Jack!" Teller had hollered as the Jeep pulled away. But Jack had leaned further out.

"Then leave me out of it!"

The last thing he had heard from Teller until a few days ago was his cackling laughter as he shouted, "Can't do that either, Jack!"

They shared another chuckle at the memory... the humor subsided and Jack smiled. "So why *were* we going to Sedona anyway?"

Teller grinned and shrugged, "Dammed if I remember, Jack, but that Bentley was sure one hell of a car."

Jack nodded, "Left-hand steering was kind of weird though."

The smile on Teller's face widened, "How would you know? You were in the back mixing drinks."

"Oh yeah," Jack laughed, "that's right. Well stocked bar as I recall."

"And you certainly put it to good use." Teller chuckled, then following a pause, he let out a long sigh.

"We've sure had us some fun, haven't we Jack?"

His longtime friend looked over and gave a satisfied nod. "Yeah Tell, we sure have."

Flush with the joy of priceless memories, Teller reached back, pulled the pack over the seat into his lap, and threw back the top flap. After a little rustling around he removed a large green stone. Holding it between two fingers, he brought it up to the window. It was unpolished and dull, but the sun behind it pulsed with a rich green hue.

Teller smiled. "And it's not over yet, Jacko. These beauties are going to finance another adventure."

Casting a skeptical eye at his grinning companion, Jack dropped the helicopter low over the tall ponderosa pines that surrounded Flagstaff as the small airport came into view.

"Great, that's *just* what I need. More of your kind of fun."

Teller feigned indignation. "Play or not pal. It's your choice."

Jack shook his head and gave a resigned smile.

"Buckle up chum, we'll be landing in ten."

= Chapter 48 =

Jack radioed the flight tower and began his babel-speak, but Teller's mind was on the upcoming meeting with Mr. Smith, so the drone of Jack going through the landing procedure was akin to a mosquito buzzing in the background. But the response that came back over the little speaker not only caught his ear, it raised his eyebrows. It was a woman's voice. A very *sexy* woman's voice.

"Welcome home, Jack. I missed you."

A rakish grin spread across his face as Teller shot Jack a look of approval.

"She sounds nice."

Jack glared and clicked the mic. "Hi, Max, clear to land?"

"This landing strip is always clear for you, Jack."

Teller chuckled, *"Nice* double entendre."

Suppressing a smile, Jack shook his head and mouthed, "Shut up." as he clicked the microphone again.

"Thanks, Max. coming in."

"And a snappy comeback." Teller grinned.

Jack switched off the radio and made a show of checking all the instruments.

"Come on Jack, who's the girl?"

Jack flicked the altimeter with his fingernail and growled, "Drop it, Teller."

"No way, Jack. This girl sounds hot, and you're single, *and* lonesome."

"Drop it Tell."

"And good lookin' may I add. Plus you've got a goddamned helicopter! What girl could resist a package like that?"

Jack said nothing, but his jawline grew tighter.

The next few minutes were spent with Jack concentrating on setting the bird down in the center of the target painted on the tarmac. That done, he shut down the engine.

Remarkably, Teller had remained quiet as Jack landed, rolling the emerald he had taken out earlier between his fingers. But as the rotors came to a stop, he looked over at his friend and grinned, "Shit, now that I think about it, I can't believe some lucky girl hasn't already snapped you up!"

Grabbing his pack, he swung the door open and hopped out, but as his feet hit the pavement, he turned, leaning into the cab and putting his elbows on the seat. Clasping his hands under his chin, he gave Jack a look of comic sincerity, fluttered his eyelids dramatically and sighed, "Gosh, Jack... wouldja marry me?" Laughing uproariously, he pushed his door closed and walked towards the terminal.

Glaring at Teller's back, Jack yanked the headset from his ears and threw it on the console, unsure whether to laugh or scream: but as he flipped the last switch, a smile tugged at the corners of his mouth and he mumbled, "Never a dull goddamned moment."

Jumping to the ground, he pulled his cap tightly to his head, shoved his fists into the pockets of his jacket, and followed Teller towards the terminal; but as he walked he noticed that the distance between them was increasing. Teller was accelerating his pace... Why would he . . . *oh shit!* Jack quickened his step, but when Teller disappeared through the automatic doors he panicked and broke into a run.

Max!

Bursting through the automatic doors he came to a screeching halt; and looking left then right, he nervously searched the area.

No Teller.

"Now where the hell did he get to?' he cursed under his breath; and knowing Teller as he did, he had a very good idea of what he was up to. Scanning the area, he spotted him next to an empty check-in booth talking to a distinguished looking

250

gentleman in khakis and a bush vest; a pilot's cap tucked under his arm. Cursing under his breath, he hustled through the scattering of travelers; praying he might catch Teller before he caused any problems.

He jogged to the left to avoid a group of Japanese tourists only to find himself in the middle of a human traffic jam.

Surrounded by a herd of noisy children, a hefty woman wrestled with a gigantic suitcase with a broken wheel. She held one crying child by the wrist while trying to keep the others in line. To his dismay, between her threats and the kids screaming, Jack only caught the tail end of Tellers conversation and an exhale of defeat escaped as the pilot pointed up the stairs to the second level of the concourse.

"I believe she's up in the tower."

'Too late . . .' He groaned as Teller shook the tall man's hand.

"Thank you very much Sir, I haven't seen my sister in over five years. This should be quite a surprise."

The pilot nodded, smiling the smile of a Good Samaritan. "Glad I could help. Max is a sweetheart."

Picking up his bag, he began to walk away; but as he glanced over Teller's shoulder he saw Jack scrambling towards them, apologizing as he bumped one person after another out of the way. Stumbling up, he grabbed Teller by the neck and leaned into his ear, panting, "Goddamn it, Tell I -"

But the pilot interjected with a jovial laugh: "Jack! How you doin'? Maxine never mentioned she had a brother!"

Glaring at Teller, Jack grabbed the pilot by the elbow and began pulling him hastily away. "Yeah, well Winston, she rarely talks about him. You know, ex-convict and all. He's kind of an embarrassment to the whole family."

Winston's smile dropped instantly, and his head snapped in Teller's direction. "Really?"

Teller was one step behind; but on hearing Jack's comment, *his* smile grew exponentially larger. Stepping up, he rested a brotherly hand on Jack's shoulder.

251

"Ahh, don't worry, Winnie, it was only Club Fed. a simple stocks and bonds fraud charge. Nothin' really."

He gave an exaggerated wink and pulled Jack closer.

"And nobody really got hurt . . . a few banks, a couple widows, an orphanage or two. No big deal." He released Jack with a rub to the scalp. "Right Jackie boy?"

Winston took a step back, and adjusting his cap flicked his wrist. "Well!" he said, examining his watch. "It's late and I've got a flight. Nice seeing you again Jack." He took an additional step backwards to assure that there would be no chance of a parting handshake from Teller. "Say hello to your sister for me." He turned and was gone.

Teller gave a cocky salute to the rapidly retreating khaki vest. "I'll be sure and do that Winston!"

Jack stood in quiet fury; and as Winston faded into the crowd he grabbed Teller by the shirt.

"What the fuck was that about!" he hissed.

"I just wanted to meet the girl, Jack. *You* started the prison bit." Jack's temper began to cool. "Yeah," he smiled, "but still, Stock fraud??"

Teller threw his arm around Jack's shoulder as they headed towards the stairs. "Come on Jack, I don't *look* like a serial killer, and you gotta admit that widow and orphanage thing was pure inspiration!"

Sighing in grudging admiration, Jack removed the arm.

"*You* are an incorrigible asshole Teller."

Tellers lopsided grin returned. "One of my more endearing qualities Laddie. Now, let's go meet your future ex-wife."

He made it only two short steps before being brought to an abrupt halt.

Jack held his wrist in an iron grip.

Teller tried to pull away, but the grip grew tighter.

"No." Jack said.

Unable to pry Jack's fingers away, Teller frowned, "What?"

"I said *no*."

Giving a final squeeze, he released Teller's wrist. "You are *not* going to screw this up, Tell. I *do not* want to see her right now! I'm dirty, I'm tired, and worst of all, I have *you* with me."

He took off his cap and rubbed his scalp. "Look. I asked you while we were in the chopper to please just let it go, and I'm asking you again. *Just- back- off!* I don't meet many women around here so let's just go to my place and clean up. *Then* we can get a beer, something to eat, and get some sleep. Christ! Don't you ever get *tired?*"

Teller cast a longing look up the stairs.

"Alright Jack. I get it," he sighed; then glancing to his left he caught their reflection in the one of three chrome pillars that supported a quarter scale jet in simulated flight. Stepping closer to the reflection he gave an exaggerated scowl at the image staring back.

"You're right, buddy, we look like shit. This is no time for me to be meeting the next Mrs. Hawkins. But do you mind if we grab a cup of coffee first?"

Breathing a sigh of relief, Jack adjusted his cap and headed towards the moving sidewalk. "Sure, there's a Starbucks down this way." Teller's grin reappeared and rubbing his wrist, he stepped in beside Jack. "What a surprise . . . a Starbucks in an airport." But they hadn't moved three feet into the crowd of travelers when a feminine voice rang out.

"Jack!"

Squeezing his eyes shut, Jack groaned, *Oh no . . ..* then turning to Teller, whispered imploringly, "Please, Tell, don't be yourself." Teller grinned and whispered back, "I take offense to that, Jack! I can be charming, just watch."

The voice called out again.

"Jack! Wait!"

Both men turned towards the voice. But while Jack stared down at the tip of his boots, Teller brazenly watched Maxine come down the stairs, her loose skirt riding above the knees of

253

what Teller couldn't help but notice were an absolutely gorgeous pair of legs.

Coming to a halt only a few feet from them, she put her hands on her hips. Her eyes roaming over Jack head to toe, she gave a disgusted, yet very sexy smile. "You need a shave, Jack."

"That's not all he needs . . ."

Teller's comment was so quiet that only Jack heard what was said: but his voice attracted her attention and her eyes grazed him, lightly lingering. With a smile, she turned to Jack and gave a slight tilt of her lovely head. With a sparkle that Teller couldn't miss, she smiled, "Who's your friend?" An awkward silence followed, and Teller stepped forward.

Putting on his most devilish smile he brought her soft hand delicately to his lips. "Hello," he said. "Names Frank, but my friends call me Teller." Allowing his lips to brush the top of her hand, she raised her eyebrows regally, pulling back with the grace of a queen at court.

"I see," she nodded, her eyes caressing him slowly, "and I see that *you* could use a shave as well, although the mustache rather suits you." Returning her attention to a flustered Jack, her smile went from sexy to amused.

"Well, Jack. Would it be too bold of me to assume that I might consider your rough, but charming friend here," she paused, granting Teller a nod, "A friend of mine as well?"

Her eyes held Jack's as she waited for him to gather his wits.

'This woman's got class' Teller smiled, then giving Jack a, 'I told you so' wink, returned his full attention to Maxine.

"Allow me to answer for my tongue-tied partner Ma'am. Jack is just a little overtired from our most recent adventures, which were both desperate and thrilling... and, if we had the time, I'm sure Jack would be happy to share. But you have caught us just as we were on our way out. As you may have noticed, while we are dirty and in dire need of a shower we've quite the busy schedule for the next few days and—"

Jack interrupted. "I'm sorry Max, we've got to go, really. I promise I'll call you when we get back. Come on Tell." He reached out, grabbed Teller's sleeve and began walking. Teller's arm followed as he was reluctantly towed away. But as they left he turned his head and called over his shoulder,

"The answer is yes!"

Maxine shot him a curious glance and he finished, "Yes, you may call me Teller,"

Jack pulled harder.

"And you may consider me a friend!" Teller shouted with a smile.

Jack yanked harder still.

A sweet laugh rang out across the concourse and she and waved, "Nice to meet you, Teller," then in a slightly louder voice called out, "Don't forget to call me Jack. You promised!" She turned and walked back up the stairs; and as she rounded a corner and disappeared from sight, Teller could not help but to admire her legs once again.

Shaking his arm loose from Jack's grip, Teller came to a full halt, but Jack kept walking away. He stood for a moment staring at Jacks back; then, with a shake of his head sprinted through the crowd. Catching up, he stepped beside his partner, giving him a look of disgust.

"You're absolutely right, Jack, that woman is *way* out of your league. I can see why you're blowing her off."

Jack marched forward, saying nothing as Teller trooped beside him, stride for angry stride. But as they passed the coffee shop Teller came to a halt. "Wait a goddamn minute!" he called out. "I *still* want a cup of coffee!"

Jack took a few more steps, then stopped, keeping his back to Teller.

"Fine!" he growled.

Teller stared at Jack's back for a moment, then walked around to look him in the eyes. "You really are a piece of work, Jack." he said, and went into the coffee shop.

A few minutes later he returned with two cups and handed one to Jack. "Hope you like iced vanilla latte."

Jack wrinkled his nose. "Kinda foo foo ain't it?"

"It appeals to my feminine side," Teller said, shoving it in Jack's direction. "You want it or not?"

Jack suppressed a smile, took the cup and began walking in silence through the concourse. Teller tagged along, watching Jack out of the corner of his eye; but Jack's expression never changed.

They soon left the building, Teller following Jack as he marched into the parking lot and pointed towards a faded old Ford truck. "There's our ride."

Teller grinned, "Hey, isn't that the same old truck you used to have?"

Jack gave a nod. "Yep."

Throwing his pack onto the seat, Teller slid in.

Jack didn't say a word. He just got in, put his coffee between his legs, started the engine and shoved shifter of the rusty old truck into gear, pointing the nose down the aptly named, 'Airport Road,' glaring through the windshield as they crossed under the interstate and turned south on old route 89A.

The silence didn't bother Teller in the least. He just stuck his head out of the window and inhaled deeply, savoring the magnificent aroma of ponderosa pines that filled the air; and with his senses fueled by the fragrance his good humor returned. A smile settled in, and he closed his eyes.

As frustrating as Jack might be on occasion, it was nice to be in the company of an old friend again. Abbott was a good man, and over the past few weeks had proven an excellent companion throughout an experience that would, in the telling, get him branded either a liar or a lunatic. But Jack, well, he and Jack went *way* back. And sitting here now, bouncing down the road watching the familiar landscape roll by, he felt very lucky indeed. Not only to have made it this far in life, but Abbott aside, to make it with at least two trusted, and true friends. One was Jake, and the other was the man behind the wheel of this truck. The man who had just saved his and Abbott's ass, no questions asked.

As they whizzed past Jackson's Grill, Teller crumpled his coffee cup and dropped it on the floor. "Hey Jack."

"Yeah?"

"We just passed a bar."

"Yep."

Teller leaned back in the seat and started whistling the tune to one of his songs. A moment later he stopped, put his left arm across the bench seat and smiled at the side of Jack's head.

"That Maxine is quite the looker."

Nothing.

Teller stretched and put a foot up on the dash. It was something that always pissed off his friend and he knew it.

Still nothing.

Teller just smiled, continuing to talk while staring through the windshield. "And altho' I may be somewhat ignorant in the wily ways of women, Jack, I *do* believe that fine lookin' specimen has got a hankerin' for your handsome ass."

He saw a slight smile trying to break through Jack's stoic facade but was enjoying himself too much to rush it. He hummed a few more bars to his song as he let the miles pass.

Finally, he turned, and looked straight at Jack.

"Hey buddy, mind if I ask you a personal question?"

Jack's mouth was tight, but he said nothing.

Teller's eyes twinkled and he smiled, "Just what the fuck is *wrong* with you?"

— — -- --- -- — —
— — — —
-- --- --

= Chapter 49 =

James's forehead rested in the palms of his hands, his fingers splayed through his hair when the phone rang. The half empty bottle teased him from the desktop, and giving it an evil look, he snatched up the phone.

"What the fuck is wrong with you Carl?" he grumbled into the receiver, "I asked you for a solution, *not* a problem."

It was the nurse in Denver.

"I'm terribly sorry to disturb you, Sir. Is this James Carson?"

Embarrassed to be caught off guard, James made an immediate reflexive switch into professional mode.

"Yes, it is. I'm sorry Miss," He squinted at the bottle. "I'm dealing with something of great importance right now. How may I help you?"

The answer came in a clipped, professional, nasal voice.

"It's your son, Sir, he's awake again and asking for you."

That's all it took. James gave in. Reaching across the desk, he wrapped his fingers around the bottle.

"Look, Miss, he's not my son, and I'm in another part of the state. What's the problem, and where's Miss Pierpont?"

"Well, that's just it, Sir. She's gone and he *is* asking for you specifically."

James sat up a little straighter in his chair. "What do you mean, she's *gone?*"

He heard the note of petty satisfaction in her voice.

"I'm *quite* sure I don't know, Mr. Carson. She said she was leaving and left. She did give me a phone number, but as the boy was asking for you I thought it best to call you first."

His suspicion was instantaneous.

Where in the hell did she go?!?

Scowling, he turned to the problem at hand.

"Yes nurse, you did the right thing. Thank you. What number did she leave?"

"One moment please." Paper could be heard shuffling in the background and a few moments later she came back on the line, giving a number with a Maryland prefix.

"Aha," it was her father's East Coast compound. *Now I know where she ran off to. Now the question is why?*

"Thank you, Miss. Now, what was Ben asking for?"

At this, the young nurse lost some of her composure. Glancing furtively around, she cupped the phone to her lips and walked away from her station. "I'm embarrassed to repeat it Mr. Carson, and these are *his* words, not mine. His exact words were, and please understand that I'm quoting him. He said, "Call my fucking uncle and have him get me the fuck out of here.""

Hearing a muffled laugh on the other end, her wounded professionalism returned. "I'm sorry, sir, but I do *not* find this amusing in the least."

Tucking the phone between his shoulder and ear, James picked up the half-empty bottle, went to the liquor cabinet, scooped his glass through the ice and poured a heavy shot over the cubes. Taking a healthy gulp, he attempted to smooth the nurses ruffled feathers.

"I apologize for the boy's language, Miss. So tell me, is he able to travel?"

Accepting the quasi-apology with a tight little smile, she felt in control again. "No, he is not. We will need to do some follow-up x-rays to make sure everything is healing properly, and even then he will not be able to travel commercially."

James stood and went to the massive plate glass window where he held the glass of Scotch up; and closing one eye, looked through the liquid. The world looked much more appealing washed in gold. With a sigh, he lowered the glass and gazed across the valley. "Well then, tell the boy that as

259

soon as he is cleared to leave I'll arrange to have him brought home. Until then, I've other things to take care of. Thank you for the call. Oh, and Miss?"

The pudgy nurse's mouth moved noiselessly. *Never* had a relative of the patient dismissed her so casually.

"Yes, sir?" she stammered.

"Do me a favor and call Miss Pierpont."

"Sir?"

"You heard me, Miss."

The nurse stuttered out, "And tell her what?" But the phone had already gone dead.

Bringing the glass up to his eye a second time, he wiggled it and view beyond sloshed out of focus.

James smiled. Confusion kept everyone off balance, and that's the way he liked it.

Now, if he only knew what Teller was up to.

— — ·· --- ·· — —
— — — —
·· --- ··

= Chapter 50 =

That's it . . .?"

Teller threw back his head and laughed, "That's *it?!?* You're avoiding that gorgeous woman 'cause you're not sure what she *wants?*" Reaching across the seat, he slapped Jack solidly on the back of the head. "Jack, Jack, Jack! I have *never, ever, ever,* been *sure* of what *any* woman *wants!* Christ almighty son, they are born wanting and they stay that way! The *only* thing that changes is that they fine-tune their wants over the years: and, fortunately for us, those years spent getting what they *think* they want is a very good thing."

Rubbing the spot Teller had smacked, Jack growled, "And why's *that?*"

"Because old boy," Teller laughed, "it means that if you are at all observant, *you* will spend a lot less time *guessing* just what the hell it is that they want, and spend more time *giving* it to them."

Jack's angry scowl slowly changed into a semi-smile.

"As twisted as that sounds, Tell, it actually makes some sense. . .. so, what do you suggest I do?"

Teller cocked his head, and slipping into his very best Irish brogue, rolled his tongue, "a've ye paid no attention atall to tha' sweet Lass's invitation ya twice blind wanker? She's made it plain what she wants . . . My suggestion, boy-o, is that ye *give* it to her." He grinned, his eyes shining with amusement.

The mood loosened and Jack laughed aloud.

"That seems like good advice Tell, but still, I must consider the source."

"Consider all you want, Jack," Teller smiled, "But the truth is still the truth."

Jack went quiet, and Teller, turning his attention back to the road began softly singing as he tapped his fingers on the wing vent glass.

Now the only sound in the truck's cab was that of the wind coming through open windows, punctuated by Teller's singing; and as they passed a deer crossing sign riddled with bullet holes, Jack swung the wheel hard to the right. Teller grabbed the wing vents strut to keep from sliding across the seat, and the pavement suddenly became a gravel road surrounded by thick forest. The rock beneath the tires was felt instantly and the worn suspension caused every bolt on the truck to clatter as they bounced across the dirt washboard.

Teller quit singing and turned to say something, but before he could utter a single word Jack aimed directly for a series of holes filled with dirty water. He smiled as they hit hard, splashing through the mud and rattling Teller's teeth.

"Jumpin' Jesus, Jack! Are you kiddin' me?" he hollered, "How in the hell do you plan on taking that classy woman out if you can't even afford shocks for this piece of shit!?"

Looking over, Jack stepped on the throttle and grinned maniacally. "Piece of shit, huh!?'

Teller turned to look through the brown water splattered across the windshield and saw that they were headed for a pothole the size of a Volkswagen. He pressed his hand hard against the roof of the cab to brace himself, but Jack swerved at the last moment and Teller grunted in pain as he was slammed against the door.

"Piece of shit?" Jack shouted and swerved again, splashing through a large puddle. An immense spray of dirty water splashed up and over the hood and a sense of satisfaction filled Jack's heart as Teller's shout filled the cab.

"And now we're driving fucking blind?!?!" he yelled, pounding on the roof.

Jack flicked on the wipers and they cleared two small, fan-shaped swaths of slime from the windshield.

"Hope you're enjoying the ride, smartass!" Jack hollered as he decided to kick it up a notch.

Peering through the mud-streaked glass, Jack saw a mini crater and veered towards it.

They hit the hole with such force that his head smacked the roof, knocking his sunglasses off and onto the floor. Cursing, he reached down, his fingers fumbling on the floorboards for his shades as he glanced in Teller's direction.

He could not believe what he saw.

Teller seemed to be enjoying himself!

He was braced with one foot on the dash, one hand pressed against the roof, one hand gripping the wing vent strut, and a shit-eating grin on his face.

Jack's enthusiasm dropped tenfold as they bounced down another mile of rough road; but with Jack's heart no longer in the game, Teller's amusement decreased as well. He was just about to apologize for ruining Jack's fun when Jack whipped the wheel again. The truck crashed through a wall of tall grass and onto a well-hidden drive.

Steering through five hundred yards of overgrown two-track road they came upon a rustic cabin surrounded by massive pines. Jack turned the key, the engine clattered to a stop, and a blissful hush fell over the area.

Teller hung his head out of the window.

The silence that enveloped them was like a sweet caress after that wild ride, and as birdsong returned to fill the silence he relaxed. Pulling his head back into the cab, Teller was just about to make a joke regarding Jack's driving skills when the trucks door slammed shut and Jack walked away without a word. He just went up the stairs, leaned against one of the supporting posts and stared at the truck.

Teller sat where he was, studying Jack through the streaked swath the wipers had left across the windshield. He had no idea that Jack felt so strongly about this woman. Maybe he shouldn't have been so cavalier in his actions and commentary back at the airfield.

Well, he thought, *there was nothing to be done about it now, and besides that, everything I said was true . . .*

Throwing open the door, he stepped from the cab, slung the deerskin pack over his shoulder, and made his way towards the house.

Jack stood on the porch; wondering what Teller was doing behind the muddy windshield and trying to make up his mind whether to be angry or amused at his meddling in his love life. But seeing Teller coming his way; a crooked smile on his face, his anger melted. Maybe he *was* a little oversensitive when it came to Max; and Teller *was* Teller after all . . . But as he hit the steps and saw Jack's expression, he held up his hands, palms out.

"Hey Jack, I'm sorry about the scene in the airport. I was just trying to get you to man up. I know you got hurt with the ex, and I just don't want you to be so snake-bit you won't give it another try . . ." he saw Jacks expression soften and he grinned. "Jack, that woman has class, she's gorgeous, and she obviously has exceptional taste in men. She's exactly what you need, and I was just trying to help."

Jack was surprised.

He knew in his heart that Teller wasn't trying to screw things up. But he had *never* heard him apologize. Instinctively suspicious he waited for some type of wiseass comment to follow. But the sincerity in his old friend's eyes eliminated any residual hard feelings. As difficult as Teller could be, through his actions and his attitude, he had cut right to the heart of the matter. With a shake of his head he looked at Teller and grinned. "Tell, do me a favor and don't do me any favors."

Teller grinned back, "Wouldn't dream of it, Jack."

Jacks smile vanished, and his expression went from forgiving to suspicious. "What is *that* supposed to mean?'

But Teller, true to style, changed the subject.

"So, you own this place?"

Jack knew he had lost. He jingled the ring of keys, "Yes, I do. It's one of the few things I still have from our smuggling days." He stuck the key in the lock, jiggled it a bit, swung the door open, stepped in, and started opening windows.

"Come on in," he called over his shoulder. But when he turned around, Teller was nowhere to be seen.

He went back to the porch.

Teller was sitting in the old rocking chair, gazing at the two tracks of flattened grass the truck had left. Looking back over his shoulder, he smiled.

"This is nice Jack. How many acres?"

"Hundred and twenty five. Come on in."

Teller whistled in appreciation but didn't move.

"Good for you."

Jack leaned against the doorjamb and nodded, "Yeah, it is," he smiled. But as he gazed through the trees, a thought suddenly struck him. "Wait a minute Tell, didn't you do *anything* with the money we made?"

For a few seconds the only sound was that of the rocker's rails squeaking on the wooden deck.; the Teller chuckled.

"Jaaack . . . How long have we known one another? My friend, the *only* thing I ever did with any money that crossed my palm was invest in trouble and put down payments on dreams." He looked up with a rueful smile. "That and spend a buck or two on the occasional willing wench."

"Of which there have been plenty." Jack laughed as he turned and went back into the house.

Teller rocked forward, pushed himself out of the chair, and went into the house. Pausing in the living room he heard noises coming from the kitchen.

"Of which, Jack," he called out, "money or women?"

Jack returned, holding two beers. Giving Teller a look that a father might give his favorite but wayward son, he held one out with a smile. "Both."

Taking one of the bottles, Teller grinned as a parade of women and good times scrolled unbidden through his mind,

"Sad but true, Jack, sad but true."

The hint of melancholy vanished, and he gave Jack a playful smile. "But let us not dwell on the past my friend. Mistakes were made and penalties paid."

Raising the bottle to his lips he closed his eyes, took a deep drink, and swept away the memories.

"What time do you want to leave tomorrow?"

Having known Teller for a long time, Jack was familiar with the look he had just seen cross his face, *and* the change of tone in his voice. *That* conversation was over.

Pulling up one of the high-backed kitchen chairs, Jack threw a leg over the seat. Resting his arms on the arched back, he set his chin on his crossed wrists, his bottle dangling from one hand. "What time is our meeting with 'Mr. Smith'?"

Teller leaned back. "We don't have a time, Jack. We talked about dinner but nothing is in stone. *I* say we get there, get ourselves situated, call the guy, and go from there."

Jack shook his head. "I dunno, Tell. I prefer to be the one who chooses the meeting place."

A slow grin spread across Teller's face. "Old habits die hard, huh Jack?"

"We don't know this guy, Tell."

Teller polished off his beer and stood. "Yeah, but Billy does, and that old fella strikes me as not only pretty damn smart, but reasonably cautious. And, as you may recall, he has apparently been peddling a fair amount of these coins for years with this guy as the go-between." he paused and held up his empty bottle. "Got any more of these?"

"Yeah, in the fridge. Grab me one too."

Jack heard the fridge open and close and Teller returned, setting a fresh bottle at Jack's feet as he swung a leg over his chair. "You're the one who's known Billy for a while buddy," he said, leaning forward. "and you told *me* you would trust him with your life. So, what's *your* take?"

Jack traded his empty for the one on the floor, and placed the new, full bottle between his legs. "Well, you are right on both counts. He *is* smart, and he *is* cautious. And I always wondered how the hell he got along on the little money he made at that bait store." A glint Teller had not seen in years lit Jack's eyes and he smiled. "So, yeah, I trust him."

"Well then," Teller grinned, "let's go meet Mr. Smith."

Immensely pleased by the spark in Jack's eyes, Teller raised his bottle and clinked it against Jack's.

"Here's to full circles."

Jack looked at him questioningly.

"Contraband and Tucson, Jack. Just like old times."

Jack gave a tight smile. "But *this* time, we're not handling anything illegal."

"*That* may be a debatable issue, Jack," Teller interjected.

"But at least *this* time we're dealing with a financial commodity rather than a recreational product."

"Think that'll make a difference in a court of law?"

Teller's smile was a practical one. "Depends on what caliber of attorney we retain." Reaching into his deerskin pack, he pulled out a clenched fist; and shaking it above his head, tossed out a handful of rough green stones like dice.

"And *these,* my friend, should pay for some pretty big guns."

Scooping them back up, he gave them another rattle and began dropping them back into the bag one by one.

"But let us not put the cart of misfortune before the horse, old chum! I don't believe our mythical friend has gone to all this trouble just to see me behind bars." He squinted, and for a moment it seemed he was looking past Jack and at some indefinable point in the future. But then his focus returned along with his smile. "I am fully capable of achieving that goal without the help of either Spanish gold or Coyotes. But, putting those negative thoughts aside, look at the phenomenal benefits I've reaped so far!"

Jack gave him a doubtful, but expectant gaze.

"Go on."

"Brother, come on! Since I fell off that wall and first spied that golden-eyed canine, I've reconnected with Kelly, relocated you, and I now have the wherewithal to spank James's ass. Metaphorically speaking, of course." Bouncing the pouch of stones and coins in his palm he continued.

"I have meet an Indian Chief who is considerably more than he appears; and while last, but not remotely least, have been introduced to a man who is a remarkable mixture of desert rat, magician, and historical library all rolled into one."

He paused then snapped his fingers. "That's *it*!"

Jack looked up. "What's it?"

"The restaurant where we used to eat! I met Linda Ronstadt there once and we ended up going to Sabino canyon and jumping off rocks into the creek."

"Christ, Tell. Try and keep your focus. What restaurant? and you're dating yourself."

"Fuck you," Teller laughed, "I was but a child at the time."

"Bullshit, Teller. I met you in Tucson, and you were no child then."

Teller's smile grew petulant. "Okay, I was an old child. Still am, so fuck you twice. The point is, I remember the name of the restaurant."

Jack laughed and asked, "Which is?"

"Mi Nidito."

A flash of recognition crossed across Jack's face and he nodded, "Yeah, I remember that place... Good food."

Teller stood. "Yeah, and nice booths where we can have a quiet meeting with Mr. Smith. What time do we need to leave here to be in Tucson by around one o'clock?"

Jack did his mental calculations.

"We need to leave this house by seven."

"Easy. Now, where can we get a bite to eat around here? I don't imagine your cooking has improved over the years, has it?"

Jack shook his head. "No Tell, if anything it's gotten worse. There's a pizza in the freezer."

"No thanks. How about that place we passed on the way here?"

"Jackson's? Not great, but its close."

"Fine, it'll do." Teller picked up his pack. "Where can I stash this?"

"There's a safe in the bedroom closet."

"A safe?"

Jack nodded. "Follow me."

Leading him into the bedroom, Jack opened the closet and pointed to a solid looking safe. He smiled, bent down, twirled the knob, and swung open a heavy steel door.

"Better safe than sorry." he smiled.

"Is that supposed to be a pun?"

"Yes, Teller." He took the pack from Teller's hands, tossed it in, spun the dial, closed the door, and walked out of the room.

Teller stared at the safe for a moment then followed Jack through the front door and onto the porch. But as Jack started down the stars he put a hand on his shoulder.

"So what's the combo?"

Jack grinned and fished the truck keys from his pocket.

"Not gonna tell you."

"What happens if you get killed or something, Jack?"

Jack's smile increased. "Guess you're just gonna have to make sure something like that doesn't happen to me pal."

Teller slid into the truck. "Watch your back."

Jack's smile grew. "Uh huh."

"Cover your ass."

"Yep."

"Just like old times then."

Jack twisted the ignition key.

"Yep, Teller. Just like old times."

— — -- --- -- — —

—— ——   —— ——

-- --- --

= Chapter 51 =

Abbott sat naked but for his boxers, his feet dangling from the dock that serviced Billy's store, dipping his toes in the cool water while enjoying the evening breeze that ruffled the thick hair covering his chest and shoulders.

He gazed across the massive man-made lake that lay out before him.

'Amazing . . . I'm quite sure the famous one-armed man never envisioned his namesake would come to this . . . an enormous evaporative pond in the middle of the largest desert on the continent; and all to power the lighting needs of that Las Vegas monstrosity Teller refers to as 'The wet dream of a Christmas tree.' Reaching into the cooler that sat beside him, he pulled out a cold can and chuckled, *'The man does have a way with words.'*

Sucking an ice cube from the rim of the can, he contemplated the twisted imagery of a Christmas tree's orgasm; smiling while attempting to delve into a psyche that could conceive of such a concept. His musings were shattered by the sudden sound of a powerful engine echoing from the canyon walls. From around the point and approaching rapidly, a sleek motorboat sped towards him. It was on him before he could lower his beer: and as he watched the muscular young man at the wheel cut it tight, sending a twelve-foot rooster tail up that soaked Abbott. The grinning driver brandished a bottle in his fist and hooted as his girlfriend raised her T-shirt, flashing a lovely set of breasts, and they were gone.

Abbott waved as they skipped across the water.

'And now nothing more than a massive playground for the future leaders of America.' He sighed as he shook the water from his curly head.

Just the night before, he and Billy had sat and conversed into the wee hours discussing this very body of water.

They had not only discussed the environmental damage created by the dam's construction, but the hundreds of native families that were displaced by the filling of a thousand fairy-tale canyons. Abbott was in full agreement with Billy on all counts, although his concerns leaned more towards the thousands of archeological sites that lay beneath these waters, while Billy's grief was tied directly to his ancestors, and the desecration of the earth and her rivers... The dogma of Manifest Destiny aside, the white man had most certainly fucked up a huge chunk of real estate in record time.

'Change comes quickly, Abbott thought as he pushed himself up, *and evolution comes in many forms. The Dinosaurs were wiped out by a single space rock while the original human inhabitants of this continent were decimated by greed and a sense of righteousness that was exceeded only by cruelty and ignorance.'* And as he looked out across the great expanse of water he considered the disparity of weaponry throughout history.

'The sonsabitches had technology on their side, they just mistook it for God.'

The boat sped by again, and drunken laughter could be heard above the screaming of the engine. Abbott shook his head. *'And **that** is the sound of the next extinction.*

Slipping on his pants, Abbott set the cooler on his shoulder and started walking towards the store.

'I wonder if Kelly's heard from Teller yet?'

— — ── ── — —

— — — __ — —

── ── ──

271

= Chapter 52 =

Kelly picked up the phone.

"Hello?"

"Hi Kelly, this is Abbott."

Her face lit up. "Abbott!! How are you?"

"I'm good. I was just wondering if you've heard from Teller?"

He could hear the deflated tone in her response. "No, I haven't, but I'm glad you called, where are you?"

Abbott was now sitting comfortably in the shade of the porch, rocking. But with his beer attached to his lip, it took a moment for him to answer. He swallowed and lowered the can.

"I'm still down here at Billy's."

Snuggling back into an overstuffed chair, Kelly looked across the valley. "I'm envious. So *you've* heard nothing either?"

A low, rumbling laugh came over the phone. "No, but I suppose it's a little early to worry, he only left yesterday... He hasn't had much time to get into any trouble."

The chiming laughter that came across the line lightened his heart. "Oh, Abbott, you have *no* idea how much trouble that man can get himself into, or how little time it takes. I assume he left with Jack?"

"Why, yes he did."

"Then he'll probably be fine. So where did our wandering hero fly off too?"

"Tucson."

"Tucson? Why Tucson??"

"Well, I guess Billy has a contact down there. Someone who can help him with those coins."

Kelly's voice gained enthusiasm. "Really??" a long pause followed, and Abbott was about to ask if she was still on the line when her voice came back, quietly this time.

"Do you think it's all real, Abbott?'

He stopped rocking. "What do you mean?"

Tucking her feet under the couch cushions, she picked up her glass, swirled the deep red liquid, frowning as the fluid distorted the clarity of the glass.

"This whole thing. I mean, coyotes, gold and rubies?"

"Emeralds," he corrected.

The casualness of his amendment lightened her concern and drew her attention away from the dark image of wine red as blood sliding down the sides of her glass.

"Okay. Emeralds then."

"Yes..." Abbott smiled, shaking his beer can he lowered it; staring as if its emptiness was a personal affront. He had forgotten what thirsty work talking to women was.

"Hang on, Kelly. I'll be right back."

Rocking forward, he set the phone on the seat and walked into the store.

His passage set the little bell above the door to tinkling sweetly, its sounds still filling the store as Abbott opened the foggy glass door of the wall cooler.

Sticking his head in he took a deep, invigorating breath of the frigid air, letting the cold organize his thoughts. Feeling clearer, he grabbed a six-pack and went back into the heat to resume the conversation. The little bell tinkled again as he took his place in his chair, settling back and securing the phone between his ear and shoulder to open a cold can.

"I'm back. So, how are things up there with James?"

"Uncomfortable," Kelly answered, "and don't change the subject."

Abbott started the chair rocking. "Alright Kelly, since you asked, here are my feelings on Teller's story. I *know* that it is true, and the events most definitely real. I was there, as were you, when he walked into camp. And I'm quite sure that you know more than I regarding the events preceding his arrival."

He paused and waited; but receiving no response, took a deep drink and continued.

"I was also the one who accompanied him on our search for the boy and witnessed firsthand the type of man that he is. And I assure you, it is one of remarkable qualities." He waited again, but the line remained silent.

Counting to ten, he asked, "Are you still there Kelly?"

Her voice came back; clear, yet the tone had changed.

"Yes Abbott, I'm still here, and I agree wholeheartedly."

Noting the subtle shift, he asked, "are you alright?"

"Yes, just trying to put this all into perspective."

At that, Abbott chuckled.

"And that is *exactly* what this is all about Kelly. Perspective.

—— —— ▬▬ ▬▬▬ ▬▬ —— ——
—— —— ▬▬ ▬▬ ——
▬▬ ▬▬▬ ▬▬

= Chapter 53 =

Teller watched as the rugged country of the Mogollon Rim passed beneath them: The White Mountains to their south, The San Francisco Peaks behind.

He turned his attentions to Jack who was grinning like a kid in a sandbox full of toys.

"Flyin' puts a whole different perspective on things doesn't it?" Teller smiled as he gazed through the glass.

Jack nodded. "That's why I never gave up the habit."

Teller's grin diminished slightly. "Well at least this habit won't kill you."

"Only if we fall out of the sky," Jack said, dipping fast and hard just to put Teller off balance. But to his annoyance, Teller remained unfazed; calmly looking at the convoluted land that spread beneath them. He did, however, turn his head and offer Jack a steady gaze. "You can't scare me, Jack, it's not our time to die." But his momentary seriousness vanished as quickly as it had arrived. "Hey, have you thought yet what you're going to do with your share of the loot?"

Jack grumbled in frustration, glanced at his watch, and made a slight correction to their heading.

Teller grinned. "Come on Jack, you can't avoid the question forever." His smile increased "Look, you're blushing!"

"Bullshit!" Jack barked. Then he growled, "I just haven't thought about it." But sneaking a sideways look at Teller's face he was undone by the twinkle in his eyes. He softened and smiled, "Well, I *have* thought about it a little…"

With some minor trepidation, Jack confessed his reoccurring fantasy of buzzing topless babes on bouncy rafts through the Grand Canyon in a brand new, blind your eyes shiny, never been a bug on the windshield, helicopter.

Teller looked at Jack for a moment, saying nothing: and in that moment, Jack began to regret the confession. But then Teller's eyes lit up, and a smile of glowing admiration spread across his face. Clapping his hands, he began laughing joyfully. "That's perfect! That's spectacular! That's a goal well worth pursuing! Jack my friend, color me impressed!"

Unable to stop his chuckling, Teller dug out two of the cups that Kelly had provided, poured coffee into one, and handed it to Jack. Filling the other for himself, he added a packet of sugar that he had taken from the airport coffee shop the day before and stirring it in with his finger, lifted the Styrofoam cup in salute.

"That's why I love you, Jack. You set realistic, achievable goals designed to satisfy the inner man."

Taking a sip, he lowered the cup. "Wait, I get to ride along, right?"

Jack set the craft on autopilot. "Only if you give *me* that sweetened coffee."

"You drive a hard bargain lad," Teller shrugged, "but it seems a fair trade." They swapped cups, and Teller raised this cup of comparatively bitter coffee into the air.

"Here's to sleek aircraft, realized dreams, and hard nipples glistening in the sun."

Jack gave a slow shake of his head and took a sip of the steaming liquid. "As usual Teller, your prosaic imagery is only exceeded by your poor taste."

Teller just grinned. "Screw you, Hawkins. I taste fine, you just haven't licked me recently."

His eyes crinkling behind his shades, Jack broke into a heartfelt smile. "I rest my case . . .."

"Good." Teller nodded. "And keep your tongue to yourself."

As Jack's chuckling laughter faded and the cabin fell silent, each man focusing on the particulars that concerned him at the moment.

Teller's thoughts had passed from the beauty of the landscape spread out below; absorbed now in the glory of Jack's dream, and on the meeting that was to take place in a few hours. This theoretically involved a great deal of money, and he was uncomfortable in dealing with someone he had never met. Teller had never been fond of blind deals. The only saving grace here was that the contact was a trusted friend of Billys. But more importantly, he had Jack watching his back.

Meanwhile, over in the pilot's seat, Jack stared through the mirrored lenses of his aviator shades thinking how completely his future had changed the moment he had picked up the nearly drowned boy on Lake Powell.

'I should have known when I flew into Durango and began thinking about Teller he would somehow manifest back into my life... he and that coyote have more in common than he realizes.'

As if on cue, Teller turned, studying Jack, all previous humor absent.

"Jack, tell me the truth. Were you really surprised when I called?"

The question pulled Jack from his own contemplations.

"Funny you should ask that."

Wrapping one hand around the cup, and the other one the control stick, he shifted his body towards Teller and sighed.

"Brother, the truth is that *nothing* surprises me when it comes to you. Altho' I gotta admit that when I heard your voice on the phone it sure wasn't what I expected."

Teller leaned back and put his hands behind his head.

"Yeah, I guess I had the advantage on that one. At least *I* knew who I was calling."

He lifted his stocking feet and pressed them against the windshield. "Well my friend, let us allow fate's fickle finger to tickle our ivories. I'm ready to sing!"

Jack blinked. "What in the *hell* are you talking about?"

Teller leaned his head back against the seat and closed his eyes. "Just feelin' like God's piano. Jeez man, show some imagination."

Jacks retort was instantaneous. "I'm not short on imagination Tell, I'm trying to decipher your cryptic bullshit."

Teller rolled his head towards Jack and opened one eye.

"It's the Coyote's will, Jack. Don't you see? Our accidental, yet fortuitous crossing of paths is going to make all of your wonderful dreams a reality! Just keep thinking wet, bouncy, nekkid girls." He waggled his eyebrows, grinned, and began to sing an impromptu song:

'Oh, the river is fast,
And so are the women,
So let's kick off our skivvies and commence us to swimmin',
with nothin' but bare skin and sun-shine how can we be blue?
Well, the nipples get hard and the peckers they shrink,
So break out the rum and let's have us a drink, Oh there's
nothing in this whole wide world that we cannot dooooo
When the dreams of my old friend Jack, they all come true!'

Teller paused and cocked his head, waiting for a response.

"Come on, Jacko! Just 'cause you don't know the words don't mean you can't sing along!" come on! a one, and a two, and a . . ."

Jack couldn't help it. He shook his head in surrender.

"I love ya Tell."

Picking up the rhythm, song filled the cockpit.

— — -- --- -- — —
— — — — —
-- --- --

278

Chapter 54

"It's a little more than just perspective, Abbott."

"No, not at all Kelly. If there is one thing my excursion with Teller has taught me, it is that *everything* is perspective. I just didn't realize *how* true it was until we were sitting on the canyon wall the day we left you and the crew with the raft and went searching for Ben. But as we sat up there looking down at you, Teller laughed and said, "They look like ants.""

Getting no response, he continued.

"At the time, I just thought it was his odd sense of humor."

At that Kelly laughed. "That does not even *remotely* represent how odd his sense of humor can be."

Abbott gave a full-throated chuckle. "I realize that now, but at the time, I just shrugged it off as an irreverent comment."

He took a long drink. "Now, however, and after traveling with the man, I'm beginning to realize that he has a true grasp of the enormity of perspective."

"Interesting phrasing."

There was a tinkle of a bell, followed by a smiling voice.

"Say hello to the little Miss!"

Abbott swiveled towards the screen door only to see Billy's dark face vanish, leaving only the image of a brilliant smile; and as the smile faded into the shadows, it reminded Abbott of the Cheshire Cat , finally disappearing as the door wheezed shut.

"What was that?" Kelly asked.

"Just Billy. He says "hello.""

Her voice brightened again. "Oh! Tell him hi!"

"I will. Now, where were we?" Abbott squinted back towards the screen door, expecting Billy to pop back through.

"Oh yes, perspective. What the Captain has forced me to realize is that we tend to judge everything from where we view it at the time."

Kelly refilled her wine glass. "That's no earth-shattering revelation."

No, of course it isn't!" Abbot replied tersely. "Nevertheless, it *is* what we do, and consequently our assumptions are repeatedly wrong. And *that* is simply due to our not having the proper perspective."

He elaborated his point at the sound of Kelly's sigh.

"You see, Kelly, y*ou* are making the assumption that the Coyote cannot be real because you're looking at it from *your* twentieth-century perspective. However, this cell phone we're talking on right now would be equally difficult to accept if you were a Navajo shaman living eight hundred years ago. Different worlds require different beliefs."

Kelly spoke up. "I don't see how that's the same thing at all, Abbott. Things change."

Abbott smiled. He was just warming up.

"It is *exactly* the same thing, Kelly, because things *do* change. The natives who lived in Cibola during the decimation of the Aztecs a few thousand miles to the South were completely unaware that they lived in Cibola. For *them* the name of that same village was Hawikuh. And to the Kings of Spain, who had only recently been made aware of this 'New World,' chose to send conquering armies across an uncharted ocean to the shores of a land filled with people who had no idea that their world was 'new,' and whom could not possibly foresee the unspeakable horrors these brutes would unleash upon them." He paused, crushed his empty can in empathy, and yanked the top off of another.

"And the Spanish, who saw their actions as destiny enforced by God's will, exhibited a level of greed beyond anything that the natives of this 'new' continent could possibly conceive. And all of this over an entirely different sense of values placed on shiny metals, and a belief in a different God!

You see, Kelly, this was the destruction of one world, and the raising of another on its ashes. All on the same globe, and at the same time . . . Who was right? Who was wrong? Each event took place, the results were the same, and each was viewed by the participants through a difference in perspective."

Abbott took a long, angry pull on his beer.

"And *our* opinion of right or wrong on this long-dead event is simply based on *our* perspective."

He paused, waiting for his pulse to return to normal.

"Abbott..." Kelly responded, "it's not hard to figure out who was wrong with *that* one."

"Yes, Kelly, *I* fully agree. I was simply making a point. Perspective can be deceiving, that's all."

At that moment, Billy walked back through the door, gave a nod of greeting, and took a seat. Abbott nodded in return.

Kelly's voice came back, "So you're saying that this whole coyote thing of Teller's is real?"

Abbott glanced at Billy, then returned is attentions to Kelly.

"What I'm saying, is that the *Coyote* certainly thinks so."

There was complete silence on the other end.

Billy leaned forward in his chair and motioned Abbott to hand him the phone. Abbott complied, and Billy spoke gently.

"I think, Miss Kelly, is that what our friend Abbott is trying to say, is that Teller is in good company, and will be fine."

Kelly's anxiety dissolved at the sound of his voice.

"Do you really think so?"

"Yes I do." He gave Abbott a reassuring smile and turned his attention to the telephone. "I have had some experience myself with Ma'ii over these many years past, and I can assure you that although he is sometimes painfully mischievous, he is never malevolent. His methods are his own, and he cares not if we understand them. He will play until he is tired of the game, or until the game is done. Either way, your Teller is in the center of it, and will be dependent on both his wits and his luck." He paused and gave a warm laugh. "And he strikes me as a man with an abundance of both."

Abbott silently raised his can and gave a smile of full agreement.

"Thank you, Billy," Kelly said softly. "I find that strangely reassuring. Although I may know nothing of this Coyote, I believe *you*, and I trust Abbott." She exhaled slowly, her heart growing warm. "And I *do* know Teller. He may be reckless, but he is a smart, and *extremely* lucky man."

Billy laughed. "That is a combination that would attract Coyote's attention. Goodbye for now Miss Kelly." Passing Abbott the phone, Abbott brought it slowly to his ear.

"Hello?"

"Thank you too, Abbott."

"For what?"

Kelly settled back into the couch, more relaxed now than she had been in days. "For everything."

A faint blush colored Abbott's cheeks, and he stammered. "But I've done nothing."

Kelly's voice grew playful. "Don't be modest you big bear. Teller said he couldn't have done this without you, and he thinks *very* highly of you. He told me how you hunted for food when you were both hungry… oh, and how you had to convince him to eat lizard. Yuck!"

Abbott's eyes widened. "He told you that?"

"Yes, and killing a six-foot rattlesnake for dinner? That was very brave."

Abbott shook his head in amusement and a grin snuck through his whiskers.

"That bastard . . .."

= Chapter 55 =

Teller watched Mount Lemmon grow closer.

Rising from the haze that blanketed Tucson, he had always been impressed by the way the ragged peak jutted out of the saguaro cactus; climbing into the sky: changing its desert finery for scrub oak and wildflowers, and, as the air cooled, pines and fir. As he admired the view, Jack checked instruments and talked to the tower. A few minutes of pilot chatter later Jack turned. "We're cleared to land buddy," He said, looking over his shades. "Another ten minutes."

"Good." Teller grumbled, stretching as best he could in the cramped cabin.

Pulling his headset away from one ear, Jack asked, "So, when's our meeting?"

"Haven't set a solid time yet Jack," Teller answered, "I had no real idea as to when we'd arrive in town. I'll give the guy a call once we're on the ground and have a car. I'm thinking we may as well get a room and spend the night. I see no point in getting right back in the air. I have no pressing appointments."

Jack shrugged. "Nor do I, partner, I say let's get us a room and discuss our strategy."

"Great minds think alike." Teller nodded.

Jack adjusted his shades, "You flatter yourself, Tell."

Teller gave a wry smile. "No Jack, I'm including *you* into my rarefied class of talent."

Jack bowed his head slightly. "Well then, I acquiesce, and feel both humbled and honored to be included in such lofty company."

"Think nothing of it, old son," Teller grinned, "just try to recognize a compliment next time one comes around."

"Duly noted," Jack smiled, and clicked the radio back on.

283

~

They were given a space near the Southwest Heli Services office and upon landing, Jack went inside to introduce himself and make the necessary arrangements. While Jack took care of the paperwork, Teller went outside, took a seat on a low brick wall, and dialed information.

Thirty minutes later, Jack joined him.

"Any luck?"

"Yeah. Hey Jack, remember an old song, Holiday Inn?"

Jack rested his hand on Teller's shoulder, "Tell, I don't have my life filed into bits and pieces of songs like you do."

Teller gave a sniff of insult and 'Tsk'd' as he handed Jack his phone. "They're simply musical reference points, Jack... like some people with their photographs. Anyway, it's an old Elton John tune, and if you're not familiar with it then the whole 'cold French fries' thing will be lost on you, so just forget it."

"Didn't mean to hurt your feelings." Jack smiled.

Teller shook his head in mock disappointment. "Alas Jack, 'tis you, not I, who are the poorer man. Musical ignorance leaves a deep hole in one's soul." He stood and started walking towards the street, leaving Jack still seated on the wall.

Teller's frequent non-sequiturs often left Jack feeling as if he had missed some part of the conversation; and as Teller walked away he felt it anew. Frustrated, he remained a minute longer, struggling to recall the tune: but short of vaguely remembering the title, failed. With a sigh, he jumped up, catching Teller as he stood on the corner, whistling happily and waiting for the 'walk' signal to change.

Sidling up to him, Jack asked. "So, what's your point?"

Teller pressed the walk button a second time. "My point, Jack, is that there is a Holiday Inn about a block away if you're in the mood for a non-descript, generic room and an order of fries. That is if room service ain't closed."

Jack glanced at his watch. "It's not even two o'clock, why would room service be closed?"

Teller cast an eye to the heavens. "Just forget it, Jack."

The sign continued to blink 'Don't walk' but Teller threw his arm over Jacks shoulder and pulled him off of the sidewalk and into the noise of the rushing automobiles; and, as he drug him along, he shouted over the blaring horns and squealing brakes, "If I have to explain the relationship of the event to the song lyrics, it negates the impact and imagery of the whole thing. Let's just get the room, locate a bar, and find a rent-a-car."

They were nearly across the street when an oncoming delivery van made a screeching swerve around them, the driver hurling an imaginative combination of obscenities as he flew by. Grinning as he pulled Jack to the curb, Teller looked to his left where an illuminated sign with the immediately recognizable Holiday Inn logo shone; the 'vacancy' brightly lit. Touching the side of his nose and raising his eyebrows, Teller performed a quite passable W.C. Fields impression.

"How fortuitous..." He smiled. Then, dropping the impression, tugged on Jack's sleeve. "Come on Jack, we got places to go and people to do. Our financial future rests on a meeting only a few hours away. It's time to call Mr. Smith."

Leading Jack through the front doors and into the lobby, Teller sang quietly: *"Oh, I don't even know if it's Cleveland or Maine . . .."*

Jack, still shaken from the street crossing followed him to the front desk, where he stood silently as a perky young woman in a green blazer looked up and smiled.

"Can I help you?"

"More than you might know," Teller winked. "But in the meantime, we would like a room."

She let the innuendo hang for a moment, her eyes resting on Jack as the tip of her tongue touched her lightly painted lips.

"King bed or double?"

"Which do *you* prefer?"

"Pardon me?"

Teller's smile remained. "King or Queen, which would you like?"

Somewhat less than demure, she answered, "I prefer King."

"Than King it is!" Teller said, smacking the desktop lightly.

"And make that two rooms, King beds in both, please."

With a sparkle in his eyes, he put his hand on Jack's back and nudged him towards the desk. "Jack, I'd like you to meet," He paused, glancing down at the nametag that nestled atop the impressive cleavage that stretched the buttons of her white blouse.

"Patty..." he grinned.

Taking out his wallet, Teller slid a credit card across the marble countertop and pulled Jack closer to the counter.

"Patty, this is my good friend Jack, who is about to become a *very* wealthy man." Leaning in for dramatic effect he whispered, "*and* he has his own helicopter."

Patty's smile grew much larger.

Giving Jack a solid slap on the back, he smiled, "I'm going to grab a beer, amigo, I think you can handle things from here." But before walking away, he looked at the pretty young desk clerk and asked, "What time do you get off work?"

"Ten-thirty."

Teller gave her his most winning smile. "Well then, Patty, Jack here will have a fine bottle of Scotch, a king bed, and coincidentally be celebrating his coming into a great deal of money around eleven. Feel free to come up and join him if you are so inclined." He turned to go, and Patty spoke up, her voice sexy, yet wistful. "What about you?"

Teller spun, and walking backwards smiled at the two of them. "Alas, dear girl, I've other obligations that will keep me into the wee hours, but please, feel free to carry on without me." Throwing a peace sign to Jack, he laughed, "See ya in the bar." Spinning on one heel, he pushed open the heavy door and disappeared into the shadows of the dark room.

= Chapter 56 =

The wall behind the bar lit up as Jack opened the door, stepped in and stood perfectly still as he allowed his eyes to adjust to the darkness. The door swung closed behind him. And Teller, responding to the light swiveled on his stool, waved, and returned to his conversation with the tall, well-groomed gentleman sporting a pencil thin mustache. The fellow leaned in: apparently enraptured with Teller's story.

Jack slid onto the seat next to Teller just as he finished with,

"And *that's* the difference between a sister and a nun."

The bartender sucked in a breath and sputtered, "That's terrible!" as he burst into laughter. Still snickering, he looked at over at Jack. Teller nodded and twirled a finger over the bartop.

the bartender dropped a coaster in front of Jack and shook his head. "Your friend has a very strange sense of humor." He smiled, placing a glass filled with amber liquid on the coaster and chuckling as he walked away.

"MaCallan do?" Teller grinned.

Giving a nod of approval Jack took a sip, followed by a big smile. "Yessss . . ." then setting the glass down, he tipped his head back towards the lobby.

"But what was *that* all about?"

"Nothing, really." Teller grinned. "Just corrupting young minds." He lifted his empty bottle and pointed it at the bartender. "Hey Terry, I'll take another."

Terry set down the glass he was polishing and smiled.

"Sure thing Teller."

Jack looked at his friend inquisitively but Teller just shrugged and sang, "I've got friends in looow places."

Jack brought his fingertips to his forehead. "This is *not* starting well . . ."

Picking up the glass, he tried again. "No Teller, what I meant was-" Teller held up his hand; swiveling his stool so he faced Jack. "I assume you're talking about the pretty girl at the desk?"

"Yes, Teller, *that* is what I meant."

Picking up the fresh bottle Terry had just set on a fresh coaster, Teller looked into Jack's eyes.

"Are you one hundred percent onboard with me on this whole thing?"

Jack was first surprised, then slightly offended.

"Of course I am, Tell!"

"Good." Teller clinked his bottle against Jack's glass of Scotch. "Then consider Patty onboard entertainment."

"What...?"

"Jack. She's a big girl. She'll either show up at your room or she won't . . . all *I* did was plant the seed of potential."

Reaching into his pocket, he took out one of the gold coins and slapped it on the bar. "But I'll bet you this," he said, tapping it with a forefinger. "That she's knocking on your door by eleven thirty." He cocked his head and raised his eyebrows.

"Well?"

Scooping up the coin, Jack bounced it in his palm.

"I'll take that bet," he said, slipping the coin into his pocket. "Either way I win."

Teller's smile faltered. "Wait a second partner. If she shows you gotta give that back! That's why it's called a *bet.*"

Jack finished his drink, shaking the ice as he smiled, "Fat chance . . .."

The light in Teller's eyes returned, and he motioned Terry for two more drinks.

"Now you're in the game, son! But you're using the title to *my* song."

"What? That's against the rules?"

Teller laughed and slapped Jack on the back. 'Hell no! For that you get bonus points! Keep the coin, Hawkins, you're right. Either way you win."

As the two men sat chuckling, Terry wiped the spot in front of them and set down fresh drinks. Teller handed him a twenty and turned back to Jack.

"Give me your phone, amigo, it's time to call our destiny."

Jack took the phone from the pocket of his flight jacket.

"I thought you didn't believe in destiny."

"No Jack," Teller smiled, "I don't believe in *destinations*. They have a habit of getting in the way of the journey."

While Jack pondered the statement, Teller took a piece of paper from his shirt pocket, spun the stool in a circle and dialed.   A few minutes of muffled conversation followed: then Teller swiveled back to hand Jack back his phone.

"Okay, amigo, dinner's set for seven."

Jack glanced at his watch. "That gives us about an hour and a half." Teller nodded and turned back to the bar.

"Hey Terry, got any recommendations for a rent-a-car?"

The bartender shrugged, "They're all about the same."

Teller laid a fifty on the bar. "Yeah, that's what I thought. So who's the nearest?"

"Enterprise is across the street."

"Well, that's convenient." Teller nodded, turning to Jack.

"Hang here amigo, I'll go take care of the car."

Teller spun off of his stool; but as he did Terry stepped up to the bar. He was a little shy, but felt emboldened after watching the two men's interaction.

"Wait a sec, Teller, you seem like a guy who might appreciate old cars."

That got Teller's attention.

Returning to his stool, he rested his elbows on the bar and leaned towards Terry. "Yesss?" he smiled.

Tongue-tied by Teller's steady gaze, the young man picked up a glass and began polishing nervously. But Teller, not being the patient type, reached out and laid two fingers on Terry's arm. Terry ceased the buffing immediately.

"Don't keep me in suspense young son. Why do you ask?"

Lowering the glass, Terry looked up into Tellers eyes. He was still nervous, but Teller's gaze was calming.

"Well, my Grandfather died a few months ago and left me his old car. I'm no mechanic, and I've got two daughters . . ."

Teller smiled. "You have my deepest sympathies."

It took a moment, but Terry chuckled and continued,

"Thanks, but they're only eight and nine."

"Then I'll offer my commiserations ten years in advance." Teller grinned.

That broke the ice. Terry gave a heartfelt laugh.

"Anyway, he left me this old Buick. I was going to sell it and put the money into a savings account for the kid's college fund... do you think you might be interested?"

Teller stood straight. "That all depends on the car. What is it?"

"I'm not sure. It's been sitting in his garage for the past three years." His eyes dropped, and his voice held a note of sorrow. "He hardly ever drove it once my Grandmother died."

He began buffing the glass again as he talked.

"It's a huge thing with a big grill. A convertible if I recall correctly . . . a road something or other."

A smile lit his face and he looked up from his buffing.

"God, he loved that car."

Teller raised his brows; "Roadmaster?"

Terry snapped his fingers. "Yeah! That's it!"

"Do you remember anything else about it?"

Terry thought about it for a moment. "Well, when I was a kid he would let me sit in his lap and steer . . . the thing had a steering wheel like a hula hoop."

Teller was excited at the prospect, but still cautious.

"Does it run?"

The young man shrugged again.

"Don't know. It did when he died. But like I said, it's sat in that garage for the past three years."

Teller reached across the bar and wrapped his hand around Terry's wrist, putting a stop to the nervous buffing.

"Terry, if the car is what I think it is, you've got a buyer. And don't worry. I'll give you a fair price. But if you're trying to scam me," a spark flared behind Teller's eyes but quickly passed and his smile returned. "But we just don't have the time right now. Listen... we're staying here in the hotel. Give Jack here your phone number and I'll give you a call tomorrow. In the meantime, pour another drink for my friend while I go rent some more immediate form of transport. Jack, what time is it now?"

"A little after four."

"Cool. I'll go get a car, take a shower, and meet you back here at six thirty." He got up and walked through a door in the back with a sign above it lit in green reading: "exit".

The bar lit up as the door swung open, then went dark as it wheezed closed. Both men watched him go; and as Terry placed a fresh drink in front of Jack, he asked, "Is he always like this?"

"This what?"

"This easy to get along with."

Jack tipped his cap back. "Only when things go his way." Taking a deep sip of his Scotch he smiled. "Which seems to be a surprising amount of the time."

— — ‗‗ ‗‗‗ ‗‗ — —
— — — ‗ — —
‗‗ ‗‗‗ ‗‗

= Chapter 57 =

"What's that supposed to mean?"

Abbott stumbled over the question.

"What?"

Kelly tucked her toes further under the couch cushions.

"What do you mean; 'that bastard?'"

"Slip of the tongue, Kelly."

"Dear, sweet Abbott." Kelly laughed. "I know how full of shit Teller can be, and I also know that the guy is like a real-life MacGyver when it comes to tight situations. So, knowing him, I kind of figured that he was the one who did the hunting."

"And most of the cooking," Abbott added.

There was a pause; and in that moment of silence Abbott heard the tinkle of ice against crystal as she laughed lightly.

"No surprise."

Abbott felt the need to defend himself, but before he could work out how, he heard the ringing of a phone in the background. "Hang on a minute," Kelly said. "Let me get that."

He heard her lay the phone down, then heard her muffled voice in the background; and although the individual words were indecipherable the tone was unmistakable. Feeling more uncomfortable with each passing moment, he was considering hanging up when she came back on the line.

"I'm back."

"Who was that?"

"That was James."

He could feel the resentment in her voice.

"He wants me to meet with some attorney to discuss the signing over of Teller's shares. And just the way he was talking

292

I can tell that he up to something. I can fully understand what Teller meant when he said that James is a great businessman, but a brutal business partner.

Abbott was at a loss. What advice could *he* give? And so he gave her the only advice that came to mind. "All I can suggest is that you not sign anything until you talk to Teller."

"No shit!!" She snapped. It had sprung from her lips quickly and was immediately followed with, "I'm sorry Abbott, I didn't mean that."

She couldn't see but as he said, "I know." he smiled, and reaching down to the floor, found that he had only one beer left. *Damn . . .* Hang on Kelly, I need to take care of something."

That something was getting more beer. Popping the last can in preparation he took a swig, got up from the rocker, went into the store and headed directly for the cooler where he stood in front of the frosty glass doors.

Holding his open beer in one hand, he tucked the phone carefully between his ear and his shoulder, reached out, and grabbed the cold steel handle. Unfortunately, not only was the seal tighter than expected, the condensation on the handle made it slippery as well. His hand slipped from the cold steel, his shoulder dropped, and the phone fell from his ear.

Automatically reaching out to catch it before it hit the ground his arm clipped the protruding tip of a rotating rack of miscellaneous goodies; spinning and knocking the beer from his grasp where it fell with a crash at the same time the beer hit the floor and exploded at his feet. Looking down at the bags of snacks scattered about and the liquid pooling at the soles of his boots, all the frustration of the past few weeks burst forth.

"Great puckered assholes!" he shouted. "It seems I'm fucked again!"

Billy was at the cash register bagging some snack items for an older couple that were down from Maine hoping to catch a few fish. But at the sound of the crash and Abbott's odd expletive, everything stopped and the three of them turned slowly to stare at Abbott.

The old man's jaw hung loose, while his wife stood unblinking, her eyes big as saucers; while Billy, struggling not to laugh kept bagging the groceries.

Poor Abbott stood motionless and embarrassed.

In the ensuing silence, Kelly's muted voice could be heard shouting from the phone that lay somewhere on the linoleum.

"Abbott . . . Abbott!! What happened!?"

The seconds ticked by... finally, with a mortified shrug, Abbott picked up the still foaming beer, put it to his lips, and drained the remains of the can: and refusing to look over at the counter, set the empty on the floor, stepped on it, then got down on all fours and began searching for the phone.

It had come to rest beneath the potato chip rack.

The couple at the counter were still rigid with shock; but Billy just chuckled. "Don't worry 'bout him folks. "He shrugged, "that's just Ole' Crazy Joe, Uranium prospector from up in the Henrys. Must have lost his mule." He smiled and handed them their change.

The couple gave Billy a dazed nod as if that explained everything; then turning, walked through door and into the shade of the porch; and as they went down the steps and out to their car, Billy heard the old woman say in thick New England accent, "Whye, I'hve never heud such language!"

To which the husband responded, "I *know* Mahtha, its the heat . . . does crazy things to the people out heah."

Meanwhile Abbott, having fished his phone from beneath the chips, stood the rack back up, re-clipped the snacks to the display, and ambled over to the counter where he stood beside Billy and watched the couple hustle the grandkids into the car and drive off in a cloud of dust.

Abbott turned to Billy. "Couldn't find that mule."

Billy looked at Abbott, held for a moment, and burst into laughter as Kelly's voice screamed from the phone in his hand:

"ABBOTT!"

Abbott gave a guilty look and brought the phone up to his ear. "Sorry, Kelly, I had a minor mishap."

"God, it sounded like you got hit by a truck!"

Abbott shook his head. "Naa, I got hit by a gravity storm."

There was a pause, and the tension left her voice. "Sounds like one of Teller's lines."

"Yeah," Abbott chuckled, "he used it on me when I jumped and hurt my ankle. He said he stole it from Jimmy somebody."

She laughingly asked, "Are you alright then?"

"I will be in a beer or two."

Hearing that, she relaxed and her voice came back, warm and reassuring. "If that's all you need, then you're fine."

Abbott pressed the phone between his ear and shoulder as he reached into his pocket and pulled out his wallet.

"Hold on a sec, Kelly."

Looking at Billy, he started counting ones out on the countertop. "How much do I owe you?"

Billy held up his hands, palms out.

"No Abbott. Teller said I was not to charge you for beer."

Abbott quit counting. "He said *what?*"

Billy smiled as he pushed back the bills.

"Teller said the beer was on him. He told me to tell you that you could consider it his version of the never empty cooler trick." He looked slightly perplexed, but the smile remained.

"He said you would understand."

Abbott stuffed the crumpled bills back in his pocket and smiled a huge smile. "That *bastard*."

Kelly's voice buzzed directly into Abbott's ear from the phone that rested on his shoulder.

"*Now* what?!?"

— — -- --- -- — —
— — — — —
-- --- --

= Chapter 58 =

Teller led Jack to a booth in the back of the restaurant. The two large bench seats were a deep red vinyl separated by an off-white table edged in chrome. Teller slid in, his back against the whitewashed wall. Red brick was visible in places where the rough stucco had been strategically removed in order to simulate an 'old hacienda' effect.

"Why the booth in the back?" Jack asked.

Teller smiled, but his eyes held no humor. "Tough for the enemy to get away quickly if there's any problem."

"Expecting trouble?"

"No," Teller countered, "Just naturally cautious."

Jack's head bobbed in agreement.

"So, how are we supposed to recognize this Mr. Smith?"

Teller had no time to respond. A cute waitress stepped up and set a tray of water glasses on the edge of the table.

"Just the two of you?" she smiled.

"No," teller smiled back, "one more will be joining us."

"Very well." She nodded, setting a menu in front of Jack; but as she placed Teller's menu her fingertips rested lightly on the back of his hand: and while she smiled at them both, its warmth lingered on Teller.

"My name's Susan and I'll be your server this evening. Would you like something to drink?"

Teller responded to her touch with a sly smile. "Very well, Susan, and yes we would. Would you please me bring a Negra Modello and a frosted glass?"

He glanced at Jack. "You?"

Jack sighed and held up two fingers. "Make it two."

Susan gave a perky waitress smile. "Alright! I'll be right back with those." She walked away, her skirt swaying.

Jack shook his head. "How do you do it?"

Teller's attention was on Susan's hips as she stepped up to the bar. He smiled, blinked, and turned to Jack. "Do what?"

Jack tipped his head in the bars direction. "That."

Both men looked back across the room to see Susan leaning shoulder to shoulder with another waitress. Words passed between them, and the two women turned towards their table. Susan whispered into her friend's ear, and instantaneously that indefinable, mysterious smile that women share spread across both faces. Susan's friend gave them a wink and turned back to the bar.

Teller scooted into the corner of the booth, kicked his feet up across the bench and smiled. "I don't know partner, but it bothers Kelly too."

"Yes, Teller I'm quite sure it does," Jack sighed, "but it bothers me for significantly different reasons."

Amusement shone in Teller's eyes and he leaned forward.

"What are you complaining about son? By eleven thirty tonight *you* will be entertaining a beautiful, buxom young lady; drinking champagne from her doubtlessly sweet chalice, whilst I, on the other hand, will be alone with my other hand. No sir, Mr. Hawkins, I shall tolerate no complaints from you tonight." He lifted his beer to finalize the statement, and as he did, he saw Susan point a tall and deeply tanned man in their direction.

"There's our guy," Teller said quietly as he stood and waved the tall man over, watching closely as the fellow made his way across the floor. The man was lean, dark, and muscular; his clothing casual but expensive. He was clearly a man who spent the majority of his time outdoors but still carried himself with a calm, professional assurance. He also looked oddly familiar.

Puzzling, and not at all what Teller had expected.

He made his way through the crowd, stepped up to the table and held out his hand. "You must be Teller."

"I am…" Teller said, taking the warm hand in his he gave a firm shake. Letting go, he stepped back. "And this is my partner, Jack Hawkins." Jack stood; taking the proffered hand. And as they had discussed earlier, motioned Mr. Smith into the booth against the wall.

Susan arrived moments later.

Setting Teller's frosted glass down she poured, bringing the foam to the rim perfectly and finishing with a bright smile. She poured Jack's glass as well, but with none of the deliberate attention. Jack gave Teller a withering glare but his aggravation diminished as Teller smiled and mouthed the word: 'Patty.'

The newcomer was too busy admiring the waitress to catch the exchange: then she turned her smile on him.

"Can I get you anything?"

"Just water for now. Thank you."

She gave a nod. "Be right back..."

Mr. Smith watched her leave appreciation evident in his gaze; but the moment she was gone he took the opportunity to begin the conversation.

Laying his hands flat on the table he began.

"Alright gentlemen, I'll be candid. The only reason I am here is due to Billy's request." He paused, leveling his gaze at Teller, who met it unflinchingly.

The slightest of smiles played at Mr. Smith's lips as his eyes turned from Teller, resting firmly on Jack.

"Mr. Hawkins was it?"

Jack nodded.

"Billy said that you were a good man and that I could trust you." But on turning back to Teller, his smile loosened, growing larger as it crept across his dark features. "*You, however, came more ambiguously recommended.*"

Leaning back, he studied Teller's face.

Teller steepled his fingers under his chin. "And?"

Before he could respond, Susan arrived with a glass of water and another menu. "Anything else right now?"

Neither Teller nor their guest spoke.

298

Jack smiled up at her. "Not quite yet, give us a few more minutes." She paused, then slipping Teller a curious glance, smiled, "Sure." And tucking her pad into her apron, went to a table across the aisle.

"And..." Mr. Smith said, "Billy told me that since you were the brother of Coyote, I should keep in mind that you were also a brother to *him.*"

Jack's mouth fell open: then he propped his elbows on the table, laid his forehead into the palms of his hands and moaned, "Ahh Jesus..."

Teller however, showed no emotion.

"Hmm, and that means?"

Mr. Smith picked up his glass to take a drink, but the ice gathered and the diverted water ran down his chin. Pulling a napkin free from the chrome dispenser, he dabbed dry, crumpled the napkin, and turned his dark, strangely familiar eyes to Teller. "That, my friend, means that I will help you in any way that I can, with whatever it is that you may need my help."

Taking a second, more cautious drink, he smiled.

"So, tell me, just what *is* it that you have that might require my services?"

Teller's expression remained cautiously amused. He studied Mr. Smith for a moment longer, then, with a slight nod, reached into his pocket, removed a coin, and laid it on the table.

Eyebrows raised, Mr. Smith picked up the piece and turned it in his hand. "More of these? I see no problem here."

He set the coin back on the table in front of Teller.

Teller's countenance remained passive. "Good. I was reasonably certain that you could handle *those.* But before we go any further, may I say that I would be much more comfortable calling you something other than 'Mister Smith'"

The dark man's face broke into a brilliant smile that was maddeningly familiar. Recognition danced on the edges of Teller's awareness but he could not *quite* place it.

Mr. Smith's smile remained as he reached across the table and held out his hand for the second time.

"Yes, of course. My name is William Gaagii Knowles, but you can call me Junior."

Jack raised his head from his hands and studied 'Mr. Smith's' profile. Now that the kinship had been brought to light there was no doubt of the relation and the smile was the clincher.

Billy had always been tightlipped about his family and Jack had always wondered why, but *this* was a surprise!

Teller however, broke into a huge smile of his own as he wrapped both his hands around Junior's.

"Truly a pleasure." He laughed.

Their laughter drew Susan's attention and she looked eagerly his way: but as he dismissed her with a wink and a shake of his head, a table of rowdy college boys began banging on their table. Donning her waitress smile, Susan unenthusiastically went to attend their demands. Teller grinned, returning his full attention to Junior.

"Your Granddad is a crafty old fella ain't he?"

"Yeah," Jack interjected. "He has never once mentioned that he had any children, much less grandkids."

With a smile that rivaled Billy's best, Junior did his grandfather proud. "As a matter of fact, Jack, he has a couple of great-grandkids. I have a daughter and two sons."

"Son of a bitch!" Jack grumbled. "How come he's never mentioned it?"

Junior shrugged. "Probably never had reason to."

Teller winked at their new broker, then looked at Jack.

"Yeah Jack, some of us don't give personal information out to just anyone."

"Screw you, Tell," Jack said with a grin, "I've known the man for years and he's never said a word."

"Relax, Jack." Junior's eyes held sympathy but his smile never faltered. "My Grandfather never mentioned it because of the very reason you are here tonight."

Both Jack and Teller sat, waiting for further explanation.

Tapping the coin that lay on the table with his forefinger, the brilliant smile vanished. "These gold coins..." he said in a low voice, "it is these coins that are the reason for his secrecy." He paused, leaning closer, his voice lowering to a near whisper.

"I've no idea how you two came across these, but coins *very* similar to this one have been a clan secret for generations." Studying the two men for their reaction, Junior went on.

"And I don't know how much my Grandfather has told you but these coins have helped our people for many, many years, and up until now *no one* has been aware of this source of income."

Sliding the coin off of the edge of the table and into his palm, Teller looked up. His expression serious, but his green eyes twinkling. "As I said, Junior, Billy is a crafty old goat. He has told us virtually nothing. Hell, he didn't even give us your real name. He told us only to come down and talk to you, and that you *might* be willing to help us. But he made no promises."

With a nod, Junior leaned back into the booth.

"That is logical, Teller. Knowing my Grandfather, I imagine he simply wanted us to meet. He knew that I would make my decision as to whether I could, or more importantly, whether I *would* help you based on my feelings, not his."

Teller nodded and finished the last of his beer. Leaning in, settled his gaze on Junior. "And can you?" he asked quietly.

Junior's smile started slow: but quickly spreading, lit his face. "As brother to Coyote, how can I refuse?"

Teller's smile gradually increased until it rivaled Junior's.

"I am *very* glad to hear that."

Raising his eyebrows, he held the coin up between his thumb and forefinger. "So, what is one of these worth?"

Junior held out his hand and Teller dropped the coin into his palm. Following a quick examination, he handed it back.

"These are of the same stamp, the same weight, and the same origins of our family's coins; so, consequently, their value will also be the same. My company has been moving these slowly and cautiously over the past many years. The last batch we moved fetched a little over fifteen hundred per coin."

"Umm hmmm." Teller gave a tight nod.

With no further preamble, Teller removed the rabbit skin pouch from the pack at his side and slid it across the table. Cocking his head, he grinned, "Alright. Now then, what do you think you could do with these?"

Junior glanced down at the rabbit fur container: then, lifting, his eyes remained on Teller as he picked up the pouch by its leather ties. To Teller, it was obvious that Billy's grandson was weighing the value of this new relationship as well as the value of whatever the pouch might hold.

With a final nod, Junior made his decision.

Loosening the ties, he tipped the soft fur container sideways and shook it. Three fat, irregular shaped stones fell into his palm and his dark eyes grew wide. Rough, uncut emeralds were the last thing Junior expected.

His eyes widened and his lips moved: but he said nothing.

Covertly bringing the stones close to the candle that flickered near the wall, he took note of how they absorbed the soft yellow light. Their subtle beauty hushed all conversation, making the ticking of Jack's wristwatch the only sound at the table.

Finally, Junior broke the silence.

"Wow." He said, bouncing them in his palm, estimating their weight. "Wow!" he repeated and looked at Teller with a smile.

Teller grinned; then raising his face to an imaginary moon, gave a coyote howl. The area around their booth went silent while other diners turned, startled. But Teller simply smiled.

"Nothing to see here folks, just expressing my joy. Please return to your dining."

The howl had also attracted Susan and her friend's attention. Lifting his hand, Teller gave a little wave.

— — -- --- -- — —

—— ——   —— —

-- --- --

= Chapter 59 =

James paced the carpet. His calls to Casey had gone unanswered and his messages unreturned. And to make matters worse, he had not heard anything back from Carl regarding his demand that Kelly sign over Teller's shares.

Goddamnit, do I have to do everything myself!' He paced furiously. *What the fuck do I pay these monkeys for anyway?*

Stomping to his desk, he picked up the phone and dialed Kelly's number directly. *Busy. Damn!* He hung up and hit auto dial. Carlton answered.

"Hello?"

"Carl!"

"Yes, Mr. Carson?"

"Did you talk to Miss Rowan?

"Yes sir."

"And what did she say?"

Looking longingly at the drawer that held the bottle of Pinch, Carl then glanced at the clock on his desk: only nine a.m. He squeezed his eyes shut, and with the foreboding of a man checking the knot on the noose he was about to hang himself with, prepared to kick the chair from under his feet.

"She said, and I quote: 'Screw him, I'm not signing anything until I talk to Teller.' Unquote."

To Carlton's utter astonishment he did not receive the lambasting he expected. There was absolute silence on the other end of the line. And as he waited nervously, his hand crept towards the drawer. He paused as his fingers touched the drawers handle.

"Mr. Carson?"

Nothing.

He removed the bottle and unscrewed the lid.

Silence…

Determining that that this was unquestionably a situation where discretion was the better part of valor, Carlton said nothing, pouring two fingers of liquid courage into the glass that still sat from the night before and lifted it to his lips.

James' suspicious voice startled him.

"She said that she wouldn't sign?"

With a sigh of regret, he lowered the glass.

"Yes sir."

"Until she spoke with Teller?"

"Yes, sir."

James struggled to hold his temper. "Have you gotten all the paperwork drawn up?"

"No sir, not all of it. I needed to have the final accepted figures before I could −" James exploded, cutting Carlton off.

"The final figures are *exactly* the figures I gave you yesterday! Thirty percent on the goddamned dollar! Now draw them up!"

"But Sir," Carlton interjected, "The original figures were fifty percent."

James' voice burned through the telephone.

"Are you questioning me?"

"No Sir! of course not! I'll get right on it."

Pouring the contents of the glass down his throat, Carlton swallowed and with a quick refill, brought it to his lips.

— — -- --- -- — —
—— —— — —— ——
-- --- --

= Chapter 60 =

Plucking a string of cheese from his bottom lip, Teller finished his last bite of Relleno, pushed the empty plate to one side, and daintily dabbing at his chin tossed the greasy napkin onto the plate and leaned back to study Billy's grandson.

The conversation during the course of the meal had been both enjoyable and informative. But as the evening wore on, Teller had been finding it increasingly difficult to continue referring the man across the table as 'Junior'; despite the man's assurances that he did not mind in the least.

In Teller's opinion the moniker did not fit the tall, regal, well-dressed man young man in the slightest. In fact, once it had been divulged that William Knowles the Third's middle name was 'Gaagii' it was more difficult still: for while he found the unusual middle name curiously poetic, when told that the Navajo word 'Gaagii' translated into 'Raven,' everything froze.

Teller's mind jumped back: back to the very beginning of this insane journey: to when the enormous black bird had grabbed him by the shoulders in his dream fall; rescuing him from the rocks below, only to take him to a snow-covered mountaintop. It seemed a lifetime ago... and while his eyes watched the dark man's lips move, his ears heard only the sound of the wind as he was released, followed by the muffled 'thump' of his body plowing into the snowbank. He was so profoundly immersed in the reality of the memory that when Susan touched his shoulder he recoiled, blinking the three of them back into focus.

Having taken drink orders from the other two men, she was waiting for his response; but now all eyes were on him; each showing varying levels of concern.

He squeezed his eyes shut again and the memories scattered. "I'm sorry, what is it you want?"

Susan's hand lingered for a moment longer. Then, with an inquisitive tilt of her head she smiled. "Your drink order . . . what would you like?" He ordered another beer; but Susan glanced curiously before walking away.

Deciding to let the peculiar coincidence pass, Teller turned his attentions to the discussion Junior and Jack were now involved in: but as the two spoke, Teller attempted to find a more fitting name for their new financier. He had used William once and had even slipped in 'Raven' a few times, but that felt false on his tongue; so, unhappy with his limited options, he decided to simplify the whole thing and just go with: 'Young Bill.'

He was using it in mental conversation when Susan arrived with a tray of fresh beers and clean glasses.

With practiced efficiency, she put the tray on the table, scooped up the dirty plates with balanced precision, and set the tray on the empty table directly behind her. Then, setting a fresh glass in front of Jack, she poured his beer perfectly; placing not quite empty bottle in front of him. He smiled his thanks and smiling in return, she refilled Junior's water glass with no fanfare. But on turning to Teller, her body language transformed. Wrapping her delicate fingers around the base of Tellers glass, she tipped the bottle; but the liquid poured a little too quickly and the foam expanded, spilling over the edge of the glass and running down her manicured nails.

"Oh my," she sighed, and laying her finger on the top of the glass, ran it around the rim gathering up the excess. Then, bringing her finger to her mouth, she slid it slowly between her lips; just as slowly drawing it out while giving him a pouty smile.

"I hope you don't mind a little head."

Teller's eyes twinkled. "Not at all sweetheart, but I prefer my beer in the glass."

Junior's mouth fell open while Jack just laid his forehead into his hands yet again.

"I'll try and keep that in mind," She smiled sweetly: then, turning, walked away: three pairs of eyes following every movement of her skirt.

Juniors eyes finally returned to Teller; wide with a combination of awe and envy. "What was *that?*"

Rubbing his face in frustration Jack looked between his fingers at the men.

"That, Junior, is something I wish I could bottle."

Teller simply smiled and shrugged. "Just lucky pheromones I guess."

Jacks hands dropped to the table and he glared at Teller.

"Are you trying to tell me that even your *stink* is lucky?"

"Shut up, Jack." Teller laughed, lifting his beer and returning to the discussion before Susan had arrived.

"So, Young Bill, if you don't mind my asking," But in mid-sentence, his eyes were drawn to the table to where two pieces of paper lay folded next to his glass. Pausing in his question he picked them up and following a quick perusal, smiled.

One was the bill, which he slid across the table where it came to rest in front of Jack. On the second she had written her phone number. He slipped that one into his pocket. This did not go unnoticed, and Jack gave a sad shake of his head along with a, 'tsk tsk'.

Purposely ignoring him, Teller again returned his attention to Young Bill. "So, as I was saying. What do you think those rocks might bring?"

Junior sat for a moment, still overwhelmed by the scene between Susan and Teller. But then, with a smile and a little shake of his head, he reached under the table to the briefcase at his feet. Bringing it up, he opened it and removed a jeweler's loupe along with a white handkerchief.

"Well, Mr. Teller. Give me a moment."

Centering one of the rough emeralds on the clean linen, he peered through the Loupe. "Impressive" he muttered, "*Very* impressive."

Teller looked over at Jack and waggled his eyebrows.

"I like the way this man thinks."

Jack nodded in agreement.

Turning the stone this way and that, Junior examined it from every conceivable angle. Seemingly satisfied, he folded the hanky into the briefcase, dropped the loop into its silk bag, and closing the lid leaned back into the booth to regard Teller through slightly suspicious eyes.

Teller, perfectly composed, stared back. "Well?

"Well," William said. "these are very high-grade South American stones, most likely from Colombia. Where did you say you got these?"

Teller's expression was unreadable. "I didn't."

Junior waited, but as it quickly became obvious that Teller was not likely to provide any further information he continued.

"Very well... these appear to be Colombian stones and that is quite fortunate as Colombian emeralds happen to be some of the finest in the world."

"And?" Teller prompted.

"And these seem to be excellent examples of Colombian emeralds."

Looking to Jack in mock incredulity Teller shook his head.

"Jeez Jack, this guy is as ambiguous as his Grandfather!"

Junior smiled at the compliment. "So, where did you get these?"

"Why?" Teller countered.

"Because," Young Bill answered. "I am not going to touch them until I know where they came from. Now, the coins are no problem . . . I've been funneling their like through a treasure salvage company I own down in Florida for years, and no one questions Spanish coins as part of long lost sunken galleons swag. But these my friend, *these* might raise some eyebrows. So I must ask you again, *where* did you get them?"

Teller saw his options were limited.

"Same place I found the coins."

Junior turned, and looked skeptically at Jack who smiled and shrugged. "That's the truth."

Junior's dark eyes went back to Teller. "Really?"

"Really."

"Wow," he almost whispered. "Does my grandfather know about this?"

Teller nodded, "Yep."

"All of it?"

Teller's temper flared. "Well, not every damn detail, but he knows enough to have sent us down to meet you. Do *you* think he would have risked his grandson, or his own future for that matter, if he weren't comfortable with the situation?"

Junior's black eyes held steady. "No, he would not."

Seeing both men getting defensive, Jack held up his hands. "Relax, Tell, he's not interrogating *you,* he's covering his ass."

Junior smiled and tilted his head in Jack's direction.

"He's right, you know."

The tension dissolved. "Hell," Teller exhaled, "I'm sorry gents; it's just that the story of how a damn Coyote led me to these stones and coins is a long one… One I don't care to repeat again and most certainly not tonight." He lifted his glass to his lips, but it was empty. Grumbling in annoyance he looked around but Susan was nowhere to be seen. He turned back to Junior. "I'm almost afraid to tell you how I think they got there, but I'm sure you are well aware of how the gold came into your family's possession. Personally, I believe the tales are related: but the point is really this. These stones are no riskier than the coins if the coins present no risk." He looked to Jack and gave a questioning twirl of his finger above the table. Jack nodded and Teller got up and walked in the direction of the bar. As Junior watched him thread his way through the crowd, he puzzled at his conflicting emotions. He felt in his heart that Teller was true: but still, in his business it paid to be cautious.

He turned to Jack. "Do you believe him?"

Jack looked into the younger man's eyes, his gaze steady and sure. "Yes, I do." His tone left no room for doubt.

William Gaagii Knowles nodded imperceptibly.

"Then it is settled."

The two men sat in silence until Teller returned holding three beers by the neck in one hand while trying to unfold a napkin with his teeth and remaining free hand.

"Where's your girlfriend?" Jack chided.

Teller managed an "Mmphh," around the napkin as he set down the bottles and opened the folded paper. Giving it a quick read he looked up, and with his trademark grin, handed it to Junior. "It's for you."

It read: *'the rough looking blond is Susan's, but I go for the tall, dark, handsome type. Meet us at the Shanty near the college after eleven.'* a lipstick kiss had been placed under the handwriting next to the signature: 'Shelia.'

Junior read it and refolded the napkin with a shy grin.

"The Shanty is a bar."

Teller's smile held. "Yeah, I figured as much," He handed young Bill one of the bottles. "You game?"

Junior's shy grin blossomed into a full-blown Knowles mega-smile. "Hell yeah! I'm divorced!" But just as quickly the smile dropped a few kilowatts, and he looked at Jack and Teller. "What about the two of you?"

Teller shook his head. "Sorry my friend, I have a woman who might frown on such extracurricular activities, and I believe Jack here already has a date for tonight." Turning to Jack, he smiled and shrugged, "Unless you'd rather go along with Junior, after all, as you mentioned earlier, nothing is in stone. So, she may or may not show up."

Having not been privy to the substance of the napkin, Jack sat with a puzzled expression on his face during the entire exchange. Therefore, his response to Teller's question was; "What in the hell are you two talking about?"

Teller laughed and plucked the note from Junior's hand. "This…"

Jack read the lipstick note, and as he did a smile crept across his face. "What do I always say, Tell? There is just something *special* about college towns." He handed the napkin back to Junior. "It's nice to have a choice, but I'd hate to disappoint the young lady. I best stick with . . ." He looked to Teller, "what was her name again?"

"Patty."

"Yeah, Patty. Sorry Junior, you're on your own."

Young Bill looked not only disappointed but slightly lost. Seeing this, Teller tried to comfort him. "I'm sure you'll be fine lad. After all, you will be in the company of *two* lovely young ladies." At that the mega-grin returned full force. "That's right!" he laughed; but then he paused and looked to Teller, his anxiety plain. "Wait! What'll I tell Susan about you?"

Teller gave a smile and a shrug. "Tell her that she would have only broken my heart. Now, let's get back to business. How much are those stones worth?"

It was with no small degree of difficulty that young Bill switched back into fiscal mode.

"Okay. A top-grade Colombian emerald," he picked up one of the stones and held it between his fingers, "Such as these, will fetch anywhere between fifteen hundred to three thousand per carat." Teller and Jack turned to one another, their smiles matching tooth for tooth.

Young Bill chuckled and continued. "Now, these are rough so that makes it difficult to see any inclusions. However, I don't see any conspicuous flaws on the ones I've examined so far. But keep in mind that you're going lose thirty to fifty percent of the weight once they're cut." He tossed the meatball-sized stone up and caught it. "This one will be worth about eighty thousand retail."

Teller's face went numb for a second: then looking at Jack, he mouthed, *"wow."* then turned back to Junior.

"And how much if we sell them just like that?"

"How bad do you want to sell?"

"How many *can* you sell?" Teller countered.

Young Bill leaned slowly back, falling instinctively into negotiation mode. "How many do you have, and how quickly do you want to get rid of them?"

Teller leaned in, closing the distance Junior had created.

"I have two hundred and eighty-seven of varying sizes, and I'm in no hurry at all."

Junior choked but quickly recovered. *"How many?"*

"Two hundred and eighty-seven," Teller smiled. "But some of them are smaller than that."

"And how many coins?"

"Seven pouches and two gourds. I would guess close to two thousand."

Jack lowered his bottle as his face went pale.

"Holy shit!" he gulped. "I had no idea..."

Reaching across the table, Teller patted him roughly on the cheek. "Suddenly that new chopper doesn't seem all so far away now does it?" Smiling at Jack's continued gulping like a fish out of water, Teller turned back to young Bill. "Think we can we work something out?"

Junior's eyes focused on the wall over Teller's head as he sat quietly, working out the figures, as well as the logistics of the numbers he had just presented with.

A few final calculations and he nodded.

"Yes Teller, but please, give me a day or so. This is a far larger undertaking than I had imagined, and there are several things I need to think about. Where are you two staying?"

Teller glanced over to Jack.

His eyes were closed and a silly smile lit his face. The thought of this sudden, and substantial cash flow had transported him into his river fantasy. Physically, he was there in the booth: but his head was over a canyon far away . . .

Teller was sorely tempted to slap the idiot grin from his face, but out of appreciation of the purity of Jack's vision he refrained. Instead, he refocused on Junior.

"We're at the Holiday Inn, under the last name of Hawkins. Here's Jack's cell number." he reached out and took the damp napkin out of Junior's briefcase; quickly scribbling the digits next to Sheila's. Junior saw what Teller was writing on and snatched it back in panic, quickly checking to make sure he hadn't written over the girls' numbers. They were still legible. Tucking it away in his shirt pocket he smiled. "Fine, I'll call you tomorrow. Oh, and Teller, you *do* understand I will take a percentage for every transaction."

Teller spread his hands as if nothing could be more evident.

"Absolutely, Young Bill. I would expect nothing less. The more pressing question would be what percentage you feel is fair." Again, his grandfather's genetics were in joyful evidence, captured within the smile that lit William's face.

"Normally I charge twenty," he said through his grin. "But for the brother of the Coyote and friend to the Navajo Nation, I will reduce it to ten."

Teller's smile struggled to equal Billy's grandsons, but fell a few hundred watts shy. Nonetheless, it won Junior's full trust.

Teller held out his hand. "Easily done."

Young Bill grasped the outstretched hand firmly, nodded, and checked his watch. "I need to get home and shower if I'm going to meet the girls."

"Yes you do," Teller replied and looked over to Jack, who was still lost in his fantasy, his foolish smile lingering on his lips.

"Just a minute, I need to retrieve my pilot."

Giving Jack a gentle kick to the ankle, Jack returned to earth, grunting and blinking as he was pulled away from his shiny new chopper, and a canyon full of pretty girls.

Laughing, Teller slid from the booth and standing at the table's edge looked into Young Bill's face; solemnity replacing all previous humor. "Just so you know, young Bill, a man's handshake means more to me than any contract. I will stand by my word, whatever we do. But I expect no less."

Junior's smile was one of both pride and respect.

"I can appreciate what my grandfather sees in you, Teller and you may expect honest and fair dealings when working with me."

He stood, back straight, his pride making him taller.

"I am a rarity in this world. I am an American Indian who is an attorney not only for the Navajo Nation, but one who is the central financer for a major salvage company in the Caribbean." The smile that graced them was one of satisfaction in his achievements. "My main objective is to buy back the land that was stolen from us and attempt to heal the wounds inflicted by the people who initiated our decimation by using the very gold they produced from the rape of our peoples and our land."

Teller's smile reflected his understanding.

"As a man who truly appreciates irony, I applaud your efforts young Bill, and look forward to working with you."

"You will hear from me in the morning," Junior said, "but now I need to get going. I've got to meet—" Giving Teller a guilty smile he reached into his pocket, unfolded the crumpled napkin, and read the signature. "Sheila, yes that's it, Shelia." But as he stepped towards the door to go, he stopped again and turned around, a question evident on his face.

"Was she the pretty one?"

Teller laughed. "Of course! She's *beautiful*."

Junior practically ran from the restaurant.

They watched him go, and Jack looked at Teller.

"Was she?"

Teller scooped the tab from the tabletop and handed it to his partner. "Hell, Jack, I don't know. I wasn't paying attention. Now go pay up, I'll see you in the car."

Jack looked at the bill, frowned, and called out, "Hey Tell, you expect *me* to cover all of this?" But Teller was already going through the front door, whistling a tune Jack had heard somewhere, but just couldn't place.

— — -- --- -- — —

— — — —

-- --- --

= Chapter 61 =

"What was that?"

"Nothing..."

"Bullshit Abbott, I distinctly heard you say, 'that bastard."

Abbott stammered out, "That's *not* what I meant!"

Kelly's laugh came over the line, and his apprehension vanished. "Oh Abbott, I know, with him it's practically a term of endearment. What did he do this time?"

Abbott's eyes went to Billy, who was leaning back on the counter, arms crossed, all smiles.

"He won't let me pay for any beer!"

"And that's a problem?" she laughed.

"No! Well, yes, it is. I can pay for my *own* beer."

Suddenly the sound of a gong rang through the room. Kelly looked up at the beautiful antique clock that Teller had found God knows where, its pendulum swinging, sitting on the mantle of the river-rock fireplace.

"I'm sure he's aware of that Abbott. It probably has something to do with all the beer you brought on the raft trip. He may not always show his appreciation at the time, but he rarely forgets."

The clock gonged a second time.

Kelly couldn't see, but Abbott was looking at the old Navajo. "Funny you should mention that. Billy just told me that's pretty much what he said."

"I'm not surprised. So Billy's there?"

"Yes, would you like to talk to him?"

"No, just ask him if he has Jack's phone number." She could hear the murmur of voices in the background, followed by laughter as Abbott came back on the line.

"Yeah Kelly, he's got it. Hang on." There was a moment of silence, and Billy's voice came on. "Hello, missy. You wanted Jack's number?"

"Yes, I do, Billy. How are you?"

"Fine as I can be. Your friend Abbott is keeping me quite entertained."

She smiled. "You know, I didn't realize just how funny he was until Teller showed up. There's something about their combined chemistry."

"Yes." Billy chuckled. "Teller does seem to bring out the unusual in those around him."

"Yes he does," Kelly agreed with a low, warm laugh.

"Could you give me that number? I want to try and get ahold of one of them." She wrote down the digits on a small notepad as Billy read them off.

"Thanks, Billy, and give Abbott a kiss for me."

Billy laughed, "I think I will wait for you to deliver *that* message."

He handed the phone back to Abbott.

"Yes?"

"Abbott?

"Yes, Kelly?"

"Take care of yourself. And if you hear from either Teller or Jack, have them give me a call."

"You got it Kelly, and ditto."

Abbott hit the disconnect button and turned to Billy.

"You think they're okay?"

Billy's black eyes stared into the distance as if he were listening. A few seconds passed and a peculiar smile crossed his face.

"Yes Abbott, everything is fine."

— — -- --- -- — —

—— —— — —— ——

-- --- --

318

= Chapter 62 =

Teller tossed the keys at Jack. "I'm tired and I need to think. You drive."

Jack navigated the rental along the streets of Tucson, staring through the windshield while struggling to grasp the enormity of the numbers that were discussed over dinner.

Running them through his head multiple times, he turned and looked at Teller who sat low in the passenger seat, his head against the seatback, eyes closed.

"Do you realize the amount of money we're talking here Tell?"

Teller rolled his head towards Jack, opened one eye and smiled, "Yes, Jack, I do. The figures come out to roughly twenty-three million U.S. dollars, minus ten percent."

Jack shook his head slowly and breathed out, "Jesus . . .."

"Jesus indeed . . ." Teller chuckled, pushing himself straighter in his seat. "That adds up to somewhere around seven-point six mill for each of the Musketeers. But don't get too excited just yet, Jacko. We're not going to get it all at once, and it has *got* to be buried deep in paper. First, we'll need to get a corporation formed. Then we-" Teller stopped, laughed, and slapped the dash. "Hell, I'm putting the horse before the cart. We can deal with the dirty details later. Right now we need to do a little celebrating! Swing into the next liquor store and I'll buy a bottle of Scotch for you, and a decent bottle of champagne for your well-endowed guest of the evening." He lay back against the seat to stare through the window at the lights of Tucson; and as they idled at a red light he saw a liquor store next to a Safeway.

"And there's one now. Pull in!"

Teller leapt out and disappeared into the store. Jack waited, tapping his fingers on the steering wheel and wondering just how much helicopter seven million would buy.

Fifteen minutes later the passenger door swung open and Teller slid in with a happy grin holding a paper bag and a dozen roses. Putting the bag in the back seat, he laid the roses on the seat between them.

"Candles and champagne are in the bag."

Jack gave him a quizzical look.

"Come on dumbass, ever hear of romance?"

As he pulled out of the parking lot, Jack gave Teller a frustrated smile. "Damn it Tell, *we* should be celebrating! This is the kind of thing people dream about happening!"

Teller chuckled, his eyes bright in the oncoming headlights.

"Jack, old son, starting tomorrow you and I can begin to enjoy our newfound fortune, and continue to do so for the remainder of our all-too-short lives." He gave a small sigh at the thought, but returned to his optimistic self in the next breath.

"But tonight is tonight! And besides, Jack, it's all perspective. I want you to realize that at this very second, there are ten million young men out there fantasizing what *you* are about to experience... a lovely woman in an anonymous hotel room, anxious to drink champagne, and lusting to perform who knows what type of perverse sexual acts upon your unsuspecting self."

Jack grinned. "Tell, you are a *master* of inspiration. Think she'll show up?"

"I've already bet a coin on it," Teller smiled. "And it turns out that bet is worth around fifteen hundred bucks. So yeah, I guess you could say I'd lay money on it."

"Oh yeah... the bet," Jack laughed. "Pretty girls and money too!" But his smile suddenly vanished. "Think she'll like champagne?"

"Amigo," Teller laughed, "I've yet to meet a woman that wouldn't drink champagne, and what you don't drink you can pour on her."

Jack smiled, the corner of his eyes creasing as he let the image soak in. With that vision firmly burned into his mind, he draped a wrist over the wheel, talking as he steered.

"So, what are *you* gonna do?"

Teller shrugged. "I'm going to make a few phone calls. We're going to need cash a lot quicker than Young Bill's efforts are going to be able to produce, and I need to get some legal wheels turning."

"Why don't you talk to Billy?"

"About what?"

"Come on, Tell," Jack said, shaking his head in the attempt to remove the image of champagne-soaked, candle lit thighs from his mind. "Think about it. Billy has been dealing with these coins for years, and Junior is already obviously familiar with the whole process. It seems foolish to go outside the existing framework." He lifted his hands from the wheel and spread them as if nothing could be more obvious.

Teller smiled at his partner. "Once again Jack, great minds think alike. My train of thought was on the same track. But the problem I'm talking about has nothing to do with the Three Musketeers financial future. No, the pressing issue at hand for me is one of severing old ties while making sure I retain my existing account."

Jack frowned. "James?"

Teller nodded. "Yep, so tonight I need to talk to Kelly and see how things are going up in Colorado. That prick owes me a considerable amount of money..." Teller cocked his head. "That is, of course, provided he hasn't already figured a way to fuck me out of it." but then his smile returned. "Again, the cart before the horse. Besides, with her watching over his snaky ass, things will be all right till I return."

The next few miles were spent discussing the future, but they had not gotten beyond tomorrow when Jack pulled into the parking lot of the Holiday Inn. Checking his watch, he smiled. "It's ten thirty Tell, what you want to do?"

Teller grinned. "I said it before Jacko, tonight is not about me." Reaching over the seat he grabbed the bag containing the bubbly and candles and passed it to Jack. "Its about you, and I want *you* to go up to your room and prepare for your guest of the evening: you know, create a little atmosphere... me, I'm going to go to the bar and negotiate the purchase of a classic automobile." Teller swung his door open, and as his feet touched the pavement he turned and smiled.

"Good luck, Jack, and don't do anything I wouldn't do."

Jack returned the smile, his grin shining in the dim light of the parking lot lights.

"That leaves a lot of room for mistakes."

"Yeah..." Teller winked, his eyes twinkling in the cars dome light. "But as there is very little I wouldn't do, it also leaves considerable room for success. Have a good night, Jack."

He pushed the door shut and walked away. And as he passed through of the ring of illumination cast by the mercury vapor lamp, Jack laughed quietly. "I'll do my best, Tell."

~

Pausing at the back door of the bar, Teller pulled a comb through his hair and walked through, the door wheezing shut behind him as he scanned the room.

It was a typical airport crowd. A few out of towners, some local folks trying to unwind after work, and a sprinkling of fairly attractive women; but the predatory gleam in their eyes marked their profession.

Squinting through the dim light, he unintentionally made eye contact with a tall black girl in a platinum-blonde wig. She flashed him a toothy leer and tugged at the hem of her leather miniskirt as she spun off of her stool, moving towards him with an extravagant swaying of hips. He smiled sweetly and gave her a limp wristed 'shooing' motion.

With a pout, she sat back down to resume her wait.

Turning to hide his smile he saw Terry behind the bar laughing. Having witnessed and thoroughly enjoyed the interaction; particularly Teller's response, the young bartender blew him a kiss and lifted his towel, fluttering it from his fingertips in greeting. Teller grinned and twirled onto a stool.

"Give me a beer, sweetheart."

Draping the towel over his shoulder, Terry set a cold beer on the bar, popped the cap, and with an exaggerated lisp, asked, "So where's your *friend?*"

"Don't you be getting any funny ideas about me just 'cause I refused the advances of some skanky hooker."

Terry dropped the act and snapped his towel in the blonde's direction. "Who? Chantell? She's no skank, she's a traveling man's companion." Teller looked over just as 'Chantell' slid under the arm of a very drunken businessman in an expensive suit. Turning back to the bar he shook his head, "Poor guy."

"That's free market capitalism for you." Terry shrugged.

Spinning in his stool, Teller watched as Chantell led the stumbling man out through the door. His loafer slipped off unnoticed, and was left on the carpet as she pulled him away,

Teller laughed and raised his beer. "Here's to America, land of the free, where any ho's dream can be realized."

Terry squirted some club soda into a glass and clinked it against Teller's bottle. "Hear, hear!"

"And hotel rooms rent by the hour." Teller added.

Terry nodded. "God bless America!"

"Not just America, Terry," Teller laughed caustically, "God bless this entire whorehouse of a world."

Tipping his bottle back, he drained it.

"Let's change the subject." He smiled. "Think we could take a look at that car tomorrow?"

"Sure," Terry shrugged. "I don't see why not."

"Great." Teller tapped the bar top with his knuckles. "What time do you get here?"

"I open this place up at ten. What time you thinking?"

"Probably around noon." Dropping a twenty on the bar as he looked up at the clock on the wall, he slid from his stool.

"I'm going to go up to the room and make a phone call. I'll see you tomorrow." Terry fluttered his bar towel at Teller, who smiled, gave him the finger, and pushed through the door.

As he made his way through the lobby, he glanced at the bell desk as he passed. Patty was gone, and a different, attractive young woman was dealing with a late check-in. Her eyes lifted over the red-eyed traveler's shoulder and she smiled. He smiled back. He was beginning to appreciate Jack's fondness for college towns.

~

Lying back on his bed, Teller randomly changed channels with the remote. The thought of calling Jack crossed his mind but he decided against it. If Patty was there he didn't want to disturb him, and if she was a no-show, which he seriously doubted, he didn't want to hear Jack bitch about it.

He checked the time. It was almost midnight.

A little late but a plan was formulating and he needed to talk to Kelly. He hesitated for a moment but picked up the phone, thinking about the meeting they had with Young Bill as it rang.

He counted the rings. He was going to let it let it ring ten times and hang up: but on the eighth ring a sleepy voice came on the line.

"Hello . . .?"

As tired as he was, he still smiled at the sound of her voice.

"Hi, Kell."

Her voice perked up. "Teller! Where are you?"

He smiled and kicked off his boots. "Jack and I are down in Tucson takin' care of a little business."

The relief in her voice was tangible. "I was worried."

"Come on, Kelly," he chuckled. "There's not much point in worrying. I'm either alright or I'm not."

324

There was a second of silence, and she came back, an edge creeping into her voice. "I never said there was a *point* in it. You just require it."

"Okay, okay, I'm sorry! I'm fine, *we're* fine. So, how are things up there?"

She flopped back onto her pillows and laid her arm across her forehead. "Just what you'd expect. James is an egotistical asshole who is trying to get me to sign a stack of papers immediately. I can only assume he wants to steal something before you get back."

Teller gave a laugh of appreciation and affection. "You are absolutely right, sweetheart, and it's not *some*thing, it's *everything*. Hey, is he talking to you directly, or through that east coast whiz kid?"

There was a short pause. "Carlton?" Kelly asked.

Teller turned down the volume on the television.

"Yeah, that's him."

She laughed softly. "He's a good guy, Tell, he just *works* for James, he's not part of the empire. As a matter of fact, he's never been too fond of James, and he has, or had, a major thing for Casey not so long ago." She giggled, "And Casey thought it was cute, which pissed James off to no end."

The wheels started turning in Teller's head.

"So *that's* why James treats the poor guy like shit, huh?"

She was silent. "I never really thought about it before Tell. He does treat poor Carlton badly doesn't he?"

"Yes, he does Babe, and that may play in our favor."

A smile spread across Teller's face. The seed of a plan was beginning to sprout. "Tell you what Kell. You give old Carlton a call tomorrow and propose a meeting. Just him though, we don't want James there just yet. Tell him whatever you have to, but get a feel for not only James' wants, but for where Carlton stands."

Kelly sat up in her bed and stuffed pillows behind her back. Now she was fully awake. "Can you be a bit clearer?"

325

As his plan gelled, Teller spoke quietly, almost as if to himself. "Find out if he has any loyalty to James. See if he is unhappy . . ." His voice faded for a moment; then returned strong and in charge.

"Everyone has a price Kelly, and we need to find out what Carlton's is. In the meantime, tell him you would like to cash in a few shares. I need some money."

"But the shares are still in your name," she argued, "*I* can't cash them."

Teller's mind was already there. "Right. Okay, have him call me at this number. But I want *you* there so I can give him verbal permission to release some funds. I may need to go to a local bank for a notary, but it might not be necessary with you as the recipient."

Kelly gave a smile. *This* was the man she fell in love with.

"How much do you need anyway?"

"A hundred grand."

Her mouth fell open. "What! Why?"

"Kelly," Teller's voice dropped an octave. "What I do with my money is *not* up for discussion." Then his tone lightened marginally. "Trust me darlin,' a hundred K is a small piece of *that* pie, so relax. There are greater things afoot, but I don't have the time to tell you about it right now. Just get Carlton on the horn with me tomorrow at ten thirty and to be ready to wire the money to a bank in Tucson."

Kelly nibbled at the torn edge of a fingernail. "Alright Tell, but when are *you* going to be back?"

"Should be in about a week with drive time."

"Drive time? What are you talking about? I thought you flew down there with Jack."

"I did Kell," he laughed merrily, "but life is subject to change. Be prepared for a road trip when I get back."

Kelly giggled. His delight was infectious. "A road trip where?"

"We're goin' for a ragtop ride to visit an Indian chief on the banks of the great still waters.

326

Kelly dropped her finger from her lips and her brow furrowed. "Teller, what are you *talking* about?"

Teller blew a kiss through the telephone. "You'll see. Now get some sleep, I'll talk to you in the morning."

She could still hear his laughter as the phone went dead.

Holding the phone at arms length, she giggled, "You bastard."

— — ‥ ‥‥ ‥ — —
— — — —
‥ ‥‥ ‥

= Chapter 63 =

The phone rang.

Pushing the papers in front of him aside, Billy set down his coffee and pulled the phone closer.

"Hello?"

"Hello, Grandfather. Do you have a minute? I would like to talk with you."

Billy's smile chased the shadows from the room. "Of course, Little Raven! for you I always have time. What is it today?"

To his Grandfather, William Gaagii Knowles III would always be 'Little Raven' and Junior minded not at all.

"I wish to speak to you concerning the two men you sent to meet with me."

The wattage of Billy's smile, if possible, increased.

"Ah Yes... my old friend Jack, and *his* friend Teller. A most interesting man, don't you think?"

Junior pulled the office door shut. This was a private conversation and Sheila was in the next room sleeping.

Following a night of dancing and drinking, at which she proved more than adequate, her true skills revealed themselves between the sheets and Junior had silently thanked Teller more than once during the course of the evening.

He refocused on the current conversation.

"Most interesting yes. But Grandfather, I get the impression he is dangerous as well."

Billy's laughter rang over the phone, "Of course he is! Coyote would not choose a meek or helpless man to pursue as he has this one. No, there is something much different here. There is a larger game being played now, and we cannot yet see its purpose. But take heart, little Raven, and be thankful he has chosen to include us in his game. Not many men receive such privilege." He paused, and when he spoke again it was softly, as if to himself. "Coyote has been in my life for as long as I can remember, and in my forefathers before me."

A moment of silence followed, and Billy's voice regained strength as his concentration returned to the present, and back to the conversation at hand.

"And now he has brought something new into both our lives. Be glad, Little Raven! Help this man as you have helped the people. I think this Teller will bring satisfaction into your work, and pleasure into your life."

Junior turned his face to the door leading to the bedroom, and with images of the previous night still fresh, a lusty smile danced across his face. *'The latter, he has already done.'*

As he struggled to suppress those reminiscences a smile reflecting his lineage spread across William's face.

"So, Grandfather, are you saying I should do all that I can for this man?"

Billy set the steaming cup on the desk.

"Yes, I am saying that, but your heart will give you advice I cannot. Listen to it well."

William leaned back in his chair. As always, his grandfather's words brought him strength and guidance.

But then his grandfather added, "And remember, Little Raven, one's friends are often delivered in odd packages."

Young Bill smiled at the wisdom of that.

"Yes, I will remember, and thank you, Grandfather."

— — -- --- -- — —
— — — — —
-- --- --

329

= Chapter 64 =

Standing naked in the kitchen with a towel wrapped around her hair like a turban, Kelly held the ringing phone to her ear with her shoulder as she poured her coffee.

A voice on the other end finally answered.

"Hello?"

"Good morning Carlton!" She smiled, delivering the greeting with as much cheer as she could muster this early. She was *not* the morning person Teller was.

"Miss Rowen?"

"Call me Kelly, Please."

"Um, sure, *Kelly*... how may I help you?"

Kelly kept the smile on her face in the hopes that its presence might reflect in her voice.

"I was thinking over our brief conversation yesterday and realized we really should talk."

For the first time since this whole thing regarding Teller and his shares of the Company started, Carlton smiled.

"Wonderful! I'll call Mr. Carson."

"No, no, Carl!" Kelly blurted, cutting him off. "Don't do that! I think our first meeting should be just the two of us, you know, so you might explain things to me in simpler terms." She paused, and added, "We *both* know how James can get."

At the mention of James' name, Carlton's hand went to the drawer that held his bottle of Pinch, but he stopped himself in mid-reach. *'Like Pavlov's dog,'* he thought, pulling his hand back and dragging it through his hair. "Yes, I *do* understand Miss Rowen. So where would you like to meet?"

'Good,' Kelly thought, continuing with Teller's plan.

"Why don't we just meet at your office? Really, anywhere else might seem suspicious."

"Of course." Carl nodded. "How stupid of me. So then, *when* would you like to meet?"

Kelly went the bedroom, opened the top drawer of her dresser and took out a pair of panties. Stepping in, she pulled them on, and with a snap of the waistband checked herself in the mirror. *Hmmm.*

Glancing over at the clock that sat on the nightstand she said, "How about thirty minutes?"

Carl's eyes went again to the drawer. "Sure Miss Rowen," he sighed, "thirty minutes will be fine."

"Great!" she smiled, picking a low-cut sweater from the adjacent drawer and holding it up. "And Carl," she said as she turned left to right, "Please, call me Kelly."

"Oh, yes! I'm sorry. Then I'll see you in thirty minutes, Miss Kelly."

"Yes, perfect, goodbye, Carl."

Tossing the phone onto a pillow she laid the rest of her outfit on the bed; changing colors and matching blouses until she felt she had it right.

Twenty minutes later, emerging from the bathroom she looked into the mirror and smiled in satisfaction.

Jeans tight, but not too tight, a soft sweater showing just the right amount of cleavage; low heels and a scarf. The look was sexy but not slutty. Perfect . . .

Teller would approve.

Finishing her coffee, she smiled as she remembered what he had said back at the campfire that morning after they had been reunited. *"Coffee soothes the savage bitch in you, at least for a little while."*

How true.

Taking one last look, she cocked her head, giving the reflection a coy smile. *What would Tell call this look?* Then, as clearly as if he were next to her she heard his voice whisper in her ear. *"Subtly fuckable."*

Giggling, she glanced over to check the clock again. Good, just enough time to brush her teeth.

Five minutes later she put her keys in her pocket, grabbed her purse and closed the door.

~

"Good morning Miss Row, um, Kelly, please, come in."

Carlton's smile was pleasant, but she could see that he was nervous. It was obvious that he was wary of the unexpected call, and more so by her insistence they meet alone. Gesturing towards a plush high-backed chair, he extended an arm.

"Please, have a seat."

Kelly held his eyes as she backed into the chair and sat, crossing her legs slowly and bequeathing a smile that could melt ice.

"Thanks for seeing me on such short notice, Carlton."

He immediately relaxed, basking in the warmth of that smile but just as quickly became self-conscious as he made an effort to bring his attention from the contents of her sweater to her face. Pulling out his desk chair, he settled in, leaning back in an unsuccessful attempt to appear casual and in control.

"So," he said, fiddling with his tie. "How may I help you?"

Kelly almost felt sorry for him.

"Well," she smiled, "I'm here on Teller's behalf."

Uncrossing her legs, she leaned towards him, locking her blue eyes on his. "But, as I am sure you are quite aware, *I* am now also involved." She pulled back, demurely re-crossing her legs, and kicking one shoe loose, she dangled it from her toe, her eyes holding his gaze.

"Yes Miss Row– I mean Kelly," he gulped, "I am aware of the business arrangement between Mr. Carson, Mr. Teller and yourself." A tiny bead of sweat broke out on his forehead. "But how may I be of help to you *today?*"

She decided she had better get to the point.

"I need a favor, and I need it now. But more importantly, I don't want you to inform James about it until our business is done."

At the mention of James' name, Carl's eyes went directly to the drawer holding the bottle: and in a herculean effort to maintain his dignity he slipped his hands under the desk to hide their slight trembling.

"I'm not sure I can do that Miss Rowen."

Kelly realized she needed to change tactics.

Rising from the chair, she stood at the edge of Carl's desk and placed both hands on its polished surface. She leaned forward and a whiff of the perfume she had dabbed between her breasts wafted in Carlton's direction. Subconsciously inhaling, he began blinking rapidly as she purred, "Carl, all I'm asking is for you to make a phone call."

Looking up from her sweater, and into her eyes, Carlton found himself both frightened and aroused.

"A phone call? To who?"

Kelly knew this was the moment that would make it or break it. Abruptly her demeanor became one of playful innocence.

"Oh Carl, don't be so suspicious." The pink lipstick she had lightly applied parted to reveal a dazzling smile, and flopping back into the plush chair she winked, "Hey, do you have anything to drink in here? It was a rough night and I could use a little 'hair of the dog."

Carlton squinted through his glasses, trying to discern if this was some sort of trap set by James. But as if reading his mind, Kelly crossed her legs again, but this time she let her ankle rest on her knee, assuming a more masculine pose.

"Come on Carl, relax. This is between us. I know James is a prick! Don't let it ruin our friendship. Break out a bottle and let's talk." Her words were cathartic, and his suspicions dissolved. With a smile of camaraderie and relief, he reached to the drawer that held the Pinch.

— — -- --- -- — —

— — — — —

-- --- --

333

= Chapter 65 =

Teller woke to ringing.

Blindly fumbling with one hand, he slapped at the lamp on the bedside table and missed altogether. The second swipe knocked the TV remote to the floor, and the third made contact with the phone. He lifted the receiver.

"Yeah?"

The voice on the other end sounded abnormally cheerful for this time of the morning.

"Hello, Mr. Teller? This is Carlton Fisk."

"Who?"

"Carlton Fisk, sir." The happy voice stated. "I take care of the company books for your Telluride Corporation."

Teller kicked off the covers and sat up. "Oh, *that* Carlton Fisk!"

The man chuckled. "Yes, Sir, *that* one."

Teller heard feminine laughter, and the tinkle of ice cubes against glass followed by Carl whispering, "Please be quiet, Miss Rowen, I'm only doing what you asked of me."

Teller smiled in spite of himself.

"Well then, good morning Mr. Fisk, I appreciate the call."

"Well Sir, Miss Rowen made it quite clear that you wished to speak with me."

Teller swung his legs out of bed. "And that I do sir, that I do. But would you be so kind as to put *Miss* Rowan on the phone for a moment please?"

There was silence, followed by the murmur of voices.

"Hi Tell."

"Good morning Miss Rowen. Have we been drinking?"

"No more than necessary." came the reply.

Teller grinned. "And how goes the mission?"

There was the clink of ice, followed by a swallow. "We're on the phone, aren't we?"

"Yes, we are." He laughed.

On the morning he had asked her to go back and keep an eye on James he had done so with full faith that she could handle the task. But this showed she was not only thinking outside the box, she was giftwrapping it and providing first-class delivery. This pleased him immensely and he flopped back onto the bed.

"Good job, Kell. So, what have you talked about?"

Kellys voice came back sounding surprisingly sober.

"Only that you needed to talk to him without James's interference, that you have an offer that may prove mutually beneficial, and of course, what a complete asshole James can be." In the background he heard Carlton laugh and exclaim, "Here, here!"

"And," Kelly continued, *"how* tired he is of his hard work going unappreciated by this organization."

Teller's voice reflected his admiration, but it was also colored with humor. "An absolutely stellar job, sweetheart, but before you put him back on, may I ask you what you're wearing?"

She gave a husky laugh. "What look would *you* have wanted me to go for?"

He considered for a moment, and answered, "Subtly sexy."

"Right concept," she laughed. "But different adjective."

She handed Carlton the phone before he could reply. And for one brief moment Teller hovered in that gray area between pride and jealousy. How good *did* she look? But he already knew the answer to *that* question.

He smiled as Carlton's voice came back on the line.

"Yes Sir?"

The poor bastard never had a chance.

335

"Hello again, Carlton. Am I correct in assuming you and Miss Rowen have had a pleasant chat this morning concerning some of my more immediate goals?"

"Yes, Sir, we have. We have also discussed some monetary consideration for my discretion in this matter."

Teller raised his eyebrows. He detected more a note of professional negotiator than that of your run of the mill bean counter.

"Yes, of course, Carl, and I've thought through several options. Perhaps you could tell me which is more practical under the circumstance, or, which you might prefer."

Carlton's voice was discretion personified. "Very well Mister Teller, please share your thoughts."

Teller smiled. The game was beginning.

"Okay Carlton, here's what *I'm* thinking. I need one hundred thousand dollars."

Swallowing an ice cube, Carlton choked and stammered out, "Mr. Teller, that's a *lot* of money!"

Teller chuckled, "Yes, it is Carl, but that's only half the story, and we can do this one of several ways. First, you can either sell or trade one hundred thousand dollars' worth of shares,"

"What!?"

"Relax and hear me out Carlton. Last time I checked the shares were worth around four fifty a share, right?"

"Yes, Sir, just under five hundred."

"But James wants to buy them all at fifty percent of their value, correct?"

At the mention of James' name, Carlton poured a dram into his crystal glass. "That is what he *claims* he is going to do, yes."

"No need to be nervous, Carl" Teller laughed. "I am well aware that James would like nothing more than to screw me out of *everything*. But I am nowhere near the weasel he is, and *that,* my friend, is why we are having this discussion. And that is also what's going to save *your* young ass."

Again, the sound of ice could be heard in the background as Carl replied, "Go on."

"All right then Carl, here is my alternate proposal. You can unload three hundred shares quietly. That will give you one hundred and fifty thousand dollars. You then wire me the hundred K, give Miss Rowan forty-K, and *you* keep the balance. Not only is that fifty thousand company dollars James can't swallow, it leaves *you* with a nice chunk of change in your pocket for your efforts."

He waited, but there was only silence on the other end.

"Or," he continued, "you can simply wire transfer me one hundred thousand out of the account to a bank down here."

"But Sir," Carlton stammered.

"Hang on, young son... there *is* more to this plan. I *am* still a signer on the account, am I not?"

"Yes Sir, on the business account."

"And is there that much in that account?"

"Well, yes, of course. That much and more, but Mr. Carson will notice that transfer."

Teller shrugged. "First, so what? and second, why? aren't *you* the head accountant?"

"Yes, I am, and because of my position, Mr. Teller, I have to give him a financial report at the beginning of every month."

"Does he read it?"

Carlton sighed. "No, I don't think so, but the rest of the firm also gets the report."

"Okay," Teller nodded, "Then we'll do it this way. And Carl, you *will* do it this way."

Again, Carlton began to protest. "But Mr. Teller..."

Teller stood and started pacing the floor. He could think more clearly when he was moving.

"Relax Carlton, this is all on the up and up. Is Miss Rowen still there?"

He could hear some of the tension go out of Carlton's voice. "Yes, she is."

"Good. We'll turn this into a conference call in just a minute." Teller's voice changed. Where before the tone had been conversational, it was now the voice of command.

"Okay, Carl, here's where we stand. My original agreement with James was that if he treated Kelly well, I would sell him my shares at fifty cents on the dollar; with Kell, excuse me, Miss Rowen, receiving the money from the sale. Is that your understanding of the arrangement?"

Carlton winced at the change in Teller's tone.

"Yes, Sir."

Teller continued. "But knowing James, he has no doubt asked you to pressure Miss Rowan into signing over all my shares at less than the fifty percent figure with an immediate cash buyout."

Carlton was impressed. "Why yes. How could you possibly know that?"

Teller's voice grew cold. "Carl, I've known James for a very long time, and his ethics followed his moral compass overboard years ago. But that regrettable fact aside, this is what we are going to do. *I* am going to fax a signed release in Miss Rowan's name, making her the sole owner of my stock in the company. *You* are going to draw up the paperwork agreeing to James' purchase of ninety percent of said stock at the price he and I agreed on: which was *Fifty* percent of the current value."

Carlton sputtered, "But Mr. Teller!"

"Reee-lax Carlton,"

Teller looked over at the clock ticking on the dresser.

"As a good faith gesture, you are going to wire one hundred thousand dollars to a bank account number I will provide. This will act as a guarantee of both parties' acceptance of the terms provided in your contract."

"But Sir!"

"Quiet, Carl, and let me finish. If you were paying attention, you'll recall that I specifically stated *ninety* percent of my stock: the remaining ten percent I am going to give to *you*."

Poor Carlton nearly choked. "Me! But why?"

338

"Carlton," Teller gently chided. "You have taken care of my interests in the Company, as well as put up with James' abuses for these past few years and I have never once heard you complain. Consider this my reward for services provided, and James' penalty for his lack of gratitude."

Carlton lowered the receiver and stared at Kelly, his jaw slack, processing what he had just heard. It took a few moments, but he finally regained his decorum.

"That is most generous Mr. Teller, but I'm not sure Mr. Carson will approve, you see-"

"*Fuck* Mr. Carson!!!" Teller roared.

The restrained fury in Teller's voice ripped through the phone, terrifying Carlton. Draining all color from his face as he fell back into his chair.

Teller took a breath; and while his volume dropped a notch, the cold anger was evident.

"Carl, I do not give one *shit* whether James approves or *not*. Mr. Carson agreed to the fifty percent. You may tell him that after your discussion with me, he has only one of two options. He can man up and stick to our agreement, or I will *never* sell him my half, and within the year I will *own* this fucking company. And once I do, I will bury his ass so deep he and the Devil will share zip codes. *Those* are his options, and he knows me well enough to know that I'm serious.

Do *you understand me?"*

The vehemence in Teller's voice rattled Carlton. Pouring two more fingers of scotch into his glass, he brought it to his lips and swallowed it in one quick gulp.

"Yes Sir, I do."

True to form, Teller's anger passed like the wind and his voice regained its prior cheerfulness.

"Grand! Okay then Carl, put us on speaker phone."

Carlton's shaking finger pressed the intercom button.

"Hi Kell, you there?"

Laying her palms on the desktop, Kelly leaned down to speak into the phone, worried at the lack of color in Carlton's face. "Yes, Teller I'm here. Good grief, what did you say to Carlton?"

"Ahh, hell, Kelly, I just had to explain how things work and reality scares some people. But I also informed him that he is to be rewarded handsomely for his efforts."

"So everything's okay?" She asked, glancing at Carl, who, while still looking dazed, slowly shook his head. The pallor was fading and a smile had begun to spread across his face. He picked up his drink, leaned back in his chair and stared up at the stamped ceiling.

Kelly watched the shift and relaxed. "Alright then, I guess everything is fine. So, what's up?"

Teller's voice was clear and commanding. "The short story is this. I am going to go to find a bank with a notary while Carl draws up an agreement involving a good faith payment in exchange for my signing over my stock to you."

She took a seat on the edge of Carl's desk. "And?"

"And once he receives my signature, he is going to write a bank draft and wire the hundred grand to Jack's account."

Her forehead wrinkled, "How does Jack feel about that?"

"Oh, he'll be delighted."

"You don't sound overly sure about that, Tell." She happened to look Carl's way again and saw that his eyes had drifted from the ceiling to her. He was nodding along in what seemed to be agreement, but then she noticed where his eyes were focused. "Cool it, Carl!" she hissed.

Teller's voice came across the speaker; sharp and deadly as a blade. "What's wrong?"

The venom in Kelly's eyes drilling through Carl's spectacles and into his heart, he nervously began looking in every direction but hers. Her anger quickly cooled; replaced with pity. "Everything's fine, Tell, I think Carlton is just excited about this sudden windfall. That's all it is, right Carl?"

Blushing with embarrassment and panicked at the threat in Teller's voice, he looked up repentantly.

"Yes! Yes, that's all it is, Mr. Teller."

Gulping the Pinch that remained in his glass he scrambled to put this turn of events back in order. With the whiskey warming him, his voice gained authority; becoming steadier as he refilled the glass to the top.

Setting his eyeglasses on the desk, he rubbed his eyes with his thumbs. "I'll get right to the paperwork, Sir, and I'll have the first draft ready by the time you call back. And thank you, Mr. Teller. Thank you *very* much." He turned, went to the wall cabinet, and began pulling documents from the top drawer.

Kelly giggled and sat down. Maybe she *had* drank just a *little* too much for this time of day.

"What did you give him as a reward anyway?

"Ten percent of my shares."

"What!!?"

Carlton turned his head and she lowered her voice.

"Are you *crazy?*"

"No more than usual," he laughed. "Besides Kell, that still leaves you with ninety percent, and the poor guy deserves something for putting up with James."

"True. But Teller, that's a *lot* of money."

Teller's voice came back. "Small potato's babe. There are greater things afoot than I have time to explain right now. Just make sure Carl gets those papers drawn up. And make *very* sure he doesn't call James in a moment of weakness. I'll call back as soon as I have something more to tell you. Bye."

The phone clicked and Kelly sat very still, chewing on her bottom lip while listening to the dial tone.: but then a slow smile spread across her face as she dropped the receiver in its cradle and drew her scarf over her shoulders, covering the cleavage her sweater had revealed.

Her job here was done.

~

On the other end of the phone, Teller smiled. *'Well, that worked out better than I expected. I'm sure glad she's on my side.'*

341

Picking up the receiver, he dialed 9 for the desk. A pleasant voice answered, and he asked to be put through to Mr. Hawkins room. On the fifth ring Jack picked up, giving a groggy and annoyed whisper. *What?"*

Teller saw no need to make his voice anymore cheerful than it was; although even if he hadn't been as pleased as he felt he would have done so just to aggravate his old friend.

"Mornin' Jack!" he sang. "I trust you slept not at all."

"Screw you Tell…" Jack grumbled, but Teller could hear the smile behind his gruff whisper. "What time is it?"

"Time for you to tell me in one sentence how the evening went."

Jack let his eyes scan the room.

Three of the many candles still sputtered, and there was dry wax pooled at the base of every one. A half-empty bottle of scotch sat next to two glasses, one lipstick smeared, while a pair of red panties hung from the empty champagne bottle that stood on the nightstand. His eyes drifted from this background of debauchery to the pretty girl lying next to him. She lay on her back, her lips parted, snoring lightly. He watched the sheet rise and fall with her breathing, smiling at the single, enormous breast peeking out from under the sheet.

Well," he smiled, rubbing an eye. "If Penthouse was still around I'd write a letter."

"It is." Teller laughed, "And I would *insist* you share your adventures with the world if only you were literate enough to write."

"Once again, screw you, Teller." Jack mumbled, leaning down and brushing a gumdrop-sized nipple with his tongue.

"Leave me alone, I'm going to work on a p.s. for my letter."

"Wait!" Teller shouted.

Jack flopped back and brought the receiver to his ear.

"Make it quick."

"I need the name of your bank, and your business account number."

Jack adjusted the pillow behind his head as Patty rolled over and slid her hand under the sheet.

"Why?"

"Because I'm going to have some money wired to the account."

"Why?"

Teller was getting impatient. "Just give me the number."

Patty gave a sleepy smile and a squeeze.

Jack sighed. "Sure. I'll get back to you with that in a little while."

"I'll give you one hour. That should be plenty of time." He glanced at the clock. "Meet me at the bar at noon." He paused, and smiled, "And Jack,"

"Yeah?"

"Don't do anything I wouldn't do."

Looking around at the room's condition, and then down at the impish expression on the face of the girl in the twisted sheets, Jack grinned, and his voice grew fainter as the receiver was dropped into its cradle.

All Teller heard was: "Too late for that."

— —   -- ---- --   — —
——   ——   ——   ——
-- --- --

= Chapter 66 =

James looked down at the screen of his ringing phone: it was Casey. His first reaction was anger. Anger based on the fact that he had been forced to wait for *her* to call *him*. But he glossed over his resentment with a teeth-clenching smile.

"Hello, Casey... *where* have *you been?*"

Her tone was friendly but not apologetic in the least.

"You know damn well where I am James. I saw no more point in waiting at the hospital than you did. There was nothing I could do to help and the nurses seemed quite capable."

It was difficult, but James maintained his temper.

"That may be true. But *I* had things that required my attentions *here.*"

At that, Casey gave a husky laugh. "Oh James. First, I find it insulting that you think I've nothing better to do than wait in that hospital. Secondly, and at the risk of sounding cruel, Benny is *your* family, not mine. And remember, *James,* it was you who sent him on that little trip in order to spy on Kelly... What she does with that handsome devil Teller means nothing to *me.*"

Knowing *that* little dig would get his attention she expected an immediate reaction: but he remained surprisingly silent.

A full minute ticked by with still nothing.

Pouring herself a cup of jasmine tea, she decided to break the silence. "As I said, *James.* Benny was in competent hands and as there was nothing more for me to do there I decided to come home. So, have you heard back from the hospital?"

James had nearly hung up the moment she had mentioned Teller's name. But refusing to give her the satisfaction of such a juvenile reaction, he swallowed and continued in a cold, professional manner.

"Yes, Casey, as a matter of fact I have. One of the nurses called yesterday. Apparently, Ben wants to leave."

"And?"

James gritted his teeth. He was still angry at her flippant remark regarding Teller. Why did she *insist* on pushing his buttons when it came to that guy? He took a deep breath.

"*And*, she said they needed to keep him under observation for a few more days for

Maternal warmth returned to Casey's voice.

"So he's going to be alright?'

"It seems so." but then he spoke her name: "Casey," and with the shift in tone she felt a resurgence of wariness.

"Yes?"

"When are you coming back?"

Her suspicion diminished, she allowed herself a tiny smile.

"Why, do you miss me?"

"Goddamn it of course I do."

His obvious discomfort pleased her immensely. Picking up her teacup, she leaned back into the soft sofa cushions.

"I was thinking of returning later this week."

"Good. I'm glad to hear that. Would you do me a favor when you do?"

She sighed. "What is it, James?"

"Would you pick up Ben at the hospital and bring him back to Telluride?"

Casey looked over the lip of her teacup and through a pair of French Doors that opened onto a patio, where, surrounded by thick irregular slabs of Flagstone the clear waters of an infinity pool glistened in the sun: and just beyond those clear waters, a flag emblazoned with the family crest fluttered from the mast of a sleek sailboat that rocked in the oceans gentle swell: as slow and steady as a metronome. The sight of that emblem, and the immense wealth and power that it symbolized brought her strength.

345

Setting her cup on the polished surface of a dark walnut side-table, she answered. But her voice held no hint of acquiescence.

"Yes, James, I will be happy to do that. Benny needs someone he knows to be there." Her voice grew cool. "But if I grant you this, you must be willing to do something for me in return."

Now it was James turn for wariness: he knew there was always a trade-off for any favor given.

"And what would that be?"

"Give up this ridiculous pursuit of Kelly. It's embarrassing for you and demeaning to me. This really is your last chance, James. You *need* me. *Your* problem is that you are just too blind to see it... are you willing to do that?"

James had known this was coming. As a matter of fact, he was surprise it had taken this long; and, in his heart he knew she was right. But his pride would not let him back down. His mind churned. How could he phrase an acceptable answer while promising nothing? As he grasped at straws the phone on his desk rang.

Looking to the ceiling, he gave silent thanks.

"Hang on a second, Casey."

Already upset with the morning's events, all his frustrations were unleashed on the caller. *"What is it?"*

"I'm sorry Sir, but this is the hospital. Have I caught you at a bad time?"

James answer was brusque. "No, no, you're fine, it's just that I'm in the middle of something very important. Make it quick."

While the nurse was polite, she was guarded as a result of her last two conversations. "You asked me to call when your son was ready to leave our care, Sir."

"No, Miss." he contradicted. "I *asked* you to contact Miss *Pierpont.*"

Her manner turned coldly professional. She was *not* going to allow him to lead the discussion yet again.

"Sir. You are listed as the *only* family member. So it is *you* that I am required to contact. It is also *you* that the boy has asked for so please don't make this difficult. Your son −"

"He's not my son." James interrupted.

Admirably, he nurse managed to maintain her composure.

"Fine. Regardless of how you are related, the boy is ready to be released, and he's asking for you. What would you like us to do?"

Laying the phone down, James began massaging his forehead with his fingertips while the small, tinny voice continued to buzz from the little speaker like the drone of a mosquito. It continued for a moment more, then stopped. A moment later the voice returned, but louder.

"Sir? Sir, are you still there?

With an extravagant sigh he picked up the phone.

"Yes, nurse, I'm still here. Tell the boy I'll have someone there to pick him up... what's today?" He checked the date on his watch. "The day after tomorrow at the latest."

"Yes Sir; I will tell him. And thank you."

"No problem. Whatever he wants, just add it to the bill."

"Very well, Mr. Carson."

"Which that asshole Teller is going to pay," James mumbled.

"Pardon me?" The nurse asked but the line was already dead.

Glad that the call with the nurse was over, but dreading the conversation to come, James picked up his cell phone.

"Casey? You still there?"

"Yes, James." she answered, splashing a cube of sugar into her tea. "So, what was *that* about?"

Rocking back in the cushions of his plush chair, he swung his feet up onto the desk and gazed at the ornate stamped copper ceiling. It was in the same style as Carlton's office, but Carlton's ceiling was tin and that small distinction pleased James to no end. "*That* was our fat little nurse," he said, sucking on his tongue as if the words left a bad taste in his mouth.

"Apparently Benny's ready to leave..." his feet dropped to the floor and his tone changed to one of coercion.

"So you *will* pick him up on your way back?"

Twirling a lock of hair around her finger, Casey smiled.

"That all depends. Will you promise to stop this foolishness with Kelly?"

James clenched his teeth.

'Fuck it. I don't have time for this shit now . . .'

Trying his best to sound repentant he sighed, "I'm sorry Casey, you're right. Come on home, we'll talk about it then."

But Casey, hearing the duplicity in his voice, answered, "You don't sound as if you mean that in the slightest, James."

It took every ounce of willpower to keep his voice steady.

"Casey," he said, clenching his jaw, "just come home. You're right, I *do* need you, but I need you to pick up Ben on the way. I know you think I'm a selfish asshole, but I'm having some serious problems here with Teller. He is making the negotiations of my buyout extremely difficult."

Casey smiled, silently applauding Teller. But James was so self-absorbed that he didn't bother to wait for her response; and disregarding her entirely, fell into his hopeful vision of the future.

"Do you realize what that would mean? It means that *I* would own this *entire* company! No more Teller! No more of his fucking games... no more of his *bullshit!*" Leaning back in his chair a huge smile crossed his face. But then he suddenly remembered she was still on the line. Struggling to erase his cheerful tone, he attempted to replace it with supplication.

"Just come on home. Please."

Her resolve wavered but she held fast.

"I'll come back, *and* I'll bring Benny, but we *will* finish this conversation upon my return."

There was a click, followed by silence.

James stared at the phone. *'Damn it,'* he thought, *'this time she's serious.'*

Setting his jaw, he dialed Kelly's number.

— — ‑‑ ‑‑‑ ‑‑ ‑‑ —

— —   — —

‑‑ ‑‑‑ ‑‑

Chapter 67

Taking the stairs two at a time, Teller's hand slid down the rail. He was feeling good, his room was on the second floor, and he didn't like elevators.

The bright Arizona sun caused him to squint as he burst into the lobby, shining through the big windows to highlight the worn carpet at his feet; as well as the other aged elements of the room that had been masked by the artificial lighting of the night before; and as he walked past the bell desk he sang,

"You ain't seen nothing till you've been, in a motel baby, like a Holiday Inn . . .'

The young man behind it looked up, acknowledged him with a perfunctory smile, and went back to whatever he was doing. Teller nodded and glanced up at the wall clock.

Noon on the nose. *'Damn, I'm good'* he smiled as he stepped through the bar door and paused, allowing his pupils to dilate.

Behind the bar, rag in hand, casually buffing the inside of a highball glass stood Terry; his white shirt buttoned down and hair slicked back. The image made Teller think for the briefest of moments of the bartender in *"The Shining,"*

Moving into the gloom, he leaned both elbows on the bar and gave Terry his best Jack Nicolson grin.

"Hello, Lloyd."

The joke sailed over Terry's head.

"Morning, Teller." he smiled.

Teller just shrugged. It wasn't the first time his humor went unappreciated. Ordering a Bloody Mary, he glanced around the room. They were alone but for a forlorn figure hunched over his glass at a table in the corner. Looking closer, Teller saw that he was the same businessman that Chantell had drug out the night before and now sat slumped over the table; looking worn and considerably worse for wear. Sliding onto a stool, Teller tipped his head in the wrinkled suit's direction.

"That poor son of a bitch sure looks like he's been through the ringer."

Terry paused to hold up the glass up he was buffing and look at the blurry figure through the glistening glass.

"I'm sure he got his hundred-buck's worth."

Teller swiveled his stool back to face Terry.

"A hundred bucks!? Holy shit! I guess a C-note doesn't buy what it used to."

At the sound of Teller's exclamation, the bleary-eyed fellow looked up, gave a half-smile, and turned back to his whiskey.

"No, I guess it doesn't." Terry laughed, placing the glass on the shelf and looking at Teller, hope plain in his eyes.

"You still want to take a look at the car?"

"Hell yes," Teller grinned, "But I hope the paint is in better condition than Chantell's was."

Terry smiled and a sparkle Teller hadn't noticed before shone in his eyes. "Well, the trunk's not as big but it's probably cleaner."

Teller's grin vanished; replaced by a look of disgust.

"*That,* my friend, is a truly ugly image."

Waving his towel in a wide arc that encompassed the dark room, Terry shrugged. "That's what happens to a nice young man when he is forced to work in a bar like this."

"You have my deepest sympathies son. Teller laughed. "And I like your style . . . but who's going to hold down the fort while we're gone?"

Terry just smiled.

Pulling a bottle of J.W. Black from the top shelf he picked up a clean glass and tossed his towel into the sink.

"Got it covered."

Locking the cash register, he poured the whiskey and walked over to the only occupied table in the room.

"Hey Joe, would you mind watching the place for an hour or so?"

Joe looked up from his empty glass.

With the tired countenance of a man beaten by events he was still handsome behind red eyes: eyes that crinkled at the edges as he accepted the fresh glass.

"Sure Terry," he smiled, dribbling whiskey over the melted ice cubes in his glass. "Be happy to, and thanks."

Observing the exchange, Teller again noted the wrinkled suit and silently tagged the disheveled fellow: *'Rumpled Joe.'*

Terry laid a hand on Joe's shoulder. "No problem. You know where things are, serve anyone that shows up and I'll see you in a little while." He turned to Teller and motioned towards the exit. "Let's go."

Stepping behind, Teller followed Terry through the back door. It was still early; but the heat radiating from the east-facing wall was intense and the transition from the cool dark of the bar to this flash-bulb oven was brutal. Teller squeezed his eyes shut to block the blinding light but it still burned through tightly pinched eyelids. Desperate, he began slapping at his pockets: searching for his old pair of Serengeti's…locating them he slipped them from their case, set them on the bridge of his nose and with a sigh of relief, opened his eyes.

Thanks to the rose tinting of the lenses he now viewed a more pleasantly colored world. The rose coloring could not, however, silence the noise nor make the industrial scene any less unpleasant. Turning to look at the Tucson-Nogales highway, a stream of seemingly never-ending traffic whizzed by; and beyond the airports concrete communication towers airliners floated in the sky, dwarfing the smaller private aircraft that circled the airfield.

The bright heat, combined with the bustle of civilization left Teller feeling dazed. Smacking the roof of the car, he laughed,

"It's not the heat, it's the humanity."

Again, the joke was lost.

Giving a shrug, he opened his door and was hit with a blast of baked upholstery hell. He fell back, fanning the door to assist in the heats escape; and as he waited he looked across the car's roof. "You do that often?" he asked.

Terry, being a Tucson native, ignored the heat and slid onto the hot cloth seat without reservation.

"Do what?"

Teller pointed back towards the building. "Let someone else run your bar."

Terry smiled, "Naa, but Joe's kind of a special case. He flies in twice a month, stays for a couple of nights, and tips well. Besides it's only noon, a little early for a crowd. He'll be alright." He motioned for Teller to get in. "Come on, it's not far." With a nod, Teller slid in, rolled down his window, and laid his arm across the seatback.

"Well then, drive on, driver!"

Taking the side streets rather than the freeway, Terry negotiated the back roads with the familiarity of a local boy while Teller gazed out the window in silence; but ten minutes into the ride and waiting for a light to change Teller turned and smiled, "Scenic route eh?"

It took a few seconds for Terry to recognize the reference.

"No, well, yeah, sorta." he shrugged, "really it's just habit. I don't like the freeway."

A kindred smile crossed Teller's face.

"I understand completely lad, I avoid them whenever I can. I'm a scenic route kinda guy myself." He turned in the seat to study Terry as he drove. "So tell med young son, what's the story with this car of yours?"

Slightly intimidated by Teller's scrutiny, Terry kept his eyes on the road. "Well, there's not much more to it than I've already told you. But hang on, we're almost there."

Making several seemingly random turns, they suddenly found themselves driving through a much older, and much wealthier, neighborhood that rested in the shadows of the Santa Catalina Mountains.

Terry followed the road as it entered a wide canyon; winding past beautiful turn of the century homes hidden by ancient cottonwood trees. Teller smiled and sniffed the air. This deep-rooted and elegant neighborhood reeked of old money.

Turning onto a smaller lane that ran between two enormous boulders, Terry came to a slow stop, the bumper nearly touching an ornate wrought iron gate.

"Well, here we are," he smiled and stepped out.

A few moments later the gate swung open, Terry slid back behind the wheel, and the cars tires thumped over the red bricks of the driveway.

Teller stuck his head out of the window, impressed by the beauty of the trees that lined the drive. Glass-smooth trunks supported graceful branches that spread above them, creating a thick green canopy that filtered the sunlight through broad, heart-shaped leaves interspersed with twelve-inch seedpods that hung from branches like giant green beans: but as they emerged from the trees dappled shade, he pulled his head back in; turning his attentions to the home at the end of the drive: a beautiful red brick and timber manse; complete with requisite gables and ornate cornices. He smiled. Passing beneath the trees majestic canopy, he had recognized them; but could not recall their species. He did, however, recognize the era of this homes construction.

As Terry pulled beneath a Porte Cochere that stretched from the entry stairs and over the driveway, he leaned against the door and looked across the seat at Terry. "Copper or railroad?"

"Excuse me?"

Pushing his door open with his foot, Teller stepped out, spread his arms, and repeated, "Copper or Railroad? Robber Baron or industrialist?"

Terry also stepped out of the car, but the baffled expression remained. Teller spread his arms wider. "This! How did your grandfather make his money? This place represents an era, and it was an era of wealth."

"Oh, sorry Teller," Terry said as he closed the car door. "I wasn't sure what you meant." But he still didn't answer. He just turned and went up the steps, stuck his hand into the jaws of one of the four-foot tall lion sculptures that guarded either side of the entry door. Running his fingers over the stone tongue, he stuck his arm down the marble beast's throat, pulled out a key and inserting it into the old lock, slowly pushed the heavy door open. Cool air rushed out, gloriously refreshing after the heat of the city. Teller smiled and continued his line of questioning.

"What I meant Terry, is that up in the Rockies, homes such as this were built by fortunes made in gold and silver, or by the railroad barons. Down here it was mostly copper and such. This place reminds me of one of those."

Terry stood at the threshold for a moment, then shook his head and stepped in. "No, I don't think my grandfather was involved in anything like that."

Teller followed for the first few steps then came to a stop.

"Hmmm, not what I expected," he said, taking in the huge, empty room. Not even a picture was left hanging on the wall.

An expression of sadness darkened Terry's face.

"Yeah, the family pretty much cleaned the place out. They're *still* fighting over the house, not to mention the other scraps that Grandpa forgot to put in his will. I think he expected to live a little longer just to piss off some of the greedy relatives."

He gave a short laugh, like a bark, and turned to Teller, who shrugged, and gave Terry a sad smile. "Happens every time."

Terry nodded. "Yeah, I know. but he *did* leave a few specific items to some of us grandkids. Come on, I'll show you the car. It's out here." He started across the stone floor of the entry and into an enormous wood-paneled living room.

Teller followed, his eyes drifting to the vaulted ceilings and carved crown moldings. Impressed with the craftsmanship, he happened to look down to the floor and noticed that they were leaving footprints in the dust. Unbidden, his mind went back: back to similar footprints that had been left in the red dirt as he had walked away from his truck: footprints that had no doubt disappeared by now. Shaking his head at the many turns his life had taken since that day, he looked up to see Terry disappear around a corner. Spurred forward, he caught up with him in the kitchen, and stopped midstride.

It was enormous; walls of cupboards and counter space with a monstrous old wood and gas stove dominating most of the wall to his right. The thing looked large enough for commercial use. Walking over, he laid a hand on its cold iron surface. Its solidity helping to reel his mind back to the present, he ran his hand along the curved chrome of the cooling shelf and asked,

"What's with this?"

Taking an old iron hook from the wall, Terry stuck its curved end into one of the cast-iron cover plates and lifted. As it rose, Teller thought he could see the past drift up through the black hole; rising like smoke and drifting away; and hearing distant laughter, felt himself drift with it.

Terry's voice brought him back.

"My father told me that our grandparents used to entertain a lot. I guess they held *huge* parties that a lot of well-known people would attend, and this kitchen was the focal point of the get-togethers. I don't remember, I was the youngest of my family, and only remember a few holidays we spent here before my grandma got sick."

Teller turned from the past. "Sorry."

Terry brightened, "Don't be, I still have wonderful memories. Altho' I can't for the life of me understand why my grandfather left *me* his old car." He dropped the plate back on the stove and smiled, "Come on."

Teller followed across the yellowed linoleum to a paneled door that separated the kitchen from the garage and wrapping his hand around the faceted glass knob, swung the door open to total darkness. They both stood for a moment and Teller would later swear that he felt the house sigh.

Reaching into the shadows, Terry's fingers skittered across the wall for the switch. Teller heard a 'click.' And a bare bulb hanging from the rafters lit up, pushing back the gloom and lighting a large tarp that covered what appeared to be a submarine.

The car had been put on blocks, and with the pressure removed the wide white sidewalls were smooth as new, and the bottom half of the chrome "Moon" hubcaps peeked from beneath the tarp. Walking over, Terry grabbed a corner of the dusty tarp with either hand.

"You ready?

Teller nodded.

With a snap he yanked the tarp back.

Dust exploded into a cloud, the motes sparkling in the light of the bare bulb: whirling in the shadowy light; twirling and dancing in the dank warm air as the tarp fluttered to the floor. There, under a single sixty-watt bulb, was the car of his dreams.

He was suddenly struck with the same sensation he had felt as he floated weightlessly in the green water following his fall from the cliff above the river.

A glorious and sublime timelessness.

He smiled, half tempted to do another jig. But instead he stood perfectly still, basking in the dreamlike joy of this vision.

Holding his breath he let a few minutes pass; and once he had decided he would not awake, he moved into the dim light, laid his palm reverently on the sleek curve of the front fender and began walking slowly forward, letting it glide along the smooth paint towards the grill. As his fingertips touched the chrome ring around the headlight he closed his eyes and pressed his fingers to the textured glass.

A beatific smile spread across his features.

A voice from the shadows interrupted his bliss. "Jeez, Teller, that's a look most guys would get stroking a lingerie model."

Teller's eyes remained closed, the fingertips of one hand reading the texture like Braille; the other resting on the curve of the hood. "Yeah," he smiled, "but there's no woman that will ever feel this solid, *or* this smooth at sixty-seven years old."

Dragging his hand along the hood to the left fender, he walked towards the driver's door, sliding his palm along the curve, and smiling the same blissful smile. Reaching the driver's door, he opened his eyes and pulled the handle. The door swung open and the unmistakable smell of old American automobile upholstery was released into the stale air of the garage. Teller sighed, "God! That is a smell you never forget."

"I know!" Terry laughed. "It reminds me of my Grandfather."

Eying the young man thoughtfully, Teller smiled. "Hold onto that memory son. You're likely to be the last generation that will ever relate that scent to your childhood. I'm afraid the stink of vinyl and plastic will be the odor embedded in your children's olfactory banks." Sticking his head into the car, he took a deep breath and stepped back, closing the door with a satisfying 'thunk.' The displaced air scattered the dust motes in another dazzling display.

"You may find this hard to believe," Teller said, still admiring the sweep of the hood. "And my telling you this will definitely *not* help my bargaining position, but I have wanted this car for many, many years."

Leaning against the fender, Teller probed Terrys eyes for hidden falsehood; but whatever he might be he appeared guileless. Feeling somewhat reassured, Teller still had to ask

"*Why* would you want to sell this car?"

Troubled by the intensity of Teller's gaze, his answer was one of honesty. "Well, I told you the day we met that my grandfather had left me his old car. I also told you at the time that I have no interest in cars. I have kids, and I need the money. And then, well, I don't know Teller, I had just sort of forgotten about it. I mean, it's just been sitting here since he died. But the minute I saw you it just popped in my head. That *you* were the guy I should mention it to." He paused, looking at the old Buick with new appreciation. Then, with a smile of insight, he rephrased, "That *you* were the guy that should *have* this car." He gave the perfect convertible top a pat.

"Apparently, I was right."

Teller raised his eyes to the heavens, pleasantly baffled by the continuing synchronicity his life had assumed.

"And I couldn't agree more." He grinned.

Turning back to the car, he opened the door and slid across the spotless upholstery. A sense of euphoria enveloped him as he glanced at the gauges. The car only had fifty-four thousand miles on the odometer.

A nineteen forty-eight Buick Roadmaster ragtop in perfect condition? This is to good to be true.

Sitting with his hands on the wheel, Teller closed his eyes; soaking in the bliss of his good fortune. But on opening them he caught a flash of blue. Leaning closer, he examined the item that had caught his attention.

Set into the dash, below the chrome ring of the clock was a three-inch tall, carved turquoise coyote. One *very* much like his. But unlike the one he had found in Estebanico's cave, *this* one was sitting on its haunches, its open muzzle pointing towards the sky. Giving a silent, laughing curse, Teller looked up at the felt headliner and mumbled, '*you're just not going to leave me alone are you?*

Sliding out of the car, Teller walked over to Terry, took him by the elbow and led him to the passenger door. Pointing at the inlay, he spoke between clenched teeth.

"What is *that* doing there?"

Terry broke into a huge smile. "I don't know, but it sure is cool, isn't it!"

Teller did *not* share Terry's enthusiasm.

"Its cool factor is not the point Terry. I mean, *what* is it doing *there?*"

The young man pulled his elbow from Teller's grip.

"Like I said. I don't know. It's just always been there. My Grandfather said he got it from some Indian he knew up on the Navajo Rez, so he had it set in the dash. It was supposed to bring him luck." He turned and gave Teller a quizzical look. "Why? What's the big deal?"

Teller gave a weary shake of his head. "Just curious, that's all." Pushing the door shut he leaned against the fender and crossed his arms. "You know," Teller said, his eyes narrowing. "You never *did* tell me how your grandfather made his money."

Terry's expression was one of unfeigned innocence.

"That's because I never really knew. I was just a kid so he never talked to me about it. I just knew he had money."

He smiled. "Teller, the only time my Grandpa would ever open up was when we were driving around in this old car. He used to tell me wild stories about some Indian Chief he knew up north. Stories about gold and turquoise, and Spanish Conquistadors! I just thought he was a cool old guy with great stories. But as I got older I started thinking that he was just full of crap."

Teller grew quiet. "Did he ever mention any names?"

"No," Terry said, scratching his head. "No, none that I can remember anyway, why?"

"No reason. Hey, what time is it?"

Terry glanced at his wristwatch. "Oh, shit! We need to get back! It's almost two!" He took a step, but Teller dropped a firm hand on his shoulder, stopping him in his tracks.

Turning him around, he looked straight into his eyes.

"Are you absolutely sure you want to sell this car?"

Terry gazed unflinchingly. "To you? Yeah."

Following a second of complete silence, an odd mix of joy and relief lit Teller's face. "I am *very* glad to hear that. Now we just need to talk money."

"Money huh?" Terry snorted, "I believe you gave up any economical edge when you began to drool."

They followed their tracks back through dust on the floor and Teller's laugh echoed throughout the empty house.

"Your right, Lad, but I know something that you don't."

Terry paused. "Really? What's that?"

Teller's eyes twinkled.

"I know that the Coyote *did* bring him luck."

= Chapter 68 =

A sudden sweep of blinding light fanned across the bar as the rear exit door swung open, and two figures stood backlit like aliens in a low-budget space movie. Jack lifted his arm to cover his eyes: but blind or not, he recognized the voice that spoke from the blur. "I should've known you'd be here."

He and Joe had been swapping lies about each's previous night; Joe still nursing the whiskey Terry had left while Jack sipped on the beer he had helped himself to from the cooler behind the bar; and as the door wheezed closed the room returned to blessed darkness. Jack slowly lowered his arm and picked up the bottle. "This is where you told me to be."

Jack couldn't see Teller smile, "Oh, yeah." and while he sensed Teller sit down beside him he remained blinded by the unexpected onslaught of sunlight.

"So where's your date?" the voice asked.

A smile played across Jack's face. "She's still up in the room."

"Ahhh, wore her out did you?" Teller laughed, then called out, "Terry, would you be so kind as to bring us a round?"

"Hey Tell," Jack drawled. "Didn't you say that Penthouse was still being published?"

Terry put the drinks on the table, but it was Teller that passed them around.

"Yeah, Why?"

"Cause I want you to write the letter for me. It's kind of unbelievable, and you're a better liar than I am."

"Now Jack," Teller frowned. "we both know that's just not true. Your lies are legendary." Looking up he shouted, "Hey Terry, bring a glass of cold water over with the next round."

Terry called back, "Sure."

Lowering his bottle, Jack gave Teller a sideways glance. "Water for what?"

Teller grinned and pushed back his chair. "To give you something to soak your poor pecker in. It must be hurtin' after the rodeo that young lady put it through."

Hearing that, Rumpled Joe burst into laughter.

Jack smiled and called out over his shoulder, "Better make it a tall glass!"

At that, Teller leaned back in his chair and looked at Jack through shining eyes. "Now see, there's what I mean, Jack. Who's the better liar?"

Terry walked into the laughter, purposefully placing a large pitcher of water directly in front of Jack.

All three men looked up, their expressions framing varying degrees of puzzlement. But Terry shrugged, "Just covering all possibilities."

Jack's grin grew while Joe cackled into his glass of whiskey and Teller sighed, "Oh Please, you'll only encourage him." But he still pulled out a chair. Terry sat and turned to Teller.

"So, what do you think the car is worth?'

Jack's grin faltered. "What car?"

Teller smiled and gave him a pat on the head. "Never you mind stud. Much like your fantasy filled adventure of last night, I too, have found my dream ride."

Jack's expression became a mix of amusement, satisfaction, and bewilderment, and seeing this, Teller pushed the pitcher in front of him. "Relax, Jack. All that this means is that there's a chance you might be flying home alone and I'll meet you at Billy's place later. In the meantime, soak your swollen gonads, *and* your ego in that pitcher of water. It'll help to shrink them both. I have business to discuss with Terry here."

Rumpled Joe put down his glass. "I'm running with the wrong crowd. *You* sonsabitches are funny!"

Terry chuckled while Teller turned, raising an eyebrow.

"That may be true, Joe," he grinned. "But we're a tough

bunch to keep up with. You best stick to Chantell. At least with her, you know how dirty your gonna get." He winked at Jack and leaned back in his chair. "Now Terry: about that car."

"Yeah," Terry said, growing pensive. "About that car. You got me thinking about some of the things my grandfather told me when I was a kid and we were driving around . . . we never really went anywhere, we just drove and he would talk. This was after my grandmother died. I didn't realize it at the time, but I guess he was lonely." A look of regret crossed his face and he gave a wistful smile. "But before Grandma died they used to take off for weeks in that old car. They wouldn't say where they had been but they always came back in great spirits, and with a trinket or two for the grandkids." Teller saw happy memories behind the young man's eyes; but then he stopped in mid-thought. "Ready for another round?"

Yeas rose from the table and Terry's melancholy faded. He smiled, snapped his bar towel, and went to the bar.

Taking advantage of Terry's momentary absence, Teller turned to Jack. "Do you have that bank info?"

"Yeah Tell, I do, but why do you need it again?"

"Because, mes amigo, I want to deposit a big chunk of change into that account."

Suspicion clouded Jack's face as he lifted his beer to his lips. "And, my friend, I again must ask you. Why?" Taking a sip, he shook his head and set the bottle down. "Man, that's just not doin' it for me this morning." Calling over his shoulder, he said, "Hey Terry, cancel that beer order and just bring me some more water, wouldja?"

Teller pointed. "You've got a pitcher of water in front of you."

"Yeah, I know," Jack smiled, "But it's been tainted."

Teller just couldn't resist. "Well, then you shouldn't have dipped your taint in it."

Jack gave Teller a look of long-suffering affection.

"God, Tell, I would *hate* to live in your head."

364

Teller just smiled, "Aww, it's not so bad Jack, at least *I* appreciate my jokes."

The ensuing laughter was interrupted as Terry returned, setting a fresh a glass of water in front of Jack, along with the other two men's drinks. Jack's chuckling diminished and he looked at Teller. "So, I repeat the question a third time. Why?"

Teller seemed genuinely offended.

"Jack, do you not trust me?"

Theirs was a friendship that spanned many years and many adventures; and while Jack knew Teller was not easily hurt he could be quick-tempered about some things.

Reaching across the table, he patted Teller's forearm.

"Trust has never been an issue partner, but even *you* have to admit that you have made questionable decisions in the past, and I *do* have legitimate business concerns to consider."

The wounded aspect in Teller's eyes dropped. He shifted in his chair, pinning Jack with a piercing gaze. "Be that as it may, *Jack*," he said, all humor leaving his smile. "You either *are* a Musketeer or you are *not*. One for all and all that bullshit... your share is assured, regardless. But right *now* I need this one little thing. So, tell me... Are you in, or are you out?"

This was not the first time Jack had seen this look. Teller may be lighthearted, he thought, but the man could chill your soul with the cold fire behind those eyes. It was then that Terry happened to return, walking unwittingly into the exchange. He could feel the tension building around the table but then Jack smiled. "I'm in." he said, raising his glass. "All for one, and all that bullshit . . .." and as quickly as a spring storm it was over. Teller smiled, and the feel of camaraderie returned.

Reluctant but curious, Terry asked, "Share of what?"

Teller's reaction was relaxed. And although he was smiling the impression of imminent danger was as threatening as a coiled rattlesnake.

"*That,* Terry, is none of your concern."

Slowly turning his gaze back to Jack, he said, "I'm glad to hear it, Jacko. You and I will finish this in a minute, but right now I want to hear the rest of the boy's story."

But pushing back his chair, Jack stood and stretched his lanky frame. With a sigh and a smile, he reached over the table, took a pen from the bartender's pocket, and picked up a clean napkin. With a quick scribble, he slid the napkin next to Teller's bottle. "There's your numbers Tell." He smiled and picked up his glass. "You do whatever you need to do. You know I'm always on your side." Tipping it back, he rattled the last piece of ice into his mouth and bit down with a crunch. "But I'm going back to my room." As he walked away Teller called out. "So the ice water helped?"

Jack turned, "Yeah, but the cold shriveled the poor thing all up. I'm gonna go see if I can find somewhere warm to put it for a while."

Teller laughed, "Shall I tell the front desk we'll be here for another night?"

Jack's answer hung in the dark room as he walked out the door.

"I *hope* so."

With a bright smile, Teller turned his attention back to the two men remaining at the table. "You see my point, Joe? There are no rules and with the game always changing it's difficult to keep up." Picking up the napkin with the bank information, he folded it, slipped it into his shirt pocket, and looked at Terry.

"How about getting me one more beer my young friend? I'll meet you back at the bar and we'll talk numbers."

Terry nodded and Teller turned his smile to Joe.

"No offense amigo, but this conversation is about to become very private."

Joe nodded. That he was undeniably out of his element was painfully clear: and hard on that thoughts heels came the depressing realization that he must soon return to his mundane daily life. Releasing a despondent sigh of acceptance, he reluctantly pushed away from the table.

"No offense taken" he smiled. "I not only understand, I've got paperwork to attend to anyway." Then he turned to Terry.

"As always, Terry, Thanks. I'll see you in two weeks." Rising, he held out his hand.

"Sir, it has been *most* interesting. I wish you luck."

Taking Joe's outstretched hand in both of his, Teller gave a squeeze. "It has been a pleasure as well Joe, and thanks, a little luck always helps." He watched Joe's disheveled back disappear through the door; and as usual, a song popped into his head.

Shuffling rhythmically towards the bar he began singing, "Every girl crazy 'bout a sharp dressed ma-an.'

Terry laughed, and began snapping his rag in time, and as Teller slid onto his stool he flashed a grin that Terry was beginning to appreciate.

"Alright then son," Teller said, leaning across the bar. "Just what was it you remembered about your grandfather?"

Terry pushed his towel across the bar in front of Teller.

"I remembered where he told me he got that coyote."

= Chapter 69 =

Kelly sat on the sofa, legs folded and feet tucked beneath, waiting for Tellers call. Her performance at Carlton's office had left her exhilarated but feeling somewhat cheap. Why *was* it that men were such suckers for tits? She had once asked Teller why men seemed to be so easily manipulated, but he had simply laughed and given her a warm kiss.

They were getting dressed for a romantic Valentine's Day dinner, and she had been standing in front of a full-length mirror, cupping her breasts; giving rise to the question.

"It's not stupidity, Kell," He explained, "It's just that we are simple souls who have most everything we need but that little thing between your legs, and *that* is one of the things we want most. So, in exchange for that little slice of heaven we are willing to go through a fair amount of hell."

Resting his chin on her shoulder, he smiled at their reflection then slowly ran his hand down her arm to her hip and around her belly, finally coming to rest between her legs, producing a sharp intake of breath. Nibbling her earlobe, he whispered, "And don't for one minute try and tell me that women don't go through the same shit just to have that little slice filled." Giving her rear a little pat, he walked away, leaving her to step into her panties with a smile and a bit of a blush.

Thirty minutes later as she stood matching the color between three different dresses with her pumps he returned, coming up from behind to wrap his arms around her waist. Kissing her neck, he whispered another, 'filling the slice' comment, accompanied by a sensual caress up the inside of her thigh and a strategically placed, tantalizing tickle.

"Yeah," she had said, lifting her face and returning his kiss. "But *we* get to choose the filling."

Teller chuckled as he worked down her neck, "Of *that* there is no doubt." The panties had come off, kicked to the foot of the bed.

Later that evening the two of them sat next to the restaurant's fireplace, the remains of a sumptuous meal on their plates and the fires flickering flames reflecting the rich magenta of their cabernet. His green eyes twinkling, Teller had reached across the table and taken her hand. "And it is moments such as this that make all that stupidity worthwhile."

It had taken a minute, but she recognized the reference from earlier that evening.

Squeezing his hand, she smiled and raised her glass.

"Here's to lovely, lovely stupidity."

~

The buzzing of the cell phone shook her from her pleasant daydream. Returning her reluctantly to the present.

"Yes?" she gruffly answered.

"Hi, Kelly. It's me."

Her jaw tightened. "James… what do you want?"

He hated it when she was dismissive. "Don't be like that dammit, we need to talk."

"So talk."

James struggled to hold his temper: he was walking a fine line and he wanted her cooperation.

"I need you to come down to the office and sign some papers. We need to get this transfer of ownership started. You understand, it's a lot of legal mumbo-jumbo, and I want to make sure you and Teller get what you deserve."

A smile crossed her face, but her voice did not betray her thoughts. "I'm quite sure you do, James, but I'm waiting to hear from Teller on how to proceed with this whole transaction. I do know that he would like to finalize it as soon as possible."

369

James was taken aback but not surprised. He was, however, immediately suspicious.

"You've spoken with Teller?"

She couldn't help but smile. "Of course, James. After all, it is *me* he's giving half the company to."

In the moment of silence that followed she could almost hear molars crack, and his voice came back strained.

"Yes, right, of course. I'm having Carl draw up the contract to the agreed-on price."

Kelly interrupted; "Which is fifty cents on the dollar, correct?"

James' voice grew tighter still. "Yes, yes, of course. Minus legal fees and a few other minor miscellaneous costs."

"Yes, of *course*," she mimicked.

She was enjoying this entirely too much.

"I'll tell you what, James, I'll call you just as soon as I've heard from Teller. Okay?"

James glared at the phone. He *hated* being dismissed.

"Fine, Kelly, but have him call me, would you?"

"I will James, bye."

James held the dead phone to his ear. With a quiet fury he hissed, "That is *no* way to treat your future business partner."

Leaning back he squeezed his eyes closed, took a moment to regain his calm, and dialed Carlton.

— — ‾ ‾‾ ‾‾ — —
— — — — — — — —
‾‾ ‾‾‾ ‾‾

= Chapter 70 =

"Really?" Teller's caviler grin vanished and his intensity returned. "Where did he say he got it?"

Pushing a fresh beer in front of Teller, he began polishing an already sparkling glass.

Teller watched him for a moment.

"Nervous?" he asked amicably.

"No, no, this helps me think. It was a long time ago, Teller, and it really wasn't that big of a deal at the time. Grandfather had taken my little sister and I up to the north end of Lake Powell for some bass fishing. He took us every year or so, and we always went to some little marina that was run by this old Indian guy."

"Do you recall his name?"

"No, I don't. It was something very forgettable, but I do remember what he called his grandson 'cause I thought it was so cool."

Teller rolled his eyes to the ceiling and mumbled, 'Puppet.'

"What's that?" Terry said.

"Nothing," Teller smiled and picked up the bottle. He didn't take a drink, he just sat smiling, swinging it like a pendulum between two fingers. "So, what was the name?"

"Little Raven. Just how cool is that?"

"That is *far* beyond cool, Terry," Teller said, shaking his head. "As a matter of fact, I'd go so far as to call it cosmic. But how does that little coyote tie in?'

"Oh yeah, the coyote... well, what happened was that my sister and I had caught some fish off the dock and we went looking for the grownups to help us clean them. We found grandpa where he always was, down at an old trailer talking to

371

Little Raven's grandpa." Terry smiled at the memory, and the smile reflected the little boy he was then.

"It was always fun because we got to run around and do whatever we wanted. The old Indian guy said that we wouldn't get hurt 'cause we had a spirit guide on our side. I never knew what that meant, but I guess my granddad believed it 'cause he let us run wild and we never did get hurt. Anyway, we went down to the trailer for help cleaning the fish, and Grandpa told my sister and me to get a fire started. We did, and after dinner we were sitting around the fire and the old Indian gave that coyote to my grandpa and told him to keep it, but to put it somewhere safe. Because, he said, someday he would need to give it to someone else."

Terry set down the glass he was buffing and looked wonderingly at Teller.

"Do you suppose that he meant *you?*"

Teller let out a deep sigh. "Terry, if someone had told me a month ago that I would be sitting in Tucson, in the bar of a Holiday Inn, buying a pristine 1948 Buick with a turquoise coyote set into the dash from a bartender, I would have asked for some of whatever they were smoking. But son, a *hell* of a lot has happened since then. Now all I can say is yes, I think that car was meant for me, and tell you that your grandfather's old Indian friend is a new acquaintance of mine. An old fella by the name of Billy."

Terry's face lit up. "That's it! That was his name!"

"I thought as much." Teller nodded. "Did your granddad ever mention anything about gold or gems?"

"No," Terry said, searching his memory further. "But I think he did something with some salvage company down in Florida."

Teller pursed his lips into a tight smile as he tore the label off the bottle. "Right. Okay, but all he left you was that car?"

"Yeah, like I said, the family has been fighting over everything that wasn't mentioned in the will, but that old car was given explicitly to me in writing. Funny thing was, I could never figure out why."

Teller's smile returned. "I think I know why, Terry, but it's a pretty goddamned complicated story. So let's leave it at this. Your grandfather was a smart fellow who knew how to keep his mouth shut. You still want to sell the car?"

Terry picked up another clean glass and began polishing. "Yeah."

"Good." Teller nodded. "Then I'm going to make you an offer. I will make it only once, and I expect no argument over the price or the terms. If you accept, I will pay you, and you will sign over the title. After that, it's done, over, finished. Does that sound fair?"

Terry was reluctant to commit. But so far Teller had given him no reason not to be trusted. He set down the shiny glass and smiled. "Sure."

"Good again. Do you drink?"

Terry opened the cooler, pulled out two beers, and set them on the bar. "I do."

Teller looked at the Budweiser Terry had placed in front of him and shook his head. "This is a *happy* time, Terry. Please, remove that swill, and replace it with something palatable."

"Oh! Sorry," Terry muttered as his smile vanished.

Shoving the unacceptable beverage back into the ice, he fished out a Heineken, wiping away the ring the Bud bottle had left and setting a fresh napkin down along with the beer.

"Most people around here drink Bud."

"I'm sure they do." Teller smiled "But I'm not most people." He took a slow drink, set the bottle down, and leaned forward. "We have established the fact that you want to sell, and I want to buy. So, here's my offer." He paused and brought the bottle back to his lips; enjoying the fretful expression on Terry's face as the suspense built: trying hard not to laugh as the speed of Terry's buffing increased.

Finally, he smiled. "I will give you sixty thousand dollars for that car."

Terry nearly choked.

"What!"

"Sixty K. That's what I want to pay for the car."

Coughing into his buffing towel, Terry struggled to catch his breath, stuttering "W-w-why . . .?" through the material.

Teller took another slow pull on his beer. "Because that is what it's worth to me."

Terry coughed again and gave Teller incredulous look.

"But it *can't* be worth that much!"

Teller's eyebrows went up. "It's probably not, but that isn't the point, and I didn't say that was what it was *worth*. I said that is what it's worth to *me.*" He smiled and tipped his bottle towards the astonished young man.

"Look Terry, your grandfather left you nothing but this car right?"

Terry nodded.

"You have kids and you need money, right?"

Again, Terry nodded.

"Well, I just *happen* to have some money, I *love* this car, and you don't need it. Am I right so far?"

"Yeah, Teller, that's all true, but that's still a lot of money for an old car."

Teller grinned, his eyes shining with amusement. "But it's got a coyote in the dash."

Terry shrugged, "So?"

"So I like coyotes!" Teller laughed. "Look, I said I would make a one-time offer. I've made it. Do you want to sell the car or not?"

Terry might have been confounded, but he wasn't stupid. Throwing his towel over his shoulder, he held out his hand and smiled, "Sold!"

Teller took Terry's hand in a firm grip. "Good. Negotiations are now officially over."

Looking over Terry's shoulder at the old Seth Thomas clock, he gave a disappointed frown and let go of Terry's hand. "It's too late for paperwork today, so how about this. I'll meet you here in the morning, we'll grab some breakfast, go to the bank, and finalize the deal." Terry was in a state of semi-shock, but he nodded along.

"By the way," Teller grinned. "I hope cash works for you."

"Cash?" Terry sputtered, "What am I going to do with that much cash?"

Teller shrugged. "Not my problem lad. Just make sure you have the title with you. First we'll go to the bank and I'll get the money. Once that's taken care of, we'll head over to the motor vehicle department and complete this transaction."

Laying a twenty on the bar, he shuffled across the floor singing, "Every woman I know, crazy 'bout an automo*beeile* shoop de do do do doop." But on reaching the door, he turned.

"See ya!" he laughed, and with a wave, pulled the door open.

Silhouetted in the lobby's light, he shone like a spirit; and for the briefest of moments Terry wondered if this was all a dream. Then the door wheezed shut; leaving Terry speechless and alone in the dark and quiet bar, silent now but for the ticking of that old clock on the wall.

~

Teller reached in his pocket to make sure he still had Jack's phone; he did, and as he walked through the lobby he looked at the clock behind the check-in desk. It was twenty minutes slower than the bar clock. He frowned, but then smiled, '*Oh yeah. Bar time . . . just goes to show, it's all relative*'

Laughing with the joy of the strange twists of life, he took the stairs up to his room two at a time, flung open the door, flopped onto the bed and took the phone from his pocket. He figured Jack was either napping or otherwise occupied, so he dialed Kelly's number. She picked up on the first ring.

"Hi Tell!"

"My, my, but don't we sound cheerful. What's got you so chipper at this hour?"

"I just got off the phone with James."

"That can't bode well."

"What do you mean?

Teller laughed, "I mean, my dear, that considering the circumstances, if you are as pleased as you sound, then James must be proportionately miserable."

She laughed. "Yes, I hope so. And I imagine that right now he's wondering just what you're up to."

The warmth of her laughter brought on a great longing for her company, and joy infused him. His happiness was equal parts love for her, and the pleasure of ruffling James' feathers.

"Well, let him wonder. Do you think Carlton will follow through?"

"Sure, I can't see why he wouldn't. You made him one hell of an offer, and honestly, I don't think he has much in the way of loyalty, *or* fondness for James."

"Good. That's two points for our side. You got a pen and paper? I've got some numbers for you."

He heard some rustling on the other end, and she came back, "Okay, I'm ready."

Smoothing the wrinkled napkin across his knee, he recited the account information.

"Alright, Tell. I've got it, now what are they?"

"Those are the numbers of the account Carlton is to deposit the money from the sale of the stock. I'm sure I don't need to say this, but you stay with him and make sure he gets it right."

"Of course, but when are you coming back? you'll need to be here for the paperwork, and you *know* James is going to shit bricks when he finds out what you've done."

Teller chuckled as he folded the napkin back into his pocket.

"James can shit bricks all day long, Kell. I haven't *done* anything… I've simply exercised my option to cash out a small percentage of what I own. The rest, as agreed, will be signed over to you, and *you* will then sign over the promised ten percent to Carlton. Speaking of, is there any indication that James is going to try anything hinky?"

She laughed again. "Teller, you know James. He hasn't said or done anything specific, but he's undoubtedly up to something. But with the help of your unbelievable generosity, and my cruel stroking of the poor guys testosterone with that subliminal slut act, I think we've won over an ally."

Teller gave an appreciative chuckle. "All's fair in love and war, Kell, and really, James can't do anything but try and cheat us through fine print. And, as *I* still need to approve and sign off on the final transaction, all *you* need to do is make sure he sticks with the agreement that we made at the lake. But listen sweetheart, if it comes to it and you need to give him a point or two, do it. It'll give him a feeling of winning, and I honestly don't give a shit. Just make sure that Carlton gets that money wired early tomorrow morning. And of course, if there are any problems you can call me at this number."

Stretching out on the couch, Kelly twisted a lock of hair in her fingers and scrunched her toes beneath one of the cushions.

"What are we going to do for Valentine's Day, Tell?"

Teller blinked. "What? Why?"

"Oh," she giggled, "Just wondering..."

The question had come out of the blue; but he smiled, "That's a-ways off, Kelly, but I'll make it memorable," He paused, "I always have, right?"

"Yes Teller, you always have."

The blinking battery icon on the phone caught his eye: low power. "I gotta go kid, let me know when Carlton gets that transfer done, and make sure you have a scarf when I get back."

In reflex, she reached up and touched her hair. "Why?"

"Let's just say that my new ride will blow you away."

He laughed and hung up.

Now he was in a grand mood. Everything was coming together, filling him with nervous energy. He thought about

377

calling Jack but changed his mind. *'Naaa,* he thought as he rolled out of bed, *'more fun to bother him in person.'*

~

Knocking on Jack's door with a polite knuckle, Teller called out, "Room service."

No response. He tried again.

"Sir, room service." This time he got a muffled reply.

"I didn't call room service."

Teller rested his forehead on the door and smiled, "I understand sir, but the young lady did. She requested a bottle of our most expensive champagne and a dozen of our smallest condoms." He heard a feminine giggle as the sound of footsteps approached the door. As the lock chain rattled out of its clasp a gravelly voice growled, "We'll take the Champagne, but the tiny condoms need to go to room two-oh-six. That's Mr. Teller's room. *He's* the guy with the little dick." Jack's unshaven face peeked through the crack of open door and looked down at Teller's empty hands.

"Where's the champagne?"

Teller's reaction was quick. He pushed open the door, stepped in and looked down at Jack's nakedness with amusement. "Sorry sir, wrong room. These condoms are obviously *much* too large."

Jack pinched the bridge of his nose. "I realize I say this far too frequently, but fuck you, Tell, and what do you want anyway?"

"Just to let you know we're good for another night, and that I'm a happy guy."

"That's it?"

Teller grinned. "That's it."

"Fine. I'm ecstatic for you." He put his hands on Teller's chest and began pushing him backwards toward the door. "I'll see you tomorrow."

He had been pushed to the threshold when the phone in his pocket rang. He grinned, fished it out, and held it to Jack, who waved it away, mouthing, "You answer it."

378

Teller shrugged and answered, "Hello?"

"Hello, Teller?"

He replied noncommittally, "Yes?"

"Good, I wanted to talk to you. This is Junior."

Teller's face brightened. "Young Bill!" he laughed, what can I do for you?"

Junior's voice was warm. "No, Teller, it's what *I* can do for you. And I want to thank you."

"Thank me? For what?"

"For the opportunity to work together," A brilliant smile split Junior's face. "And for the introduction the other night."

Teller was at a loss. "What introduction?"

"To those beautiful women."

"Oh yeah," He laughed, "What was the one's name?" Sheila?"

"Yeah, Shelia… how'd that work out?"

From the smile that was spreading across Teller's face, Jack divined that whatever the conversation was about, it was extremely good news. Teller winked at him. "Glad I could be of service. So, what's up?"

Jack continued to watch Teller's face as he talked, but short of a raised eyebrow his face betrayed little emotion.

'Good poker face' ran through Jack's mind.

A nod and a smile later Tell flipped the phone closed.

"We're in business pal. Be ready for dinner tonight at six. We're going back to Mi Nidito. I'll meet you downstairs at the bar at five. And Jack," Teller slid his foot across the carpet to block the door as Jack pushed it closed.

"Yeah?"

"Shave and try and make yourself presentable. You look like shit."

Jack leaned against the doorjamb, scratched himself, and with a big smile kicked Teller's foot out of the way.

"And at the risk of being repetitive, Teller, go fuck yourself." He slammed the door in Teller's face.

Teller turned and walked happily down the hall, whistling the *'Mister Rogers'* theme song.

= Chapter 71 =

Ben sat quietly in the plush seat next to Casey.

The Gulf Stream IV had reached cruising altitude only minutes after takeoff and was scheduled to land in Grand Junction in twenty minutes.

Sipping her ginger ale, Casey gazed through the window thinking of how best to handle James. Suddenly the view went white, and the jet gave a shudder as it flew through a bank of Cumulus clouds. She reached over and clasped Ben's hand.

"It's alright, Benny, everything's fine."

Ben attempted a smile despite the contraption that was screwed to his skull and holding his jaw in place.

Through clamped teeth he asked, "Hathe you her' from Kelly?"

Casey's hand returned to her lap with a tinge of resentment. *God, why are these two men so fixated on that woman?*

"No Ben, I haven't."

"I'm going to kill him...."

It was spoken so quietly that Casey almost didn't hear. Her heart sank and she turned, not wanting to know, but asking anyway.

"What?"

Ben rotated his entire upper body to face her. "I said, I'm going to kill Teller."

Casey slumped back into her seat and closed her eyes.

Oh, Benny . . ..

And so ends Book 2.

Here is a short excerpt from Book 3, the final, rousing conclusion to The "Southwestern Songline series.

= Chapter 1 =

Carlton rolled his chair back and opened the lower desk drawer. There were now *two* bottles of Pinch stashed behind the steel cashbox. The first was standard protocol. The second was a recently added emergency backup, because if the past few days were any indication of what was to come, he was going to need them both.

Calibrating the records so the transaction would not show until the next quarterly report, Carlton had sold Mr. Teller's stock last night, deftly timing the sale at the last ring of the trading bell. Just as Teller had requested.

Removing bottle number one from the drawer, he peeled away the foil, poured his whiskey to the top of the glass, and with drink in hand, gazed at the cursor that blinked, no, *winked*, at him on the screen.

One press of a key and his life would change forever.

With the burden of his crushed dreams weighing heavily on the finger that hovered over that key, the finger dropped.

"*Fuck* James Carson . . ."

With the pressure of his finger on that key Carlton felt suddenly lighter. It was as if he were pushing himself up, and away from his past. And as that long-suffered weight dissolved, Carlton leaned back in his chair, looked up at the ornate ceiling, and smiled, "And *fuck* that ceiling too . . ."

The decision to defect was not a difficult one, and the money that Teller offered was more than sufficient incentive. But Kelly, dressed as she had been that morning . . . well, *that* made for a heady mixture.

He sniffed the air where her perfume still lingered.

'God he sighed, *'God, she was even more beautiful than Casey.'* but then immediately amended, *no, not more beautiful. More achievable.'*

Perhaps when this was all over he would ask her out.

But the moment the thought entered his head, the menacing tone of Teller's voice over the phone echoed in his ear and he reconsidered. Perhaps lunch was a better idea.

Bringing the whiskey to his lips, he glanced at the numbers on the screen again.

That James would be murderously angry was a given. But the truth was he didn't really care. Nothing he had done was illegal, or even unethical. The sale of one hundred thousand dollars worth of stock was a legitimate transaction. The stock belonged to Mr. Teller, and he was allowed sell any amount he wished without the approval of the stockholders, or without consulting the board for that matter, *and* he could sign over the remaining percentage to whomever he wanted. Which, in this case, was Miss Kelly.

Carlton sighed and closed his eyes.

The image of Kelly leaning over his desk, her auburn hair spilling over her shoulders as her breasts swayed beneath that soft sweater returned, and reluctantly shaking that pleasing, yet dangerous image from his mind, he laid his palms on the paperwork that lay spread out across the desk before him. Once these documents were signed he would own the remaining ten-percent of this transaction.

But at the thought his smile diminished. That was only providing Mr. Teller kept his word.

But no sooner had the worry materialized, it vanished, and his smile returned. James Carson *detested* Teller, and Mrs. Kelly believed in him. The combination gave him faith in the outcome.

As he rolled the figures over in his head a glorious sense of rebellion, mixed with relief filled him with joy. The money from Teller's generous offer was not enough to retire for life, but it was unquestionably more than he would *ever* see working here as James' whipping boy. Leaning back, Carlton stared again at the ceiling. When had things gone wrong?

Not so long ago, corporate headhunters had plucked him from the University and offered him this job; and from that moment it had seemed a custom fit. What more could a young man have had asked for? An expense paid relocation from the dreary east coast to a hip town in the Rockies, combined with a fine starting salary with a prestigious law firm.

It was everything an Ivy League kid could envision as a springboard for a successful career, with Casey as the gold ring. Everything seemed perfect. But then James had entered the picture and dashed his dreams. The man was an arrogant, self-centered prick who showed little respect for her, and none at all for him. No, he had no moral misgivings with what he was doing, and the thought of helping Teller mess with James' private kingdom brought him a great deal of personal satisfaction.

He smiled, *'Karma, asshole . . . .'* and picked up the phone.

~

Kelly was in the shower, shampoo dripping down her face when the phone rang. Under normal circumstances she would ignore it, but these were anxious times. With a quiet curse, she quickly rinsed, shut off the water, grabbed a towel, and wrapped her dripping hair while reaching over the sink counter to pick up the phone. Attempting to sound civil, her stress and annoyance still came through in her voice. "Hello?"

385

Carlton's sense of conviction was shaken by the antagonistic tone of her response, and he stammered out a weak, "Hello, Kelly? I'm sorry, this is Carlton, is this a bad time?"

She punched the speaker button and set the phone near the sink, "No, no Carl, it's okay, I was just in the shower. What's up?" suddenly her voice was drowned out by the noise of the hairdryer, and the image of her wet and naked flashed through his mind. With great difficulty he reigned in his imagination, struggling to recall just why he had called in the first place.

"Oh, yes, I just wanted to let you know I have the bank draft ready, do you have the information I need?"

"Yeah Carl, I do, just a sec." Brushing her hair back, she went to the closet, pulled out one of Teller's old oversized T-shirts and pulled it over her head. Tugging it over her butt she picked back up the phone. "That was pretty quick Carl, any problems?"

"No, not yet anyway, but then Mr. Carson doesn't know about it yet either."

"Good Carl, let's keep it that way for now. I'll be right over, just give me a few minutes."

"Alright Miss Rowen, I'll be waiting."

Sensing the anxiety in his voice she purred, "Carl, call me Kelly, please."

The line went quiet and she gently asked, "Are you alright?"

"Yes, just a little nervous."

"Don't be," She laughed, "you're not doing anything wrong are you?"

Carl's voice came back much stronger. "No. Nothing I'm doing will create any legal disputes."

"Good, that's what Teller said. And don't worry, he won't screw you out of anything he's promised. Whatever he offered, you'll get." A tight smile crossed Carlton face. "That's good to know Miss Rowen, because once Mr. Carson becomes aware of what we are doing I will no longer work for this firm."

Kelly teasingly responded, "And that's a problem?"

Surprising himself with a sense of power he hadn't felt since he realized that Casey was an unobtainable goal, he laughed, "Hell no! nothing has worked out for me since I took this position. Fuck Mr. Carson *and* his jerk stoner brother! I'm going to take a vacation."

"That's the spirit!" Kelly laughed, "Where do you think you'll go?" There was a second of dead silence, and Carltons voice came back strong and bright, "I'm going to Disneyland!"

"I'll be right over." Kelly chuckled.

Hearing Carlton show such strength made her happy; and knowing it would please Teller as well, she chuckled, "I'll be right over." and threw the phone onto the bed.

Pleased with the way the day was unfolding so far, she pulled the damp t-shirt over her head, finished drying her hair, and nearly skipping out of the steamy bathroom, laid out her clothing options on the bed.

Giving a critical review of herself in the full-length mirror, she turned to study her choices. *'Hmmm, sexy, or business?'*

Having already set the hook, she saw no further need to tease poor Carl, so she settled on casual business with a subtly sexy undertone. What the hell, she *was* a woman after all.

Choosing her ensemble, she spritzed some perfume into the air and walked through it. Then, performing a quick pirouette in front of the mirror she smiled at the reflection.

Perfect . . ..

Ten minutes later the sound of low heels clicked across the hall tile. Pausing at the oval mirror that hung above the low table beside the front door, she pushed a stray lock of hair into place, picked up her purse, and slipped a freshly painted finger through the ring that held her keys.

Tucking the bank information into a side pocket of the purse she stepped out into the brilliant spring day, dialing Teller as she walked.

— — -- --- -- — —

— — -- --- — —

-- --- -

＊

All three Books in The Songline Series are available on-line through Amazon and all other E-stores in both Kindle format and Paperback.

However, if you would like a 1st run, personally signed copy, just go to my Website:

DenverCDavis.com

Enjoy!

With a poet's temperament and gypsy's feet, I have lived my life with a smile and a song.

I have been a cowboy, a carpenter, a cross-country ski bum and a back-roads vagabond.

I've sipped chilled champagne on sleek jets, downed Rum on the wooden decks of Sailboats, and drank warm beer in ragged jungles.

I have slept with angels, danced with devils, broken rules, bones, and the occasional heart.

The prerequisite of my journey has always been adventure, my destination the unknown, and the road traveled is littered with memories.

www.ingramcontent.com/pod-product-compliance
Lightning Source LLC
Chambersburg PA
CBHW051315250626
47155CB00007B/2331